W9-BVR-894

The Repeat Year

WITHDRAWN
No longer the property of the
Boston Public Library.
Sale of this material benefits the Library.

The Repeat Year

ANDREA LOCHEN

BERKLEY BOOKS, NEW YORK

THE BERKLEY PUBLISHING GROUP
Published by the Penguin Group
Penguin Group (USA) Inc.
375 Hudson Street, New York, New York 10014, USA

USA | Canada | UK | Ireland | Australia | New Zealand | India | South Africa | China

Penguin Books Ltd., Registered Offices: 80 Strand, London WC2R 0RL, England
For more information about the Penguin Group, visit penguin.com.

This book is an original publication of The Berkley Publishing Group.

Copyright © 2013 by Andrea Lochen.
All rights reserved. No part of this book may be reproduced, scanned, or distributed in any printed or electronic form without permission. Please do not participate in or encourage piracy of copyrighted materials in violation of the author's rights. Purchase only authorized editions.

BERKLEY® is a registered trademark of Penguin Group (USA) Inc.
The "B" design is a trademark of Penguin Group (USA) Inc.

Library of Congress Cataloging-in-Publication Data

Lochen, Andrea.
The repeat year / Andrea Lochen. — Berkley trade paperback edition.
pages cm
ISBN 978-0-425-26313-6 (pbk.)
1. Nurses—Fiction. 2. Time travel—Fiction. I. Title.
PS3612.O246R47 2013
813'.6—dc23
2012045918

PUBLISHING HISTORY
Berkley trade paperback edition / May 2013

PRINTED IN THE UNITED STATES OF AMERICA

10 9 8 7 6 5 4 3 2 1

Cover design by Diana Kolsky.
Cover image of "Couple in the Rain" © Dmitriy Shironosov / Shutterstock;
"Umbrella Pattern" © Lorelinka / Shutterstock.
Text design by Laura K. Corless.

This is a work of fiction. Names, characters, places, and incidents either are the product of the author's imagination or are used fictitiously, and any resemblance to actual persons, living or dead, business establishments, events, or locales is entirely coincidental. The publisher does not have any control over and does not assume any responsibility for author or third-party websites or their content.

ALWAYS LEARNING PEARSON

Acknowledgments

Writing can be such a lonely pursuit, so I want to thank the many writers along the way who have made me feel like a valued part of the writing community. As an undergraduate student at the University of Wisconsin, I was blessed to work with Ron Wallace, Judy Mitchell, Lorrie Moore, Ron Kuka, and Jesse Lee Kercheval. Thank you all for believing in me and encouraging me to pursue writing.

The University of Michigan gave me the opportunity to devote two blissful years to my writing, for which I am most grateful. While there I wrote the first draft of *The Repeat Year* and was privileged to work with Peter Ho Davies, Nicholas Delbanco, Laura Kasischke, Eileen Pollack, and Michael Byers. My appreciation also goes out to Andrea Beauchamp and the Hopwood Awards program for recognizing the spark of potential in my early draft.

Thanks to The Best Cohort Ever, who didn't earn this title for no reason: Becky Adams, Kate Blakinger, Steve Dabrowski, Delia DeCourcy, Randa Jarrar, Tiana Kahaukawila, Jane Martin, Kodi Scheer, Ben Stroud, Joy Wood, and Steve Woodward. Their encouraging feedback on the early chapters helped shape my novel to what it would one day become. Becky Adams was a particular help with later drafts of the novel, and Kodi Scheer has been the kind of friend every writer dreams of having: tirelessly reading and rereading various versions of chapters piecemeal, offering wise suggestions, and never failing to boost my spirits and make me laugh.

Thanks to my agent, Stephany Evans, who is my own fairy godmother, although thankfully not of the Sherry Witan variety. Her expert guidance in the publishing world has proven invaluable. I'd also like to thank her assistant, Becky Vinters, who offered some very smart editorial comments, and everyone at FinePrint Literary Management.

Thank you to the wonderful team at the Berkley Publishing Group. Thanks especially to Emily Beth Rapoport, for being a champion for my book and giving it a home, and to Andie Avila, for her tireless efforts to bring my lifelong dream to fruition.

I am grateful to my husband, an emergency medicine doctor and an excellent resource for all things medical, who good-naturedly answered all my bizarre questions about diseases, drugs, and procedures. Thanks also to my friend Dr. Brittany Bettendorf, who read my novel for accuracy (medical and otherwise) in its later stages. Any medical mistakes made are purely my own.

I am indebted to my family for their love, patience, and support throughout the years. My parents, Mike and Linda Kurtz, and my sister, Steph Hundt, have been my biggest fans and constant cheerleaders since I wrote my first story in the third grade. It's impossible to fail with a family like them because they've always made me feel like a success.

Finally, thank you to my husband, Matt Lochen, who prayed for me every day, patiently endured my writerly moods, built me a desk and my own "writing nook," and never stopped believing in me. There aren't adequate words in the English language to express my love and gratitude to you.

calf. He was concealed under the blanket and facing the other direction. Only a few inches of his brown hair peeked out.

Had Alex persuaded her to stay over at his place? She didn't remember going home with him, only how lonesome the ICU had been—she'd been stuck working the night shift on New Year's Eve of all nights—until Alex had been called in to check on his congestive heart failure patient. He had fastened a party hat to Olive's head and kissed her at midnight. Sure, he'd also kissed Mrs. Conrad, the seventy-two-year-old wife of Olive's patient, but only because Mrs. Conrad had been determined to stay up and watch the countdown on TV. No one should ever ring in the new year alone, Alex had said.

Olive lifted the sheet to look down at her body. Oh, shit. She wasn't naked, thank God for that, but what she was wearing wasn't much better: a black camisole and hot pink underwear. She lifted the sheet a little higher to see if she could discern Alex's state of dress, but the sheet was tucked tightly beneath him. She couldn't believe this. Just when they had started to reconstruct a semblance of a professional work relationship. What had she been thinking? After working a twelve-hour shift, she typically went straight home to bed. Had they gone out for celebratory drinks instead? It was disconcerting that she couldn't remember. She felt sleazy.

She slipped out of bed and began to hunt for her navy blue scrubs. They weren't on the floor next to or under the bed. She crept to the other side of the bed and looked down at the blanketed cocoon. Alex's face was covered. He didn't stir.

No clothes on the floor. No socks, no pants, no boxers, and certainly no blue scrubs. Only a TV remote, a man's watch, and a folded newspaper littered the beige carpeting. Alex's bedroom looked less cluttered than she remembered it. Where were his skis, his swim fins? His precariously stacked medical reference books? Still, the room looked awfully familiar. She stopped in front of the dresser. Definitely not Alex's dresser, which was a huge German wardrobe, a family heirloom. This dresser was six drawers high with a scratched mahogany finish. It was as recognizable to her as her own childhood dresser, which had been painted white with pink stenciled bows.

On top of the dresser, next to a halogen lamp and a large metal Slinky, stood a silver-framed photograph of her face. It was a picture she knew well, one taken of her in college. In it, she wore a gray woolen cap with a red pompon on top. Her nose was pink from the cold; her eyes were slits against the glare of the snow. It was a picture only one person had ever admired.

"Phil?" Her voice sounded loud in the silent room.

"What?" was the muffled reply from the bed.

"Phil?" she repeated in disbelief. The lump under the blanket squirmed a little. She hurried to his bedside and gently pulled the blanket away from the face of her ex-boyfriend. His features were at once both familiar and foreign to her. A shock of dark brown hair. Neat, thick eyebrows. A long, slightly crooked nose. Brown stubble above his lip and across his cheeks and chin. A small, dark freckle under his left eye. Her breath caught in her throat as she stared down at him. Her worry dissipated and was replaced by a kind of relief. A flutter of joy.

Without opening his eyes, he reached out and grabbed Olive around her waist and pulled her toward him. "Come back to bed," he mumbled.

She resisted his embrace and took a few steps backward. "How did I get here last night?" she asked. "I don't remember coming here at all. Did you stop by the hospital?"

Phil opened his eyes. They were bottle green and flecked like a snake's skin. "I hope you didn't forget *everything*," he said. "Now come here." His arms were clumsy with sleep. He reached out again but could barely touch her where she was standing. His fingers brushed against the bare strip of skin between the bottom of her camisole and the waistband of her underwear. Her skin tingled.

"Did we sleep together?" she asked.

"If by *sleep together*, you mean have wild, passionate sex, then yes." He was more awake now and scrutinizing her. A mischievous smile touched his lips.

Olive pulled her tank top down to cover her stomach but only succeeded in exposing the tops of her breasts. She crossed her arms and tried to look stern. Surprised as she was, this was Phil. It was hard to resist smiling back at him. Phil Russell, whom she had dated and loved for over three years, and broken up with—quite badly—last February. She hadn't seen him since and had only spoken to him on the phone a few times throughout the year. Once, when she'd heard his mother, Carol, was in the hospital for knee surgery. Another time to tell him she'd found one of his Nike golf shoes at the bottom of her closet and did he want it back? She had spitefully withheld his left shoe when she'd returned a box of his belongings. He hadn't wanted it anymore; he'd already thrown out its mate.

"Look," Olive started. "I have no idea how I ended up here, and if I gave you the wrong impression last night, I'm sorry. But I really should get going now."

"Go?" His playful grin changed to a look of concern. The skin between his eyebrows puckered. "Are you feeling okay?"

"Where are my clothes?"

Phil raised one eyebrow. "In the kitchen where we took them off."

She pushed open his bedroom door, nearly hitting Cashew, who had apparently had his nose pressed against the door, in the face. Cashew was a flat-faced, swirly-furred, brown-and-tan shih tzu. He was supposed to be Carol's dog, but he had gone through such periods of doggy depression when Phil had left for college that Carol had agreed to let her son have him.

Cashew leaped and danced around Olive, wriggling and twisting into the shape of his namesake. Olive had always adored the little dog as much as he adored her. She had been almost as devastated to lose Cashew as she had been to lose Phil. But what could she have done after their cataclysmic breakup? *Hey, Phil. Do you think it would be okay if I stopped by your apartment when you're not home to visit your dog?* There had been so many casualties when they'd separated.

She scooped Cashew into her arms and walked out into the living room. Everything was arranged the same as when they'd been dating. The mismatched armchairs and futon, the glass coffee table he'd inherited from his grandmother, the bookcase crammed with three-ring binders and science textbooks, his Bowflex looking like some kind of ancient torture device in the corner of the room. Remnants of a quasi-romantic evening—a pair of wineglasses and a pizza box—rested on the coffee table. Olive glanced back and realized that Phil was following her to the kitchen in his boxers.

Of all the possibilities she could've imagined for herself

in the new year, waking up in bed with her ex-boyfriend had not been one of them. Even though she couldn't remember the path that had gotten her to his place, and even though she knew it was a mistake, she still thought it was a perversely pleasant one. Just to see Phil's sleeping face in the fuzzy morning glow had made this strange escapade worthwhile. Ten months of separation had dulled the pain of proximity for her, and seemingly for him as well. Perhaps they could even be friends now if she hadn't just messed things up by somehow landing herself in his bed. Still, she wished she could remember last night's sex. Phil was a spectacular lover.

She found a pile of discarded clothes under the kitchen table—a tangle of jeans, socks, and a turtleneck sweater. Her blue scrubs were still nowhere to be found. She nuzzled Cashew against her chin one more time and then set him down.

"Can my chocolate chip pancakes convince you to stay?" Phil asked. He opened an overhead cupboard and retrieved a bag of chocolate chips.

Olive pulled the turtleneck sweater over her head. She wanted to ask why he was being so nice to her. Had he forgotten how things had ended between them? The unforgivable thing she had done? And when she'd confessed, the way he'd held the door open for her and ushered her from his apartment and life as though she were a stranger?

"You're sweet, Phil. But trying to re-create our New Year's Eve together from last year is really too much. Wine and pizza, the chocolate chip pancakes. I don't understand why you're going to such lengths for me. Why now? What's changed?"

"What do you mean? I thought I was being original," he

said, and set the chocolate chips down on the counter. "Gosh, Cashew is going nuts! Ha-ha, pun intended. You'd think he hadn't seen you in months! I love that about dogs. Rolling out the red carpet for you even if you've been gone for only a few hours."

Olive looked down to see that Cashew was snuffling her sock with the intensity of a bomb-sniffing dog. He paused in his inspection and gave her ankle a good slurp. "But he hasn't—" she started to insist.

But Phil had already disappeared into the fridge. He emerged with eggs and milk. "Anyway, didn't we spend New Year's Eve last year in Las Vegas?"

"We spent New Year's in Vegas in 2009." She turned away from him and zipped up the fly of her jeans.

"Right."

"And we spent New Year's at your place in 2010. We watched the ball drop on TV."

"Right. Last night."

"Is this some kind of joke?" she asked. "Because I'm really not in the mood for this."

"I'm just as bewildered as you are. You seemed fine last night, but you must have had too much to drink. Maybe you should go back to bed and sleep it off."

"What I need to do is drive home and figure out what possessed me to come here last night," she muttered. Her purse was sitting on the counter next to a potted bonsai tree. It was a yellow leather hobo bag, an older purse she didn't recall bringing to work. She must have gone home to change clothes and purses last night. It seemed unlikely, but no more unlikely than spending the night with her ex.

She swung the yellow purse over her arm and took a step toward the door, but Phil blocked her with his body. She was extremely conscious of his bare chest; she had forgotten how good he looked with his shirt off. His chest and stomach looked as smooth as rock that had been shaped by rippling water. God, she'd missed that.

"You're acting really strange. I don't know if it's a good idea for you to drive."

"I'm fine."

Phil looked skeptical. "Will you call me as soon as you get home?"

She nodded. He would come to his senses by then. Whatever had happened between them last night was a mistake, much like the horrible mistake she had made last February. But standing there in his affectionate gaze, she couldn't refuse the hug he offered her. Even though he hadn't showered yet, the scent of his woodsy soap still lingered on the bare skin of his neck and shoulders. His embrace was firm and gentle, and it carried with it three years of memories.

Olive had barely reached the stairwell when she heard a door flung open and Phil's voice trailing after her. "Hang on a sec," he called. "I just remembered *I* drove last night. I'll drive you home as soon as I'm dressed. I need to let Cashew out quick, too. Just give me one minute."

"What?" she called back to him, but he had already closed the apartment door. The puzzle of last night's events was becoming more and more complex. Had Phil stopped by the ICU to visit her, or had their paths crossed somewhere else? She was tired—and a little ashamed—of trying to give shape and substance to the black hole in her memory of last night. She would ask Phil the specifics sometime soon, but right now, she didn't want to give him any more reason to be concerned about her. Frankly, she was concerned about herself. Blacking out and sleeping with her ex? Definitely not a very good way to start the new year.

She heard Phil's door open and shut again, and he was soon at her side.

"Are you sure you don't mind driving me?" she asked. "I mean, do you have the time? Because I could call a taxi or something."

Phil laughed. "Um, yeah, I have the time."

His ancient tan Mercedes-Benz was parked in one of the farthest spots in the parking lot. It was a 1987 diesel, a car he had told Olive he bought back in high school when driving a Mercedes, no matter how old, was considered cool. But more than nine years later, the thing still wouldn't die. Phil was too reasonable to trade the Mercedes in for a newer car when it was still running all right. Prudence was his religion.

He pulled out of the parking lot and turned onto Regent Street. Debris from last night's parties littered the lawns and sidewalks. Beer bottles, empty kegs, old couches with rips like wounds revealing their stuffing. Undergrads, bed-headed and hungover, slunk down the sidewalks, trying to look nonchalant in their walk of shame.

"Why are you turning here? You need to stay on Park to get on the Beltline."

"Why would I want to take the Beltline?" He made another turn onto Orchard this time, and Olive recognized every house they passed. They were relics, taken over and run down by college kids and landlords who were tired of putting in the effort. The three-story white colonial that had been converted into a law office. The green-and-maroon Victorian with the gingerbread lattice. The mossy brick house with the lawn full of political signs. The house with the missing balcony that had smashed to the ground, injuring five college students a couple of years ago.

Olive stared at Phil in disbelief as the car slowed to a stop. "Talk about a trip down memory lane," she said softly. She turned her head to look out the window. They were parked in front of her old house, a two-story clapboard painted Pepto-Bismol pink. She and her old roommate Kerrigan Morland had lived in the upstairs flat for seven years. She identified her old bedroom window. A plant was sitting there. The familiar touch made her smile, remembering the African violet she had kept in the window when she lived there. It had been the plant she'd kept alive the longest. In November, it had finally crossed over.

"So, here we are," Phil said.

"Here we are," Olive repeated. "Just as glorious and gaudy as I remembered." Phil was waiting for her. Was he waiting for her to get out of the car? A prickly shiver buzzed across the back of her neck. Something was not quite right here. The house, the street, the entire morning. She felt as though Phil were following a script while she was simply saying whatever it took to get herself offstage and back safely into the wings.

"Do you want me to come up?" he asked.

"You know that I don't live here anymore," she said, "and I haven't lived here in almost a year. Please just take me home. I'm tired. I'm tired of this. Please, Phil." She waited for his sigh of resignation. She waited for him to put the car in drive and take her back to her condo on the east side. "Phil?" She suspected he was putting together his own monologue. She could tell by the way he was flexing his lips, pursing and then relaxing them.

"You're scaring me, Olive," he said so softly that she had to lean in to hear the words that followed. "You don't remember how you got to my place last night? Well, I do, and I'll tell you every detail if it will wake you up out of this . . . *state* that you're in.

"Kerrigan wanted to have a party for New Year's Eve, and you didn't. She told you she'd keep it small, and you agreed to it. We were there, Kristin and Brian were there, Jeff was there, Robin and Lisa, Ciara, Steve. You made the sangria, Kerrigan made cupcakes with little plastic babies on top. More people kept coming, and it started to get so loud and crowded, that you said you wanted to go to my place.

"We drove over to my place around eleven o'clock. We ordered a pizza, but it didn't show up until two. We had to call Luca's about ten times to figure out where the heck the delivery guy was. Apparently, it's one of their busiest nights of the year. We watched the ball drop *twice*, once for the Eastern time zone, another time for the Central time zone. We kissed both times. I went into the kitchen to find a corkscrew for the wine, and you followed me, and we—"

"That's exactly right," Olive interrupted. She remembered the noisy party and the late pizza, the sangria and the pretense of helping Phil find the corkscrew. She even remembered Kerrigan's cupcakes and the plastic Mardi Gras babies she'd reused as decorations to symbolize Baby New Year. "Every last detail. But that all happened a year ago."

"I don't know what you mean by that! A year ago? 2009? We already agreed we were in Vegas." He splayed his fingers and drummed them against the steering wheel.

"No, I mean last year, 2010." That wasn't what she meant. That was Phil's definition. Her language was becoming imprecise. The boundaries between the years were starting to confuse her, and Phil was complicating things by making her pin numbers to years instead of allowing her to say "last year" and "this year."

"This is giving me a headache. Can we just go inside and figure this out somehow?" He formed fists with his hands and punched the steering wheel. His fists connected with the horn, and it let out a squawk like a sick bird. At the sound, a young woman poked her head out the door of the mossy brick house next door.

"Go inside? We can't. I don't know who lives here anymore."

"*You* live here. Kerrigan lives here."

"I just told you I *don't* live here, and Kerrigan doesn't live here anymore, either. She couldn't keep up with the rent after I left. She moved in with Ciara."

"Olive. Please. Just trust me."

At this moment, she couldn't have trusted him less. To trust him meant doubting herself and a year's worth of memories. But she was tired of sitting aimlessly in his car, and the sooner they got out of the car, the sooner she could disprove him.

The outside stairs leading to the upper flat on the left side of the house—these, too, were painted Pepto-Bismol pink—were rickety and unsafe. Obviously, the landlord hadn't gotten around to fixing them yet. She felt the boards sway beneath her and Phil as they made their ascent. Her hand was on the doorbell when Phil brushed it away.

"Don't," he said. "You'll wake Kerrigan."

"Right. Kerrigan. How considerate of you."

He pulled his keys from his pocket and rifled through them. He'd kept a copy of her old apartment key! She had turned in her own copy, even though her landlord had insisted he would change the locks. Phil found the key and held it up to the lock. It was Olive's turn to brush his hand away.

"We are not letting ourselves into somebody else's apartment."

He unlocked the door and stepped inside. She stood resolutely on the threshold.

"They're going to call the cops," she whispered.

"If you don't tell, I won't tell," he whispered back. He caught her hand and pulled her inside.

Peeking in on the new tenant was like returning to her elementary school and realizing how short the lockers were and how low the bubbler was. The strip of pink seashell-patterned linoleum in the kitchen looked as though it were better suited to a bathroom. The row of three giant picture windows let in buckets of sunlight but let out any warmth generated by the congested electric heater. The water-stained ceiling resembled a map of the world. But then there was the furniture. The black-and-white floral couch from IKEA. The black-cushioned papasan chairs. The red throw pillows. A geometric black-and-white rug, also from IKEA. Olive's brain needed a second to catch up with her eyes. Then she sat down directly where she was standing. She didn't collapse or keel over. Her knees didn't fail her. She just sat down. Hard.

Bristly fibers scratched against her hands. She looked

down and found she was sitting on a coir and rubber welcome mat. She scooted her butt over to read the message she knew by heart. *Did you remember to wipe?* She laughed out loud.

Phil turned around and looked down at her. He extended his hand to help her up, but she refused it. "Are you okay?" he asked, but she could barely hear him over her own laughter. The welcome mat's message wasn't even what tickled her so much. It was the ridiculousness of that fashionable, uncomfortable couch, standing in a place that Olive knew, according to all laws of nature, it shouldn't be standing in. She knew that because she had left it positioned in her own living room at High Pointe Hills Condominiums, fifteen miles away, on top of the same geometric rug. Her stupid IKEA living room set was disrupting the order of the universe.

"See? You remember now?" Phil was saying. He hoisted her up by the armpits and led her to the couch. She didn't want to sit on it, so she shook herself loose of his grip and sat with her knees bent under her on the rug. Plastic cups and paper plates were tossed everywhere. On the coffee table and rug, stuck in the cushions of the couch.

"I'm so sorry," a familiar female voice said from across the room. Olive craned her neck upward but couldn't see over the couch. "I'm going to clean this up, I promise. You won't have to lift a finger. I was going to do it before you came home, but you surprised me."

"Kerrigan?" Olive asked. Her friend's blond head peered over the couch. Kerrigan's expression was cautious, as though she expected Olive to scold her. Olive could only gape. The red pillows, papasan chairs, and party debris were crushing her. And on top of that, she sensed Phil hovering. She tried to ignore the muted conversation going on above her.

She bent forward and rested her forehead on her knees, in the agile position her dad had always identified as "the Yoga Thinker." As a child, she had curled herself inward like this whenever times seemed especially tough or uncertain. It was a way of holding the world at bay.

Chapter 2

January 1, 2011, the date on her laptop's toolbar maintained. *Revelers ring in 2011* was the top headline on an international news website, accompanied by a picture of fireworks exploding over the Sydney harbor. On her desk: a 2011 tropical beaches calendar—a Christmas gift from her mom—the same one she had used all year to record her experiences in her cramped, boxy handwriting. The calendar was still wrapped in cellophane, and when she removed the plastic, the days were unmarked, the pages crisp and white. She flipped through the images of white sand beaches, hammocks strung between palm trees, and pink-streaked sunsets. Every photograph was familiar to her; each grid of days was as blank as the next.

She hurried past February, a page she had longed to rip from the calendar last year. She could visualize the row of heavy black *X*s that had marred the page—the days of her and Phil's demise.

She paused over June. The corresponding photograph

showed two canoes floating in a cove of shallow, green water. She associated that pair of canoes with a lingering feeling of dread. June had been the month of her mom's marriage to Harry Matheson. Saturday, June 25, on the island of St. Lucia. With this memory came a flood of other events she'd faced in 2011, and she suddenly felt like to do it all over would be more strenuous than swimming upstream.

"I can't do this again," she said aloud.

She dropped the calendar, and the weight of its slippery pages pulled it over the edge of the bed. She fell back against her pillow. Perhaps it was possible to stave off the situation if she lay very, very still. Perhaps she could even subvert it with the power of her thinking. The only thing that mattered right now was her body against the pillow and bed. She closed her eyes. The white crown molding began to recede. The ceiling above her felt open and expansive, as if someone had lifted the roof off the house. But into this expansiveness crowded all the people, places, and things that had been erased from the boxes on her calendar. She saw the look on Phil's face when she told him about her transgression. She saw the yellow rental truck into which she had packed all her belongings for the move across town. She saw Alex and the haphazard crush of weeks they had spent together. She saw her mom with a gardenia in her hair. She saw an assembly of her patients, like ghosts in their white gowns—the ones she'd sent home, and the ones she'd lost.

Someone knocked on her bedroom door. Before Olive could even call out that she wanted to be left alone, Kerrigan was sitting at the foot of her bed.

"Don't go to sleep, okay?" Kerrigan said. She tickled the

bottom of Olive's foot. "Phil thinks you might have a head injury or something."

Olive laughed and pulled her foot away. "I'm fine, really. And I should be the one to know, right?"

"So then you know what year it is?"

Olive nodded and propped herself up into a sitting position. Sitting with her old friend was strangely comforting. They hadn't spent much time together since Olive had moved out. The intimacy of living together had faded, revealing how dissimilar they really were. The last time Olive had seen Kerrigan was in November when they'd gotten together for coffee. They'd still been on good terms, but things hadn't felt as comfortable and easy between them. Now Kerrigan was unshowered and still in her pajamas. She cradled a leftover cupcake in one hand.

"And you're not having visions of the future?" she asked, and licked the frosting off the cupcake ornament.

"Of course not," Olive said.

"Damn. I was hoping you could tell me if I finally meet Mr. Right in 2011."

Olive scanned her memory of Kerrigan's dating life in 2011 and sadly admitted to herself that she was pretty sure Kerrigan hadn't met him yet. There was Steve at the beginning of the year, and then a guy named Clay that Olive never got to meet. When Olive and Kerrigan had met over coffee in the fall, Kerrigan hadn't mentioned seeing anyone. But perhaps there was still hope for her in December.

Kerrigan had been watching her face, Olive realized. She quickly smiled to hide her depressing insight. "Cupcakes for breakfast?" she asked.

"Sticking to my resolution," Kerrigan said. "Never deprive myself of an opportunity for happiness."

Olive laughed. Of course—how could she have forgotten Kerrigan's New Year's resolution? Kerrigan had used it to justify calling in sick to work on several occasions, buying season hockey tickets, throwing herself an eighties-themed birthday party, and taking a trip to Cozumel with her sister.

"Want one? There's still a couple left." Kerrigan took a large bite.

"No, thanks. Did Phil leave?"

"Yeah, but I'm supposed to call him if you start acting kooky."

"His words?" Olive frowned.

"Mine."

Olive stood up and walked to the window. A gray van was parked where Phil's Mercedes had been. She watched two men struggling to slide a plaid sofa into the back of the van. Her attention drifted back indoors. Sitting on the ledge was her African violet, resurrected from the dead. She stroked its fuzzy leaves. "You're still alive." She had thrown the entire pot away when it was reduced to a shriveled, grayish stalk, and yet here it was, clay pot and all. She imagined it hurtling through outer space to get here.

"Kerrigan," she began, but when she turned to her friend's expectant face, she realized she wasn't ready to confide in anyone about these fantastic events just yet. She wasn't sure what to say exactly, wasn't sure how to describe this *thing*, wasn't sure how she felt about it. Speaking of it aloud would catapult this blurry phenomenon into the solid existence of her reality. And she didn't want to end up in the emergency room having tests done to see if she had a head injury on New Year's Day. She spent enough time at the hospital already.

"I'm going to clean up the apartment," Kerrigan said, and threw up her hands in exasperation.

"I didn't say anything," Olive insisted. She pushed the African violet an inch closer to the windowpane so it wouldn't fall.

"I know, but you were thinking about it. I can tell." Kerrigan started toward the door. "This is really bad timing, I know, but I asked Steve and a few other people over to watch the Rose Bowl later. I hope you don't mind."

Olive didn't follow sports, but she vividly remembered the Badgers' defeat in the Rose Bowl last January because it was all anyone had talked about for weeks. She sighed and tried to hide her irritation. She hadn't even spent an hour with Kerrigan, and she was already remembering all the reasons why she had eventually decided she needed to move out, move on, and start over in her own place. Even three years after their graduation from the University of Wisconsin, Kerrigan had clung tightly to her college friends and lifestyle. Almost everything she did for fun involved either a keg or a football game. Usually both. And for the first time ever, Olive had finally had her college loans paid off and was starting to make good money at her job. While living within walking distance of Dane County General Hospital had definitely been a perk, the location just hadn't been worth dealing with their noisy, drunken undergraduate neighbors.

She and Kerrigan were twenty-six, and it was about time for them to get their lives in order. But wait. Was Olive twenty-six, or was she still twenty-five? She didn't understand the rules of this bizarre happening yet, but she suspected if it really was only 2011, she was still twenty-five. This thought made her smile. Turning twenty-six had terrified her; it had been the point where she became closer to thirty than twenty. It wasn't that she thought twenty-six was old; she just had ideas of where she should be and what she would be doing when she turned thirty, and she wasn't anywhere near reaching any of those goals.

Kerrigan was still leaning in the doorway talking about football and Steve, the new guy she was dating. ". . . TCU doesn't stand a chance," she concluded.

Don't be so sure, Olive thought, but instead she said, "You know, you're worse than living with a guy. You're messy, you're always watching sports, *and* you hog the bathroom."

"You love me," Kerrigan said. "I'm going to shower now. Don't do anything crazy while I'm in there, okay? I'm supposed to be keeping an eye on you."

"I'll try not to."

She was alone again. She'd been wishing for this all morning, wishing to get away from Phil and then Kerrigan, to have quiet and solitude, but now that she'd been granted that, she realized she was left all alone with her thoughts. The tropical beaches calendar was still lying on the floor next to the bed. She picked it up and considered throwing it away. But as she bent down to drop it into the garbage, she saw the crumpled cellophane peeking out, and attached to the cellophane was the snowman gift label her mom had used.

To: Olive Elizabeth

With Unconditional Love, Mom

The sight of her mom's bubbly, even handwriting—like an elementary school teacher's—made her resolutely restore the calendar to her desk. Unconditional love. The words sent a sharp pain to somewhere below Olive's breastbone. It was far easier to accept unconditional love than to give it. She and her mom had always been close, and they'd become even closer after the death of her dad three years earlier. Last year's wedding, however, had driven an invisible wedge between them. A Harry Matheson–sized wedge.

Harry or no Harry, she suddenly had the urge to be sitting next to her mom on the squishy, paisley-print couch in her childhood home, a mug of hot cocoa in hand. Even if she didn't confide in her mom, just being in her presence would make things seem more normal and less uncertain. There were moments in her life when the only person who could offer her comfort was her mom. This was one of them.

An hour later, she stood on the doorstep of her childhood home: a gray-and-white Cape Cod in Cottage Grove. There were four cars in the driveway and a long row of them parked on the street. She'd had to park almost a block away. When she'd seen all the cars and realized what this meant—a New Year's Day party—she had almost turned around and driven home. But her need for comfort was stronger than her feeling of indignation.

A New Year's Day party was a tradition her parents had started in the eighties. They had thrown one every year and opened their house, cupboards, bar, and hot tub to their friends, family, and neighbors. Olive had been required to attend these parties until she was fifteen years old, at which point she'd been allowed to make other plans on New Year's Day with her friends. In the fourteen years of parties she'd endured, she'd witnessed Neil Diamond karaoke, a heated argument about Reaganomics that nearly escalated to a fist-fight, and middle-aged men and women skinny-dipping in the hot tub.

Her mom hadn't hosted a New Year's Day party since her dad's death. The first year had been too sad, and the following year, she had claimed that Greg had been the one who liked to do all of the entertaining, that she was just as happy to go to someone else's party or maybe even a movie on New Year's Day. Therefore, this had to be Harry's doing. They'd been married only six months, and Harry was already trying to take over her dad's traditions.

Except this was supposedly 2011. And if that was really true, it meant that Harry and her mom weren't married yet; they weren't even engaged this early in the year. So what was going on?

Olive swung the door open into the chaos of the party. Judging by the pileup of people in the foyer who were hanging their coats in the hall closet, many guests were just arriving. She recognized several faces: her aunt Laurel, her mom's younger sister, who immediately snagged her in a hug; Mr. and Mrs. Pinto from next door; and Sherry Witan, who had been in a book club with Olive's mom several years ago, who no one much liked, but who never turned down an invitation. There were other faces that looked vaguely familiar, Harry's coworkers, she suspected.

She found her mom in the kitchen surrounded by many helping hands. She was wearing an apron with a cartoon figure drawn on it that made it look like she was wearing a bikini: a tacky Christmas gift from Harry, who had a matching surfer dude–physique apron. Her dark hair was pulled into a high ponytail. The effect was that she looked like a college cheerleader instead of a middle-aged hostess. The marble kitchen island was covered in time-honored potluck dishes—the plate of deviled eggs, the red Jell-O mold in the shape of a candy cane, some kind of cheesy casserole, a tray of tortilla chips arranged around a bowl of guacamole.

"Oh, Olive!" her mom said. She pulled Olive into a one-armed hug, as her other arm was occupied stirring the barbecue in the slow cooker. "When did you get here?" Was she surprised to see Olive?

"Just a second ago." She glanced down at her mom's wedding ring. It was the white gold band with the solitary diamond—from her first marriage—not the braided yellow and white gold band Harry had given her. It was another piece of undeniable evidence that the events of 2011 had not played out yet.

Her mom followed Olive's eyes to the ring, and she twisted it self-consciously. "You're not working today?"

"No, I had to work the late shift last night."

"Really? I thought you and Phil had plans."

Olive paused. "There was . . . a big change of plans." She accepted a cup of punch from Jody Kessler, her mom's friend and fellow librarian. "I didn't know you were having this party."

"Of course you did. I invited you last week. But to be fair, I didn't think you'd come since you've been dodging these parties since you were a teenager."

"These parties? Mom, *these parties* were a tradition you had with Dad." She didn't realize how shrill she sounded until she saw Jody peek out from whatever she was doing in the pantry and then disappear as though it were unsafe to return.

"So was eating dinner and going for a walk. Does that mean I can't ever do those things again?" Though her tone was light, her smile had evaporated. Without it, Olive could clearly see the crow's-feet and the hair-thin lines around her mom's drawn lips. Not a college cheerleader. A widow in only her early fifties.

"Olive, these parties are for my neighbors and friends—*our* neighbors and friends—to celebrate the new year together."

Olive planted her palms on the cool marble countertop. She couldn't help wondering if these were the same words Harry had used to persuade her mom to host the party. Her fingers curled around the smooth edge. Shouldn't she be past all this? This back-and-forth with her mom, the subtle insinuations, each fanning the flames of grief and guilt for the other. She had struggled so hard last year to come to terms with her mom's remarriage. She took a deep breath. "The new year. Right."

Her mom leaned forward to tuck an escaped strand of hair behind Olive's ear. "Is everything okay, honey?"

The tenderness in that question made her want to burst and spill everything like a shattered decanter of wine. This was the comfort she'd been seeking—the opportunity to place this burden on someone else, someone who had the capacity to bear it, the wisdom to sort it out, or better yet, make it all go away. But this visit was not how she had envisioned it. The party guests, for one. The youthfulness and glow of her mom, for another. She had already disrupted the party enough; there was no need to bring it to a screeching halt by making her mom question her mental stability.

"Everything's fine." She took a small sip of punch. "Is Harry here?"

Her mom furrowed her eyebrows and searched Olive's face. "Of course. He's grilling the salmon fillets."

She drifted into the living room, out from under her mom's worried gaze. It was so like Harry to grill something like salmon. In her mind's eye, she could see her dad in his University of Wisconsin sweatshirt and red-and-white striped sneakers planted firmly on the deck that he had built, a bottle of Miller Lite in one hand, a metal spatula in the other. It had been only hamburgers and brats for him. The occasional steak or chicken breast. Through the French doors, Olive could see the slim silhouette of Harry at the helm of the grill, like a man tangling with an unruly beast. She didn't go outside. Instead, she walked to the picture wall. She braced herself for the worst. After the wedding in June, Olive's mom had hung up a photograph of the five of them, all standing barefoot on the beach—the newlyweds; her brother, Christopher, and his wife, Verona; and then Olive, the only one unpaired, like an unmatched sock. Her eyes sought the place where the picture had hung, which was now marked only by its absence—a conspicuous hole among the other framed memories.

She stood looking at the wall for a long time. She felt like she might crumple to the floor again, the way she had back at the apartment, so she made her way to the couch. Sherry Witan was sitting on the other end of the couch leafing through a coffee table book. Olive pulled one of the worn paisley pillows onto her lap. It was soothing to hold.

The wedding had happened. The whole year had already happened—all 365 days of it. Olive knew it; perhaps someone else knew it. Just because Phil and Kerrigan and her mom didn't remember didn't mean that she was the only one. She studied the other party guests to see if she could detect a difference in their behavior, an awareness, a kind of recognition of the absurdity of their position. Mrs. Pinto seemed to be a little off, clutching her beer bottle in both hands and surveying the room hurriedly with her small, black eyes, but Olive suspected she was just drunk. There had to be someone else. She couldn't be the only one.

She shifted in her seat and touched the edge of a folded newspaper her mom must have wedged between the couch cushions. It was often her way of quickly tidying up. Olive opened up the newspaper and began skimming through the headlines. *Dane County snowmobile trails to close. Injured bald eagle on the mend at wildlife center. UW marching band ready for Pasadena.* Nothing caught her eye, but she didn't know what she was looking for. Was she looking for an article to reassure her that others were aware of this strange loop in time, or was she looking for something to irrevocably convince her of this awful fact? The date on the newspaper was December 31, 2010. Her mom wouldn't have let something a year old stay under the couch cushion if that were the case. But it wasn't. There was no refuting the facts now. Olive bowed her head.

Her cell phone suddenly vibrated against her leg, and she wiggled it out of her pocket. It was a text message from Phil. **How are you feeling? Call if you need anything. I'm helping my mom take down her Xmas lights today. Love you.**

She stared at the message until the letters looked like

hieroglyphic groupings of pixels. How was one supposed to respond to a loving, concerned message from an ex-boyfriend who didn't remember he was an ex-boyfriend? Was there some kind of etiquette to follow? She finally settled on a reply: **No need to worry about me. I'm at my mom's.** She pressed the send button and slumped even further into the couch.

Someone sat down next to her. "Hungover?" a female voice asked with a low laugh. Her aunt, Laurel.

"Tired," Olive corrected. She pocketed her phone and sat up straighter. She could see Sherry Witan on the other side of her aunt, still pretending to be captivated by the coffee table book, but Olive had a feeling she was eavesdropping on their conversation.

"I missed you guys at Christmas," Laurel said. "I'm really sorry I couldn't be there." She was a flight attendant for Frontier and was often scheduled to work both Christmas Eve and Christmas Day.

"We missed you, too," Olive said.

"I heard Harry joined in the festivities." Laurel leaned in conspiratorially.

"He did."

Her dad, a car salesman, had never been quite impressive enough for Laurel, who had remained vigilantly single her whole life, and dated pilots and doctors and actors—or at least men who claimed to be pilots and doctors and actors—that she met on her flights to Kansas City and Cleveland and Indianapolis. Laurel found Harry's job as a professor at the University of Wisconsin much more glamorous. Wrongfully so, since he taught medieval studies, perhaps the dorkiest of all departments. She claimed a scholar was just the thing for her brainy older sister, who had been the acquisitions director at the Richmond branch of the Madison Public Library for the past nineteen years.

"Aren't you warming up to him yet?" Laurel asked. "I know it's hard for you and your brother to see your mom with anyone other than your dad, but you've got to get used to it sooner or later. For Kathy's sake."

Olive disliked when people talked down to her like that, as though she and Christopher were a pair of school-age brats reluctant to gain a new stepfather. However, she had just told off her mom for throwing a New Year's Day party with Harry—maybe she *was* a brat. "He's a great guy," she said. "He's grilling salmon right now," she added, as though this substantiated her claim.

"How nice." Laurel nodded and sifted through a handful of mixed nuts. "Nuts are good for you, right? Protein. I'm trying to lose some weight. Do you have a New Year's resolution?"

Olive didn't believe in New Year's resolutions. They seemed like something dreamed up by health clubs, a feel-good method of making it through January's postholiday blues and the guilt of overindulgence. It was so much easier to focus on a problem with your body than with your personality. So much easier to come up with a solution, too. There were products to purchase. Exercise balls, diet pills, an elliptical machine, Weight Watchers cookbooks, Pilates classes. Where was the quick fix for a character flaw like recklessness or selfishness or just downright stupidity?

"Not yet," she said. "But I probably need one. Or ten." She must have done something seriously wrong to be here. Made mistakes of epic proportions, mistakes worthy of attracting the universe's attentions. Unless it was just some random glitch in the otherwise relentless march of time. "Is that your only resolution, Aunt Laurel? To lose weight?"

Laurel's chipper expression became serious. She wiped her salty palms on her black skirt and leaned closer. "Don't tell your mom, okay? I want to try Botox. All the women I work with are trying it, and they look fabulous." Sometimes it was hard to believe Laurel was her mom's sister, they were so different.

A loud snort came from the other end of the couch, but when Olive turned to look, Sherry Witan appeared engrossed in *Barns across America* and unaware of their conversation.

"Would you excuse me for a minute?" Olive asked. "I need to use the bathroom."

She wanted to lock herself in the bathroom the way she had in third grade. Over a dinner of brats and corn on the cob, her mom had announced that Olive would have the same fourth-grade teacher Christopher had, Mrs. Katz. Christopher had been a troublemaker in her class, and Olive was horrified to think Mrs. Katz would think the same of her. Though it was painful to give up her corn on the cob with the beloved miniature corn-shaped holders, Olive fled to the downstairs bathroom and refused to come out until her dad convinced her Mrs. Katz would give her a fair shake and quickly discover what a bright, well-behaved student she was. A goody-two-shoes, Christopher had clarified.

Her dad wasn't here now to make this problem go away. She had come to this house looking for some solidity and reassurance, conveniently forgetting all that had vanished three years ago. Even though this year seemed to be standing still, time hadn't stood still in her childhood home. Everything was changing. Her mom had resurrected the New

Year's Day party tradition last year, and Olive hadn't even known about it. She hadn't been a part of it. She was ninety-five percent sure that her mom hadn't invited her last year, and if her mom had, she had intentionally misled Olive into thinking it was a different type of get-together. Somehow that seemed like the biggest betrayal—that she'd had to live a whole year of her life and return to the beginning just to find out what she'd missed that first day.

She fingered the basket of small holiday soaps her mom put out every year. These soaps were never used; they were for decoration only. There was a gold bell, a green tree, a red cardinal. Underneath the colored wax in some places, flakes of white shone through.

She knew her situation was incredible, unbelievable, unfathomable, but still she wished she didn't have to face this year again alone. She needed a confidant: someone imaginative, who could suspend his or her disbelief and just trust her. Phil was too rational; he'd insist there was some sort of explanation, maybe having to do with quantum physics, but most likely one that had to do with her mind. Kerrigan couldn't keep a secret to save her life, and her mom obviously had enough on her plate as it was.

Her face was pale and tired-looking. Her long, dark hair was knotted at the nape of her neck because she hadn't had a chance to shower yet. She looked a little unbalanced. "Maybe it is all in your mind," Olive said to herself in the mirror. She dipped her fingers in cold water and traced the circles under her eyes. She pinched the apples of her cheeks a couple of times and turned off the tap.

"I'm not crazy. I *know* I've lived this year before."

Sherry Witan was waiting to use the bathroom when Olive came out. They exchanged glances and Olive tried to smile at her because she knew most people avoided Sherry and she felt a little bad for her, sitting all alone at the end of the couch with a coffee table book throughout the entire party. Sherry squinted sternly back at her. Olive walked away.

Chapter 3

Olive's cell phone startled her awake the next morning. Tina, one of her fellow ICU nurses, was irate on the other end.

"It's ten after seven, Watson! Where are you?"

Olive was too groggy to make sense of Tina's question. She had slept poorly last night, trying to convince herself that if she believed strongly enough, she would wake up in 2012 in the tranquillity of her condo. A brief scan of her cramped bedroom proved otherwise. "I'm at home." Her voice sounded husky with sleep. She tried to clear her throat discreetly. "I'm not on till tonight. Why are you calling me?"

"You're supposed to be working the day shift this month, remember? Like we've been planning for weeks, since Jennifer's on maternity leave. And *I'm* supposed to be picking up my kids from their dad's house right now."

The day shift? Of course: last January, Olive had worked the day shift, seven A.M. to seven P.M. She had disliked every minute of it. The day shift was ten times busier with its visiting hours and grieving, beseeching family members and doctors' rounds with flocks of gawking residents and med students in tow. As someone who had been relatively new to the ICU—Olive had transferred there in October 2010 from the surgical floor—she had felt adrift in a sea of impossible demands. Taking a patient's vitals with an audience of six or more. Checking ventilators, pushing meds, drawing blood, calling for X-rays and EKGs. Bringing fathers and mothers, husbands and wives, sons and daughters back to life.

That was why she preferred the night shift, even though it put her at odds with the rest of the world's schedule. It wasn't that nothing ever happened at night. Patients worsened at all hours, and family members often watched over their loved ones through the night, but Olive looked forward to the moments when a kind of peace descended over the ICU in the early hours of the morning, when everything hung in a delicate balance.

"I'll be there as soon as I can," she said. She trapped her cell phone between her ear and shoulder and dug through the pile of dirty scrubs on her closet floor, hunting for a top that wasn't too wrinkled.

"And when will that be?" Tina snapped.

Olive felt assaulted by her tone. She knew her lateness put Tina in a tight spot, but she didn't understand the hostility in her voice. Of all the ICU nurses, Tina was her closest ally and friend. Some nights they ordered pizza with fresh mozzarella, tomato slices, and basil. Together they had imagined elaborate, fascinating lives for the intubated, geriatric patients who couldn't tell their own stories and got few visitors. Mrs. Estrada, they speculated, had danced the flamenco in her prime. Mr. Gorski, with his dyed black hair and jowls, had definitely been an Elvis impersonator. Or should've been. It had taken some time for Tina to warm up to Olive, but—

A swift realization struck her. They were back to the beginning of the year, back to the point when Tina was still wary of Olive's four-year university education and assumed Olive would look down on her own community college background. Olive had also made a series of mistakes when she first arrived that had sent her to the top of the more experienced nurse's shit list. Taking too long to start IVs, especially with elderly patients and their uncooperative, sluggish veins. Hesitating to contact the doctor on call during emergencies in the middle of the night. *It's his job, Watson. We're here, aren't we? And we aren't allowed to do anything major without him. So get his lazy ass out of bed.* But perhaps her gravest offense was showing astonishment when Tina told her that she had a seven-year-old daughter and a five-year-old son, despite the fact that she was Olive's age.

Olive sighed. Showing up late today would surely not endear her to Tina. Regaining her friendship would be another uphill battle. "Twenty minutes, tops," she promised Tina, and tried to shimmy into a pair of mint green drawstring pants. Olive could still hear her grumbling into the phone about having to call her ex-husband when Tina disconnected.

Kerrigan had a pot of coffee brewing. The wide-open bathroom door afforded Olive a view of her friend already dressed for the gym.

"What are you doing up?" Kerrigan asked.

"I have to work the day shift this month. I'm already fifteen minutes late, and Tina's ready to murder me."

"Have some coffee first. You look rough."

"No time." Olive spun in a helpless circle, trying to remember where she kept her backpack in this apartment. The coat closet.

"Five more minutes won't make a difference. Sit down and have a cup. I'll braid your hair."

Kerrigan loved to braid hair, especially long hair. She wasn't particularly good at it—some braids turned out lopsided, one strand much thicker than the others, and her French braids sometimes sloped diagonally across Olive's scalp—but her fingers were gentle and soothing. And the girl had a point: What difference would five minutes make? Tina was already enraged.

Olive breathed in the aroma of her coffee. Kerrigan sat behind her, weaving together sections of Olive's hair. She had forgotten how Kerrigan could be her own planet with a distinct gravitational pull, exerting both acceptance and a tremendous sense of calm. Olive had first experienced this her freshman year at the University of Wisconsin, her second weekend in the dorms. The first two weeks had flown by gaily with dorm-sponsored events, get-to-know-you games, and meals at the cafeteria with her roommate, Brandi. But then the second weekend came, and Brandi had left to visit her boyfriend in Whitewater. Olive would have liked to go home, too, but her parents were both too sapped, figuratively and literally, by her dad's chemotherapy treatments to make the trip to campus to collect her. She missed them terribly.

She tried to keep herself occupied. She called her best friends from high school, Maggie and Alistair, who were attending the University of Wisconsin–Milwaukee, to see how they were doing. Maggie sounded like her usual bubbly self; she'd made several friends already and they were planning a birthday party for one of the girls in her suite that night. Olive couldn't even get hold of Alistair, who she presumed had become such a man-about-town by now that he wouldn't be caught dead stuck inside his dorm room on the weekend. She sat inside her dorm room, first with the door open, hoping to attract passersby, but then after that didn't work and she started to feel like a zoo animal on display, with the door shut. The longer she stayed inside, the harder it became to come out. Loud, happy voices ricocheted in the hallway outside her door. If she came out now, they would wonder what kind of loser sat alone in her room on a Saturday night. She didn't venture out for dinner, fearing eating alone at the cafeteria, instead making a meal from her supply of snacks.

Around ten o'clock, she really needed to use the bathroom. The sounds in the hallway had dwindled; she figured almost everyone in the dorm had gone out to some frat party by then. Trying to look ill in case anyone questioned her, she made a beeline for the girls' bathroom at the end of the hall. Pushing open the door, she was startled to see someone perched in the open window in nothing but an oversized black T-shirt. The girl's hair was twisted on top of her head in a chignon and covered in what appeared to be banana pudding. Hair supplies—combs, brushes, clips, bottles, and creams—were strewn across the three sinks.

The girl turned from looking out the window to take Olive in. Her face was strikingly pretty, pretty in the way of prom queens and girls in skin cleanser commercials, but her dressed-down appearance tempered the effect. "Hi," she called from the window. "Is that your natural hair color?"

Olive touched a strand of her long, dark chocolate-colored hair, as if checking to make sure it was still there. It slithered through her fingertips, falling back against her shoulder. "Yes."

The girl pointed to the creamy mixture on her head. "Touching up my roots," she said, and swiveled in the windowsill, her bare legs dangling down, her back pressing against the wire mesh screen. "You know they always say blondes have more fun, but if I had naturally brown hair like that . . . My own natural color is more of a 'dishwater' blond—gosh, who ever heard of having your hair compared to dirty dishwater as a good thing? Yuck. Don't ever dye your hair," she concluded. "It's gorgeous. Color like that doesn't come from a bottle. Believe me, I've tried."

"Thank you," Olive replied. She felt awkward about ducking into one of the stalls now, not sure if their conversation, if it could be called that, was over, but she really needed to relieve herself. When she emerged, the girl was in front of the sinks, clearing away a space for Olive to wash her hands.

"I'm Kerrigan Morland, by the way. I'm in 410." She frowned slightly. "My mom is into all things Irish, but she didn't do her homework before she named me. It means 'one with dark coloring.'"

Olive laughed as she dried her hands on a paper towel. "Olive Watson, after my grandmother. I'm in 406."

"Oh, *you're* Olive," Kerrigan said, in a tone that worried Olive that rumors had already started about her: the antisocial girl who never went out on weekends. Kerrigan must have seen the anxiety in her eyes, because she hastily added, "I've wanted to meet you since I saw your name sign on your door. I thought to myself that anyone named Olive *must* be cool. I'm so tired of all the Brittanys and Ashleys of the world. There are four girls in my calculus discussion section named

Katelyn, except they all spell it differently. *K-A-T-E-L-Y-N. C-A-I-T-L-I-N. C-A-Y-T-L-Y-N-N-E.* Okay, I made that last one up. But seriously."

There was a long moment, and Olive fretted that she was supposed to follow this rant with some witty comment. She missed the mellow, easy banter of her high school friends. In college, every conversation felt like a contest to determine who was the smartest and funniest. How was she ever going to make friends if she could never get a word in edgewise?

Kerrigan was watching her, but her expression wasn't judgmental. "Have you seen this view?" she asked. "It's amazing." She gestured to the window ledge where she had been sitting. "You need to sit down to see it. I think it's mostly safe."

Olive wanted to retreat to her room, where it was *totally* safe, but something made her stay. Perhaps it was her awe of this girl who exuded so much confidence that she was at ease dying her hair in just her Goo Goo Dolls concert T-shirt on a Saturday night in the girls' bathroom. Or maybe it was because this was the first person who had reached out to her, truly reached out to her besides the standard "name-hometown-major" questions, and she felt grateful despite Kerrigan's obvious eccentricities.

She sat down on the ledge, tucking her knees in the way Kerrigan showed her. The screen seemed even flimsier up close. They were on the fourth floor, and if she lost her balance, it was the only thing separating her from plummeting to the cement pathway below. "What am I looking for, exactly?" she asked, eager to get this stunt over with.

"The lake," Kerrigan said. "Look way off to the left. You can just see it behind the trees."

She was right. Beyond the jagged outlines of the trees spread an amorphous bluish black that was so profound it was hard to tell if it was water or sky, earth or heaven. Lake Mendota. Olive hugged her knees to her chest. The night breeze carried the smell of the lake to her—a musty, primordial odor that reminded her of death. At that moment, she subconsciously understood that her dad was not going to win his battle with cancer and that she would one day, in the not too distant future, lose him.

"It's very pretty," she said, leaping up.

"Are you okay?" Kerrigan asked. She had rinsed the dye from her hair while Olive was at the window, and her hair now hung in golden tangles around her face. When Olive didn't respond, she continued, "I think the worst thing about this place is how *happy* everyone pretends to be all the time. I mean, you know that everyone is missing their families and their friends and their houses and their pets and their privacy. And they're all scared and confused about what they're doing here and what they're going to do with their lives, and if they're good enough, or smart enough, or whatever, but they still feel obligated to pretend that they're having the time of their lives."

Though Olive had promised herself she wouldn't tell anyone in the dorms about her dad's leukemia—she didn't want to be like Samantha Trevors from high school, whose mother had Huntington's disease and whom everybody had pitied and held at arm's length—she told Kerrigan, this girl she had known for all of five minutes, everything. And Kerrigan listened thoughtfully as though she were memorizing each of Olive's sorrows and trying them on. When two rowdy drunk girls stumbled into the bathroom, Kerrigan guided Olive into her dorm room to continue the conversation without even pausing to clean up her hair dye mess. Surrounded by satiny pillows on Kerrigan's futon, Olive felt her loneliness lift. She had never met anyone like Kerrigan before, someone who could switch as easily from being playful and outgoing to contemplative and caring as though simply flipping from one radio station to the next.

"Don't move your head around so much. Otherwise the braid will be crooked." Kerrigan pressed her palms firmly against Olive's temples.

Olive laughed. The braid would most likely turn out crooked no matter what, but she didn't mind. It was strange thinking of Kerrigan as the girl in the Goo Goo Dolls T-shirt dyeing her hair in the dorm bathroom eight years ago. She hadn't known it at the time, but Kerrigan had felt just as lonely and out of place as she had. They had become best friends overnight, in the effortless way of small children, trusting in the confidence of their instincts, never imagining that one could hurt or leave the other. How had she forgotten how essentially *good* Kerrigan was?

She wanted to hug her friend for the hair braiding, this spontaneous act of tenderness. She felt taken care of. So much of her time she spent tending to others. It was nice to have someone looking after *her* needs. It had been a long time since anyone saw to that. Probably not since Phil. She remembered his offer of pancakes and the light brush of his fingers against her bare abdomen. *Come back to bed.* Despite herself, she shivered.

"Did I get your ticklish spot?" Kerrigan's fingers fluttered against the nape of her neck.

After the caffeine and therapeutic hair braiding, Olive felt almost human again. She parked in the staff parking near Dane County General's emergency entrance and took the elevator to the second floor, ready to face Tina's wrath and the bustle of the day shift. She craved the repetitive tasks of her job. Drawing a blood sample would restore normalcy to her world. Watching the steady green waves on a cardiac monitor might help her forget the agitation of her own heart.

Tina ambushed her with a chart before Olive had even locked up her backpack. She watched reproachfully as Olive struggled to squeeze the backpack into the narrow locker. Then they set off at a clip through the semicircular ward to one of the patient rooms.

"A new patient came in last night," Tina called over her shoulder. Olive struggled to keep up with her. "Sarah Hutchinson, a nineteen-year-old UW student with bacterial meningitis. We've started her on vancomycin and meropenem. Her temperature and white count are a little high, but almost back to normal. There's an ICP monitor to check for any brain swelling. Her father is in the waiting room. He's very anxious, but I convinced him to get some rest. He'll want you to call him back in here after rounds."

They halted just outside the young woman's room. Each of the patient rooms in the ICU had a floor-to-ceiling window so the nurses could keep an eye on their patients at all times; *fishbowls*, the rooms were called. Olive stared in disbelief at the girl's familiar lanky figure beneath the pale blue cotton sheet. Sarah Hutchinson. A nineteen-year-old University of Wisconsin student. Majoring in dairy science to take over the family farm one day. An only child with a dead mother and an overprotective father. Olive listed these details off in her head as surely as if Tina had provided them.

She stepped inside the room and drew close to the girl's bedside. Sarah Hutchinson's hair was the color of sun-bleached prairie grass. A patch had been shaved for the insertion of a thin plastic tube, the ICP monitor, into a bolt in her skull. Instinctively, Olive raised her hand to touch her own hair. She remembered how horrified she had been at first by the ICP monitor and its invasiveness, the way it wormed its way into the brain, which Olive had come to view as the last place of privacy in the human body. Tubes invaded throats, catheters probed bladders, IVs snaked their way into veins and arteries in hands, arms, and thighs, yet the brain felt sacred to her, which was why she had avoided neurology as a specialty.

But now she knew that Sarah, in her unconscious state, felt no pain from the ICP monitor's presence. She also knew that the teenager would recover quickly and leave the hospital within a few days, with no signs of permanent brain damage. She could almost see the yellow balloons Sarah's father had tied to the handlebars of the wheelchair in which he had delivered her from the hospital. Sarah Hutchinson felt like a cousin. Olive leaned close to her expressionless face; even her blond eyebrows and eyelashes looked colorless and shy.

Olive's momentary paralysis prompted Tina to step into the room. "Hey," Tina said gently, misinterpreting her stillness. She touched Olive's elbow. "She's going to be okay. She got here just in time."

Olive turned around, but Tina was already heading to their next patient's room.

"Mr. Paulson came in on New Year's Eve from Green Glen Nursing Home. A seventy-nine-year-old diabetic suffering from pneumonia. It's amazing he's lived this long; I don't know what they thought they'd accomplish bringing him here. It seemed just plain cruel to intubate him. We're trying to wean him off the ventilator now. You know how that goes." Tina closed the charts with a conclusive snap that seemed to dare Olive to ask her questions and detain her any longer.

"Thanks," Olive said. She wanted to apologize for her tardiness and give Tina a valid excuse, but what could she say? *I'm sorry, Tina, but I woke up in 2011, when I thought I would be waking up in 2012, so I confused my work schedule?* Or *I've already lived this year, and reliving it is just a little disorienting for me, so could you please just cut me some slack?* But before she could construct any kind of apology, Tina left.

Only a few tufts of white hair covered Mr. Paulson's flaky scalp. He hadn't left as much of an impression on Olive as Sarah Hutchinson had, which made her feel a little guilty. She felt sorry for the man her memory had blotted out, or, perhaps more accurately, the man who had become lumped in with the hundreds of nameless, faceless elderly patients who came to the ICU with pneumonia every year. Their wrinkled, distorted features once handsome, their diminished bodies commenced a trip backward through time, returning first to infancy, and then marching onward to their death. Olive was there to make their trip more comfortable, or sometimes, if necessary at a family member's request, prolong the time until they reached their destination.

Already running behind, she hurried to take his vitals. The troupe of residents on their rounds would be inquiring after her patients soon, and she hated measuring how much urine was in a Foley catheter in front of an audience. She tallied Mr. Paulson's fluid balance and was almost out the door before she remembered the most important part of nursing, as Gloria, the compassionate nurse who'd mentored her, had put it.

She covered Mr. Paulson's tubing-free hand with her own. His skin felt like worn flannel. "Mr. Paulson, I'm your nurse, Olive, and I'm going to be taking good care of you. We're going to have you back to Green Glen in no time, watching baseball or cardinals at the bird feeder, or whatever it is you like to do there, okay? Okay."

Talking to the unconscious patients had once seemed like an exercise in futility to Olive. She had felt awkward and theatrical, like she was holding a conversation with herself. But now it came second nature to her, and it helped remind her that her patients were real people with real stories, not just bodies to be bathed and cared for.

A cluster of white coats stood outside Sarah's room. Without realizing it, Olive scanned the group for Alex. He wasn't among them. She was grateful.

Dr. Su, the attending physician, smiled when she saw Olive approach. "Your patient?"

Olive nodded and ducked into the room. Being thrust back into the beginning of her ICU career off-kilter like this made her feel incompetent and unsure of herself. *You've had over a year of experience in this,* she reminded herself. *Just chill out. You know what you're doing.* Even if no one else thought she did. And of the five people in the room—six, including Sarah—Olive was the only one who knew for certain what would happen to the college student. Although she didn't write off Sarah's recovery as an inevitability. Everything still had to be done vigilantly. No care or treatment could be neglected. That thought steadied her hands as she measured Sarah's blood pressure. She rattled off numbers to

Dr. Su and her residents, and after a brief discussion, they went on their way.

She stood at the foot of Sarah's bed for a moment and allowed herself to appreciate the weirdness of the situation. The forward momentum of the past twenty-four hours came to a screeching halt. She'd had repeat patients before—like poor Mrs. Gertler, whose body had rejected her new kidney and needed to be put back on dialysis—but never in such a literal way. She tried to imagine what Sarah had done last year after her hospital stay. She tried to imagine her studying for an economics exam or cheering at a Badger game but couldn't. To Olive, Sarah somehow existed only in this hospital bed, in this blue-speckled gown, with a patch of her white-blond hair missing.

"Miss Hutchinson, I'm your nurse, Olive," she started, and then didn't know what else to say. She patted the girl's bony foot through the sheet. "You probably don't remember me, but we've met before. You pulled through then, and I promise I'll help you pull through now."

She looked up to see Mr. Hutchinson's lanky figure obscuring the window. The stubble on his face and dark smudges under his eyes confirmed Tina's report that he'd spent the night at the hospital. He wore ribbed corduroy pants and a denim shirt and held a furry winter cap in his hands. Olive remembered the intimidation he had inspired in her last year. Now she saw him only as a man filled with sorrow and remorse. She knew he blamed himself for his daughter's sickness. He hadn't wanted her to go to college for reasons like this.

Stepping into the room, he was immediately on the offensive. "The other nurse said I could come in here around half past eight. She said someone would come get me, but nobody did."

"It's been a busy morning," she said. "But you're more than welcome to sit with Sarah now."

Mr. Hutchinson took the seat next to his daughter's bed. "How's she doing?"

"She's doing well. Her heart rate and blood pressure are strong, and her white blood cell count and temperature are steadily becoming more normal."

"Aren't there any doctors around here? No offense, but I'd rather hear this from a doctor."

"Sarah's physician, Dr. Su, just checked in on her, and agreed that she's doing quite well."

"Is he still around? I've got a lot of questions."

"She's conducting her rounds right now. She should be back soon, if you'd like to speak with her."

"Yes, I would. And why are there bubbles in Sarah's IV tubing? Couldn't one of those bubbles go straight to her heart and kill her?"

Olive straightened out a kinked length of tubing and flicked away the bubbles. "They're quite harmless." She was surprised by the way her earlier feeling of enlightenment was swiftly being eroded. She felt like strangling him with the tubing. Yet when she turned around, she saw he had his head in his hands. He rubbed his forehead vigorously. She knew what was coming next. Olive watched Mr. Hutchinson expectantly. She felt like she was waiting for an upcoming monologue in a play she'd seen before.

"I didn't want her to go to Madison," he began, head still in hands. "I didn't go to college, my father didn't go to college, and we did just fine on our farm. And now all of a sudden, folks are telling us we need some fancy college education to run a dairy? Heck, our cows don't need a diploma to know how to produce milk. But Sarah wanted to go to school; she wanted to make our farm more profitable, and I was stupid enough to let her go. And look where it got her!" Here he got choked up, and his next words came out strangled. "Deathly ill. Lying in a hospital bed like her poor mother, God rest her soul."

Olive was ready to offer him what solace and reassurance she could. She had never before known with such certainty the right thing to say to a patient's family member. "Mr. Hutchinson, letting Sarah go off to college was very generous of you. It shows how much you love your daughter. Don't think of it as a mistake. Sickness can come at any time or any place. And Sarah's strong. I know she's going to recover soon and be back to her old self. I have a very good feeling about that."

Mr. Hutchinson looked up at her and instead of relief in his eyes, she saw anger. "You don't know that. That's what they told me about my wife ten years ago, and she died within the week. So don't you make me any promises you can't keep." He stood up and looked as if he'd like to stalk out of the room, but thought better of it because he didn't want to leave Sarah. "Where's that doctor? Can you bring that doctor to me?"

She had been naïve to think that her reassurance would mean something to Mr. Hutchinson. He simply viewed it as the same kind of hollow promise that other doctors and nurses made. He didn't have a grain of trust in Olive and wouldn't believe in his daughter's recovery until he witnessed it with his own eyes. If that meant staying at her bedside for the next three days, he would do it. She didn't blame him, and yet she longed to tell him about the yellow balloons and give him something to which he could cling.

Olive was relieved to take her lunch break at one o'clock, even if she had no one to take it with. At this point in the year, she was still the new girl who hadn't quite broken into their cliques. With the stress of her morning, she didn't mind sitting alone at a round table in the hospital cafeteria. Instead of trying to make polite conversation, she had a moment to finally let down her guard and do some serious wallowing in the horrifying implications of reliving this year. She didn't think she could come back here day after day, night after night, and see the same patients over again in their various stages of dying. It was all too cyclical. It all felt so pointless. But maybe there was more to it. Maybe she was supposed to use her foreknowledge of the year to save lives. The thought was both exhilarating and exhausting at the same time.

There were two voice mail messages on her cell phone: one from her mom, the other from Phil. Hearing his voice felt like swimming up to the surface after being underwater for a long time. She pressed the phone to her ear and tried to remember this was someone she had broken up with and lived without for the past ten months. Someone who had pushed her away. Someone who had been incapable of giving her a second chance. How could he still have such an effect on her? She felt betrayed by her own feelings.

"Hey, Ollie. It's me. You must be at work. I thought you might call in sick today, but I should've known better. I guess that means you're back to your old self? I hope so anyway. My dad's in town tonight, and he asked if he could take me out to dinner, sometime around eight. I was hoping you might come along. Call me when you get off work. Love you. Bye."

Phil and his father, Charlie, shared a volatile past. For the first eight years of Phil's life, he had believed his father had separated the light from the dark and the ocean from the sky. Charlie had taken him along on short-distance hauls to Chicago and Des Moines and the Twin Cities, feeding him gas station candy and truck stop breakfasts and teaching him the science of the road. But that had all changed in 1993 when Charlie lost his job, and his drinking, which had always been a problem lurking in the corner, got really ugly. Not long after that, Phil's parents got a divorce, and Charlie became less and less a part of Phil's life, until he disappeared altogether. In the spring of 2010, he had suddenly reappeared—sobered up, attending AA meetings, and wanting to be part of his grown son's life. Phil refused at first but eventually allowed himself to be persuaded to go out to dinner. They had gone out a handful of times since then, whenever Charlie passed through Madison.

Olive couldn't imagine going out to dinner with Phil and Charlie tonight, the tense silence as steak knives scratched against plates, the banal talk of rising gas prices. But what was more, she couldn't imagine simply picking up where she'd left off with Phil, before things had fallen apart, and pretending everything was normal between them. It seemed deceitful. Where was the ethics manual for all of this? If you wronged someone in a year that you had lived through, but the year seemed to exist for no one else, had it really happened? Her conscience, always loudest at the most inconvenient times, spoke up: *Yes, of course. To you, it happened. You did it and you remember it. So you're still responsible.* But if you broke someone's heart, and the other person didn't remember, was it so wrong just to slip back into his arms? *Theoretical question,* she told her conscience before it could respond.

The rest of her shift felt like a television rerun. She couldn't remember the entire script, but she knew the shape of the day. Some events resounded in her head. The Amish family that walked solemnly through the ward like a funeral procession to visit a middle-aged woman with lymphoma. The way the day nurse manager, Toya, got the theme from *Raiders of the Lost Ark* stuck in everyone's head, because whenever she saw the respiratory therapist, whom she thought looked like a young Harrison Ford, she would hum the first few bars. (Behind his back, they all called him Indy.) A basket of teddy bear cookies on sticks arrived. They were decorated to look as though the bears were wearing scrubs and surgical masks and were sent by a former patient's family in gratitude—a family whose loved one had lived, of course; the ICU staff was rarely thanked for the care they had given to patients who died.

Before Olive left for the night, she briefed the incoming nurse, Kevin. Then she moved from room to room, dimming the overhead lights in the patient rooms to bring them the twilight they had missed.

Chapter 4

After working for twelve hours, Olive found it difficult to reenter the world. She often thought of coal miners emerging from the bowels of the earth: blinking and rubbing their eyes against the daylight, marveling that their trucks were parked where they had left them, that their homes had mirrors and electric lights and their children scrubbed-pink fingers. She inhaled the fresh wintry air and then picked her way across the slushy parking lot to her SUV.

When she had first started in the ICU last year, it had been almost impossible to reconcile her work life with her personal life. She had scoffed at Phil's complaints about his obnoxious, lazy students and her mom's anxiety that her extended family would feel excluded from the wedding. It had been difficult for her to care about what to have for dinner, or whose turn it was to pay the cable bill, or the illogical filing system Kerrigan's office had recently implemented. The stakes in that part of her life were mercifully lower; nothing could compare to the tragedies she witnessed every day. Kerrigan had once accused her of being condescending.

But eventually she had learned to dim the fluorescent lights in her mind. While the faces of her dying patients flickered before her eyes frequently, she did not bring them up at the dinner table. She did not talk about tumors like jellyfish or skin that had been so badly burned it flaked and crumbled like dead leaves. She did not talk about toddlers who would grow up without their mothers or husbands who lay weeping on the tile floor. She kept most of this to herself.

It was already pitch-black when she climbed the pink, rickety stairs to her apartment. Miserable Wisconsin winters with their scanty hours of daylight. She longed to put her feet up. To take a hot shower and crawl into bed with her hair still damp and clean-smelling. She had hardly set foot on the landing when Kerrigan greeted her at the door. Kerrigan gripped her coat sleeve and blocked her entry into the apartment.

"Were you expecting a visitor?" She took a step back, allowing Olive to stand on the welcome mat.

Olive's initial thought was that it was Phil waiting for her. Dinner with his dad, she suddenly remembered. She hadn't called him back! He was probably sitting sullenly in a papasan chair, jiggling one of his long legs in that impatient way he had.

But Kerrigan continued in a rushed whisper. "She's been here for almost an hour. One of your mom's friends, she said. I tried to tell her that I didn't know what time you'd be home and that I had somewhere to be, but she insisted on waiting for you." She backed up farther, allowing Olive an unobstructed view of the living room.

A heavy woman with graying reddish hair sat on the

black-and-white floral couch. Sherry Witan. She looked quite at home in Olive's living room, even though she had never set foot in the apartment before.

"Hi, Sherry," Olive said. "What a nice surprise." She hoped she sounded convincing. *Surprise* was definitely the right word for what she was feeling right now, but not preceded by an adjective like *nice*. She couldn't imagine why Sherry Witan was here. Olive had never seen her outside her parents' parties before. It wasn't as though they were good friends who went out for coffee and chatted weekly on the phone; she didn't think her mom even maintained a close relationship with her. At her parents' parties, Olive had never held a conversation with Sherry that exceeded the typical one-minute party platitudes. "Hi, how are you doing?" "Good. How are you?" "Great. This hummus is fantastic." "My mom's a good cook." "She is." Olive had found that she had relatively few small-talk skills. She didn't seem to notice the awkward pauses and would instead gaze intently at the speaker as though eye contact were the only crucial element in a social encounter.

Sherry didn't stand. Instead, she swiveled her head like an owl to survey Olive. "Your mother gave me your address. I hope you don't mind."

"Not at all." Olive sat down in the papasan chair closest to Sherry. "Is there something you wanted to talk about?"

Sherry ignored the question. Her eyes swept over the room, seeming to miss nothing. Kerrigan's *On Wisconsin* alumni magazines and issues of *Sports Illustrated* on the coffee table. The dusty artificial orchid. Nail holes riddled the walls and yellowish water stains bruised the ceiling. A beer bottle hid halfway behind the TV.

Olive scrutinized the living room, too. When she returned her attention to Sherry, Olive found that she was watching her as though no one had ever taught her not to stare, as though she believed she was magically concealed from public view and therefore able to watch people as hungrily and conspicuously as she liked. Olive stared back. Sherry was in her late fifties. *Large* was the best word to describe her. She carried her weight with importance and made you feel in her presence, especially if you were thin, that you were an insubstantial waif. Her facial features were remarkably refined and delicate by contrast to her body: narrow brown eyes; thin, pink lips; a small, babyish nose; finely penciled-in eyebrows. If you studied Sherry in two separate photographs, one of her face and one of her body, you would never imagine that the two parts belonged to one another, and yet they somehow seemed to work in harmony for her. Her hair was a washed-out red that defiantly revealed several inches of gray roots at her part and temples. It fell in loose waves over the shoulders of her fringed gray silk shawl.

"I'm leaving," Kerrigan called in a loud voice from the foyer area. "I'm supposed to meet Steve for dinner and the hockey game. I'm already almost twenty minutes late." Olive straightened herself up and peered over Sherry's head. Kerrigan stood as if waiting for some kind of recognition that she was free to go. She raised her eyebrows at Olive.

"Okay. Have fun. Thanks for waiting."

When Kerrigan had left, Sherry sank back more comfortably into the couch. She absentmindedly stroked one of the fringes of her shawl.

Olive had used up all her patience and soft tones with Mr. Hutchinson. She didn't want to be nice anymore; she wanted to demand that Sherry state her purpose and then go. There was so much to think about, and anywhere other than her bed right now felt like an unbearable place to be. The only thing that was preventing her from losing her temper was the memory of Sherry's well-timed snort yesterday. That and a tiny voice begging Olive to take notice: Sherry had not made this unexpected visit to her place last year.

"Did you enjoy the party yesterday?" Olive asked.

"I always do. Your mother's guacamole was excellent. I was surprised to get an invitation. It's been a while since Kathy's thrown a party, hasn't it?"

"It has." For a moment, the death of her father and courtship of her mother floated between them. And because Sherry's expression encouraged her to say more, Olive said, "Three years to be exact. Or rather, two years." She flushed.

Sherry nodded regally, as if by granting her approval, she was bestowing a favor on Olive. "And are you having a nice new year so far?"

Her question caught Olive off guard. She was about to say, *Yes, and you?* but something stopped her. There was something about the way Sherry had said *new.* Most people rushed the words *new* and *year* together as though they were an inseparable expression, part of a phrase that had become almost meaningless with use. But Sherry pronounced the word as though she were asking a question. As in: Oh, is that sweater new? As in: But is this year *really* new? "It's been kind of crazy," Olive said at last. "I'm having a hard time adjusting."

Sherry steepled her masculine fingers. Her intense brown eyes sought Olive's in a way that made Olive feel as though Sherry were physically reaching out to her, not just reaching, but pulling. At that moment Olive fully appreciated something that she had always suspected: Sherry Witan was not an ordinary middle-aged woman. She was not simply bookish or socially awkward. She was alien. Olive had been only twelve years old when her mother introduced her to Sherry, whom she was instructed to call *Ms.* Witan. Four other women had come over to their house to discuss *Tess of the d'Urbervilles*, which had stuck in Olive's head because of its funny-sounding title. She'd been quietly finishing her social studies homework in the kitchen when shouts erupted from the living room. Poking her head through the doorway, Olive had witnessed a white-faced Sherry towering over the other book club ladies. "None of you get it," she had accused. "You don't understand the sacrifice she made for him. Why did she even tell him the truth? For *love*? *For nothing.* Look where it got her."

Olive saw the same intensity in Sherry's face now. But instead of yelling, Sherry murmured, "I overheard you yesterday."

"I know." Sherry hadn't exactly been Miss Subtle at the other end of the couch with her nose stuck in *Barns across America*. "With my aunt Laurel. I heard you"—she had been about to say *snort* but thought better of it—"laugh."

Sherry shook her head. "That's not what I'm referring to. I was outside the bathroom. You said, 'I'm not crazy. I know I've lived this year before.'"

Olive felt her cheeks flush. At the very moment she had been wishing for a confidant, a nosy eavesdropper had been lurking outside the bathroom. She didn't know what to make of this. Was Sherry questioning her sanity? Would she tell her mother? Or was it possible that Sherry was experiencing the same thing?

"I saw you looking at that wall of family photographs. I

saw you studying that newspaper." Sherry listed these facts off as if they were proof of a crime. She stared at Olive.

Olive didn't break eye contact. "So what?" she asked, and sat perfectly still with her hands clasped in her lap as though she were posing for a portrait that Sherry was drawing.

"I've talked to only one other person about this before, so if I got it wrong, just forget it." Sherry scooted forward until her knees were brushing the coffee table. She and Olive were now leaning toward one another, like friends with a secret.

"Please go on."

"It's not just a feeling, Olive. It's real. You've already lived through 2011. I have, too, and I remember all 365 days of it. But here I am back at the beginning. Here we are, I should say."

Olive nodded, not trusting her voice. The mixture of relief and vindication she'd been expecting to feel—to have someone else acknowledge this bizarre occurrence—did not come. Instead, to hear it spoken aloud—spoken aloud by someone like Sherry Witan, no less—made the whole thing seem like an elaborate hoax. She felt inexplicably defeated.

"I went to bed in December 2011 and woke up the next day in January 2011," Olive mused aloud. She knew there was no taking it back now that she had spoken it in Sherry's presence. She had chosen her side, or rather, her side had been chosen for her. The surreal side. Sherry Witan's side.

"So I thought." Sherry nodded again with her magisterial grace. She removed her fringed shawl and spread it across her lap like a blanket. Underneath, she was wearing a white blouse with lace detailing on the collar and sleeves.

"Are there other people? Do you know why this happened? What are we supposed to do?"

Sherry held up her hands as though to dam up the flood

of questions. Her left hand was bare, Olive noticed. No wedding ring. She had heard from her mom that Sherry had been married something like three or four times. On her right hand was a thick-banded gold ring with a garnet the size of a grape.

"Slow down. I've got a lot to tell you, and I don't want to leave anything out," Sherry said. "I should start by telling you that this isn't my first time."

"You mean you've lived this year over more than once already?" Olive asked in disbelief. She saw the past year loop before her eyes, continuously, over and over again like the reel of a movie. She imagined 2011 was a trap. Perhaps, one by one, everyone would fall into it until the history of the world repeated and erased itself at the start and end of every year—always the same year, 2011. Or maybe it was just she and Sherry stuck here while everyone else marched forward.

Sherry held up her bare left hand again to silence Olive. "No, not 2011. This is my first time repeating it, same as you. What I meant was I've repeated other years in the past. My first was 1982. And then 1997. I had to repeat 2005 twice."

"You had to live the same year three times?" Olive asked. She felt a little light-headed at the prospect. "Why did you have to do that one over again and not the others?"

"Calm down, calm down. You look like you're going to faint. Why don't I get us something to drink? Is it okay if I do that?"

Sherry looked fuzzy and pixilated as she walked to the kitchenette. Olive rested her head against her knees. Three times? How many additional years had Sherry lived total? Four years? This would be Sherry's fifth repeat. Would Olive have the same fate?

"For heaven's sake," she heard Sherry say from the kitchen area. "You've only got beer and diet soda in here. How do you kids live? No milk? No orange juice?" Olive heard the wooden rattle of drawers and cupboards opening and closing. "Don't you have any tea?" Sherry called.

"I don't drink tea," Olive called back. She had to lift her head momentarily from her knees to respond. "My roommate does, though. There might be some in the silverware drawer. You can make some for yourself, but I don't want any."

Sherry stood before her shortly holding two mugs. One of them was a novelty mug that read, *You are dumb.* The other was a global warming mug that had a map of the world drawn on it; when you poured a hot beverage in it, some of the land disappeared. Olive chose global warming. The bitter smell of green tea rose up from it. She watched as Florida vanished.

"Thanks. I don't really like tea, though," she said, and bent down to untie her tennis shoes.

Sherry resumed her spot on the couch. "You should try it. It will make you feel better."

"I've tried tea before. It's not really my thing," Olive protested, but she took a small sip to show Sherry she was appreciative of her efforts. The green tea looked and smelled like what she imagined urine would look and smell like after someone had eaten large quantities of grass. Perhaps the tea even tasted like it, although she had no proof to back this up. "Mmm. Yeah, it's still not my thing." She pulled out the drawer of the coffee table and extracted two sandstone coasters. She set her mug down on one of them and laid the other within Sherry's reach.

"See? You look like you're feeling better already."

"I'm eager to hear what you have to say about this—" She

interrupted herself, not sure what to call it. Phenomenon? Time warp? Miracle? Curse? "This . . . *this*." She kicked her tennis shoes under the coffee table.

"I knew you would be. So let's see. Where to start? I've never done this before." Sherry looked pleased with her role as storyteller. "I've met only one other person who's repeated a year before, at least in the thirty years I've known about it. There could have been people in my childhood and adolescence who were experiencing the same thing, but I wasn't aware of it. The one other person I met was my first husband's boss, the district attorney. But he wasn't very receptive to my conversation. It was my first time, in '82, and I had just as many questions for him as you have now."

"How did you know he was living the same year over?" Olive asked.

"My husband, Clyde, kept making comments about him at home. Gene McGregor was his name. I guess in meetings he would hint at the fact that he could predict the outcome of a trial, and was insistent on the fact that if they didn't do A, B, and C, they would fail. In theory this doesn't sound that strange for an arrogant lawyer, but Clyde and some of his coworkers suspected something else was at work. They began to wonder if Gene was getting outside information and, in effect, working with the defense. There was one particular case in March of that year that Clyde told me about. Gene was in a frenzy trying to convince his staff that the evidence wouldn't hold in court and that they needed to come up with some other tactic. Clyde went out to a bar with Gene one night and Gene confessed that if he lost this case, he knew he would never find rest, and claimed he would be stuck in the 'purgatory of this year all over again.' After Clyde relayed this to me, clearly thinking that his boss had lost it, I decided to seek Gene out and confirm if my suspicions were accurate.

"It took a great deal of courage for me to go over to his house—I was only a little older than you at the time. Gene answered the door completely plastered. We had met briefly at the office Christmas party, but he couldn't conceive why one of his employee's young wives was visiting him at his home. I tried to talk to him about the big case he was working on, but he became really angry, saying that Clyde shouldn't be sharing confidential issues with me. I tried to placate him, and he invited me inside for a drink, asked me if I was lonely because Clyde was working late. I realized I had better articulate myself more clearly, so I was very blunt with Gene. I asked him if he was reliving 1982.

"I could tell from his shocked expression that I had hit the nail on the head, but he didn't want to admit it. He told me he would blow his head off if he had to live 1982 over again. I asked him if he thought failing to put an evil man behind bars had been the impetus for his repeated year, if it was the event he needed to correct before moving on, that that was my theory of how things worked. He laughed at me and told me I was delusional. I was barely out the door when he came out onto the front lawn and asked me what I supposed he should do to change the course of his year. I told him that I didn't know but I thought winning the trial would be a good start, although it couldn't hurt to focus on improving other aspects of his life as well."

"So did he make it to 1983?" Olive asked.

"He did. But I'm not sure how long it took him to get there. I cornered him at the office Christmas party and asked him to contact me on New Year's Day, but he didn't. I was too afraid to go back to his house, so I called him at the office. He acted like he hardly remembered me, like it had been years since we'd talked, not just days. He wouldn't tell me for sure, but I think it *had been* years for him."

She turned to Olive, as if suddenly remembering her presence. "But that won't happen to you. Gene was an anomaly. He was a pretty awful man, and you know what? They never won that trial."

But Olive was still trying to wrap her head around the idea of the lawyer existing in some sort of alternate reality as the rest of the world, Sherry included, had sped past him. Years of his life condensed into mere minutes for everyone else. "But didn't you just say you had to live 2005 over twice?" she asked.

"Don't focus on that," Sherry said. She tapped a spoon against her mug. The sound rang out like a chiming bell. "It will only make things worse. You have to focus on the big picture. The reason for the repeat year."

"So what you're saying is that the essential idea behind reliving this year is to correct something we did wrong last year?" Perhaps Olive hadn't been far off the mark yesterday when she'd supposed that she'd done something seriously wrong last year to deserve this fate.

"That was my theory," Sherry said. "But it's not quite as simple as that. If every time someone made a mistake, they had to relive that year, we'd all be in the same boat. We'd all probably still be in the Stone Age because we wouldn't be able to progress further than that. But as far as I can tell, there are only a few of us having these experiences."

"Perhaps it's some kind of major mistake we made that

affects the outcome of the world?" Olive offered, feeling sheepish immediately after the question escaped her mouth.

Sherry's thin, pink lips stretched into a wry smile. "That thought had crossed my mind, too. Delusions of grandeur? But I don't think we're here to assassinate any villains or warn anyone of meteors hurtling toward the earth. We're not superheroes; we're still *us*. Just with a little extra knowledge. And the things I changed—well, it's still not obvious to me how to go about this year even though this will be my fifth go of it."

"Really? What have you changed?"

"I set myself up for that one." Sherry's lips straightened into a stern line. "I want to help you through this, but you have to understand that this doesn't make us instant bosom buddies." She draped her silk shawl around her shoulders, and Olive thought she saw the return of the Sherry Witan she knew from parties: serious and aloof with an almost accusatory stare.

"If you could just give me a ballpark idea," Olive pressed.

"I'm sure you've heard rumors about my illustrious track record." Sherry gave her shoulders a slight shake as though awakening herself. "I'm probably the worst guide you could have through this. I obviously haven't learned my lesson; I've had to do this so many times."

"That means you've had a lot of experience," Olive said gently. "I'm just happy to have someone to confide in."

"So you haven't tried to talk to anyone else about it?" Sherry asked. When Olive nodded, she continued, "That's good. I made the mistake of trying to tell my second husband about it, and I ended up spending the whole year in therapy.

Which was helpful, don't get me wrong, but not really the issue at hand."

"Yeah, I think my ex-boyfriend thinks I'm a little nuts, too. I was so disoriented when I woke up at his apartment on New Year's Day. We hadn't seen each other in months, and then all of a sudden, we're back together."

Sherry traced the mug's rim with her fingers. She seemed to be waiting for Olive to expand on her situation. Olive looked down. Two large pockets were sewn along the bottom of her scrub top. The left one was starting to sag and detach from the weight of the instruments she carried with her all day. A pocket-sized procedures and pharmaceutical guide, hemostats, bandages, ibuprofen (for her), the Motorola, pens. Her pocket would soon be hanging on by a thread.

How could Sherry assert her own desire for privacy in one breath and then give Olive such a look—a look that demanded Olive's life story? It seemed an unfair expectation. She felt reluctant to admit any of the secrets that might have helped to land her here.

"We'd been dating for over three years and we broke up last February," she finally said.

"Ah," Sherry said. She set her cup of tea on the coaster.

"We had a big fight and then were on a kind of break, and I—" She couldn't form the words. Unspoken, they tasted acidic on her tongue. The burning sensation spread to her sinuses, and without warning, she began to cry. It was wholly inappropriate. Sherry Witan was the last person on earth in front of whom she wanted to lose it. She grabbed for the tissue box on the end table, but it was empty. "I'm sorry. I don't know why . . ."

"For heaven's sake," Sherry said, but her voice was kind,

motherly. She handed Olive a handkerchief that smelled of men's cologne. "You're doing all right. You're handling this quite well, actually. My first January like this, I spent in bed. I didn't shower, I didn't dress, I barely ate. By the end of the month, I was getting out of bed, but only to bring back books from the library. I read books on Buddhism, Hinduism, existentialism. I read Hawking, McTaggart, Kant, Leibniz, the ancient Greeks. I read H. G. Wells's goddamn *Time Machine*. And none of it helped. If anything, it made things worse, because I became confused, paralyzed, too scared to try anything. I went back to bed for another month, and I didn't snap out of it until my husband started talking about Gene McGregor."

Olive felt humbled. A part of her had always secretly admired the complete abandon with which some people could break down and wallow in their misfortune. Whenever Kerrigan broke up with a boyfriend, she called in sick to work and camped out on the couch for several days watching the Soap Network and eating canned pineapple. But Olive liked to be clean and eat regular meals and keep busy. Moving forward as though nothing had happened was her preferred method of coping.

The fact that it hadn't occurred to her to look in a book for the answers made her feel dimwitted. She knew who Stephen Hawking was but couldn't imagine wading through one of his scientific texts. The other names Sherry listed were only vaguely familiar to her.

But what struck her the most was that Sherry had assumed she was weeping out of exhaustion and frustration from the overwhelming prospect of reliving the year, which had blissfully, fleetingly left Olive's mind for a moment. She had been crying for Phil: the way she had hurt him and her disappointment over how things had turned out for them.

"You're doing all right," Sherry repeated. "You're already light-years ahead of where I was. You went to work today, right? That's good." She twisted the tassels of her shawl around her fingers. "So you had issues with your husband. What else went wrong last year?"

"Boyfriend," Olive corrected. "And I don't really know. You'd think it would be obvious."

Sherry frowned. "Obvious to others, perhaps. It's easy to point out someone else's mistake, harder to recognize your own. Especially because most people—except the lucky few like ourselves—are forced to live with their mistakes. So they learn to justify their mistakes, build on them, until they can look back and convince themselves that their mistake was inevitable all along, a good choice, in fact. An unwed teenage mother can look back at her unexpected pregnancy fondly six years down the road once the child's out of her hair and in school all day. She wouldn't dare go back and fix that mistake because it's become part of her life."

Olive didn't know how to respond. Was Sherry talking of her own past? She folded the damp handkerchief into a triangle. "I'm not sure I—"

"You need to think of this as an opportunity, a blessing, a second chance—not an inconvenience and a curse," Sherry said. "I know it can be difficult. I remember how frustrating, how absolutely heartrending the experience can be. In 2005, I had to watch my mother die three times." She bowed her head and looked down at her hands. "I hope 2011 doesn't hold anything that awful in store for you."

Olive thought of her dad. Why hadn't she been given the

chance to relive 2008? She thought of the patients she had lost last year—the ones who had inspired her to cut out obituaries and keep the small rectangles of newsprint on her nightstand. She wanted to move to the couch and sit beside Sherry, but Sherry's earlier comment about being "bosom buddies" made her wary. "I'm really sorry, Sherry."

"That is neither here nor there. What you need to do now is retrace your year to the best of your memory, find the sticking points, and figure out a way to straighten them out." Sherry raised her head, and Olive saw that there was no hint of tears in her eyes.

If only it were as easy as Sherry made it sound. As if Olive could simply sketch a map of her year—all twelve months, 365 days, 8,760 hours—in pencil and label the catastrophes like little land mines, mark them with red pushpins. If she reexamined her year closely now, every word she had said, every action she had done would become suspect. Had she really made her mom cry the day of her wedding when she'd suggested her mom loved Harry more than she'd ever loved her dad? Had she really moved out on Kerrigan and left her with a rent so steep she'd been forced to move in with her sister? She would mark the weekend trip to Lake Geneva with Phil and the subsequent week in February with a white flag. She felt such shame. Perhaps what Sherry had said was right; it was far easier to resign yourself to your mistakes and move on than acknowledge and try to rectify them.

"Perhaps I should get going," Sherry said. "You look like you're near your breaking point."

Once in the refuge of her bedroom, Olive began to undo her French braid, slipping off the elastic band at the end and then running her fingers through her hair. Kerrigan had woven it tightly, the way Olive liked it, so her hair would stay in place all day. The braid loosened at first and then completely unraveled. The tension in Olive's head and neck dissolved.

She closed the filmy curtains of her window and smiled at her African violet in its clay pot. "One outcome I am going to change is your death," she told it. "I promise this time around to do everything in my power to keep you alive."

Then she lay awake trying to picture the moment the year had rolled back into itself. It hadn't happened at midnight, as she might have expected of such a magical event. Instead, it had happened sometime between the hours of seven and ten A.M., after she got off work and before she woke up next to Phil. She imagined her slumbering body, wrapped up in a sheet, soaring over rooftops, trees, and lakes to get to Phil's apartment. Her furniture dispatched like something out of a children's book: her bed and dresser galloping down the road, halting for stoplights, her books flapping overhead like giant, inverted insects. But these were just the material objects. What of intangible time itself? What of the 365 days? Where had those days disappeared to?

She exhaled deeply and rolled onto her other side, squeezing her down comforter to her chest with both fists. *Sticking points*, Sherry had called the moments that had condemned them both to this repeat year. Olive thought of a scarf she had attempted to knit her first year of college. Brandi had taught her how to knit, and Olive had brought yarn and needles with her everywhere: on the bus, to lecture, to the Arboretum on sunny autumn days. The scarf had taken her five months to complete but had turned out so knotted and irregular that she had hidden it at the bottom of her closet instead of giving it to her mom for her birthday as she'd intended. But now she imagined the scarf coming undone: the knots untangling, the bumpy, woven wool separating, flying apart into pieces of colored yarn again. Blue, purple, white, and pink, the yarn rewound itself onto cardboard cones. The knitting needles fell to the ground with a clatter.

Chapter 5

Eleven hours of dreamless sleep restored Olive. She awoke with the desperation of a deep-sea diver coming up for air. Her heart pummeled her rib cage as though it had little fists. Clarity reigned over her. Last February she had begged Phil for a chance to try to make things right between them again. He had answered, "How? What will you do, Olive? Change the past?" Then the impossible had happened. New Year's Day. A second chance. She had been granted the unbelievable opportunity to *change the past*, and already two days had slipped away. What was she waiting for? She needed to see Phil. Every frantic thud of her heart articulated that desire.

She untangled the sheets from her legs and stumbled to the bathroom. As she waited for the water to warm, she mulled over the way they had met—at the farmers' market in the fall of their senior year at Madison. She had bought a paper bag of apples that had promptly dropped out of the bottom and rolled across the crowded sidewalk, bumping against Birkenstocks and tennis shoes, obstructing the wheels of wagons and strollers. A small group of people had stopped to help her salvage what she could—she couldn't remember the others now—and Phil was among them. They had nearly bumped foreheads as they'd stooped to collect the apples.

"This one doesn't seem too bruised," he said, as he dusted a squat McIntosh off on his navy blue polo shirt and handed it to her.

Their fingers touched, transferring energy between them almost like a static shock, and she raised her eyes to meet his. His eyes were the most startling shade of green she had ever seen, with a kaleidoscope pattern of amber overlaying his irises. Balanced on the balls of her feet, she would have fallen backward at the sight of those eyes and the overwhelming warmth emanating from them, had he not reached out to steady her. He helped her rise to a standing position.

"Thank you," she said with a slight question in her voice, hoping he would supply his name.

"Phil," he said, with a smile as stunning as his eyes. "You're welcome . . ."

"Olive." She was trying not to stare. His glossy brown hair seemed to glow in the morning sunlight, and his fitted polo shirt was doing little to hide his well-defined biceps and pectoral muscles. And yet there was something about his casual demeanor suggesting he was that rare and refreshing combination of a person who is both drop-dead gorgeous and completely unaware of it.

He didn't comment on her old-fashioned name, as most people felt compelled to do. Instead he pulled a couple of plastic bags filled with produce from his backpack. Within a minute, he had transferred all the vegetables and herbs into one and freed up the other for her use.

"The bruises taste the sweetest," he said. "That's what my mom always said, at least. Now whether that's true or just something she told me to stop my complaining remains to be seen." He grinned.

Olive laughed. "Well, there's one way to test that theory." She rubbed an apple against the hem of her skirt and turned it over, looking for the flat side where it had hit the sidewalk. She sank her teeth into the slackened skin, and a flood of nectarous juice filled her mouth. She looked up to see Phil watching her intently, as if committing her face to memory.

"Your mom's right," she said, wiping her mouth self-consciously with the back of her hand. "That was delicious. Would you like one?"

"Yes, I would. Very much." They had sat on the steps of the Capitol, eating their apples and talking long after the farmers' market vendors had taken down their booths and packed up their vans, and then Phil had invited her to his apartment for a dinner of spaghetti with homemade sauce seasoned with the fresh basil he had purchased.

To start over with Phil again—what a blessing! To be given a fresh start not at the very beginning, but at a place where they'd already grown so close together and shared so much. She couldn't wait to see him, to surprise him at school, and embrace him with none of the hesitation she'd felt on New Year's Day. She quickly lathered her hair with shampoo and stepped under the showerhead. The water whisked the frothy soap along the length of her body before it disappeared down the drain. Perhaps this was what new believers who waded into rivers to be baptized felt. With each plunge under the water, more and more sins were washed away, until they were left clean. Every misstep she had made last year had been forgiven. No, better than forgiven: erased.

The drive to Wright High School took fifteen minutes, thirty if traffic was congested like it was at present. Insubstantial gray snowflakes landed on the windshield and instantly melted. Phil had fifth period off for lunch, and if she remembered correctly, it ran from the precise and rather odd times of 11:14 to 11:58. In the past, she had brought him meatball subs or cheeseburgers and fries and they'd eaten in his classroom with the lights turned off and the door locked so his students wouldn't bother them. But when she'd started on the night shift, she had joined him for his lunch break less and less because it was difficult for her to wake up before noon.

She was stopped behind a silver hybrid car plastered with bumper stickers for local schools, co-ops, a greener community, and peace and tolerance for everyone. *Coexist*, one of the bumper stickers read. The hybrid inched forward a little.

What if she was already too late? What if she had missed a tiny window of opportunity to work things out with him? She was starting to feel panicked. It was already eleven o'clock. She listened to the worried message Phil had left on her cell phone last night wondering why she hadn't returned his call. Her need to see him grew stronger. All the things she loved about him, the things she'd missed about him, were rapidly coming into focus.

After that first date, Olive had suddenly felt like she was seated backward in a whitewater raft, speeding blindly toward a huge waterfall. Scary as hell, but not a totally unpleasant feeling. In fact, she found it strangely exhilarating. It was unlike any other relationship she'd had before.

She'd dated only two other guys in college: Jonathan, a political science major and passionate activist, her freshman year, and Aaron, a shy and romantic English major, her sophomore year. Neither relationship had lasted more than three months, and Olive knew she was mostly to blame for the failures. She tended to jealously protect and separate the different regions of her life. Her dad and family came first, then her schoolwork, then her friendships, and a boyfriend was somewhere beneath all that. She meted out dates and growing intimacies cautiously, as if there were a science to it all. She never told either boyfriend about her dad's cancer for fear that she'd be seen as needy.

But Phil wasn't content to abide by the conventional rules of dating. The day after they met at the farmers' market, he invited her to the driving range. He taught her to hit golf balls and regaled her with funny stories from his experiences student teaching. She told him about her clinicals and her big upcoming anatomy test, which he immediately proposed to help her study for. Olive even found herself mentioning her brother's wedding the following weekend. Phil offered to be her date, and she could see the boundaries already blurring between her regions. Meeting her family on only the fourth date? But Phil didn't seem to think anything of it.

Her anatomy test was on the musculoskeletal system, and Phil spent an hour quizzing her with a stack of flash cards Olive had already virtually memorized. But she was so incredibly distracted by his presence—he sat only three feet away in the black papasan chair—that she was struggling to come up with the Latin names. Finally she had a better idea.

She nervously dug her fingernails into her palms as she spoke. "The test will actually be a lab practicum. We'll have to identify the muscles on a cadaver, so maybe it would be more helpful if I tried to recognize them on a model."

"A model? Say, someone like me?" Phil raised his eyebrows playfully.

Olive's adrenaline spiked. She couldn't believe her own boldness. "Well, you are much cuter than our cadaver." Oh, no! What was she getting herself into? Didn't *Cosmopolitan* recommend something like two months of dating until sleeping with someone? No, wait! *Cosmo* approved of sex after the third date or whenever the time felt right, but it was a magazine primarily about sex, so probably it was pretty permissive. She tried to drown out her prudish conscience.

"I should hope so." Phil grinned and set the flash cards down on the coffee table. "Anything to help science. Where do we start?"

"The head and neck." She stood up from the couch and crossed the short distance to Phil. She brushed his forehead with her fingertips. "Occipitofrontalis." She lightly caressed his silky eyelid. "Levator palpebrae superioris." Her touch became more sure as she stroked his handsome jaw. "Masseter."

"Who knew I had so many muscles just in my face?" he said.

She pressed her finger against his lips. "It's a good, strong face." Her fingers walked down to his neck and then his shoulders, and Phil let out a sigh. "Sternocleidomastoid. Trapezius. Biceps. Deltoid."

As if on command, he lifted his arms upward for her to take off his shirt. She complied and bowed her head to kiss each muscle she named. "Pectoralis major. Rectus abdominus. Serratus anterior."

He stopped her progress by cupping her face in his hands. "Those are the sexiest words anyone has ever said to me." He guided her face toward his to kiss her, and she fell forward into his lap. Coming up for air between kisses, Phil murmured into her ear, "You. Are. Beautiful." The disapproving voice in her head was silenced. She was amazed by his gentle forcefulness; his ability to make her feel powerful yet totally helpless at the same time; the way his hands and mouth were everywhere at once but always where she wanted him to be. She had had sex before, but this was the first time someone had made love to her.

Afterward, they lay naked and breathless on the couch, covered only by a decorative throw blanket.

Phil sighed contentedly. "Not to state the obvious, but you seem to have a pretty good grasp of anatomy."

Olive laughed. "You think I'm going to ace the test?"

"I do." He rolled over onto his side to face her. "This may be a totally naïve question," he started, "but it seems strange a nursing student wouldn't have to take an anatomy class until her senior year. Shouldn't that be one of the first weed-out classes?"

Olive bit her lip. "It is. I first took it last year, but I had to drop it. I withdrew from the semester because my dad was getting really sick, and I was so worried about him that I couldn't focus on any of my classes." Lying in his arms in the most vulnerable position she could imagine, she told him about her dad's leukemia, and he listened and he held her, and for the first time ever, she didn't feel the need to cry. All her carefully constructed boundaries were tumbling down. He stripped her bare, but she had never felt safer.

She pulled into a visitor space in the parking lot behind

the school. Wright High School was a beautiful, three-story brick building with a red roof situated in a nice neighborhood. On the front façade, the classical stone pillars and clock tower with a decorative cornice seemed to belong more to a national library or Unitarian church than a high school. In the back, the hulking building cast a dense shadow that stretched nearly halfway across the football field and track.

She sat in this shadow, watching the clock on her dashboard change from 11:15 to 11:16 to 11:17. She knew she should go inside, that she didn't have a moment to spare if she wanted to catch Phil before his sixth-period class started, but for some reason, she couldn't force herself to get out of the SUV.

Phil had been a big hit at Christopher and Verona's wedding. He had a confidence and ease that were contagious, and Olive found herself talking to second cousins and members of Verona's family as if they'd been best friends all her life. He'd made an excellent impression on Olive's dad, too, who appreciated that Phil hadn't asked him once about his health or congratulated him on making it through the wedding, as so many other well-meaning guests had. Instead, Phil had shaken his hand firmly and immediately launched into a discussion about Badger football, which was one of her dad's absolute favorite topics.

"It's remarkable," her dad said to her later that evening. Phil had left their table to get drinks for everyone.

"What is?" Olive had been watching her brother and Verona slow dance. She couldn't remember having ever seen two happier people.

But her dad wasn't watching the newlyweds; he was watching Olive. He was wearing a black bowler hat to hide his baldness. During the church ceremony, Olive had thought he looked quite dapper in his tux with the old-fashioned hat. Now, she noticed the way the hat cast shadows over his increasingly angular and hollow features.

He smiled at her, softening the sharp corners of his face, as if he could read her mind. "How different you are from Phil."

"You think?" She frowned slightly.

"I do. It's—it's the way you both move through life, I guess. He's so self-assured. I've never seen someone make living look so graceful. And you're so—"

She narrowed her eyes in a teasing way. "Klutzy? Awkward?"

"I was going to say hesitant and thoughtful." His eyes strayed from her face, and Olive followed his gaze. He was watching her mom, dazzling in a bronze floor-length gown, talking animatedly with Verona's mom across the room. "But I think he'll be good for you."

"We just met two weeks ago, Dad." Olive reached across the table and rested her palm on top of his hand.

He flipped his hand over to squeeze hers. "Even so, Olive Oyl."

Olive agreed with her dad. Phil's resoluteness was very appealing. He made decisions efficiently and quickly and always followed through. He had few passions and close people in his life, but those he chose were sacred commitments to him. And he had chosen Olive. She didn't know what she had done to deserve his loyalty and unwavering dedication, but he had given it to her readily. And there was something so comforting in that, that the last barricaded region of Olive's heart, one she hadn't realized she'd still been protecting, was finally opened wide to admit him.

They biked together and ran together and took Cashew on such long walks that sometimes they got lost for hours in neighborhoods they'd never seen before. They went on mini vacations together—hiking and camping at Devil's Lake, seeing Broadway musicals in downtown Chicago, visiting the water parks and miniature golf courses of Wisconsin Dells. They graduated together and entered the workforce together—fretting about résumés, interviews, and first days.

Phil was there for her the gloomy December her dad passed away, and he was everything she needed—someone to cry with, someone to rage against, someone to sit beside in silence. She was there for him when his dad unexpectedly rumbled into town and back into his life in an exhaust-billowing eighteen-wheeler. After particularly grueling days in the wards, Phil rubbed her temples and whispered in her ear, "You're a great nurse." When he had a foot-high stack of exams to grade, Olive made a pot of coffee, picked up a purple pen, and joined in. When there were more Ds and Fs than As and Bs, and Phil's scowl was becoming deeper and deeper, Olive reminded him, "You're doing a good job. It's a hard subject for them, but look at all the Cs! These kids are lucky to have you."

They played in the snow together like children, sculpting snowmen and snowdogs and snow aliens. They went to all the festivals the city had to offer—the book festival and film festival, Kites on Ice, Art Fair on the Square, Taste of Madison. They spent the holidays with each other's families, kept hygiene essentials and clothing at each other's apartments, took care of one another when one of them had a particularly miserable cold, woke each other up in the middle of the night to relay and interpret their dreams, and rhapsodized about a honeymoon in Bali, a house with a fireplace, and a yard for Cashew—the life they would one day build together.

This was what she stood to regain.

She tapped her fingers nervously against the steering wheel. So what was she waiting for? She didn't want to admit it to herself, but an indelible stain clouded her relationship with Phil. However she tried to reason this time travel to herself, she couldn't forget what had happened between them last February. Even if Phil was blissfully unaware of their history, she was not, and it was her duty, her burden to remember. She felt like Hester Prynne bearing a scarlet letter on her breast. Surely Phil would recognize that she was not the same. Surely he would sense the one-year bridge between them.

She forced herself to move forward. To look straight ahead and ignore all the wreckage in the rearview mirror.

Entering the school always unnerved her. Even though she had never been a student at Wright (neither she nor Phil had gone there; she had attended LaFollette and he had attended Oregon), the scuffed-up checkerboard floors, infinite rows of lockers, and bursts of raucous laughter made her feel anxious and self-conscious. Naked and on display in that way only adolescents can experience. *It must be all the hormones in the air,* she thought. If someone analyzed the air content, they would probably find twenty percent estrogen, thirty percent testosterone, and fifty percent fear. How could Phil face this day in and day out? Then again, he had been popular in high school: varsity cross-country and golf, homecoming and prom court, *and* he'd made it look cool to be on the math team and in the science club. He probably didn't have the same visceral, gut-wrenching memories of high school that most people did.

She slipped past the gym, where the thuds of basketballs and the stench of sweat were emanating, and climbed the stairs to the second floor, where all the science classrooms and labs were grouped together. A Hispanic boy who looked like he was only eleven or twelve was descending as she was going up. No doubt he was a freshman, the smallest in his class, who was picked on mercilessly and prayed to every saint in the canon nightly for his growth spurt. Olive almost said hi before she realized this would be considered weird, so she smiled instead. The boy glared back at her, stone-faced, with perhaps just a trace of pity for her obvious inferiority. Touché.

The science hallway was crowded with students' old science projects. Posters highlighting elements from the periodic table papered over the green tiled walls. Colorful pipe-cleaner models of DNA swayed from the ceiling. An ancient display case housed Rube Goldberg machines, rockets, a whole taxidermy collection of birds and large rodents, and ostensibly, a human skull.

Phil's classroom was at the end of the hallway, but Olive couldn't help peeking into the classes in session as she hurried past. A chubby man in a sweater vest lectured to a room full of bored-looking students. That would be Mike Coleman, the earth science teacher. Olive had a hard time picking out the teacher in room 212, a tiny, white-haired lady, who was scurrying among the stations as her students spread something on petri dishes. The aptly named and beloved Flora Hughes of biology. One of the chemistry labs was fully occupied by a class, but the other had just a handful of students busy with Bunsen burners and graduated cylinders. A make-up quiz, perhaps, presided over by a pretty red-haired teacher. Jessica Flynn, the only female chemistry teacher, Olive deduced. Her slim figure and porcelain doll-like features seemed familiar, and then it hit Olive. The girl from the coffee shop.

Last April on her way to work, Olive had stopped to pick up cappuccinos for Tina and herself and spotted Phil on what looked like a date. The redhead had been sitting too close to him on the sofa and laughing loudly. Olive had hid behind a display of teapots and mugs and told herself in between deep breaths, "So. He's moved on. What did you expect him to do?" She had tried to be calm and nonchalant, but the line had been inching forward at a snail's pace and Phil was tucking a strand of the redhead's hair behind her ear, so before Olive had reached the counter to order and risk being seen, she had fled.

The chemistry teacher studied Olive with friendly curiosity. Olive hadn't realized she'd been frozen like an idiot in the doorway. She smiled vaguely, as though she'd been looking for something but now knew where it was, and hurried away before the redhead could ask her if she needed any help. No way was Olive letting Jessica Flynn get her hooks into Phil this year.

She practically ran the rest of the way down the hall. Phil's classroom door was closed, but the lights were on, and when she pressed her nose against the glass, she could see him seated at his desk in the back of the room, eating what looked like a bowl of soup. She rapped twice and then hurtled into the room.

Phil bolted upright in his seat, eyes wide. "Thank God it's you. I thought you were Gina."

Not the welcome she'd expected. "Who's Gina?"

"You remember Gina. I told you about her last year when she was in my class. She's a sophomore now, and she's still stalking me."

"Oh, *that* Gina. Yes, now I remember." Honestly, she couldn't blame the girl for being in love with him. She bet half the girls at Wright High School had little hearts penned into their notebooks with "Mr. Russell" doodled inside. He just looked so gosh-darn cute in his sky blue dress shirt, striped tie, and khakis with that ridiculous crease pressed down the middle of each pant leg. Standing at the whiteboard, drawing diagrams, and cracking lame jokes like: *Why did the chicken cross the road? Because chickens at rest tend to stay at rest, and chickens in motion tend to cross the road.* Honestly, how could you not fall in love with a guy like that?

"I'm so glad to see you. I was worried when you didn't return my calls yesterday." Phil slurped a spoonful of his soup.

"I'm really sorry that I didn't get back to you. I had an unexpected visitor at my apartment."

"It's okay. You didn't miss much. It just didn't seem like you, so I was a little concerned. An unexpected visitor?" He raised the bowl to his lips and drank the rest of the broth.

"Yeah, one of my mom's friends. Sherry Witan." No lies here. She would tell him as much of the truth as possible.

"What did she want?" He sounded mildly interested. A courtesy question, really. He sifted through some papers on his desk.

She shrugged. "It's not important. Did I come at a bad time?" She was trying not to fret. She tried to reassure herself that his reaction to her arrival had nothing to do with their breakup, because to him, it hadn't happened yet. It was simply the middle of a busy workday, and judging by the mounds of board work on his desk, he had been hoping to get a lot of grading done during his lunch period. She had caught him off guard. What did she expect? For him to sweep her into his arms and plaster her face and neck with kisses?

"Of course not," Phil said. "In fact, I'm so happy to see you"—here he scooped up a disheveled pile of spiral notebook paper with snibbles still attached to the edges and shoved it into a folder—"that everyone in my morning classes gets an automatic check on their board work today!" He stood up and wrapped her in a tight hug. The delicious scent of his soap made her a little weak in the knees.

He motioned to his empty bowl. "Are you hungry? I've got a whole drawer full of Campbell's and there's a microwave in the teacher's lounge. Or I have granola bars, bananas, oranges, beef jerky, some pretzels that might be a little—or a lot—stale."

"Thanks, but I'm okay. I really just wanted to see you. To talk." She searched his eyes for any reservations. There were none. There was only warmth and liquid light.

Phil pulled a student desk closer for her to sit in. It was at least two inches lower than his, and as she sat down she couldn't shake the feeling of being a teenager again, awkward and exposed.

"So how's your day going so far?" he asked.

"Not much to speak of. I literally woke up an hour ago. How are you doing?"

"Eh, you can imagine. The holidays are over and the kids are all brain-dead from winter break. Final exams for the semester are rapidly approaching, there's no end to winter in sight, and spring break is months away. The natives are a little restless." He grinned at her, and suddenly the tremendous need to apologize overwhelmed her. But she couldn't tell him about last year. He wouldn't believe her, and if he did, well, that would be even worse; their new chance at happiness would be ruined.

"How was dinner with Charlie?" she asked.

He set the bowl down, knocking his spoon to the floor in the process. It clattered to the floor, but he didn't retrieve it. "Sometimes I don't know why we do this. This pretending."

Adrenaline flooded her bloodstream. *He knew.* Had the full force of last year's events and all its unworthy moments abruptly come back to him like an amnesiac remembering his true identity? Or had he known all along and simply been putting on an act of starting over with her? She gripped the metal bar on the edge of the desk. "What do you mean?"

"Pretending we're a normal father and son. I can see how hard he's trying, but sometimes it feels irrelevant to me. Last night, I was looking at him across the table, and I couldn't help thinking, 'Who *is* this man?' He's not the dad I adored as a little boy. But he's not the guy that wrecked everything, the one I've blamed and pinned all my hatred on since then. He's someone else, you know? This old guy with this sad, droopy mustache, and I have no idea how he spent more than a decade of his life, except that he wasn't here."

She relaxed her grip and sank back against the hard plastic seat, but her overwrought brain could hardly make the switch from one crisis to the next. She'd been on the defensive, and now she had to change over to the supportive girlfriend role. "Phil, I . . ." She didn't know what to say. It was a role she hadn't filled in a long time, and she had always felt slightly out of her depth when Phil spoke about his dad. Both their dads had left them, but Phil's had left willingly. And his leaving had been a blessing to his family compared to the holy mess he'd been making of their lives.

Phil bent to pick up his spoon. "It's okay. I don't expect you to know what to make of that revelation any more than I do. Sometimes I just surprise myself how detached I feel and how little I care about him. I guess I feel like a bad person."

"Never. You are the best person I know." She unfolded herself from the small desk and stood by his side. She wanted to put her arms around him and lay her head on his shoulder, but she was afraid a student might walk in. She squeezed his shoulder instead. "Tell me more about the dinner."

"I'd rather not," he said. "You came all this way to see me, and I don't want to waste precious time talking about him. We've only got . . . oh, about fifteen minutes before my students come barging in, demanding to know who the hottie is."

"Ha." She reached across him and lifted a silver ball from his Newton's cradle, letting it fall against the others. Click-clack, click-clack, click-clack.

"The last time you visited, Taylor Roquemore and Dominic Spain caught a glimpse of you and started a rumor that you were a supermodel."

"It must have been from far away," Olive mumbled. "And still this Gina is after you?"

She started to drift through the classroom, examining all of his toys. She had once thought that studying his apartment or closet or childhood bedroom would give her the insight she needed into his complicated and sometimes frustratingly opaque mind. But now she knew the key to understanding Phil was his classroom. Everything in the room—the posters on the walls with cheerful, motivational slogans (*Today is a great day to learn something new! Just because something is difficult doesn't mean you shouldn't try; it means you should just try harder. Even Einstein asked questions! Physics is Phun*^{2}*!*); the ramp with its matchbox cars; the stopwatches and balls of all kinds (golf balls, softballs, bouncy balls, volleyballs, a bowling ball); the springs, pendulums, magnets, and tuning forks; the calorimeters and voltmeters—told a story about Phil. He trusted in Newton's three laws of motion, the laws of thermodynamics, the electrostatic laws, gravity, the speed of light, the speed of sound. These principles followed reliable equations with reliable constants. They could be counted on time and time again. They would always do exactly what he expected them to do. The laws of physics would never fail him.

While she'd been inspecting a prism hanging from a suction cup on one of his windows, deep in thought, he had come up behind her. He planted a soft, stealthy kiss on her collarbone and then backed away, as if nothing had happened.

She laughed at his innocent expression. He was all but whistling with his hands clasped behind his back. "I've missed you," she said, before she could stop herself.

But he surprised her. "I've missed you, too. It seems like we haven't gotten to spend much time together—like this—lately." He looked as if he were going to say something more, but didn't. He lifted a strand of her hair to his nose and inhaled deeply. "God, you smell good."

She couldn't believe the way her body responded to his proximity. She had expected to feel guarded and hesitant around him at first. They had been separated for ten long months. Shouldn't there be a period of readjustment? Probably it had something to do with the hormone-saturated air. And it was hard to feel tentative when he was looking at her like that. Her memory of his eyes hadn't done them justice—they were an even more brilliant shade of green than she remembered. The yellow flecks dotting his irises looked almost golden.

"This morning I was thinking about the way we met," she said. "Do you remember?" The snow was coming down more heavily now; the flakes were white and fat and blotted out the gray sky.

"Of course I do. You were wearing a white skirt like a petticoat and your hair was in two braids." He reached over and tenderly divided her hair into two loose pigtails. "Why don't you ever wear your hair like that anymore?"

She shook out her hair, letting it fall down her back. "I don't remember that."

Phil perched on the edge of a desk, in a way she was certain he scolded his students for on a daily basis. "When I saw you drop those apples, I knew it was my chance. Thank God for your clumsiness. Otherwise, I might not have gotten up the courage to talk to you."

"Hey! I wasn't clumsy." She lunged forward, pretending she was going to disturb his precarious balance, and he laughed and straightened. "The bottom of the paper bag broke. The apples were too heavy for it."

"That's right. Well, thank God for that paper bag, then. It certainly played its role in our fate."

"Do you really believe we were destined to meet?" she asked.

He nodded and took a step closer to her. "Don't you?"

She had never believed in fate before, instead preferring to believe in her own free will. While the apples had created an introduction for them, if she and Phil hadn't hit it off, nothing would've come of the incident. It had been her decision to accept his dinner invitation. Their mutual decision to start a relationship. She had made some good choices, some bad—that was for sure—and she'd accepted the consequences.

But Olive was starting to seriously reconsider the idea of destiny. Perhaps they *were* meant to be together, but her free will had led her astray. Now fate was bringing them forcibly back together. What was this repeat year for if not to restore Phil to her?

"I'm starting to think something like that," she said with a smile.

"Good." Phil ambled back to his desk and retrieved a granola bar from one of the drawers. "You're positive you don't want anything? I forgot to mention I have something in here that's either chocolate-covered raisins or mouse turds."

"Gee, tempting, but no thanks."

He took a large bite of his granola bar. "You seem to be feeling a lot better."

"I'm fine."

"You were really disoriented on New Year's Day."

She forced a laugh. "I was loopy. Sleep-deprived."

"I've never seen you like that." He frowned. "You didn't remember what we'd done the night before. It was almost like you'd blacked out. You didn't seem to know where you lived. You said something about Kerrigan living with her sister. You were really agitated. You seemed almost mad at me."

She looked down at her hands. "I don't know what to tell you, Phil. I was exhausted. This working the night shift is really getting to me. I'm tired all the time. My circadian rhythm must be out of whack."

"Then maybe you need to ask them to put you on the day shift because this schedule does not agree with you." He crumpled up his wrapper and tossed it into the garbage can.

"Well, I'm on the day shift this month, so we'll see how it goes, okay?" She tried to add a note of gentle finality to her tone.

But he would not be so easily swayed. "Your behavior was really disconcerting. I'm worried about you, Olive, and I feel like there's something more to this. Is everything okay?"

She was unsure how to proceed. He was opening up a safe space for her. A space to confess her problems, but he couldn't even begin to fathom the depth of what was troubling her. She knew this was the moment, if not exactly the ideal place, to tell him the truth about her repeat year. He was concerned, sympathetic; he might even humor her and pretend to believe until she'd found a more scientific way of convincing him. But if he agreed to believe her story—that she had seen the future, so to speak—he would eventually ask questions. He would want to know what had happened in the year and why she thought she was reliving it. And how could she possibly respond to his questions without disturbing the fragility of this fleeting, shimmering second chance?

She had chosen to tell him the truth last year. She had confessed her infidelity to him and he had given up on her. What made her think he would react differently this time? Where had her honesty gotten her last year?

But the infidelity had technically not happened yet, and Olive would not allow it to happen this year. She realized that telling him the truth had never really been a serious possibility. She needed to protect him; she needed to protect his unmarred image of her.

"I had had this really strange dream, and I just couldn't shake it," she said.

"What kind of dream?"

She spoke softly. "Everything had changed. Kerrigan had moved out and I lived somewhere else, on my own. You and I had broken up. It was a terrible dream."

Phil looked thoughtful. His hand hovered over the folder he had so hastily filled with ungraded homework assignments earlier, but he didn't touch it. She couldn't tell if he was buying her story, or if he was puzzling through the other strange things she had said on New Year's Day. At last he said, "Maybe your subconscious is trying to tell you something. Are you sure everything's okay?"

The concern written on his face made it difficult to answer. It was now or never. She could do what was right or she could do what was best. For both of them.

"Everything's great," she said. "I think my subconscious was trying to remind me how good I have it." She squeezed his hand. "How lucky I am to have you."

He squeezed her hand back and then grabbed the folder. "Not to ruin the moment, but you probably need to get going in the next five minutes before the bell rings and there's a stampede in the hallways."

Olive looked up at the clock. Eleven fifty-three. "Good idea."

"Will I see you tonight?"

"You can count on it, Mr. Russell."

Chapter 6

Olive was on her fifth cup of coffee. The transition back to third shift had been brutal. Her eyes felt gluey, and it seemed like every breath she took was followed by an irrepressible yawn, yet somehow, she had survived the night. It was now eight in the morning. Her replacement, Kelly—the flakiest nurse on the ward—had called in sick. It had taken Toya, the nurse manager, forty-five minutes and ten calls to guilt someone into taking Kelly's shift.

"I'd lay off the coffee if I were you," Toya told Olive as they convened at the nurses' station. "You're going to give yourself heart palpitations."

While Olive's heart did seem to be beating abnormally fast, she suspected it had more to do with her anxiety about the upcoming weekend than her caffeine intake. It was the Friday of her fateful trip to Lake Geneva with Phil. She had to get home to pack and take a long nap so she'd be well rested for tonight. She wanted everything to be perfect this time around.

"Well, look who it is. My favorite employee," Toya said as Christine arrived to relieve Olive. Olive quickly briefed the incoming nurse on her patients, and then the two older women shooed her away and ordered her to go straight to bed.

In the elevator, she mentally ticked off reminders for the weekend. She needed to pack warm, comfortable clothes. She needed to persuade Phil to drive her SUV instead of his Mercedes. She needed to be simply wowed by the shabby cabin in the woods, his choice of a romantic getaway. She needed to avoid all talk of her job. She needed to stay awake.

The elevator doors slid open to a view of the lobby. A small crowd pressed forward as Olive struggled to step out. Among the crowd was a woman who looked suspiciously like Sherry Witan at first glance. Olive looked again. "Sherry?"

Sherry looked like a rabbit caught in a cage. She quickly thrust her hand out to prevent the doors from closing, much to the displeasure of the other passengers. "Hold your horses," Sherry grumbled as she pushed her way off the elevator. Sherry eyed her. "Olive," she said. The doors closed behind them with a ding. "You look like shit."

"I just worked thirteen hours," Olive said defensively. She suppressed the urge to comment on Sherry's own bedraggled appearance. Sherry's unkempt hair was streaked with even more gray than normal, and there were shadows under her eyes the same shade of lavender as her shapeless overcoat. "What are you doing here?"

"What do you think? I'm here to visit you."

Olive was about to scoff at that when something stopped her. It had been a month since Sherry's first unexpected visit with her offer of guidance. Olive hadn't seen hide nor hair of her since that day. But now at a pivotal moment in Olive's year, Sherry had popped up again. It was almost like she was her fairy godmother. Olive rubbed her aching forehead. Oh man, she was sleep-deprived. Sherry—a fairy godmother?

Sherry dug in her crocheted handbag for a handkerchief and blew her nose. She looked at her watch and then up at Olive. "You need someone to talk to, don't you? Why don't I buy you a cup of coffee?"

The hospital cafeteria was slow at that time of morning. Only a few careworn residents and family members hunched over breakfasts of nuked eggs and sausages. Sherry chose a cinnamon roll caked with icing, then put it back, and filled a disposable cup with hot water. Olive took Toya's advice to lay off the coffee and let Sherry buy her a bottle of apple juice instead.

"Did you know that apple juice is a natural laxative?" Sherry asked conversationally as she pulled an Earl Grey tea bag from her purse.

"You don't say."

Sherry glanced at her watch. "I know you probably want to get home to bed, so let's cut to the chase. How has your month been? Any difficulties?"

Every single day had been difficult. Every day she second-guessed herself, comparing her memory of last year to her present actions. Sometimes it felt like she was digging a hole with dirt continually raining back down on her. How was she supposed to know if she'd made progress? This wasn't *Groundhog Day*, where Bill Murray knew at the end of his day if he'd fixed things or not. She would have to wait until the end of the year to find out. It was something she didn't like to dwell on.

"My relationship with Phil has been going well. This weekend was actually a big turning point for us last year."

Sherry cocked her head and stirred her tea.

"He surprised me with a trip to a cottage in Lake Geneva, and one bad thing just seemed to happen after another. His car broke down, and we were stranded in the cold for hours. By the time we got to the cabin, we were both pretty crabby, and I said some things I probably shouldn't have said. I was just so disappointed about the cabin. I mean, that's Phil's idea of romance, not mine. Initially, I thought maybe he was taking me to Chicago so we could see a play or musical. But no. He wouldn't have thought of something like that."

She paused, conscious of her resentful tone. She took a deep breath.

"I could tell Phil was really hurt. He'd tried to do something sweet for me, and I blew it. I apologized. He apologized. We decided to try to start the night over. He went out to get some firewood. I had this patient who I was really worried about—an eighteen-year-old kid with multiple stab wounds. He's upstairs right now, and I know he's going to be okay. But I didn't know that then, so I called to check on him. Phil came back with the firewood when I was on the phone. He got pissed off when he realized I was talking to the hospital and accused me of never being able to separate myself from my job.

"We had another big argument. He told me that ever since I'd started in the ICU he felt like he was losing me, little by little. That I never shared stuff with him anymore. When I tried to explain that I didn't share as much with him anymore because he overreacted like he had just done, he said, 'I just want you to protect yourself. You get so involved with each of your patients, it's like it was with your dad all over again. I can't bear to see you like that. I'm not asking you to stop caring for your patients. I'm just asking you to distance yourself a little, get a little perspective . . .' He reminded me how I had helped him keep his sanity when he had first started teaching and he'd brought home mountains of work with him and lain awake every night, fretting over what to do differently, how to reach one student, how to help remove another from a bad home environment."

Olive paused. She wanted to stop now, but she couldn't. But how could she admit to Sherry something she couldn't even admit to herself? The words she'd suppressed in her memory of the very idea that *she* had given him. She'd been so furious with him, unable to see that his suggestions came from a loving place, instead fixated only on the belief that he couldn't possibly understand because he had never witnessed death and he'd never experienced the loss that she experienced almost weekly, and it was cruel and insensitive of him to try to deprive her of that hard-won truth. *Maybe it's not as easy for me to close my heart off,* she had said. *Maybe I'm not as good as you at cutting people out of my life just like that.* It was petty and mean, a sucker punch to the soft, vulnerable parts of Phil that he had revealed and entrusted to her over the years, and she didn't need to elaborate for him to understand and the light in his eyes to flicker out.

"I threw it back in his face," she summarized for Sherry. "Phil said he was going to 'cool off' and take a walk in the woods. I was so exhausted that I fell asleep before he came back. The next day we decided to cut our stay short and leave early."

She twisted off the cap of her apple juice and took a swig. It was strange that Sherry hadn't interrupted her, and that even now, at what could've presumably been the end of her story, she wasn't volunteering her wisdom.

Sherry watched Olive with her shrewd, unblinking eyes. "So why did you break up?"

"I cheated on him," Olive said in a small voice. "He wasn't speaking to me the following week. I felt so alone and so uncertain. I was here at the hospital working, and I had a really rough night. Alex, a resident, was working, too. And he was there for me. He seemed to really understand me." She turned the bottle cap over and over between her fingers. "The next day Phil called me. He said he knew we could work things out, that we'd just had a bad night. I knew I had to tell him about Alex. I thought he might be able to forgive me over time. But he changed his mind about us pretty quickly."

She tried not to envision Phil working out on his Bowflex, a reflexive habit he had whenever he was worried or depressed. When he'd called to apologize, she had suggested they continue their conversation in person, that there was something important she needed to tell him. But she nearly lost her nerve when she walked into his apartment and found him seated on the enormous black-and-silver contraption, the veins bulging in his arms, the machine's black rods bending as easily as wheat swaying in the wind. He stood up immediately when she entered, his face sweet and eager with forgiveness. In retrospect, that was what had hurt her the most: his sweet expression before he found out the awful truth.

"Well, aren't you are a sight for sore eyes." Phil squeezed her in a sweaty hug, Cashew dancing frantically around their ankles. She could feel Phil's heart lub-dubbing under his cotton shirt, hardy and unafraid. She almost chickened out then.

"I've missed you so much," she said. Her words were muffled by his chest.

He gently released her. "Me, too. I'm such an idiot for hassling you about your job. I'm really proud of everything you do. I just worry about you sometimes. But I know you're your own person and you'll figure out a way to handle it, even if it's different from my way. Just know that I'm always here whenever you want to talk." He took a long pull from his water bottle.

She couldn't stand there letting his bittersweet apologies wash over her for one more minute. "Phil, do you think you could sit down? I need to—"

"Can I just change out of these sweaty clothes first? I thought maybe when we're done talking we could go to the Lion's Head Pub for a bite to eat." He wiped the perspiration from his temple with the hem of his T-shirt, revealing the landscape of his abdomen.

Her resolve weakened. It would be so much less painful to keep her mouth shut and go out to dinner and act as if nothing had happened. But the guilt would consume her like a slow burn; she knew that. And Phil was the best person she knew, the biggest-hearted, the truest, the most honorable. If she couldn't put her trust in him, well then, she didn't know what she could believe in anymore. They required complete honesty from each other. They had both made hurtful mistakes before, but none as hurtful as this. But he would forgive her. She would find a way to make him understand and then regain his trust.

"Please sit down. I need to tell you something." Beneath the thin mattress of the futon, she could feel the metal frame, as bony and sharp as cracked ribs. Cashew immediately bounded onto her lap, and she stroked his velvety ears.

"All right." He draped a green towel around his neck and sat down.

She didn't know how to get started. What could possibly be an appropriate prologue to soften such unbearable news? "I tried calling you for a week, but you wouldn't return my calls. I thought we were through. That you didn't love me anymore."

"That I didn't love you?" He blew out an exasperated sigh. "Ollie, by now, you should know how I operate. I needed some time alone to think about us. And when I did, I realized how stupid I'd been." He grinned boyishly at her, dabbing his forehead with the towel.

She suddenly felt like shaking him. "But I didn't know that! You can't expect me to read your mind. I'm just trying to explain to you how I felt. Not as an excuse, but just so maybe you can understand where I was coming from and why I did it."

His smirk vanished. "Olive, *what did you do*?"

She couldn't meet his eyes. "I slept with someone." The statement pervaded the air like poison. Spoken aloud, it sounded too blunt, too appalling; she sought to qualify it somehow, but everything she could think of sounded like a cliché from a daytime talk show or soap opera. "It only happened once, and it will never happen again. I just felt so miserable and confused. I thought I had lost you. But I never meant to hurt you." Out of the corner of her eye, she saw Phil's body stiffen.

A hush fell over the room, punctuated only by their soft breathing and the musical jangle of the tags on Cashew's collar as he restlessly shifted position. Seconds dragged into minutes, and still Phil didn't speak. Finally, she gathered enough courage to face him. He was sitting ramrod straight, his hands pulling the ends of the towel around his neck as taut as a noose.

"Phil?"

"What do you expect me to say, Olive?" His tone was subdued. He stared straight ahead.

"I don't know." She paused, anxious for him to jump in and give her the opportunity to explain herself, but he remained silent. "Something. *Anything.* Please, Phil."

He took a deep breath and released it slowly as though the act of exhaling pained him. "Do you love him?"

"No. Not at all. The only person I love is you." She hated how ardent and rehearsed she sounded.

Another minute passed. Cashew hopped down from the futon and returned with his raggedy stuffed squirrel. When no one attempted to take it away from him, he sprawled dejectedly on the floor.

"Is it someone I know?" Phil asked, relaxing and then tightening his grip on the green towel.

"No."

"Someone you work with?"

"Yes," she whispered. "Phil, I'm so sorry."

He slumped forward. When he finally lifted his head, he looked at her for the first time since she'd confessed, and his tortured expression scissored through her heart. She had never seen him in so much pain before. Not when he talked about how his father had screamed insults at his mother while he hid in the kitchen pantry, counting the stacks of canned goods, arranging and rearranging them by name, then type, then expiration date. Not even when his favorite student, Kelsey, the brightest kid he'd seen come through

Wright High School and a natural in physics, had dropped out of school so she could get a job to support her younger siblings and addiction-riddled mother. This pain was so much worse, and she was the reason for it.

"I didn't mean to hurt you. I was at work, and my patient died. Her daughter and husband were there, and it was so sad. I kept thinking about my dad, and I was so heartbroken about us—I thought you were breaking up with me. It was one of the worst nights of my life, and you weren't there." She left the rest of her accusation unspoken. *You weren't there . . . for me.*

He shook his head as if he could erase this information. "This is what I was trying to explain to you last weekend. I don't *have* you anymore. And this proves it."

"No! You still have me. This was a mistake. A terrible mistake, and it will never happen again."

"You're not listening to me, Olive. We have a problem, and it's not going away. We used to tell each other everything. But since you've started working at the hospital, if something upsets you there, you confide in one of your coworkers because you think I won't understand. That I won't even try to understand. That's a problem. Something happens between us—we have one fight—and you're ready to hop in bed with someone else. That's a *big* problem. If you don't know by now how much I love you—if you don't believe in us enough . . . it's . . . you'll never . . ."

She clung to fragments of his speech as if they were a tattered parachute. *How much I love you. Believe in us.* "I do know, Phil. You make me feel so loved. But you scare me sometimes. You shut yourself off from me for a week. You can't expect me to be a mind reader and just know that you still feel the same way."

Cashew stood up on his hind legs, propped his front paws on the futon frame, and started licking Phil's knee. Phil pushed the little dog away. "No! Bad dog. Get down."

Phil jerked his knees toward his chest. At that moment, it wasn't hard for her to imagine what he had looked like as a ten-year-old. "Did you ever think that I wall myself off from you because you do the same to me?" he asked.

"To punish me, you mean? But that's not fair, because I don't intentionally try to push you away. I chose my job and everything that comes with it. You didn't. Is it so wrong for me to keep some of it to myself, especially when you've been so clear about not wanting to hear it?"

"That's rich, talking about fairness and punishment, Olive. You slept with someone else."

"Not to hurt you. Not to *punish* you."

"Why, then?" His tone was painfully earnest. He wanted the truth.

She bit her lip. It tasted salty from tears she hadn't realized she'd been crying. "I don't know. To stop myself from hurting."

"I'm supposed to be the one to stop you from hurting."

"Well, maybe I don't always want that to be your role. Maybe I don't always want to have to be comforted and fixed by you, Phil." She barely felt the bars of the futon's metal frame digging into her flesh.

"Okay. Now I can see we're getting somewhere. Let me repeat: Are you in love with him?"

"No!" she cried. "I already told you no."

"That's right. And you love me, and you never meant to hurt me. This was all just a mistake." Sarcasm hardened his words.

She closed her eyes and took a few deep breaths. When she reopened them, the apartment looked different somehow. Darker. Less familiar. The sun had disappeared behind a cloud. Cashew was nowhere to be seen since Phil's scolding. "Phil."

"What?" He didn't look at her. His eyes were trained on the window.

"Do you think you can ever forgive me?"

"I don't think you want my forgiveness. You want something else. Something that I apparently don't know how to give you."

"That's not true. Please just tell me you still love me and that you will try to forgive me for this someday."

Every part of her body waited apprehensively—her heart, her teeth, her nails, her spine, all bracing themselves for his answer. She tried to recall the warm and open look on his face when she'd walked into his apartment but found she couldn't. His face was expressionless now, his eyes distant. He was building a barricade so that she could no longer reach him.

"Phil? Please. You're doing it again. You're shutting me out."

He leaped up from the futon and crossed his arms. The veins in his arms protruded as if they were thorny vines tangled around his skin. "Dammit, Olive. You don't get to come over here, tell me you cheated on me, and then accuse me of shutting you out. How do you want me to treat you? It's a survival mechanism, you know."

"I know," she murmured.

"I think—I think we'd better say good-bye." He uncrossed his arms, and they tumbled to his sides. His sign of resignation.

She fought the urge to disagree and persevere. She had never understood his desire to extricate himself from a fight, regroup, and return cold and levelheaded to negotiate peace. In the heat of battle, she could see the green hills ahead, the shaft of sunlight breaking through the storm clouds. If she could just push her way a few feet further, if they just could endure another hour or two—but she knew this was what he needed. And if this was what he needed, by all means, this was what she was going to give him.

"All right, I understand. But please, let's continue this soon. Can I call you later tonight?"

"You don't understand. I think we need to say *good-bye*, Olive." He turned away.

His meaning blindsided her. It was as if the earth had been knocked out of its orbit and was now speeding toward an unknown galaxy. Never had she thought they would just . . . end. Stop. Cease to exist as an *us*. "I screwed up tremendously, I know, but I can make this right somehow—"

He kept his back to her, his straight, broad shoulders as unyielding as body armor. "How? What will you do? Change the past? Change who we are?" Still refusing to look at her, he walked to the door.

She hastened to follow him. She rose up on her tiptoes so that her face was level with his, so that he couldn't look away. His eyelashes were wet and matted, but his eyes were as hard and opaque as jade.

"But I love you so much, Phil."

"I believe you." He swallowed, and his Adam's apple bobbed like something lodged in his throat. "But I can't love someone who treats me this way. I thought we wanted the same thing, but I guess I was just lying to myself. We're not so different from anybody else after all." And then he had opened the door, and it had taken Olive a full minute to realize it was for her.

Remembering their breakup made her feel the heartache anew, as raw and tender as if it were a fresh physical wound. To have him stare at her, disillusioned, as though he weren't quite seeing her anymore. It was more unbearable than if he'd shouted obscenities at her. She shuddered. She would do everything in her power to prevent it from happening again.

Sherry was observing her with pursed lips. The purplish circles under her eyes looked even darker in the harsh cafeteria lighting. She exhaled deeply. "That's a sad story, kiddo."

An understatement, to say the least. Olive didn't know what she'd been expecting from Sherry, but she had certainly expected more than that. She felt like she'd just bared her soul to an apathetic cashier at the supermarket. *That's a sad story, kiddo. Now did you want paper or plastic?*

Two white-coated female interns sat down at the end of their table. They both looked like they hadn't slept for several days. Sherry and Olive momentarily watched them try to stomach the rubbery scrambled eggs.

"I know it probably seems like this at your age," Sherry started, "but it's not always about men. Romantic relationships. My first repeat year I devoted to trying to make things work with Clyde. Then, years later, I tried again with another man. But I think I missed the point both times."

"What are you trying to say?" Olive asked warily. Her feelings toward Sherry were swiftly escalating from mild irritation to full-blown anger.

"I'm not necessarily saying you should break up with your boyfriend. I'm just suggesting you try to spend more time improving other aspects of your life, too. Men come and go. But your friends, your family—they're stuck with you for the long haul."

This sounded extremely hypocritical coming from someone who seemed to have no family or friends to speak of. Sherry didn't get it. Olive knew what she wanted, for the first time in a long time. She was hopeful that Phil was the key to this year—if not the whole picture, then a large part of the picture. Sherry knew nothing about Olive's relationship with Phil. Her advice was wildly frustrating. She came around only once a month, yet pretended to know everything about Olive and what was best for her.

"I appreciate your time, but I really need to get some sleep now," Olive said, biting back all the other things she wanted to say. She rose from the table. She must have spoken a little too loudly, because the female residents turned to look at her.

"Everyone wants their own happily-ever-after," Sherry said. "And why not? Maybe you'll have yours with Will—"

"Phil."

"—and maybe not. The point is: This year is bigger than all that. You have to think holistically."

"No offense, Sherry, but doesn't that contradict what you told me last month? You told me to find the 'sticking points' in my year and straighten them out."

Sherry threw up her hands. "Are you recording everything I say in your diary or something? Fine. Let's revise that, then. Your approach should be to see both the big picture and the individual moments *at the same time*."

Olive couldn't help it—she rolled her eyes. Something

about Sherry brought out the irreverent teenager in her. “Thanks, that’s helpful.”

“You’re welcome.” Sherry fished out a cracked tube of lipstick from her purse. “Remember, I warned you that I’m not very good at this.”

Right on both counts, Olive thought. Sherry had warned her, and she was terrible at this. “I really need to get home. I have a big weekend ahead of me.”

Without the aid of a mirror, Sherry began to coat her lips in a greasy, uneven layer of salmon pink. She held up her garnet-ringed finger to stall Olive. “You want something quotable for your diary? Perhaps the only piece of wisdom I’ve gained in all my repeats?”

The lipstick did nothing to improve her appearance. Between the bags under her eyes, the slapdash makeup, and the three inches of gray roots taking over her otherwise orange hair, Sherry looked a little deranged. Better suited to be spouting Bible verses and premonitions of the end of the world from a cement podium in Library Square than Olive’s trusted advisor and guide in this strange time warp.

Sherry clutched her lumpy handbag to her chest. “In a repeat year, it is easy enough to change your actions, but it’s a lot harder to change your heart. And it’s impossible—” She paused, suddenly distracted by something or someone over Olive’s shoulder.

Olive turned around but saw only a group of orderlies and a doctor entering the cafeteria.

Sherry’s eyes flicked back to Olive. “It is impossible,” she repeated, “to change someone else’s.”

Chapter 7

By the time Olive got home, her head felt waterlogged. She closed the curtains against the bright sunlight and fell into bed still wearing her dirty scrubs and tennis shoes. What seemed like only minutes later, a loud knock woke her up.

"Wakey wakey," Kerrigan chirped. "Phil just called to say he's on his way. I heard your phone ringing and ringing, and guess where I finally found it? The fridge! There's a missed call from your mom, too. Wait a second. Have you even packed? Where's your suitcase?"

"What time is it?"

"Four o'clock. You almost slept the whole day." Kerrigan parted the curtains, revealing a darkening sky.

And she still hadn't gotten more than six hours of sleep. There was a dull pain in her hip, where she'd been lying on a forgotten hemostat in her pocket. She hung over the edge of the bed and peered under the dust ruffle for her red suitcase, which was regrettably, as Kerrigan had suspected, still empty.

Remembering the chilliness of the cabin last year, she

began haphazardly filling the suitcase with sweatshirts, flannel pajama pants, and wool socks.

Kerrigan supervised her progress. She pulled out a pair of flannel pajama pants with a horror-struck look on her face. "What the hell is this?"

"Pajamas."

"These are the kind of pajamas you wear when you've been married thirty years, not what you pack for a romantic getaway. Where is your lingerie drawer? The second drawer? I'll handle the packing from here. You go shower. You look and smell like something National Geographic dug from the ice."

Olive had packed mostly babydolls and negligees the first time she and Phil had taken the trip, but she couldn't explain this to Kerrigan. What with all the fighting that had gone on that weekend, she hadn't had the opportunity to wear any of the lingerie. And to top it off, the thermostat had been set at a fixed sixty degrees, with only a meager supply of firewood to stoke the fireplace. She planned on sneaking a pair of pajama pants back into the suitcase when Kerrigan wasn't looking.

When she came out of the bathroom wearing khakis and a striped sweater, Kerrigan gave her a critical look.

"I hope you're wearing a thong under there."

Olive crossed her arms. "Kerrigan."

"I'm just saying. You're going about this in a totally different way than I would."

"I can see that." She held up a large bottle of lubricant that had been laid conspicuously on top of her socks.

"It's a two-in-one: massage oil *and* a personal lubricant. Quite possibly the best product ever invented."

Olive laughed, and suddenly her anxiety was swept away. Without realizing it, she'd been building this weekend up to almost mythic proportions—The Weekend That Ended It All—when really, it was just two and a half days with the man she loved. Two and a half days for them to relax, have fun, and get closer to each other. She'd been experiencing the jitters an actress feels as she's about to walk onstage for opening night; now she understood that if her relationship with Phil was really going to stand a chance, this weekend couldn't be a performance. It had to be real. It had to come from the heart. And that would be easy.

It wasn't difficult to persuade Phil to drive her SUV. He seemed skeptical when she improvised a weather report about an impending snowstorm but agreed anyway that her four-wheel drive would be safer for the trip.

"I'm surprised," he said, as he merged onto the highway. "I thought you'd be begging me nonstop to find out where we're going, but you don't seem the least bit curious."

"Oh, I am. But it doesn't matter as much to me because I'll be happy wherever we're going as long as I'm with you." She reached across the center console and squeezed his knee.

He turned to her with a look of pretend exasperation. "Do you mean to tell me that we could've gone to the Super 8 on East Wash, and you would've been just as happy?"

"Just think of it this way. I'd be happy with you anywhere, but you get bonus points for creativity."

"Points, huh? And how do I redeem these points? I hope they add up faster than my credit card rewards."

"Oh, they will," she said, and kissed him on the cheek.

The drive to Lake Geneva was blissfully uneventful. No bad fuel pump, no two-hour wait in the cold for a tow truck.

They checked in first with the owner of the cottage, who lived in a separate house on the wooded property and assured them (in response to Olive's inquiry) that there was plenty of dry firewood in an unlocked tool shed. When they drove up the gravel road, Olive was surprised to see that the cabin was actually quite lovely with its knotty wood siding, asymmetric sloped roof, and high, circular windows. Her memory of it had been heavily influenced by her bad feelings associated with the night. But here it was, and it wasn't some shabby, hokey cabin in the middle of nowhere. It was handsome and rustic and yes, okay, so maybe it *was* in the middle of nowhere, but that added to the romance. The trees standing sentinel around the bungalow seemed seductive in their offer of privacy.

Inside, almost every surface was of scrubbed, sweet-smelling pine: the walls, the slanted high ceiling, the rafters, the floor. The cottage consisted of one main room sectioned into areas—bedroom, living room, kitchenette—and a bathroom. A white brick fireplace grayed with soot was the focal point of the room. Above this fireplace hung a painting of a black Labrador, triumphant with a lifeless duck in its mouth. Ducks of all species swam across the blue of the bedspread, and a painted wood mallard and his mate sat atop the wardrobe. Every detail was familiar to Olive.

"Oh Phil, I love it," she said, and she wasn't just saying it to please him. "It's absolutely perfect."

Phil deposited their luggage beside the bed. "It looks a little different than it did on their website." He ran his finger over the sooty bricks of the fireplace with distaste.

"Well, I don't care what it looked like on the website. It

looks gorgeous in person." She wrapped Phil in a tight hug. "Thank you for surprising me."

He bent down and kissed the crown of her head. "I'm so glad you like it! I had my doubts, you know, because you're not much of a nature lover. Well, come on, you're not! But—well, I'll tell you why I chose this place later. Brr. It's a little chilly in here. Why don't I get a fire going?"

They sat on the floor in front of the fireplace eating peanut butter and strawberry jam sandwiches and drinking champagne. Olive took off her wool socks, which were just a little too toasty, and wiggled her bare toes.

"We forgot to make a toast," Phil said when they were almost finished with the bottle. He poured them each a few more drops of champagne, making sure the glasses were equal. "To our future together," he said. They clinked glasses. Olive mentally tacked on to his toast, *And to second chances.*

Warm, drowsy, and a little buzzed, she stretched out and laid her head in his lap. "Tell me about the nature of time."

Phil laughed. He ran his thumb lightly along her jaw. "The nature of time? You mean from a physics standpoint?"

"Yes." She closed her eyes and listened to the crackling fire. Behind her eyelids, the world was soft and orange.

"Well, there are two theories actually. Newton and Einstein believed that time is its own dimension in the universe and that it flows along at a constant pace in a linear, sequential order. But there were other philosophers who proposed that time is a concept invented by humans to catalog and reference our experiences in relation to each other."

Olive opened her eyes. "And which do you believe?"

"Newton and Einstein, of course. They have the math to

back it up." He stroked her hair, and her body tingled from her scalp to the nail beds of her toes.

"There are just two theories?"

"No, those are just the most accepted theories. Civilizations have been trying to explain time for hundreds and hundreds of years. You've probably heard of the Mayan calendar? The Mayans believed that time was cyclical."

She propped herself up on her elbow. "Cyclical how?"

"I don't know really. Something to do with the seasons and the movement of the planets and understanding the past to predict the future. But they also believed in sacrificing people." He cocked an eyebrow. "Why the sudden interest in physics?"

She pretended to be insulted. "Sudden interest? I've always found physics fascinating. Do you think it would ever be possible to fall out of Newton's so-called linear time?"

"Fall out of?" His eyebrow shot higher. "You mean like time travel?"

"No, of course not!" Olive walked her fingers along the floor toward his knee. "I mean, like now. With you. Is it possible for us to extend this moment, thereby thwarting the confines of time?"

"Yes. Definitely. Here, let's try this." He leaned forward and gave her a long, dizzying kiss. "Did that work?"

"I can't tell yet. What do you say we slip into that big old whirlpool tub together?" she asked. Her fingers started to follow his pants inseam up his leg.

"How'd you know about the whirlpool?"

"I poked my head in the bathroom when I was unpacking the food," she lied, as her fingers advanced farther.

"Do you think it's big enough for two?" He grabbed her frisky hand and helped her up.

"We'll make it fit."

The water filled the tub slowly. She sat on the wooden edge of the whirlpool and wrapped her legs around his waist. The thrumming rush of the water and Phil's deep kisses made her forget herself. They undressed each other, then stepped into the knee-high water. Nestled in his arms, in the soothing warmth of the water, Olive felt miles away from all her concerns. Her nerve endings felt like they'd woken up from a long sleep; every inch of her skin was alive to Phil's mouth and caresses. In this space, she was no longer a duality—Olive past, Olive present; she was only one Olive, and this Olive knew what she wanted. There were no second guesses. She stopped thinking about the year as a whole and focused only on this moment. It was more happiness than she deserved.

The next morning they ate doughnuts in bed and got the sheets full of powdered sugar. They gave the bathtub another try, this time in a more functional way and by taking turns. He washed her hair and body, paying special attention to her breasts to make sure they were extra soapy and clean. She sat on the ledge behind him in her terrycloth bathrobe and rubbed his shoulders and trickled a cup of warm water over his head and down his back. It made him shiver with pleasure.

"Are you up for taking a little walk?" Phil asked later that afternoon. "I want to show you around the area. It's really beautiful."

"You bet." She rolled on an extra pair of socks before lacing up her hiking boots. She put on her down-filled winter jacket, fleece gloves, and pompon hat. He took one look at her and burst out laughing. “What? I want to stay warm,” she said defensively.

“I’m not taking you on an Arctic expedition, I promise,” he said.

They walked out into the crisp, sunlit day, the only kind of day found in February in Wisconsin when it’s below freezing and there’s still snow on the ground for the sun to reflect off—when everything is brilliantly, blindingly blue and white, and shimmering like a mirage. Phil walked ahead, hands thrust deep into his jacket pockets, weaving a path through the naked trees, and Olive followed.

He stopped at a fork in the trail. “I think the lake is down this way.” He chose the path on the right that wound down the hill. The path was pretty steep, and she had to hold on to tree branches and his arm from time to time. “We’re almost there.”

With about thirty feet of their climb down the hill left to go, a view of the lake opened up below them. It was frozen solid and sparkling in the winter sunlight. It was small—more a pond than a lake, really—and shaped like an eggplant with the small end to the east and the fat end to the west.

“It’s stunning,” Olive said.

They descended the hill and began to walk slowly side by side along its snowy shore. Phil was on her left-hand side at first, but he awkwardly stepped around her so that he was closest to the lake. He reached for her fleece-gloved hand, and she accepted his, which looked red and blotchy. She hoped he wasn’t getting frostbite. She tried to warm his hand with her own.

"Do you see that tall fir tree across the lake?" he asked.

There were many tall trees across the lake. "Which one? What's a fir tree look like?" He quickly pointed, and she followed his arm. "Yes, okay. I see it now. What about it?"

"The guys and I camped at that site last summer."

"Oh. Is this where you went fishing?"

He dropped her hand and returned his to his pocket. "There was this old guy camping with his grandsons a few sites away, and we got to talking to him one night and found out he used to own this land a long time ago."

"Are you sure he wasn't just pulling your leg?" she teased. Despite the extra pair of socks, her feet were starting to feel a little numb. She stamped them to warm up.

"No, he was serious," Phil said. "He told us the name of the lake." He paused for dramatic effect. "Lake Olive."

Olive laughed. "That's a good one."

"I'm not kidding. The man said he named the lake after his wife." Phil stopped abruptly. "And I knew it must be the lake's real name right away because I'd never seen a more beautiful lake before, and I've never seen a girl more beautiful than you."

She stood next to him and looked out at the iced-over lake. It was bleak-looking now, but she imagined it looked pretty in the summer with ripples and waves and reflections of the sky. "Thank you, Phil," she said.

"I knew when he told me that that I'd have to bring you here one day. I've been in love with you for three years, Olive." His tone was suddenly formal and scripted-sounding. "Three transformative years. You've made me so happy, and I want to spend the rest of my life making you as happy as you've made me." Surprised, Olive turned around to discover him bent down on one knee in front of her in the snow. "Olive Elizabeth Watson, will you marry me?"

She couldn't move or speak. She could only stare. She was sure her mouth was hanging open. Was he serious? He must be serious. He couldn't be kidding. There he was, oh my God, yes, there he was producing a little black velvet box from his jacket pocket and then opening it, and there was a diamond ring inside it. His face was pensive and white as the snow. He was waiting for her to speak, but what could she say? The simplicity and clarity she'd been experiencing since last night clouded over as the weight of last year's events returned to her.

She couldn't, shouldn't say yes, knowing what she knew. They had frustrations and misunderstandings lying in wait for them. They had gone on without each other last year. They had dated other people. A month after their breakup, she had left him a voice mail: *I don't think I'll ever stop loving you, Phil. If you ever feel you can get past this and forgive me, please call.* But he had never called her back. She had tried all measures to mend herself—work, Alex, more work. Phil had given up on her, but she, she had remained permanently halved. Was it possible that he had felt incomplete without her, too? Maybe his wary heart had disallowed him from returning to her. She supposed now she would never know.

How could it be that their relationship was balanced on such an extreme precipice? Marriage one way, total dissolution the other?

It struck her then with a bolt of certainty that this proposal had been on Phil's agenda last year, too. That was why he had wanted the weekend's events to go so perfectly, and that was why he had been so frustrated when they hadn't. The night had gone so horribly wrong that he had decided not to propose to her, not to even let her know his intentions. And then a week later, she had done something that made Phil change his mind about her forever. She reeled at the thought of how badly she had hurt him. Had anyone in her family known about his intentions? Had he asked for her mom's permission to propose? Had he told Kerrigan? No one had ever let on to her.

"Phil," she said, her voice barely above a whisper. Tears welled up in her eyes. "Please stand up. Your knee must be freezing."

"It doesn't matter," he said. "All I care about right now is hearing one little word from you. Say yes, Olive."

It should've been so simple to say yes, but guilt thickened her tongue. Sherry's words sounded like an alarm in her head. *It's easy enough to change your actions, but it's a lot harder to change your heart. And it's impossible to change someone else's.* She could perfect this weekend with her foreknowledge, and she could control her body's reckless impulses. She could wear Phil's ring. But what if it wasn't enough? When it came right down to it, they still had unresolved issues, and until they worked through those, she couldn't be fully confident in their love.

"You are so sweet, Phil. But marriage is so . . . permanent. How do you know—how can you be so certain—that we're meant to be together forever?"

He looked into her eyes with disbelief. "Without a doubt, Ollie, you are the only woman I want to spend the rest of my life with."

She pictured the way his handsome face had shut down

when she'd revealed her betrayal, and then the way he had tenderly brushed back the redhead's hair in the coffee shop. "You *don't* know that," she said, and her words came out a little more harshly than she had planned.

Phil rose to his feet. He still held the open ring box in his right hand. He brushed off the snow on the knee of his pants with his left. "Yes, *I do.* Don't you want to spend the rest of your life with me?"

"I love you, Phil." She mopped up her tears with the fingers of her fleece gloves.

"I love you, too. Don't you want to be with me forever?"

"I don't know," she whispered. "I'm not ready to answer that question, yet. I need more time."

"I can't believe this," he said. He snapped the ring box shut and thrust it back into his jacket pocket. "I thought you would say yes. I thought we felt the same way about each other."

"Please don't be angry. I'm not saying that I feel any differently about you or that I wouldn't consider one day marrying you—"

"Gee, thanks. That makes me feel a lot better. Just what every guy who's proposed wants to hear." He kicked a hard chunk of snow onto the icy surface of the lake.

She didn't know what to say to make this better. She doubted there was anything she could say.

"Let's just go back up to the cabin." He set off up the hill without looking back to see if she was behind him. She had a hard time keeping up with him, and he didn't offer her his arm this time. Her calves were aching from the climb, and her lungs were burning from breathing so heavily by the time they got back to the cabin. He went directly into the bathroom and slammed the door behind him. Olive collapsed onto the couch.

When the bathroom door finally creaked open, he was across the room before she could even look up. He held her face between his hands. They felt cool against her scalding cheeks.

"I'm sorry," he said. He kissed her eyelashes, then her nose and forehead. "I shouldn't have roared at you like that."

"I'm sorry, too." She managed to catch his lips and press them against her own. "I wish you knew how much I wanted to say yes."

He twisted his fingers through hers. "You can still say yes."

Founding a marriage on secrets and lies was out of the question. She told herself it would be unfair to him if she said yes, since he didn't truly know what he was getting himself into. He didn't understand the woman she was or what they had been through together in a previous time. There was no way she could accept his proposal without first telling him the truth, but there didn't seem to be a way to tell him the truth, either.

"I don't want this to break us up. I'm not ready for marriage yet, but I don't want to lose you." She squeezed his hand.

"Okay," he said simply.

They didn't make love that night. They left the next day in the late morning. Things weren't hostile or tense between them. A casual onlooker wouldn't have suspected a thing. But they both knew things had changed between them. The silliness and affection they had so openly displayed before was all but gone. Olive was reminded of the drive back to Madison last year when she had then, too, pointed out a huddle of brown-spotted cows just to have something to say.

Chapter 8

Oh, man. I still can't believe you said no," Kerrigan said. It had been her unrelenting chorus for the past week, as if the current strain on Olive and Phil's relationship wasn't enough of a reminder.

Olive ignored her. She brushed her hair into a ponytail and snapped an elastic band around it. It was a Friday night, and they were in Kerrigan's room. Kerrigan was getting ready to go out; Olive was getting ready for work.

"Has he taken back the ring?" Kerrigan persisted. She threaded a pair of gold-beaded chandelier earrings through her ears. In the ICU, Olive wasn't allowed to wear earrings or necklaces, perfume or nail polish. Not even clear nail polish.

"I don't know. We're not talking about it. It's kind of a touchy subject, you know?" Olive sat down on the desk chair and crossed her arms. In her faded green scrubs, she felt frumpy next to her friend. She wished she hadn't agreed to let

Kerrigan wear her red halter dress. Kerrigan had the eye-catching cleavage Olive lacked and the dress required.

"I know, I know," Kerrigan said. "It's just *you and Phil.* Phil and Olive: the cutest couple I know. I can't get over it. You guys are so perfect for each other. I wish I could find that." Despite her careful primping, she looked miserable. She and Steve had called it quits a few weeks ago.

"You will," Olive said. "In a dress like that, probably sooner rather than later."

Kerrigan blotted her red lips on a tissue, crumpled it up, and tossed it into the wastebasket across the room. She had bombarded Olive with questions the moment she'd gotten home from the trip, and when Olive had finally told her that she had refused Phil's proposal, they had cried together about it. It had felt so good to share her problems with someone other than unsympathetic Sherry that she had been tempted to tell Kerrigan the whole truth. A fleeting temptation, but one that was now resurfacing.

Tonight was the night she had cheated on Phil. She longed to confess to Kerrigan the mix of uneasiness and shame she felt. Surely, Kerrigan would have something consoling to say. With her own checkered past, Kerrigan was not one to judge; she would probably want to hear all the dirty details.

Yet whenever Olive tried to formulate in her head how she would convince Kerrigan of her extraordinary situation, it sounded ridiculous. *Do you remember how you thought I had a head injury on New Year's Day? Well, the reason I was acting so strange is that I'm caught in some kind of time warp. I've actually seen the future. Well, at least one year of it.* No, that wouldn't do.

"It's going to be okay, sweetie," Kerrigan said. "Why don't you give him a call?"

On the short drive to Dane County General, Olive tried to do just that, but Phil didn't answer his phone. She left him a message: "Hi, honey. I'm headed to work now. I wish we were spending the night together instead."

Her mom beeped in as she was leaving the message. She hurriedly switched over. "Hi, Mom. I don't have a ton of time to talk right now. I'm driving to work. How are you doing?"

"I'm good. Look, I know you're busy, but I thought maybe if you have a free moment tonight, I could stop by for a late dinner and bring some subs, or we could go to the cafeteria. I'm not picky."

The thought of having her mom there as emotional support was appealing, but then she would probably have to share the details of last weekend and listen to stories about how wonderful Harry was. "I appreciate the offer, but I just don't think I'll have time tonight. Friday nights are always hectic. Maybe sometime next week?"

The ICU was in its usual tumultuous, transitional period when she arrived. Gloria was shepherding a middle-aged couple into the Family Room, and Olive knew that their loved one had probably just died, and they were now about to learn this unbearable truth—a pain with which Olive was all too familiar. An unusual number of specialists milled around the ICU; she recognized Dr. Nichols from cardiology and Dr. Dumont-Gray from nephrology. The deceased patient had probably been an organ donor. Now, in this critical window, it was important to secure the family's permission to begin the organ procurement process.

Tina was at the nurses' station talking to Toya. They were both eating brownies from a white bakery box. Alex was thankfully nowhere to be seen. Olive's plan was to stay as far away from him as possible.

"Brownie?" Tina offered. "Gloria brought them as a birthday treat."

"Maybe later. I think I'd better check in first."

"You're taking over for Jennifer tonight," Toya said.

Olive found Jennifer, the new mom, typing rapidly at one of the computer stations outside a fishbowl room. She was wearing pale pink scrubs. Jennifer always wore pastel-colored scrubs; during the later months of her pregnancy she'd looked like an Easter egg. She swiveled on her stool to face Olive.

"You're not going to like this." She tapped a finger against the spiky green lines on the computer monitor. "You'll have only one patient tonight because she's circling the drain. Mrs. Gardner was brought in this morning. End-stage renal disease, congestive heart failure, and emphysema. I don't expect she'll make it through the night."

Betty Gardner. Olive pictured the old woman's frail, hunched body, her translucent skin and the web of purple veins beneath. She could almost smell the cloying scent of rose talcum powder and urine. She wasn't the first patient under Olive's care who had died—there had been five others before her last year—yet she was the first patient who had died on Olive's watch. Her family was the first that Olive had comforted, or rather had tried to comfort—Mr. Gardner had advanced Alzheimer's. Alex had requested she be there when he broke the news.

"Her daughter's in the waiting room. At the first sign of a downturn, she wants to know so she can make sure her dad's here for the end." Jennifer slid off her stool. "Ask Tina if you have any questions. The new resident's on tonight, and he can't find his ass with both hands."

She was referring to Alex. Olive smiled tightly and accepted Mrs. Gardner's chart.

She took the vacated seat. Behind the glass lay the old woman's motionless body. The chart and the ill patient it described felt damning. She had forgotten about Betty Gardner in the context of this night; she had thought only of her own tawdry, trivial affairs. Now she was starting to understand the connection between these two events. How had she not seen it before? Her raw sense of culpability and failure had blinded her.

The chart offered no answers, no loopholes; it read like a death sentence.

"Mrs. Gardner, I'm your nurse, Olive. You're in good hands tonight."

Olive squeezed the old woman's gray nail beds. She pressed down on her breastbone. No response. She felt like she was handling a corpse, a woman who had literally been raised from the dead. She had been the one to wash Mrs. Gardner's body last year and prepare it for the morgue. She knew she would be repeating the procedure again tonight. The thought made her light-headed. She sat down on the edge of the bed.

What was the point of this? To make these poor people suffer all over again? If there was nothing she could do for her patients anyway, then why taunt her with the possibility? The cosmos had a cruel sense of humor.

"Olive."

She leaped up at the sound of Alex's voice. It was almost

as if she had summoned him through her thoughts. He was like some kind of wicked reply: the universe wasn't through with her yet. His light brown hair and beard were shaved close and looked fuzzy to the touch. He wore his wrinkled white coat over pale blue scrubs that matched his eyes. His presence filled the room. Her body felt extremely conscious of his as he walked to Mrs. Gardner's bedside.

"I'm glad you're on tonight," he said. Both last year and this year, he had made much of their both being "new." Like Olive, he had initially been intimidated by Tina and some of the other nurses. "Is this your first time losing a patient?"

He had asked her this last year. Then the question had seemed premature to her; she hadn't picked up on the inevitability that all the other staff sensed when a patient was about to pass.

"It feels like it," she said.

"I know what you mean. It never gets any easier, does it?" As he pulled the loop of his stethoscope from his lab coat pocket, his arm brushed softly against hers. She wondered if his body had a recollection of hers, if somehow it had secretly retained memories separate from his mind.

She held the clipboard against her breasts like a shield. "Only if you want it to."

Alex looked up at her with startled eyes. Not the answer he'd been expecting.

It was a lesson she was still learning. When she had first started nursing, she had taken every death personally, like she was losing her father all over again. Every patient lost under her care was a little piece of death she would carry around with her until the end of her own life. But the alternative seemed so unfeeling. Tina and the other nurses could crack jokes and banter back and forth about contestants on *American Idol* before the body of a deceased patient was even cold. It was a coping mechanism, she knew, but not necessarily one she thought she would ever adopt. There had to be something in between. Olive had been called a bleeding heart before, but her heart no longer had the same plasticity and tenderness—it was scarred and worn beyond repair.

Alex warmed the bell of his stethoscope with his breath before touching Mrs. Gardner's skin with it. "I lost my first patient in medical school," he started, "my very first day of my internal medicine rotation. A middle-aged man came in complaining of a horrible headache. He begged me for some pain medication, Tylenol, anything. I left the room to check with a resident. When I came back in, he was unconscious on the floor. He died within minutes. A subarachnoid hemorrhage."

Olive had heard this story before. It was obviously one that had left a deep impression on Alex; it had stuck with her as well. "That's awful," she murmured.

"The resident had never seen anything like that before, either, so he tried to make a joke out of it. Called me Dr. Death. They called the man's wife at work to ask her to come to the hospital. I remember this because it was so strange—she worked at a travel agency that planned big-game hunting safaris. They made me stay in the room to learn how to break the news to a family member. She didn't believe that he was dead until we showed her."

He smoothed the white hair off Mrs. Gardner's forehead. "You should contact her family now," he said. He prescribed a dosage of morphine, squeezed Olive's shoulder, and left the room.

Olive administered the morphine, watched the labored

rise and fall of the old woman's chest a few moments longer, and then left the room, too. She wished she could leave the ICU, the hospital even. She didn't feel strong enough to handle this again. The woman she was now seemed a lot weaker than the woman she had been.

It was nine twenty-five. Mrs. Gardner's daughter was watching a rerun of *Friends* in the otherwise empty waiting room. She was somewhere in her fifties or sixties, a woman who had probably once been very handsome, but time and misfortune had aged her severely. She was still bundled in her winter jacket and a pink scarf, despite the fact that it was unusually warm in the waiting room.

She stood up when Olive entered the room. "Anne Delaney. How's my mother?"

"She's hanging on, but we don't know for how much longer. Dr. Carpenter suggested you contact any family you wish to have with you."

"I should call Michelle to bring my dad." Anne said this without any conviction. She looked at Olive for affirmation.

Last year, Olive hadn't known who Michelle was. She had thought she was a sister, a daughter, a partner maybe. Now she knew she was the home health aide. She had a sudden image of Mr. Gardner, a giant of a man, strangely dignified in his plaid pajamas. With his advanced Alzheimer's, he hadn't understood the reason for the late-night ICU visit, hadn't even recognized his wife's name. He'd become agitated and mean. Olive suspected he had brought more sorrow than comfort to his grieving daughter, but she didn't feel she had the right to instruct Anne to do otherwise.

"That's your decision, Anne. I know it's a difficult one."

Olive rubbed Anne's upper arm, but she didn't know if the woman could feel it through her heavy jacket.

"It will be after ten o'clock by the time they get here. He's normally in bed by eight. And I just don't know"—here her voice broke as she stifled a sob—"if he'll even remember." She covered her face with the tail of her pink scarf like a child. "If you had loved someone for sixty-one years but couldn't remember that now, would you still want to be there at the end?"

In nursing school, they had taught her how to deflect personal questions, as well as moral or value judgments. The trick was to turn it around on the person with a question about them. *What do you think about that? How does that make you feel? What religion do you practice?* It didn't fool the persistent patients, and Olive knew Anne deserved better than that.

"Yes, I would. But it would be hard. It *will* be hard."

"Thank you." Anne unwound her scarf and removed her jacket. "I think that's the right decision. I owe it to my parents."

"Would you like to see your mother before they arrive?"

"Yes, please. I'll be there as soon as I've made my call."

She had been given the chance to avert something of a disaster, and she hadn't gone through with it. The memory of Mr. Gardner, Anne, Michelle, Alex, and herself all locked together in that room distressed her. It would've been so easy to say, "No. Don't worry him. You can tell him tomorrow in the familiarity of his own home. He can say good-bye to her at the funeral." She knew nothing good could come of this. So why had she agreed with Anne?

Because it was Anne's decision to make, not hers. And

Anne had seemed to want some reassurance that she was doing the right thing. While Olive didn't know if it was the right decision, the Gardners weren't her parents. Their story was not hers to revise. She seemed to be there only to bear witness.

She took Betty Gardner's vitals and then returned to her post at the computer station outside the room. What had at first seemed like a new road filled with so much possibility now felt like a well-worn path she had already trod and couldn't break out of. Anne went into her mother's room, held her hand, and talked to her. Only moments later, she left. Olive sat sentinel on the stool for what felt like hours. She had no other patients to attend to, so she had no reason to leave.

Nothing seemed to be in her power to change. She couldn't save Mrs. Gardner's life. She couldn't even protect the woman's daughter from unnecessary heartache. She hadn't fixed her problems with Phil.

A change in the heart monitor's steady beeping rhythm brought Olive back from her thoughts. She hurried to Mrs. Gardner's bedside. After a quick survey of the machines, she discovered that the pulse oximeter was the culprit. Mrs. Gardner's oxygen saturation levels were dangerously low. Olive turned up the ventilator to one hundred percent oxygen. The old woman's chest rose with each whoosh of forced oxygen, but her skin remained bluish and clammy, and her saturation levels didn't rise. Feeling as if she were caught in a dream she'd had before, Olive removed the oxygen bag from the wall and began ventilating Mrs. Gardner herself, with quick, measured pumps. "I need help in here!" she called.

Tina was immediately by her side. She whipped off her

stethoscope and listened to the old woman's chest. She suctioned her lungs and listened again. "I can't hear any airflow in there. Listen, Watson, there's no hope for her anymore. All we can do now is make sure she's not suffering." Tina injected another dose of morphine into the IV.

She had known what was going to happen all along; she just wasn't ready to accept it. Tonight's events had unfolded as swiftly and relentlessly as they had last year, and there didn't seem to be a damn thing she could do about it. She stared down at Betty's face as she forced the air into her uncooperative lungs. Her forehead was high and angular, her long nose beaky, her blue lips drooped downward.

Olive's hand was cramping up from her rhythmic squeezing of the oxygen bag. She turned to see Alex enter the room.

He reached across the bed and placed his hand over Olive's, which was still compressing the bag. "You've done all that you can. She's gone. It's time to stop now."

Olive gave the bag one last squeeze and then slowly removed the plastic mask. Last year, she hadn't been able to peel her eyes from the cardiac monitor's dips and dives, anticipating that one final flat line, the moment when it was all over. Now she continued to watch Betty.

"Twenty-two seventeen," Tina announced as the old woman's body gave its last weary shudder.

Olive wanted to flee. She didn't want to participate in what happened next. But Alex was inadvertently blocking the door.

"I understand the family is in the waiting room and that you've established a rapport with them," he said. "Would you please bring them to the Family Room?"

Mr. Gardner, plaid pajamas and all, was sitting awkwardly next to his daughter. He didn't seem to fit in the chair. It took both Anne and Michelle to raise him to a standing position. He shuffled along well enough on his own, with only his daughter's hand gently placed on his elbow.

The Family Room was painted a sunny yellow, but that hardly disguised its purpose. Scratchy gray couches lined the walls. End tables in between were stocked with tissue boxes and pamphlets. Only one picture hung on the wall—a framed photograph of a rainbow arcing over a rural landscape.

Alex introduced himself. "I have some very sad news. We did everything we could to revive Betty, but she died a short while ago." He launched into a brief explanation of how her body had shut down and the measures they had taken.

It was strange to watch the three figures on the couch. Anne, already resigned to her mother's death, was stoically watching her father's face. Mr. Gardner was scowling down at his hands in his lap. Only Michelle, the paid help, reacted in a typical way. She gulped and wrung her hands and reached for a tissue to dab her eyes. "Poor Betty."

"Dad, did you hear what the doctor said?"

Mr. Gardner glared at his daughter.

"Mom was very sick. She passed away. She's gone now."

Mr. Gardner didn't talk, but he seemed to be listening to Anne. His eyes didn't leave her face.

"Are you okay, Dad? How are you feeling?" She patted his knee.

"Don't touch me! You're not going to lock me up in a goddamn hospital. I want to go home!"

"It's okay, Dad. It's me, Anne. Your daughter. We'll go home in just a little bit. We're here at the hospital because of

Mom. Do you remember your wife, Betty? She just died. It's very, very sad. We're all very sad."

Mr. Gardner tried to stand up. He hoisted himself up partway, and then fell back down onto the seat.

"Would it help if he saw her body?" Alex asked.

"No," Anne and Olive both said in unison.

"It will just make him more agitated. He's not usually like this. He's not good in unfamiliar places," Anne explained. "I thought I would try, but I guess I'll have to wait until he's more lucid—"

Mr. Gardner was trying to stand up again, and this time, Michelle assisted him.

"Get off me!" he shouted. "I don't know you! I want to go home."

"I'm going to take you home, Walt," Michelle said.

"If there's anything further I can do to help, please let me know," Alex said to Anne.

Anne looked from Alex to Olive with pleading eyes. "He loved her so much. He put in a Japanese garden in their backyard because she always wanted to see Japan but was too afraid to fly. He's going to ask for her in the morning. And the next morning. And the next. I don't think he's ever going to realize what he lost."

Because Olive had lost a parent before and knew there was nothing anyone could really say to lessen that pain, she hugged Anne. The older woman seemed surprised at first, but then she embraced Olive the way Olive suspected she wished her father would embrace her.

What made Olive the saddest about the Gardners was that everyone wanted to be enshrined in someone's memory. It was the only way of living on after death, really: in the minds of loved ones. Memories were the only things that made aging bearable, a way of reverting to better, simpler days. Mr. and Mrs. Gardner had been robbed of that.

She needed to tell someone. Someone who would care, someone who would try to understand. Someone who would remind her that she was loved and cherished.

Olive blindly found her way to the locker room. She sat on a bench with her knees tucked into her chest. She needed to talk to Phil, but it was almost eleven thirty. She didn't know where he was or what his plans for the night had been. Perhaps he was already in bed. Her desire to talk to him was so strong, however, that she decided it was worth the risk of waking him up.

He answered on the fourth ring. "Olive?" he shouted into the phone over the din of a noisy bar. "I thought you were at work."

"I am. Where are you?"

"Castaway's with Brian and Jeff. Is something wrong? You never call me from work."

"Phil, I—"

"Hang on a second. I can't hear a thing in here. I'm going to go outside."

"No, don't. Really, it's not necessary. I just wanted to—"

A huge swell of music and laughter rose up, and she could barely make out his next words. "Olive? I'm going to call you back, okay? I can't hear anything you're saying."

"No, really. It's fine. Have fun. I'll talk to you later."

She cradled her cell phone in her cupped hands. It seemed unthinkable that Phil could be at a bar with his friends right now, while she was here, alone, inundated with feelings of grief, failure, and self-pity. Last year he had asked her to share this part of her life with him. He had said he wanted to help her protect herself from too much sorrow. But at times like these, their worlds seemed almost irreconcilable. And how could she really explain the twofold loss of Betty Gardner?

She contemplated calling Kerrigan. But no, Kerrigan was probably still at a bar or club, too. Only then did she think of her mom.

The locker room door swung open, and Alex stepped inside. He was holding the bottom of his blue scrub top away from his stomach. A long drip of blood clung to the fabric. Olive froze.

"Excuse me," he said, and gingerly lifted the shirt over his head. He balled it up in his hands, the bloodied side in, and stood in front of her, naked from the waist up. He was not as muscular as Phil, but his body was long, tan, and lean. The body of a swimmer. He seemed to want something from her.

"Oh," she said. Of course. "Scrubs with body fluids on them go in the biohazard hamper." *Body fluids?* Why couldn't she have just said *blood*? She stood up so that the bench was between them.

He deposited the shirt into the hamper and shut the lid. "I was putting in a central line," he said. He opened his locker and pulled out a fresh blue scrub top. He bent at the waist to put it on, and Olive could see the familiar tattoo of a caduceus, a winged staff entwined by two serpents, on his shoulder blade.

She started making her way to the door. Everything was a direct echo of what had happened last year. She needed to remove herself from this situation as quickly as possible.

"That was the most depressing thing I've ever witnessed. Are you doing all right?" he asked.

Last year she had come unhinged at this question. She hadn't cried for Betty Gardner. She had cried for Mr. Gardner, who didn't remember enough to cry for his beloved wife. She had cried out of fear that things were over with Phil. She had cried for her dad, who had died too young and wouldn't get to walk her down the aisle one day, if that day ever came. She had cried for the dread that possibly one day she might die alone and forgotten. Alex had held her. He'd rubbed her back and whispered things like, "You did everything you could for her. She's not suffering now," and "They'll be reunited one day," and when he'd inclined his head to kiss her, she hadn't resisted. Instead, she had accepted his mouth like it was her only chance at salvation. She'd had a chance to come to her senses and stop. He had asked her, "Is this okay? Do you want to go somewhere more private?" and she had followed him back into the Family Room, the scene of tragedies, where they had locked the door behind them. In essence, with that desperate act, Olive had been trying to ward off death. Dispel the stench of it that seemed to cling to her. Prove that she was young and recklessly alive.

She looked at Alex, who didn't remember all that had passed between them. She knew he would readily comfort her again if she only gave him the chance. Last year she had craved reassurance and understanding, and Alex had given that to her. She hadn't even given Phil the opportunity to do the same. His frustration with her work preoccupation had made her believe that he wouldn't even try to understand. Now she realized how unfair that had been. If he loved her, he would try. If she loved him, she owed him the chance to try.

Though the rest of the night had been almost an uncanny

replication of last year, this was one incident she was going to change. “I’m okay,” she told Alex. “Thanks for asking.” She pushed open the locker room door. The door paused briefly on its outward swing, allowing a couple of seconds for her to look back, but she didn’t, and the door completed its sweeping arc and closed behind her.

She returned to Betty Gardner’s room. Olive freed the old woman’s body of all the tubing and wires. Then she bathed her as gently as she had been taught to bathe the newborns in her obstetrics clinicals.

A little after two, she called Phil again, tucked in the corner of the break room next to the antiquated microwave and TV. It was clear she had woken him up. Before he could ask her about her earlier call, she told him everything about the Gardner family. He didn’t interrupt. He didn’t comment or ask questions or offer consolation. The only way she knew he was there was by his breathing, but his reverent silence made her certain he was listening to her every word.

Chapter 9

The days grew longer. The sun shone with an intensity unusual for late March, melting the hills of dirty snow. Only a few gray patches remained, protected by the constant shadows of buildings. The front yard of the pink house offered up a bizarre assortment of abandoned objects. Disposable plastic cups, flattened beer cans. A solitary purple stiletto, one raggedy black mitten. Unaccountably, a three-hole punch.

Olive's mom had invited her and Phil and Christopher and Verona over for dinner. She knew what tonight was: the engagement announcement dinner. Phil hadn't been here for this last year—she had faced it alone and blundered it quite badly—but she felt certain that with him in the mix, everything would carry on more peaceably. He had that effect on people. She felt like a better person with him by her side. But she was slightly worried that her mom's news might hit too close to home for him with their own unsuccessful engagement still lingering unspoken between them.

They took Olive's SUV for the twenty-minute drive to her mom's house; Phil's Mercedes was in the shop as predicted—at least by Olive—for a new fuel pump. The sun had set only moments before, and the sky was a luxurious shade of blue. Everything looked muted and surreal, like viewing the world through gauzy fabric; even the sooty, diminished snow on the side of the highway looked picturesque.

Olive turned off the radio and straightened up in her seat. "I'm pretty sure my mom asked us over tonight to tell us they're getting married."

"Wow. That's big. What makes you think that?" Phil asked, swiveling in his seat to watch her profile.

"They've been together for almost a year now. He's at every single holiday and nonholiday family function. They threw a New Year's Day party together. They flew to Arizona to visit his mother in January, and they're learning how to retile the upstairs bathroom together." When she stacked it all up, it did make a pretty compelling argument. Why hadn't she seen that last year? Everything seemed so obvious in hindsight.

The windows were starting to fog up. Phil turned on the defroster. "You seem okay with this. *Are* you okay with this?"

Since Harry had started dating her mom last May, Phil had heard Olive's many complaints about him. He was too old for her mom—six years older, to be exact. He was divorced and not on great terms with his ex-wife and daughter, who lived on the north side of Chicago. He wore cuff links and had perpetual coffee breath. He had an annoying habit of trying to supply words for people. He bought her mom opera tickets, and because she was too nice to tell him she hated the opera, they kept going. He tried to win Olive over by name-dropping campus locations: "It was so nice outside yesterday, I ate my lunch at Union Terrace" or "I was hiking up Bascom Hill the other day when . . ."

"I don't have a choice," she said. "They'll get married with or without my blessing. I just want my mom to be happy." And as difficult as it was for her to admit, in the first five months of the marriage, Olive's mom was the happiest she had seen her prior to 2003, when her dad had been diagnosed with leukemia. It was one of the questions that had nagged at Olive the most before the wedding: Would Harry make her mom truly happy, or was her mom simply lonely? She knew the answer to the first part now, and she wasn't so sure it mattered anymore if her mom's desire for remarriage stemmed from loneliness.

Phil's knees bounced up and down; he was always such a restless passenger. "Good for you. Well, Harry has some pretty big shoes to fill. Your dad was one of the best men I've ever known."

"Oh, he won't be filling my dad's shoes. There's no way." Olive dug her fingernails into the steering wheel. "I will never think of him as my dad, or probably even my stepdad. He's just Harry."

"Okay." Phil turned his face toward the window.

"I'm sorry. I didn't mean to snap at you. What you said was very sweet, and I know my dad thought the world of you, too. I'm trying to be very Zen about all of this, but I don't think I will *ever* see what my mom sees in Harry."

"I don't know about that," Phil said. "Professor Matheson attended the coronation of Charlemagne."

She grinned. "Professor Matheson thinks March Madness is a seventh-century plague."

Phil snorted. "That's a good one."

"Thanks. I've been saving it for the right time."

It was an inside joke they shared. When Olive's mom had first introduced her to Harry, Olive had immediately started "researching" him. She had checked out the medieval studies department web page and Harry's individual profile. She had Kerrigan put her ear to the ground for any university rumors. She even found a website where students rated their professors. Though overall Harry's marks were high, one of his students had written in the comments section: "Professor Matheson attended the coronation of Charlemagne. Archbishop Stephen Langton plagiarized the Magna Carta from Professor Matheson. Professor Matheson thinks Hoobastank was a city in the Byzantine Empire." The last one was Olive's particular favorite. She wondered if Harry had ever seen the website.

They pulled up to the gray Cape Cod with its slanted roof and white shutters just as Christopher and Verona were pulling up, too. Olive hurried to remove her seat belt, but Phil caught her hand. Expecting some last silly words of encouragement, she gazed up at him, but his expression was solemn.

"You didn't tell your mom about my proposal, did you?"

"No. No one knows." She freed her hand, which he had almost crushed in his grip.

"Good."

It felt like such a cold note to end on, but he was already opening his car door. Christopher and Verona called out to them, and suddenly they were hurled into the spotlight, quite literally, as the motion sensor lights snapped on, illuminating the front lawn and white picket fence.

Christopher and Verona had brought a bottle of wine. Even with the foresight of a year, Olive would never be as prepared and well mannered as Verona.

They were a handsome couple: Christopher was tall, dark, and attractive, and Verona was his complementary opposite—petite with alabaster skin and blond, baby-fine hair. She owned a sweater set in every color. She was a PhD student in the math department, working on her dissertation on algorithmic randomness.

"Olive! Have you done something different with your hair? It looks so pretty in curls."

Phil and Christopher clapped each other on the back as if they were old buddies. Christopher wrote articles for a progressive online newspaper and did freelance web development on the side. He and Verona had three dogs—a chocolate Lab named Fanny, a Corgi named Dixon, and a Papillon named Lola. Though Christopher and Phil had little in common besides a love for dogs, they held each other in very high esteem. Christopher had been especially disappointed with their breakup last year.

Their mom was waiting, framed in the doorway, squinting against the brightness.

Inside the house, everything had been carefully orchestrated. A row of pillar candles had been lighted on the mantel. Soft piano music streamed from the stereo. Bruschetta slices had been daintily arranged on a china platter and laid on the coffee table. They were told the shrimp primavera—Harry's specialty—would be ready in fifteen minutes.

When Olive had walked into this last year, it had felt like she had mistakenly stepped into someone else's living room. Who was this woman in the beige silk blouse with a string of pearls? Certainly not her mom, who wore the same flowery dresses to work almost every day and had never owned a valuable piece of jewelry in her life, aside from her wedding ring. If they turned the stereo on, which they rarely did, she had popped in a James Taylor or Joni Mitchell CD. Dinner had never been an "affair" before. She had thought her mom was trying to be a different woman for Harry. Or even worse: that her mom had been wishing for a life like this all along.

Now that she knew what tonight really meant, she noticed subtleties she hadn't the first time around. Her mom offered Phil something to drink three times, forcing Phil to finally agree to a glass of sauvignon blanc the third time. Harry had armpit stains right through his tweed blazer. They were both incredibly nervous. They were trying hard to make everyone enjoy themselves because they were striving for a favorable outcome—acceptance.

"Olive, can you give me a hand with the salad?" her mom asked. Harry made a motion to get up, but she shook her head slightly and he remained seated.

"Sure," Olive said, and followed her mother into the kitchen. She didn't remember this impromptu chat happening last year. Displayed prominently on the marble kitchen island on a white porcelain pedestal was her mom's famous chocolate cake. "Oh, yum. For us?"

"Of course it's for you," her mom replied. "Don't tell your brother. It was meant to be a surprise."

Her mom's chocolate cake was so notoriously delicious that it had once sold for three hundred dollars at a silent auction fund-raiser for the library. The recipe was her mother's, Olive's namesake, who had passed away the week before Olive was born. She baked it only once or twice a year so it could retain its special, sought-after status. Last year Olive had seen the coveted dessert as some kind of bribe, but now she knew better. The chocolate cake was a peace offering. It was supposed to be a reminder that they would still be the same family—it wouldn't be all bruschetta and shrimp primavera from here on out. It was a reminder that her mom was still the same woman underneath it all. Still, it was hard to know if this was the whole truth.

Her mom handed her a knife and a tomato, and Olive set to dicing it on a pull-out cutting board next to the sink. "I'm sorry we still haven't gone out for that dinner yet," Olive said. "Things have just been so busy at work lately. Maybe we can go next month."

"It's fine. I understand." It was the same airy, yet knowing response her mom had used with them in their teen years. *You can't come to the family reunion because you have too much algebra homework to do? It's fine. I understand. You came home after curfew last night because there was a brief power outage at the party and all the clocks stopped? It's fine. I understand.* "I know you and Christopher like Thousand Island. What kind of dressing does Phil like?" She pulled two dusty gravy boats from the cupboard and started rinsing them out.

"He likes anything, but ranch is his favorite. Look, Mom, you really don't need to make more dishes and use those. The plain old bottles are fine."

"I don't mind." She toweled the silver gravy boats dry. "This clawfoot one was my mother's. When I was a little girl, it always reminded me of Aladdin's magic lamp. When Laurel was about six, I convinced her if she rubbed it just the right way, a genie would pop out and make all her wishes come true."

Olive laughed. She slid the cutting board out of its slot and guided the diced tomatoes into the salad bowl with her knife. "Was Aunt Laurel very disappointed?"

"Not at all. It worked for her." Her mom poured the Thousand Island dressing into the gravy boat. "She played with it for the rest of the summer until my mother had a big Sunday dinner one day and found out her gravy boat was missing."

"I don't think I've ever heard that one before. It doesn't sound like Aunt Laurel at all."

"Laurel was very imaginative as a girl. Until she discovered boys, that is." She returned the bottles of salad dressing to the fridge.

"It sounds like you were also very imaginative," Olive said.

"Ah, you know me. I was always a reader."

The salad was ready now, and there was no longer any pretense for being here in the kitchen together, but Olive could tell her mom still wasn't satisfied. She lifted the lids of pots on the stove and opened both the fridge and oven as though she were looking for something but couldn't quite remember what. They both decided to speak at the same moment.

"I think I know—" Olive started, as her mom blurted, "Is everything okay between you and Phil?" "—what tonight's dinner is for."

Her mom reacted first, her face coloring. "What do you think it's for?"

"Did Harry propose?"

Her mom could've been a debutante preparing for her first dance, twirling happily in front of a mirror, then suddenly standing stock-still as she realized that someone was watching her, unsure of how her giddiness would be perceived. "Yes, he did. And I said yes." The expression on her face was half defiant, half afraid, and Olive remembered with what frustration her mom had told her before the wedding last year, *"There is no other person in the world who can make me doubt myself like you."*

"Mom," Olive said, stepping around the kitchen island to embrace her. "I am so happy for you." She stirred up memories from last fall and winter—Harry and her mom's frequent trips to the farmers' market and subsequent exotic dinners; the way Harry had lied about knowing how to ice skate and then fallen and sprained his wrist, all in an attempt to make her mom happy—and she tried to really mean the words she'd just said, to really feel the happiness in her heart. When her mom squeezed her back and then beamed at her, Olive found it wasn't very hard.

"You have no idea how much that means to me," her mom said, and Olive could hear the tears, close to brimming over, thick and tremulous in her voice.

Yes, I do, Olive thought, as she remembered all the times she had withheld this joyful acceptance, when it was the only thing her mom had wanted from her.

"We were going to tell everyone over dessert," her mom said, suddenly looking stricken. "Do you think you could act surprised? I don't want Christopher to think I told you before him."

Olive grinned. "Of course."

"So about you and Phil—"

Harry poked his head into the kitchen. "Need any help in there, Kathy? I would hate for my noodles to be . . . the opposite of *al dente*, whatever that may be. Overcooked? Mushy? Limp?"

Olive tried not to laugh at Harry's mention of limp noodles. She was glad Phil was in the living room, out of earshot; he probably wouldn't have been able to contain himself.

"No worries," her mom said. "I turned down the flame a minute ago. And we're all set in here. Would you mind setting these salad dressings on the table for me?" She handed the gravy boats over to Harry and, as soon as he left, raised her eyebrows questioningly at Olive.

"Everything's fine," Olive said. "We're fine. We're great. Terrific." With each adjective, she felt less and less convinced. But now was not the time or place to tell her mom about Phil's proposal and her refusal.

Her mom held the glass salad bowl tightly to her chest. "All right. I understand." And with these words, she let Olive know she was only temporarily letting her off the hook.

They situated themselves in a boy-girl pattern around the dining room table; last year, there'd been an empty chair next to Olive's that had made her feel like an outcast. This year, Olive and Phil were across from Verona and Christopher, and Harry and her mom were seated at the head and foot of the table. Olive was stuck next to Harry, who liked to explain his every culinary choice at great length.

"Do you know what the secret of perfect shrimp primavera is?" he asked her. He was still wearing his tweed blazer, and three neat drops of sweat balanced just under his hairline. Harry had a crown of thick, brown hair ironically circling his otherwise bald head.

Olive tried to look politely interested, but all she wanted was to get Phil alone and ask him why he had wanted to know if she'd told anyone. Was it just his bruised pride, or was it a sign of something more serious? It worried her.

"There's actually more than one secret." Harry winked. "I prefer penne noodles, for their firmness, to the traditional spaghetti or linguini. Also, I find most recipes for the dish a tad bland, so I add a dash of pepper flakes to mine for a little kick. And lastly, I always use fresh basil from the farmers' market at Capitol Square."

Olive perked up at this last tip. Fresh basil from the farmers' market? She looked over at Phil to see if he had caught this and was also reminded of their first meeting, but he was engaged in a conversation with Verona about the challenges of teaching physics and math to disinterested students.

Harry noticed he'd gotten her attention. "Aha," he said, leaning in. "You wonder how I can possibly get fresh basil in March? One of the vendors I frequent gets a weekly shipment from California, and I don't know how they do it, but you'd never know it's flown two thousand miles to get here."

She speared a penne noodle and wished she were eating one of her mom's specialties instead: pork chops and sauerkraut, pot roast, or her dad's favorite, meat loaf. "I'm not much of a cook," she said. "I can hardly—"

"Boil water? Fry an egg?" Harry offered.

Olive shot her brother, who had been watching this exchange, a meaningful look. Harry's verbal tics bothered him just as much as they bothered her. Harry had tried to call Christopher "Chris" early on with little success.

"Olive. Do you know who I saw at the library the other day?" her mom called down the table. "Sherry Witan. It sounds like she's taken quite a liking to you."

Phil turned to Olive with interest. She hadn't told him anything about Sherry since her first unexpected visit. All other conversation stopped as everyone turned to study Olive.

"Sherry Witan?" Christopher gaped. "If you ask me, that woman isn't rowing with both oars."

Olive's mom tried to look stern, but the corners of her mouth turned up a little. "Well, I think it's very sweet of you, Olive, to take an interest in her like that. Sherry doesn't really have anyone in her life since her last husband died." There was a short, loaded pause before she hurried on. "Her only son just left for college last year, and apparently he refuses to come home or even talk to her on the phone. It's a very sad situation."

Sherry had a son? Olive didn't know why she found this so surprising. With all those marriages, it seemed likely that at least one of them had produced children, and she was certainly under no illusions that she knew everything there was to know about Sherry Witan. Sherry told her almost nothing about herself. She wanted only to analyze Olive's problems as if it were a spectator sport.

"That's your book club friend, Kathy? The one who attends all the readings?" Harry asked, seemingly just to get back in the conversation.

Olive's mom nodded quickly. "She's the one with the—"

"Red hair and impeccable knowledge of *The Canterbury Tales*."

"That's the one," she said with a smile. She seemed to find Harry's interruptions charming. Olive wondered what she'd think of them five or ten years from now.

"What's her son's name?" Olive asked. Next to her, Phil was discreetly trying to remove the mushrooms from his shrimp primavera. He had mounded a little pile of them on a mauve rosebud on the china, as if they'd blend in.

"Heathcliff."

"After *Wuthering Heights*?" Olive asked her mom.

"I'm not sure."

"How do you know it wasn't after the fat cartoon cat?" Christopher asked with a laugh, and Phil joined in.

Naming her child after a dark and doomed romantic hero definitely seemed like something Sherry would do. This was a conversation they had not had last year. Olive was so wrapped up in this new development that she momentarily forgot about the business at hand. Therefore, when Harry and her mom stood up to clear away the dishes, she felt her stomach do a series of back handsprings. But what did she have to be worried about? She'd already come to terms with it (well, almost), and her mom already knew that she knew about the engagement. All she had to do now was act surprised for Christopher's benefit. But the memory of last year's dinner was so awful that she couldn't help feeling slightly squeamish.

"Let me help with that," Verona offered. Always the model daughter-in-law.

"No, no. That's quite all right," Olive's mom said. "There's chocolate cake for dessert. We'll be right out." And she and Harry hurried into the kitchen loaded down with dirty plates.

Phil reached under the table for her hand. "What do you think? Is this it?" he whispered.

She squeezed his hand back, grateful for the gesture. *We're still a team,* it seemed to say.

Her mom and Harry reentered, carrying the cake on its porcelain pedestal. Olive's mom set it at her end of the table and sat down. Harry stood behind her and placed his hand on her shoulder.

"Kids, we have some news." She didn't call it *good news.*

Just *news*. She made brief eye contact with Olive and then focused on Christopher. "Harry and I are getting married."

Something bordering on hysteria bubbled up in Olive. She'd witnessed this announcement once before, already attended the wedding, and her mom had just conveyed the same information to her only minutes before, and she was supposed to act pleasantly surprised? Charmingly delighted? The downright ridiculousness of it made her feel like she was in a Shakespearean comedy—irony wrapped in irony upon irony. She gulped her wine and tried to figure out what a normal reaction would be at this point. She decided to play it safe.

"Congratulations, Mom! Congratulations, Harry."

"That's great news," Phil said, a little too cheerfully.

"Have you started planning the wedding?" Verona asked. She leaned against Christopher as if to prod him into speaking. He looked like he'd just been told one of his dogs had been hit by a car.

"Yes, actually," Olive's mom said. "We're planning a June wedding, because Harry won't have to take off then. We'd like to do something small, one of those destination weddings on a tropical island. Of course we'll want all of you to be there with us."

This was the part where last year Olive had told her mom that she didn't know if she'd be able to take off work since she hadn't accrued much vacation time yet. She couldn't believe her own thoughtlessness. She hadn't thought through what she was going to say then, had just spoken the first words that came to her lips, which had been a declarative statement that pretty much meant she wouldn't come to their wedding. Then she'd excused herself from the table, gone outside, and walked repeatedly around the house. When she'd come back inside, the table was cleared and everyone had moved to the living room and was talking quietly. Her mom wouldn't look at her. In Olive's own defense, she'd been taken aback. It had been only a little over two years since her dad's death. Wasn't there a longer, more respectable waiting period required for widows to remarry? And how could her mom possibly be considering marrying this man who was nothing like her dad? Someone her dad would've found insufferable?

Christopher finally spoke up. "Isn't that a little fast? I mean, that's only three months away." His teeth were gritted.

"We've been thinking about it for a long time," Harry said with an awkward chuckle. "June can hardly come fast enough. I can't wait."

"Oh, I bet you can't," Christopher said, under his breath but loud enough for everyone to hear.

"My college roommate did a destination wedding in the Bahamas," Verona said. "It was the most gorgeous wedding I've ever been to. They said their vows in the meadow behind these plantation ruins at sunset—"

"No one wants to hear about Shelly's disgusting glorification of Caribbean slavery that she tried to pass off as a wedding," Christopher said. "This is about *my mom's* wedding. To another man."

Verona folded her napkin and carefully laid it next to her plate. "Excuse me, everyone. I need to use the restroom."

"Christopher," their mom said softly. "She's just trying to help."

He narrowed his eyes. "I know what she's trying to do, and it's not going to work." He cast his insistent gaze on Olive, but she didn't know what to say. "Look, Mom, we know you miss Dad; we do, too. But you don't have to marry the first guy that comes along just for companionship. We'll spend more time together. That Jane Austen tour in England you keep talking about? Well, maybe Olive and I can take you for Mother's Day."

"That's a nice thought, Christopher, but this isn't just about companionship. And he's not just the first guy that came along. I love Harry."

A long silence followed. Olive didn't know how long. It felt like minutes, like her heart had paused its continuous clenching and unclenching, and she remembered how her dad had called her Olive Oyl, and her brother Columbus, and her mother Hepburn. "I look nothing like her!" her mom had insisted. "You're right!" her dad had bantered back. "You're much prettier!"

"And I love your mom, too," Harry said at last. Olive was embarrassed to see that his eyes were slick with tears.

"We hope you'll be very happy together," she murmured. Her brother glared at her mutinously.

Christopher had handled this so much better last year. He hadn't said these things. Granted, after the dinner he and Olive had spent an hour on the phone commiserating, but at the table, he'd been as good as gold. What was different? It was like their reactions had totally flip-flopped. Last year Olive had been the inconsiderate, selfish child, and Christopher had been the tactful, supportive one. Olive wondered if she had unwittingly helped Christopher maintain his cool last year by being antagonistic and voicing his opinion for him. She felt like she'd failed him. Why hadn't she thought to prepare her brother for this?

"I'm going to check on Rona," Christopher said, pushing his chair away from the table.

"Oops," Harry said. "Forgot the forks and plates." A contingency plan. He disappeared into the kitchen. And so Phil and Olive were left alone with her pink-faced mom, who was wielding a knife.

She stabbed into the cake. She carved a large slice, and then had no plate to put it on, so she continued cutting the cake into equally huge wedges. "Greg, Greg, Greg," she muttered, seemingly to herself, although Phil was sitting only a foot away. "Why did you have to be so goddamn good?"

"Mom, I'll talk to Christopher," Olive said. "He doesn't mean any of it. You just caught him off guard, that's all."

"Shhhh, honey. It's all right," her mom said, waving the carving knife vaguely in the air. "Let him have his reaction. Your dad would've appreciated it."

A few minutes later, Christopher and Verona came back to the table, blank-faced and subdued. Harry returned with the plates; six forks dangled precariously off the stack. He looked around warily. Olive's mom dished up the big slices, and they were passed around the table. Dessert required less conversation, and Olive found that everyone was taking larger bites and chewing longer than necessary. Olive's mom asked Phil about the upcoming season of the boys' golf team he coached at Wright. It was a relatively unfamiliar sport for most of his high schoolers, so his team rarely made it to regionals, let alone sectionals or state, but Phil enjoyed it all the same. From this, they moved to a discussion of how the University of Wisconsin campus was changing since Olive and Phil had graduated and finally, to Phil's delight, their March

Madness brackets. The topic of the wedding was not brought up again.

Olive tried to talk to Christopher on their way out, but he shook his head. "You said nothing. Nothing. Just 'Congratulations' and 'We hope you'll be *ever* so happy together.'" He clasped his hands under his chin, raised his shoulders, and batted his eyelashes, doing an impression of her. "I thought we were on the same page about Harry."

"Let me call you later. I can explain—" But Christopher just brushed past her.

"Don't worry. He'll come around," Phil said. He'd suggested they take a stroll around the neighborhood before the drive back to Madison because it was such a lovely, unseasonably warm night. He'd always admired her family's neighborhood with its impressive brick houses, old-fashioned streetlights, smooth white sidewalks, and cul-de-sacs. Phil had grown up in an antiquated farmhouse in the country with no neighbors for miles.

"I don't know about that," Olive said. "You don't have any siblings, so you don't know the wrath of one. And Christopher is a champion grudge holder. He's still mad at me for stealing his favorite Pound Puppy and decorating it with pink and purple puffy paint."

"You forget my mom comes from a family of seven sisters, and someone's always in the dog house. They take turns."

"I should've warned him. He would've handled it better if I had told him ahead of time." She was beginning to think what a good ally Phil would be in all of this. Tonight he had held her hand when she'd needed his strength. He had spoken up and tried to defuse the situation. She wished she could tell him the whole truth. He usually had such sound advice.

He was logical and fair and tried to view a problem from multiple points of view. He would get her safely through this situation with her family. If only she could confide in him.

"Warned him? But you didn't know for sure, right? Cut yourself some slack. You had just as much right as Christopher to get upset, but you were much more mature about it. He's the one who should be brooding over his conduct, not you."

Olive hugged her thin jacket to her sides. If Phil only knew how the tables had been turned. "I almost started laughing when my mom said it. It just seemed so funny, you know? Not that they're getting married, but the pomp and circumstance of it all. The candles, the music, the china, the wine. 'Kids, we have some news.' It all felt so rehearsed, I almost lost it. Can you imagine? I was almost in tears thinking about how my dad used to call her Hepburn. What is wrong with me? Why can't I just be happy for her?"

They continued down the street in thoughtful silence. When they came to the end of the block, Phil grabbed her hand.

"You can't just manufacture emotions," he said. "You feel what you feel. When my parents got divorced, everyone felt so sorry for me. But really, it was probably one of the happiest times in my childhood. Finally, my dad would leave my mom and me alone. At least that was the idea."

Phil had told her only pieces of his childhood and adolescence at a time, ashamed of their dissimilar upbringings and circumstances. His parents had divorced when he was ten years old, which was years after Charlie had started disappearing for months at a time, only returning home drunk and belligerent to ask Carol for money. Even after the divorce,

Charlie would stop "for a visit," as he put it, when he was in the area, regardless of whether they were home. Phil would return from school never knowing what might be missing from their house: the window air conditioner, gardening tools, the framed collection of rare coins Charlie had given him for his seventh birthday. They reported the thefts to the police, and Carol got a restraining order, but nothing seemed to help.

Then one evening when Phil was a sophomore in high school, he and his mom returned home after an all-day golf tournament to find a semi cab parked in their driveway. Phil pleaded with his mom to let him go in and confront his dad or at the very least, call the cops, but she made a quick U-turn and drove to one of his aunt's houses to spend the night instead. As far as they could tell, nothing had been taken, but it appeared that he'd slept in Carol's bed, showered, and made himself some breakfast (there was a telltale crusty skillet in the sink). He'd ripped a sheet of paper out of Phil's geometry notebook and left it on the table like a note, but there was no message written on it, as if there were no words for him to explain himself. After that night, they didn't hear from Charlie for nine years; they hypothesized that he was either locked up or dead. Phil had admitted to Olive once that he'd preferred the latter possibility. But in April 2010, he showed up again—out of jail and six months sober—and Phil had been working on forgiving him ever since.

"Oh, Phil," she said. "You went through so much. That was a terrible situation for you."

They had stopped in front of a home with a pair of rooftop dormers and two white columns supporting the front porch.

As a child, Olive had been reminded of a friendly face. Phil pulled her into a hug and rested his chin lightly on top of her head.

"And you don't think losing your dad to cancer at fifty-one is a terrible situation? And then trying to single-handedly pick up your mom and hold the pieces of your family together? No wonder you're a little suspicious of Harry. You have every right to be protective of this family."

"Thank you for that." She wiggled out from under Phil's chin and looked over his shoulder. The sky was thick with clouds, not a star in sight. Against the sky, the stark, intricate branches of a tree looked like black lace.

"Did you return the ring?" she whispered into his neck.

"Why? Have you changed your mind?" He drew away from her and looked down into her eyes.

"I guess I'd just feel a lot better if I knew you still had it."

"Would you?" He smiled and started to amble back toward her mom's house.

She followed him. "Phil, I—"

"Want to get engaged now since it seems like the 'in' thing to do?" he teased in a playful tone. "That Harry's a trendsetter."

She tugged on his arm until he stopped in his tracks.

"Of course I still have the ring, Ollie. Did you really think I'd give up on you that easily? I've known I wanted to marry you since May third, 2008."

"May third?"

"We were sitting on the pier when a pair of ducks came along. You wanted to feed them, but we had nothing to give, so you ran to the Union and came back with a bunch of stale hamburger buns. The ducks had left by then, but they came back when you started tossing bits of bread into the water. Soon, we had a whole flock of them surrounding us on the pier, and you were so happy. You were laughing and trying to toss the bread far to the little ones who couldn't get up close to the pier. You're always looking out for others. Even the timid ducks. You're so loving. So kind."

She didn't deserve him. Her conscience clamored to correct him. She was unfaithful, petty, selfish. Too afraid to fess up to her mistakes.

He linked his arm through hers and pushed her forward. Olive's house was in view now. It didn't look like any of the lights were still on. Harry and her mom had retired for the night. Or maybe Harry had left, and her mom was all alone, sitting on her bed, looking at a wedding photo on her nightstand.

"I've never told you this before, Ollie, because I didn't want to make you sad. I wanted to save it for the right time. The week your dad died—" His voice quavered, and he paused. Her dad had been like a father to Phil in the year they'd known each other. Phil let out a deep breath and continued. "I asked him for his blessing to marry you one day. He knew he wouldn't be there to walk you down the aisle, but he said it would make it a little easier to say good-bye to you knowing that you wouldn't be alone and would never be without love in your life."

She was so engulfed in emotion, she couldn't speak. Her tears made the glowing streetlights look like small comets. He continued to guide her, and Olive wondered if her dad had known she would need someone like Phil to watch out for her, especially in the years following his death.

Chapter 10

"We've got a full house," Gloria said. "The ER just called, and they want to send up two MVC victims from that Beltline accident, but we don't have a single empty bed."

"I can free up a bed," Kevin said. "I've got a patient recovering from a modified radical mastectomy. The OR sent her up earlier this morning for observation because she was a little too hypotensive, but she's doing fine now."

"Great. Send her down to oncology." Gloria picked up the phone to call the ER.

Kevin turned to Olive. "I think she might still be a little loopy from the anesthesia. She's been saying some odd things. Do you think I should tell Gloria before we transfer her?"

"What kind of odd things?" Olive asked.

Kevin frowned. "A lot of mumbling about years, particularly 2011 and 2012. She doesn't seem to know what year it is. Then something about being trapped here as punishment for something she'd done wrong. I couldn't make most of it out."

Olive gingerly set down her coffee cup for fear she'd spill it in her excitement. Was it possible that there was another person experiencing a repeat year right here in the ICU? She'd known there was a reason she'd said yes when Toya had called her this morning to see if she could come in and work extra. Last year she had turned her down, maintaining that she already had plans for the day, inventing a bridal shower for her mom on the spur of the moment. Really she just hadn't wanted to go out in the rain.

But today had been different—still raining, but different. Phil was at a weekend golf tournament with his team in Waukesha, and a certain restlessness that had nothing to do with the weather had crept over her. Except for her reconciliation with Phil, she was starting to realize that she hadn't deviated too far from last year's path. She needed to make more changes, take more risks. She needed to put herself in a place she hadn't been last year and see what happened. So when Toya called, before she could come up with an excuse to stay home, her lips said yes.

Now she was glad she had. Her willingness to come in to work today had maybe put her in the path of another repeater. Maybe one that needed her help.

"Can I see her?" Olive asked Kevin. She was trying not to get her hopes up too high. Lots of people mumbled strange things when they were coming out of anesthesia.

"Be my guest. Just hurry."

Kevin's patient's room was one of the few rooms that actually had an outside window. Rain dribbled down the glass, blurring the world outside. The lights were dimmed. A lumpy figure was partially concealed under the gray blanket. Red hair fell across the pillow.

"Sherry?" Olive whispered.

She seemed smaller. Her chest looked vulnerable and caved in where her right breast had been; the hospital gown hung awkwardly over the spot. Sherry's face was stripped, makeup free: no eyebrows, a pale shapeless mouth. If it hadn't been for her tiny, round nose and red-and-gray-striped hair, Olive wouldn't have been sure that it was her.

Sherry opened her eyes. She didn't look surprised to see Olive. Maybe she thought she was just another nurse.

"How are you feeling?"

"Like someone just chopped off a part of my body," Sherry muttered. She clutched at the blanket with her IV-taped hand and tried to pull it up over her shoulders. The tubing caught and the needle tugged at her skin. Sherry flinched.

"Let me help you."

Sherry's face crumpled like the face of a child on the verge of tears. She flung her hand out, caught Olive's hip, and left it there. She held on to Olive. "I didn't go through with it last year. I did it now. I did it."

Kevin poked his head in the room. "What do you think? All clear? The ER patient's on the way."

"She's doing well," Olive said, and gently returned Sherry's hand to her side. "Much more alert and awake. I think she'll be just fine." She looked down at Sherry. "Your blood pressure has normalized now. You don't need to be in the ICU anymore. We're going to transfer you to the oncology inpatient floor, where they'll take really good care of you, and you'll have more privacy, a nicer bed, fewer machines. They'll probably keep you overnight." She lowered her voice so Kevin couldn't hear the rest. "I work until seven o'clock tonight. I'll come visit you then." She didn't know if Sherry had heard or understood her. She looked eerily indistinguishable from any of Olive's patients.

The ICU was so demanding the rest of the day that Olive had very little time to think of Sherry. Yet as she changed the dressing on Mr. Ewing's abdominal wound, she thought: *breast cancer.* Probably very advanced if they'd removed her whole breast and lymph nodes. As she filled Mrs. Bhadra's feeding pump, she wondered if anyone had known about Sherry. Had her mom known? Did Sherry's son know? Her ex-husbands? Had Sherry confided in anyone? And as she tried to complete her charts for the night, one question kept floating up to the surface of her consciousness: What had happened to Sherry last year?

At ten after seven, Olive made her way to the oncology floor. It was well after visiting hours, but she didn't think anyone would bother her wearing her scrubs and ID badge. She looked at the patient board behind the nursing station for Sherry Witan's room number.

Sherry was in a double room, but the other bed was unoccupied. Propped up by pillows, she was watching a baseball game with the sound turned low. Her eyes flicked briefly to Olive as she entered the room and then back to the TV.

"Do you like baseball, or is this the only channel you get?" Olive asked.

"I've made a lot of money through the years predicting the outcomes of games," Sherry said. "Watch this. Braun's about to hit a triple."

Her color was improving. Plummy like a baby in an incubator. Sherry had the sheet pulled up as far as it would go—up to her chin—as if to disguise her altered body. Olive sat down in the upholstered chair beside the bed, and still Sherry's eyes remained on the TV.

"When were you diagnosed?" Olive asked.

Sherry shook her head. "Last thing I want to talk about."

"Tell me about your son, then. Heathcliff."

She turned to face Olive, her lips stretched as thin as taut rubber bands. "Are you always this impertinent with your patients?"

"You're not my patient."

Far away, a baseball bat cracked, and the crowd roared. Sherry shifted in her bed.

"He's nineteen. Studying at the University of Michigan. He's handsome like his father: my second husband, Norman. Got stuck with my temperament, though."

"Does he know about this?"

"No one does. And they're not going to." Sherry fumbled for the remote, which was tangled up in the sheet.

"What about this year, Sherry? Why do you think you're here? What are you changing?"

"I don't want to talk about this. I didn't ask you to come visit me. You wouldn't even have known if you hadn't wandered into my room by accident."

"Do you really think that was an accident? I wasn't even supposed to work today. This year—someone—*something* is bringing us together. I want to help you, Sherry."

"I'll bet you twenty bucks the Brewers win in extra innings."

"Sherry."

A steakhouse commercial came on. Country-western music filled the room; a steak sizzled on a grill.

"Do you know what simply bewilders me? The fact that I'm given the chance to live some years over and not others," Sherry said.

Olive thought of her dad and how they had driven to Lake Mendota four months before he died. She and Christopher had taken turns pushing his wheelchair; her mom had walked beside them. It was a humid August morning, and a foul stench rose up from the lake, but Olive's dad made them all stop and watch the crew team skimming across the water like mayflies. She would've given almost anything to relive that moment with her dad.

"For example: 1994. Nineteen ninety-four was a train-wreck. We'd moved to Waco for Norman's job. Heath was two and slowly draining away my will to live. There was this supermarket—I can't remember the name of it now—but they had free childcare while you shopped. I'd spend hours at the supermarket and come home with just a box of cake mix or a bottle of Worcestershire sauce. Norman went out of town for a business trip one week, and I was at my wit's end. I didn't know anyone in town, and I was dying to see the new *Little Women* film adaptation. I asked the lady next door to watch Heath for a little while, so I could go to the theater.

"But when I came back two hours later, she didn't answer her door. All the lights were off, and her car wasn't in the garage. I called the police. They asked me all these questions that made me seem like an awful, negligent mother. I'd left my baby with a total stranger to see a movie? Where was my husband? I had to call Norman and ask him to come home early. He was furious with me. He'd left for four days, and I'd lost our son.

"It took them forty-eight hours to find Heath—the worst

forty-eight hours of my life. Our neighbor had driven him all the way to Fort Worth, where her daughter lived. Not a hair on his head had been harmed, thank God. It was hard for the police to know if she'd had any malicious intentions or if it was just some misunderstanding, mostly on my part, so they didn't book her with much. I, however, was under permanent suspicion from then on. Even my toddler didn't seem to trust me.

"I prayed on New Year's Eve that I would be given a chance to relive the year and fix my mistakes like I had ten years earlier. But I woke up the next morning in 1995."

Olive kept quiet. She suspected that Sherry wasn't finished yet. The neck of her hospital gown had fallen forward as she talked and revealed the bloodied pink edge of a bandage.

"Then, two years later, my prayer was answered." Sherry laughed bitterly. "But I didn't want it then. I thought my life was finally getting better. Norman and I were separated. I'd moved back to Madison. Heath was in half-day kindergarten, and he spent the summer with his dad. I'd met someone new. But boy, was I wrong about everything. I met your mom that second time around. She got me a part-time job shelving books and invited me to join her book club. What an angel your mom is."

Sherry sank back into her pillows. "If you're waiting for a moral, there isn't one. I'm just babbling. See? Didn't I tell you the Brewers would win?" She turned off the television, and suddenly the room was silent.

Olive moved closer to the bed. Her chair scraped against the floor. "You told me to think of this year as a blessing. A second chance. Can't you see that's what you've been given? You can beat this, Sherry. I'll help you."

"But why not 2009, a missed mammogram? Or 2010, my year of failed homeopathic remedies? Why 2011, when it's already too late?" She gestured helplessly toward her lopsided chest. "I'll tell you why. Because repeat years aren't just redoes for quick fixes. They're last chances."

Olive scrambled to come up with something to say to give Sherry hope. She could tell her that nearly every year the number of women who died from breast cancer decreased by one to two percent. Or she could encourage her to open up to Olive's mom about this, so she wouldn't feel so alone. But what she really wanted to suggest was that Sherry contact Heath and try to reconcile things with him. However, all of these sentiments sounded like something you would tell a dying patient.

A young nurse with glasses came into the room carrying an IV drip bag. She seemed startled to find Olive there. "How are you feeling, Ms. Witan?"

"Like I'm missing a piece of myself," Sherry said.

"She needs her rest now," the nurse said to Olive. She detached the empty IV bag and hung up the new one. "It's okay to grieve for the loss of your breast," she said in a practiced voice to Sherry. "Many women do. Have you considered reconstructive surgery?"

Olive lingered in the doorway for a moment. Sherry didn't seem to notice when she left. She slipped her arms into her jacket sleeves and wondered if she'd accomplished anything at all by coming here.

"Hold on," a voice called after her. It was Sherry's nurse. "Ms. Witan wanted me to tell you she's glad you came." The light winked off the nurse's glasses.

Olive wished she could go home to Phil and tell him about

Sherry. She wouldn't even be able to reach him by phone tonight because he was taking the boys out for pizza and bowling. He'd be driving home late tomorrow afternoon. She thought about going straight to bed.

Outside, she inhaled her first breath of nonhospital air since six forty-five that morning. It smelled of car exhaust and worms, but it was still lovely. The rain had finally let up, and everything seemed the better for it.

Chapter 11

When she got home, it looked like every light in the second story was switched on. Even her own bedroom light. She dragged her feet on the stairs, anticipating something she probably didn't want to walk in on. But Kerrigan was alone. Olive found her in her bedroom, wearing a glittery black dress, pawing through the closet. When she heard Olive come in, she turned around and held up a white, gold-sequined tank top.

"What do you think of this? It doesn't look like something you'd own, which is why I like it so much, I guess."

"What are you doing?" Olive asked. She threw her backpack on the floor and inspected her African violet, which was looking a little thirsty. Despite her best intentions, it was difficult remembering to water it weekly.

"Don't tell me you forgot. You promised me we'd go out tonight."

That was before Olive had known she'd get called in to

work. "I worked twelve hours today, Kerrigan. I'm a little tired." She dumped a half-full glass of water from her nightstand into the clay pot.

"You're always tired. It's not even nine o'clock. You're turning into a little old lady." She tossed the sequined top at Olive. "Put it on."

It was difficult negotiating these awkward intersections in her life. Her thoughts were still with Sherry in the hospital. With the lost little boy. Olive fingered the sequins. She wanted to keep her promise and be a good friend to Kerrigan, but a noisy, crowded bar was the last place she wanted to be right now. She didn't feel up to pretending to have a good time.

"This is our last chance for a girls' night out," Kerrigan said. "God knows when Phil gets back tomorrow, it will be back to twenty-four-seven coupledom for you." She struggled to squeeze some loose hangers back into the closet. "So what do you say? You're only twenty-five once."

The first bar they hit was Castaway's, a tropical-themed bar popular with the twenty-somethings. Brightly patterned fabric like sarongs draped across the ceiling, hurricane lanterns lit the tables, and the bartenders wore hideous shirts. Olive was momentarily reminded of St. Lucia, where she would be headed in less than two months. She tried to stay in the moment and think of this as another time-space experiment, like today at work had been. She was breaking the pattern, forging ahead into uncharted territory. What else had she missed last year by staying home?

"Here we are. The first round's on me," Kerrigan said as she deposited two glasses as large as cantaloupe halves on the table. The slushy pink liquid inside made Olive guess they were strawberry daiquiris. A sparkly glaze of sugar coated the rims. Kerrigan lifted her glass high. "To my best friend, who I love, but who needs to loosen up." She clinked glasses with Olive. "Now loosen up."

Kerrigan told her about the text messages she'd been receiving from Steve, asking her to meet up with him, as if they hadn't broken up months ago. She rhapsodized about the resort in Cozumel where she and Ciara had stayed last month, and how the maid had folded their towels into different animals—a swan one day, a rabbit the next, an unbelievably elaborate elephant on the last day. It was all for tips, of course, but still she hoped the resort Olive would stay at in St. Lucia did towel animals. She talked about the student worker in her office whom she wanted to sleep with. He was Indian American and had the most beautiful eyebrows she'd ever seen.

"They probably frown on office romances at the university," Olive said. "And besides, don't you think he's a bit young for you?"

"I didn't say I was going to sleep with him. I only said I *wanted* to."

That was the problem—there wasn't much of a difference between those two things in Kerrigan's world. It was one of the many things about Kerrigan that Olive envied. She doubted that Kerrigan would ever be made to repeat a year. Kerrigan seemed to live with no regrets.

Two daiquiris, three mojitos, and a mango margarita later, Kerrigan suggested they walk to a bar down by the Capitol. It wasn't until they were only a block away that she mentioned Steve would be there.

"Kerrigan! I thought this was supposed to be girls' night

out." A blister was developing on Olive's left pinky toe, and her right heel felt raw and abraded. She wasn't used to walking long distances in heels.

"It is, it is. I just want him to see me in this hot black dress and remember what he's missing."

They passed an abandoned shop with a royal blue awning. Up ahead loomed a stretch of high-rise condominiums. A brief feeling of déjà vu stole over Olive. She looked up and down the street, trying to determine why this area felt familiar to her, but the more she tried to place it, the less familiar it looked.

The place was called Heureux Hasard, and it was more of a bistro than a bar. A jazz quartet was playing on a small platform in the back. The regulars were older and more sophisticated than the Castaway's crowd—probably in their thirties or forties, buying whole bottles of wine instead of just by the glass, eating steamed mussels and roast beef au jus even though it was after midnight. Olive suddenly felt like a silly undergrad in her sleeveless, sequined top, but she had such a nice buzz going, she didn't mind much.

They both spotted Steve at a booth in the back, so they chose a table in the storefront window. The waiter took their order—two glasses of pinot blanc and a plate of Brie and crackers—and then carded them. Olive found this so funny that she couldn't stop laughing. She twisted her hair into a loose bun to lift it from the back of her neck. After the long walk, it felt downright balmy in the bistro.

"He's not even looking over here," Kerrigan complained. "Do you think he's with that black-haired girl?"

"It doesn't matter. He's not worth it. He's just playing mind games with you." Olive let her hair tumble down. She cupped the bulb of her wineglass and looked into its pale liquid as though she were gazing into a crystal ball. "You will meet someone new very soon. A rodeo cowboy. His name will be . . . Clay."

Kerrigan snorted with laughter. "I like that. That's good. Now tell me what will happen to Steve."

Olive waved her hands in front of the glass, nearly knocking it over. "Alas. I see only bad things for Steve. Painful urination. Genital warts. Penile discharge."

"Oh my God. Did you just say penile discharge? You're so much more fun when you're drinking."

Olive was glad Phil was out of town, so he wouldn't see her like this. He hated when she drank too much and worried about her safety. When he went to bars, he drank only one or two beers before switching to soda. Being raised by an alcoholic father had made him a very cautious drinker. He'd seen firsthand the destruction alcohol could cause.

The waiter brought over another round of drinks. "Compliments of the gentleman in the back booth," he said.

"Pathetic," Olive scowled. "We don't want them. He can't buy you back with drinks. Send them back." She felt bold and infallible. It was nice to focus her energy on this smaller, more manageable crisis.

"Is there any way we can keep them but you tell the gentleman we sent them away?" Kerrigan asked the waiter. He shook his head and left with the tray of drinks. "Well, that was dumb. We had free drinks, and now we have no free drinks. Hey, this hot guy is totally staring at you. Two o'clock. Be cool."

Olive glanced over her right shoulder but saw only a table of women.

"Sorry. My two o'clock. Your, um . . . Oh, shit. He's coming over here."

The hair follicles on the nape of her neck contracted. She busied her hands with the cheese knife, cutting herself a notch of Brie. In the moment before he spoke, she felt certain she knew who it was, just as she had instantly recognized Sherry earlier today. Improbable. Unlikely. But what about this year wasn't? She was being led by mysterious cosmic forces with unknowable designs. That and Kerrigan, who had dragged her unwittingly right into his neighborhood. Now she knew why these streets seemed familiar.

"It *is* you," Alex said. "Why did you turn down my drinks?"

Olive looked up at Alex. "We thought they were from Steve—her ex." She concentrated hard on appearing sober, as it suddenly became apparent to her that she was not. "Kerrigan, this is my coworker, Dr. Kerrigan. Er . . . Carpenter. Alex, this is my friend, Kerrigan Morland."

"Please. Call me Alex," he said, as he shook Kerrigan's hand. He turned to Olive. "I hope I'm not interrupting. I'm here with some friends, and I was surprised when you came in. I've never seen you here before."

"She's never been here before. She doesn't get out much," Kerrigan supplied.

"Same here," Alex said with a smile. "Occupational hazard. Would you both like to join us?" He looked different in his jeans and black dress shirt, untucked, without a tie. Less like the Alex she worked with. More like the Alex she had had a summer fling with last year. The way he was looking at her right now made it difficult to believe he remembered nothing of their past relations.

Olive's alcohol-soaked brain was struggling to keep up with her accelerated heart. "Thanks, but we—"

Kerrigan nudged her under the table with the toe of her shoe. "We'd love to," she finished. "We'll be right over." Olive gave her an openmouthed look, but Alex didn't see it because he was already pointing out his table. He stepped away, and Kerrigan started gathering her purse, her wineglass, and the plate of Brie.

Olive slapped the table with her palm. "What the hell, Kerrigan?"

"Come on, live a little. You know cute doctors are my favorite kind of doctors."

Neon warning signs flashed in Olive's head. *Bad idea, bad idea, very bad idea.* Why did fate have it in for her? What was up with that? Two months had passed since she had walked away from Alex in the ICU locker room, and she'd been doing a damn good job avoiding him since then. But now here they were, at midnight in a dusky bar with a bass for a heartbeat. Perhaps it was the universe's idea of a "man walks into a bar" joke. Or was this some kind of temptation: Phil out of town, and Alex the carrot dangling in front of her nose, waiting to see if she'd bite?

"Well, I won't bite," she said adamantly, and flung her purse over her shoulder.

"That's good to know." Kerrigan led the way to Alex's table, which was conveniently located only two booths away from Steve and company's.

Alex was sitting with two other residents that Olive thankfully didn't recognize: Jim Bilkers, an emergency medicine intern, and Anoop Mehrotra, a second-year internal medicine doc. When they caught a glimpse of Kerrigan in her little black dress, they fidgeted in their seats and self-consciously patted their hair. She and Kerrigan sat on the same side of the booth with Alex, and Olive was dismayed to find that in this close proximity, her thigh almost touched his. She pressed her knees together and tried to take up as little space as possible. They ordered a round of drinks, and Kerrigan was all smiles and laughter, at her most flirtatious with her ex only a few feet away.

Apropos of nothing, Alex said, "Olive is the most badass nurse in the ICU."

"In all our years of friendship, I never figured you for a badass," Kerrigan quipped.

"Badass how?" Jim asked, and gulped his beer. He wiped his mouth with the back of his hand. "Telling off doctors?" Olive could already tell he was the type of doctor Tina would call a *nump*, a Narcissistic Über Macho Prick.

"No," Alex said. "But this girl is not afraid of anything or anyone. Last week we had a gangbanger recovering post-op from multiple gunshot wounds. When he woke up, he was crazy as a wildcat, trying to yank out his catheter, and complaining we were starving him. He was NPO, of course." He paused to translate for Kerrigan, "Nothing by mouth. So I was not looking forward to dealing with this dude. But then here comes Olive, and she walks up to his bedside, and says nice as pie, 'Sir, we were able to save your life. And I know you're very uncomfortable, but you're still recovering. If you let me help you get better, I'll make sure you get some barbecued ribs soon—' Because that's what he'd been begging for. And just like that"—Alex snapped his fingers—"the wildcat became a kitten."

"Hard core," Anoop pronounced, and grinned at Olive. He had kind brown eyes and was drinking a Tom Collins. Definitely not a nump.

"I don't know about that," she said, blushing despite herself. What Alex had described was true, but Olive had never imagined herself as being particularly brave in her actions. The patient had been younger than her, and she hadn't viewed him so much as scary as scared. Tina had once grudgingly admitted to Olive that she had a way with patients, but even then, Olive had viewed this as the more ho-hum gift of "people skills" or "communication skills." Not a lack of fear. Not bravery, as Alex was trying to convince the table.

Jim vied for the floor and told a story about a young man who came into the ER after his hand had been severely mangled by his snowblower. The wound was so grotesque that the admitting nurse, who had over twenty years of ED experience, had thrown up on the spot. After Jim described his heroic efforts to save the man's hand, he concluded with, "What kind of idiot sticks his hand into a snowblower? Since then, I've been surprised by the sheer number of idiots I see on a daily basis. You would not believe how many people get shitfaced and then decide to climb up on ladders and clean their gutters. Big mistake."

Anoop relayed an encounter he had with an eighty-nine-year-old veteran who had served in World War II. In his chest X-ray, Anoop had discovered a bullet lodged in his diaphragm. Though everyone else was astounded that this man had managed to live a perfectly healthy life with a two-inch lead bullet embedded in his chest, the old man seemed only mildly surprised. In fact he didn't say much of anything, until Anoop started asking him when he'd been injured in the war. "Lord, I didn't get shot in the war," he replied. "I got shot by my fool brother-in-law two years after the war."

Olive took a small sip of her wine and risked a glance at Alex. He was shaking his head and laughing. He caught her looking at him, and they maintained eye contact for just a moment too long.

Kerrigan elbowed her in the ribs. "Is medical stuff all you people talk about?" she whispered.

"I'm afraid so," Olive whispered back. "Why don't you say hello to Steve?"

"He left like half an hour ago. You realize it's almost closing time, right? I'm going to call us a cab." She snapped open her cell phone and stalked away from the table.

"Need a ride home? My car isn't parked too far from here in an underground garage. I live in Metro Place," Alex said.

"Not after how much you drank, Doctor. We're taking a cab," Olive replied. Phil would never forgive her if he found out she'd gotten in the car with someone who'd been drinking. He wouldn't mind that she and Kerrigan had joined cute doctors for drinks—Phil had never been a jealous boyfriend—but if he learned she'd been hanging out with irresponsible drinkers or *being* an irresponsible drinker, it would really disappoint him.

"All right, all right." Alex waved the waitress over so he could pay their tab. "I'm glad you decided to join us. It's fun talking shop, isn't it? We should definitely do this again."

Olive stood up, and purple spots danced in front of her eyes. "Thanks. I had fun. Good night, Alex. It was nice meeting you guys." She walked carefully to the front of the bar and found Kerrigan, who was tucking her cell phone back into her purse. They stepped outside together into the shock of the night air to wait for their cab.

Kerrigan was uncharacteristically quiet. She leaned against a stop sign. Her hair, which had been perfectly styled and hair-sprayed for extra body, now fell flat against her skull because of the moisture in the air.

"What's wrong?" Olive asked. "You're the one who wanted to sit with them. If it had been up to me, we would've left an hour ago."

Kerrigan didn't reply. She gazed off into the distance.

"Since when are you someone who can't hold her own in a conversation?" Olive sat on the damp curb, not caring if she ruined her skirt. "I'm sorry I didn't try to keep you more involved, but I've never had to worry about that before."

Kerrigan slowly focused her eyes on her friend, but still she didn't speak. There was something both accusatory and sad in her eyes.

Olive slipped her fingers into the heel of her shoe; dried blood rubbed off on them. "Is this about Steve? Because frankly I think you're better off without him."

"This is not about me! This is about you! And Alex! What is going on, Olive? Do you have a *thing* for this guy?"

Olive hurriedly glanced behind them, but the street was empty. Alex and his friends must have slipped out the side exit. "Lower your voice, Kerrigan. Nothing is going on between us. Why would you even think that?"

"He's clearly into you. He was persistent in getting us over to his table, then he talked you up to his friends, and his eyes hardly left you the whole night."

"So? That doesn't mean that *I* have a thing for *him*."

"Then why did you giggle at his friends' stupid stories?

And why did you play with your hair so much? And why didn't you mention your boyfriend, not once, the whole time?"

"You have no idea what you're talking about. I tried to tell you I didn't want to join them, but you wouldn't listen to me. I've been trying to stay away from him, but it's more complicated than that."

"Are you kidding me? You're frickin' cheating on Phil?" Kerrigan looked like she was going to cry.

"Shhhh! Stop shouting, and stop jumping to conclusions. Let me try to explain." She laid her forehead on her knees and took a few deep breaths. When she looked up, she could see the Capitol building; the white granite glowed in an almost unearthly way in the moonlight.

"I'm about to tell you something very strange. But please just listen to me and try to keep an open mind, okay? No interruptions. No questions until I'm finished. Okay?"

Kerrigan still looked sullen, but she sat down on the curb next to Olive, five feet away, and started to unstrap her high heels.

Olive told her about New Year's Day and how she had woken up in the wrong year. She told her about Sherry's visit and disclosure. The bad trip to Lake Geneva last year, the horrible mistake she had made after it, and Phil's subsequent reaction.

"He couldn't forgive me, so we were just *over*. We went on without each other for the rest of the year, and then New Year's Eve 2011 came along. I was working in the ICU, living in a condo on my own, and then—*boom*—the next morning I woke up in bed with Phil in his old apartment, and it's like nothing happened." She stood up on the curb in her bare feet and balanced on the edge. "Something wonderful is happening to me, Kerrigan. I've been given a fresh start with Phil." She stretched her arms open to the night sky. "With everything."

She turned to Kerrigan. "Do you believe me?" She tried to keep the pleading, childish note out of her voice. It was so important that someone she cared about understand her and what she'd been through.

Kerrigan raised her hand for Olive to help her from her seated position. "I'm sorry you've been going through this alone, sweetie. It's going to be okay. It's all going to be okay." She shielded her eyes with her palm as a pair of headlights focused on them. Their cab had finally arrived to take them home.

Chapter 12

It didn't take long for Olive to discover that Kerrigan didn't really believe her. The next morning, she lay in bed until almost noon, headachy and nauseated, flip-flopping between reactions of delight and complete horror at what she had confided to Kerrigan the night before. How thrilling to have another confidante (who wasn't Sherry) in her repeat year! Yet the things she'd told Kerrigan! Oh, God, almost everything about Phil and Alex. And Kerrigan, bless her heart, was not always the most closemouthed person. The first time Olive had met Kerrigan's sister, Ciara had asked how she was doing after a minor surgery she'd had to remove an ovarian cyst. Olive's own brother and sister-in-law hadn't even known about the procedure.

When she finally stumbled to the fridge for a glass of orange juice, she found a note stuck there with a Bucky Badger magnet.

Good morning, Crazy Girl! Hope you're not too hungover. Tailgating and Brewer game today—won't be back until 7:00 or so. Stay away from alcohol and cute doctors, okay?

Olive ripped up the note and hid it under some paper towels and a banana peel in the trash. Crazy girl? That didn't sound very promising. And it wasn't. When Kerrigan got home that night, she told Olive all about the game and avoided any mention of last night's exploits. Olive cautiously followed her lead. The next night, as Kerrigan was leaving for a party, she called over her shoulder, "Any mystical hunches tonight, roomie? Will I meet the man of my dreams?" It was then that Olive knew with certainty that Kerrigan had viewed her bizarre admission as a joke. A stupid, drunken joke. And the note and teasing quip were her ways of letting Olive know she was forgiving her foolishness as well as her flirtations with Alex.

She tried to feel relieved. It was like confessing to a crime in a burst of conscience, and then realizing the other person was asleep or hard of hearing. Safe again, thank goodness. She tried not to feel hurt or offended; if their roles were reversed, she doubted she would've believed her absurd monologue, either. But a small blot of hopelessness started to grow in size. If her own best friend didn't trust her enough to believe in the repeat year . . .

And then two weeks after their girls' night out, Olive returned from a run to find Kerrigan sitting, chin in hand, at the bottom of the pink stairs. The sun was still high overhead, even though it was early evening. Olive slowed to a walk and wiped the sweat from her brow. Her heart was already pounding from the exercise, but it sped up when she saw Kerrigan waiting for her. Something had happened. Something that had shaken Kerrigan up very badly. Her eyes glittered in a familiar way: the way Olive's had when she'd looked into the mirror at the start of the year, questioning her own sanity.

"Hey," Olive said. "Is everything all right?" She pulled her sneakered foot against her butt and stretched out her sore quadriceps. Kerrigan stared at her as though a sparkly white horn had just sprouted from the middle of her forehead. Olive released her foot and tried to step around her.

Kerrigan's skinny arms shot out to block the stairway. "We need to talk."

Olive backed up. "Sure. Out here?" The yard looked particularly public and wide open with its huge swath of parched grass and constant parade of passersby on the sidewalk: runners, bikers, skateboarders, couples strolling hand in hand.

"No. We'd better go inside." Kerrigan stood up and trooped upstairs, looking back once as if to make sure Olive was following her.

They sat in front of the box fan in the living room. The breeze cooled Olive's flushed skin and fluttered the loose strands of hair that had escaped her ponytail. Kerrigan sat at the other end of the couch, her knees bouncing nervously.

"I met someone today. Clay Brennan. He ropes calves in rodeos. I need you to be totally honest with me. Did you set me up with him?" She gave Olive a hard look.

Olive stared back, unsure how to respond. She suddenly remembered the silly, offhanded prediction—which had been a very real prediction—she had made about Kerrigan's love life that night. It had now come true, and Kerrigan was spooked. "No," she finally said. "I had nothing to do with that."

"Dammit, Olive. You told me I would meet a rodeo cowboy named Clay, and I did. So either you arranged for us to meet, or . . ."

"I can see the future?" Olive suggested softly.

Kerrigan leaped up from the couch and strode to the window. "What the hell is going on? You spouted all this nonsense about time travel that night we went out, and I humored you because you were drunk, and I thought you were inventing some crazy metaphor to make yourself feel better about having feelings for someone other than Phil. But then I meet this guy that you told me I would meet, and suddenly I'm wondering how much more you know about what's going to happen this year." She turned to face Olive, and the late sunlight illuminated her silhouette.

"I was telling you the truth that night," Olive said. "I've already lived 2011 once before. I went to bed at the end of the year—New Year's Eve—and woke up at the beginning of the same year—New Year's Day."

Kerrigan crossed her arms and chewed on her lower lip. "If that's really the case, tell me who will win the World Series."

She laughed. "You know I don't pay attention to sports!" She bet Sherry knew who would win, though. "Ask me something I'd know."

"I don't know! Tell me something impressive. Convince me."

Olive scanned her memory of the year for a piece of information capable of converting a nonbeliever. There were no election results to report, and many of the major news stories she could've impressed Kerrigan with, like the killing of Osama bin Laden, had already happened. Reciting her patients' health problems wouldn't mean much to Kerrigan. She suddenly realized how wrapped up in her job she had become since college, how much a part of her identity it had become. She'd been so busy just surviving last year—just getting through her first year in the ICU, getting over Phil, trying to get settled into her new life on her own—that she hadn't paid much attention to the world at large.

"Well, in December, all the U.S. troops will finally be withdrawn from Iraq, and the war will be formally declared over."

Kerrigan leaned against the back of the couch. "Holy shit. You're serious." Her weight rocked the couch backward, so that it stood on only two legs, and Olive was momentarily off-kilter, feeling as though she would fall.

They lay on the geometric rug with their legs propped up against the couch, a bag of red licorice between them. Kerrigan had wanted to hear first about her own life, and Olive repeated what little she knew—the move to Sun Prairie, her continued employment at the university. Though she didn't come right out and tell her that their close friendship had become strained and distant last year, Kerrigan seemed to pick up on it. "Was I happy?" she asked, and Olive had to admit that she didn't know. At one point, Olive thought she might be crying, but when she turned to check, Kerrigan seemed transfixed by the water-damaged ceiling instead. One large yellowish patch looked like a shark to Olive; another small stain resembled Louisiana.

Then Kerrigan wanted to hear about Phil and Alex, and Olive found herself admitting details she hadn't allowed herself to dwell on since the start of the year. How the loneliness in the weeks before her mom's wedding had led her back to

Alex's arms. She'd told him that their affair had ended her relationship with her longtime boyfriend. He told her that he'd been engaged to someone throughout most of medical school, but he'd called it off because they hadn't had anything in common anymore, hadn't understood each other. Since then, he'd vowed to date only other doctors—or nurses, he added for Olive's benefit.

They fell into a nocturnal rhythm, sleeping until four in the afternoon, eating BLTs at the kitchen island. Most of their time was spent at Olive's condo because the complex had a large, kidney-shaped swimming pool. Since many of her neighbors came home from work and ate their dinner at that time of day, they often had the whole pool to themselves. Alex swam laps, and Olive sunned herself in the late-afternoon rays. Sometimes a stray kid surprised them as they touched each other teasingly in the shallow end.

At work, they acted as if nothing was going on but fooled no one. When Alex tried to kiss her in the locker room, she slipped out of his grasp, still haunted by their first encounter. Before they fell asleep in the mornings, they talked about their shared patients in great detail, but Olive soon found this was the only thing she could talk to him about. He was enthusiastic about her mom's destination wedding, encouraging her to take scuba lessons, missing the point entirely. And when she tried to explain the loss of her dad, he was more interested in the type of leukemia he had and what kind of treatments they had tried than how his death had affected Olive.

Kerrigan rolled over onto her side so that they were facing each other. "I'm sorry I made us join him and his friends for drinks. I would never have done that if I'd known. There's clearly still something between you guys."

"No." Olive shook her head. "Weren't you listening to me? He's not right for me at all. I want to be with Phil."

"Of course you do. But that doesn't mean you're not still attracted to Alex. You work with him all the time, he's hot, and he thinks you're badass. How could you not be attracted to him?"

Olive didn't answer. Alex was a risqué diary page she wanted to tear out entirely. Why couldn't Kerrigan just leave it be?

Kerrigan paused, as if waiting for a response, and when she didn't get one, she asked, "Did you ever try to get back together with Phil?"

She tried not to think about the pathetic voice mail she had left that he had never returned, the nights of insomnia where she longed to call him and pour her heart out, the days when she drove out of her way just to pass the high school and glimpse his car. When she heard through the grapevine that his mom had had knee surgery, she called to hear him say in a tight voice, "She's fine. Thanks for calling." After she saw him in the coffee shop with the redheaded teacher, she began to fathom how far gone she and Phil really were.

She shook her head. "He wouldn't take me back."

"And presumably he doesn't know any of this now?"

"No."

"This is why you turned him down when he proposed?"

"Yes."

The fan turned the pages of a magazine on the coffee table.

It was dark now. Olive didn't know how late it was. She waited for Kerrigan to ask when she was going to tell Phil the truth. She waited for an indictment to come, but if Kerrigan was thinking it, she didn't say anything.

Olive sat up. She reached for a piece of licorice, one of the last left in the bag, and curled it around her finger like a ring. She had wanted to feel reassured in the way these talks normally reassured her. Sprawled on the living room floor or hanging off the end of Olive's bed, eating licorice or gummy bears or microwave popcorn like a couple of thirteen-year-olds, they had talked about *everything* in their eight years of friendship. They had talked their troubles into nonexistence, swept them into a place so far away from the pink house that they ceased to matter. And though the living room was bright and safe, and Kerrigan, who now knew the whole truth about her repeat year and actually believed her, was close beside her, Olive's troubles had not gone away; they were only waiting for her on the front stoop, nosing against the door like stray cats, begging to be let in.

Kerrigan sat up, too, drawing her knees to her chest. "If I were you, I'd go for it. Say yes. God, you're lucky. It's like you've got fresh eyes to reevaluate your life. Sometimes I feel so directionless. Like I'm just groping around in the dark."

"I still feel like that." She realized it was a kind of apology, for being the one who'd been given a second chance. For not doing better.

Kerrigan walked to the window again, but with the lights on in the apartment, Olive didn't think she could see beyond her own reflection.

"Is Clay worth my while?"

"I don't know how to answer that. I never met him. Besides, what makes a relationship 'worthwhile'? Do you have to end up marrying the guy?"

Kerrigan didn't turn around. "Just tell me how long we last."

"Two or three months, maybe. But listen. This isn't just *my* year. You can change outcomes, too. Maybe Clay is the one for you. Maybe you didn't give him a fair shake the first time around. Or maybe not. Just don't give up, Kerrigan."

"Even though half the year is over, and I've accomplished nothing? Even though you've just informed me I have nothing to look forward to in the second half? More monotonous work, another breakup, moving in with Ciara when you move out on me?"

Olive had seen her get this upset on only one other occasion. When they'd met in college their freshman year, Kerrigan had had few female friends. Most of the girls in their dorm were intimidated by her effortless beauty, her ease with boys. It had been difficult for Olive to accept at first, too. Then one night, Olive and Kerrigan came home to find that someone had carved the word *SLUT* into Kerrigan's door. Kerrigan had broken down like a small, vulnerable child. Olive soothed her, and together they covered the door with postcards from Olive's collection—a Japanese woodcutting of a snow-capped mountain, a black and white of the Arc de Triomphe—and vintage *Vogue* covers. Still, it had been hard to forget what was etched into the wood underneath, and they were both ready to move out of the dorm at the year's end, but not before Kerrigan had discovered the vandal's identity and started a dormwide rumor that the girl was sleeping with her chemistry professor to get an A.

Olive stepped alongside Kerrigan and met her ghostly

eyes in the window reflection. "You don't see me going anywhere, do you? I'm not moving out. And as for this knowing what the future holds—well, it sucks, and I'd be one to know, right? It can make you feel trapped at first, like you don't have the power to change anything. But you have to get past that. You have to get to a place where you realize you're the only one who's been standing in your way all along."

She was finally starting to believe that herself.

"Master of my fate, captain of my soul, and all that garbage?" Kerrigan asked with a hint of a smile.

"Yes," Olive said. "All of that garbage." She started to close the blinds. "You're not going to tell anyone, are you?"

Kerrigan rolled her eyes. "Who would believe me?"

Chapter 13

It was a hot, muggy afternoon. Olive's black steering wheel scorched her hands, so she drove with her fingertips. College girls in sundresses and flip-flops walked lazily down the streets. Sailboats drifted in the distance, looking like bobbing seagulls as she curved her way around the lake to Maple Bluff.

The weeks leading up to her mom's wedding had spilled into each other like waves at high tide. June 25 had seemed so far away, but now it was already the day before they left for St. Lucia. Olive couldn't believe she was almost halfway through her year. All her good intentions—helping her mom prepare for the wedding, reaching out to her brother, checking in on Sherry after her mastectomy—had never become more than intentions.

When she wasn't working, she and Phil were taking Cashew to the dog park, eating at little sidewalk cafés on State Street, or tumbling into bed together. Just the other day, she'd gotten off work at seven in the morning, positively ravenous for him. Instead of going home to bed like she usually did, she picked up his favorite coffee drink, a large hazelnut latte, and drove to his apartment. He answered the door with his shirt unbuttoned, his tie slung around his neck, and his hair still damp from the shower, and she couldn't help herself; she'd thrown herself into his arms and almost made him late for his first-period class. After he managed to leave, she burrowed into his bed and slept for eight hours, then showered, climbed back into bed, and waited for him to get home for another round. It was intoxicating, just like the year they had first met, and she felt like a lovesick college student again.

But she hadn't heard from Sherry since their chance encounter at the hospital, and the image of her—washed-out, vulnerable, alone—gnawed at Olive and disrupted her otherwise rose-colored summer. Sherry needed help, even if she didn't want it, and Olive was clearly the one to give it. She was most likely the only one in Sherry's life who even knew about her breast cancer, and she was definitely the only one who knew about the repeating. There were only sixteen hours to go until her flight, and she hadn't even started packing, but she needed to see Sherry.

Maple Bluff was a wealthy village, where the governor himself lived in a mansion. Many of the houses overlooked the lake. There were no sidewalks and many of the snaking roads were so steep that other cars and houses appeared only when you were almost on top of them. Olive didn't know how Sherry could afford to live in Maple Bluff. While her house was on the side of the road that didn't overlook the lake and was substantially smaller than many of the surrounding homes, it still had an impressive log façade with giant picture windows. As far as she knew, Sherry held no steady job. She suspected she had inherited money from one or all of her past husbands.

She rang the doorbell three times, but no one answered. She was about to give up and leave, when she wondered if Sherry was outside, out of earshot. The lawn on the side of the house was less cared for than the front yard. Spidery weeds grew, and the grass was taller and drier and made Olive's ankles itch. As she made her way around back, the landscaping became more and more unkempt. There were no fences separating the lots, yet Sherry had created the impression of one with shaggy trees and shrubs, clinging vines, and knee-high grass. Olive stuck to the only path now, a twisting trail of flat river stones.

"Sherry?" she called into the dense greenness.

"Who's there?"

Sherry was squatting in front of a bush with glossy, heart-shaped leaves. She used the plastic watering can on the ground to push off and stand. Wearing an orange cotton smock and a floppy straw hat, she looked like a drooping, exotic flower. The symmetry to her chest had been restored, and Olive wondered if she'd had breast reconstruction surgery or was wearing a prosthetic.

"Hello," she said, sounding almost happy to see Olive. She wiped her hands on her dress, leaving two wet smudges that clung to her thighs.

"I hope you don't mind. I rang the doorbell. I wanted to see how you're doing."

"It's a new day," Sherry said with a little shrug. She carried the watering can to the patio and motioned for Olive to follow her. "Do you like my garden?"

There were no flowers. No vegetables as far as Olive could

tell. The ground cover was thick; no pathways cut through it. It looked like a miniature jungle, overrun by weeds.

"It's very green," Olive said. "Very peaceful."

Sherry laughed once, a sharp, barking sound. "Robert would be spinning in his grave. He put in delphiniums and pansies and chrysanthemums and feverfew and hired a gardener to look after it. It was really lovely, but time-consuming, and rather stifling, and after Robert died, I let the gardener and the garden go. This suits me better." She set the watering can on the bottom step. "Wait here. I have something for you."

The patio needed another coat of stain. Two brown wicker chairs sat beside a mosaic-topped table. A stack of paperbacks balanced there, looking like they'd been left out in the rain, their covers rippled, the pages stamped into a permanent wave. On the top was Kate Chopin's *The Awakening*.

Sherry returned, a large cream-colored envelope in hand. "Don't think I forgot. This is for your mom and her beau. I've been meaning to mail it, but now here you are."

Olive accepted the envelope, which felt heavy in her hand. She could imagine a pair of doves embossed on the front of the card and a congratulatory message inside about a lifetime of love, a new beginning. "Thanks. I'll make sure they get this. How are you feeling?"

Sherry sat down heavily. "You caught me on a good day. I'm constipated, my abdomen is swollen, my feet feel like they're burning, everything tastes like metal, and I'm tired and achy all over." She lifted her hat, and even before she had removed it, Olive knew Sherry's hair would be thin and wispy, if not totally gone. She remembered the way her dad's thick, brown hair had fallen out in clumps almost overnight and never grown back.

"Chemo," Olive stated.

With the hat gone, she could see that Sherry's face was a little pinker and puffier than usual. Her scalp was peeling, and the hair that covered it was gray and threadlike. Without her characteristic red hair, Sherry's face looked naked and old.

"Four treatments so far," Sherry said, replacing the sun hat. She peered at Olive from under its brim. "So, what's the significance of the wedding? In the context of your repeat year, I mean."

The change in topic was not lost on Olive. She crossed her legs and shifted in the worn wicker seat. "I wasn't very accepting last year. I made things pretty hard on my mom."

"Ah." Sherry slipped on a pair of large tortoiseshell sunglasses. Behind the brown lenses, her eyes were unreadable.

Eager to restore the conversation to the matter of Sherry's health, Olive rushed on, "But now I've come to terms with it, and Christopher's giving her a hard time instead. Maybe if it were anyone other than Harry."

"Well, he's certainly not as handsome as your father, but he's not without all appeal," Sherry said. "He's very attentive and physically fit; he reads medieval poetry. He cooks for Kathy, and he wants to broaden her horizons, and God knows at our age, a woman needs her horizons broadened. I remember when they first met, when Harry gave that reading on *The Canterbury Tales* at the library, and—"

"What reading at the library?" Olive interrupted. When her mom had introduced her to Harry last spring, she said they'd met in yoga class, which had seemed too bizarre to be untrue.

"There was a special spring reading series at the Richmond branch, UW professors discussing their work and fields of expertise, and Harry was one of them. He really knows his Chaucer. After the reading, they started talking and really hit it off, and Harry stayed so long that he ended up helping Kathy take down the chairs."

"When was this?"

"A few years ago. Maybe 2008?"

"Two thousand eight?" It was several degrees cooler in the garden. Olive suddenly felt chilled in her shorts and tank top. If what Sherry said was true, her mom and Harry had known each other for three years. They had known each other before Olive's dad had died, and they had lied about it.

"Yes, it must have been 2008 because it was around the time Robert had his first heart attack." Sherry inhaled deeply. "Can you smell that freshness? That's photosynthesis in the process."

Olive poked the sharp edge of the envelope into her palm. Just because they'd met each other at a library event three years ago didn't mean anything, she reprimanded herself. It could've been a coincidence, a fluke. But why the need for secrecy then? When they'd reconnected in yoga class and started dating, why hadn't Olive's mom explained the wacky circumstances to her? God knows Harry would've loved to interrupt and supply words for *that* story. Unless they had felt guilty . . . Yet why the guilt if they had done nothing wrong, nothing that needed to be hidden? Her thoughts were becoming more tangled than the foliage in Sherry's yard.

"Sherry, do you think my mom and Harry have had some kind of relationship going on since then?" She hadn't realized she was going to voice the question until it burst between them into the moist, cool air.

Sherry tipped her sunglasses down to study Olive with her

Check Out Receipt

BPL- North End Branch Library
617-227-8135
http://www.bpl.org/branches/north.htm

Tuesday, December 2, 2014 1:47:15 PM

Item: 39999045632963
Title: The bluest eye
Material: Book
Due: 12/23/2014

Item: 39999071200735
Title: The repeat year
Material: Paperback Book
Due: 12/23/2014

Total items: 2

Thank You!

cool, brown eyes—eyes that had seen everything and seemed no longer surprised at the scandals and injustices of the world. "I honestly wouldn't know. Perhaps you should ask your mother."

Olive hugged herself with goose bump–covered arms. How could she possibly ever ask her mom that question? Its implication was too awful. *Did you cheat on Dad while he was on his deathbed?* In the ICU, she'd witnessed husbands who'd abandoned their wives in their greatest time of need—cancer, multiple sclerosis, a stroke—and the nurses viewed it as one of the greatest sins of men. Olive couldn't decide what was worse—the husbands who divorced their sick wives or the husbands who stuck with them and quietly saw other women. She had never heard of a wife who'd deserted her sick husband. Her mom had been by her dad's side every step of the way, lovingly feeding him and giving him his medications, even when he insisted he couldn't taste anything and the medicine was a waste of time. She had taken him everywhere he wanted to go no matter how complicated it was to get him there, especially after he needed a wheelchair: the lakeshore path, the House on the Rock, even Memphis to see Sun Studios, Graceland, and the Lorraine Motel where Martin Luther King, Jr., had been assassinated. She had been the picture of a devoted wife. But a picture . . . or the real thing?

Olive couldn't believe she was even allowing herself to think these thoughts. Her initial reason for coming seemed foggy and far away. Out of the corner of her eye, she could see Sherry's round, pink forearm resting on the table. Cold, unflappable Sherry Witan, who could disclose information that Olive's mom might have had an affair while her dad was still alive without batting an eyelash. Only days before the wedding, when Olive had finally made peace with their marriage! And after Sherry had called Olive's mom an angel . . . how could she? Olive had been wrong to think that Sherry had changed, that the person she'd seen in the hospital bed was the real Sherry, someone crying out for help. The real reason she'd reached out to Olive back in January was to puppeteer someone else's failures.

Olive raised her head. "Have you told your son?"

Sherry didn't respond immediately, and Olive wondered if she was going to pretend she didn't understand. But then Sherry muttered, "I tried calling him. He won't answer his phone."

"Did you leave a message?"

"It seemed unkind to leave him a voice mail about cancer."

"Unkind, yes. But then maybe he'd call you back."

Olive couldn't tell what emotions, if any, were flickering behind those dark glasses. At that moment, it wasn't too hard to empathize with Sherry's son. Whatever Sherry had done to warrant this silent treatment, this excommunication from his life, she had probably deserved it. Even so, Heath had the right to know what was going on with his mother's health, and Olive felt that with absolute certainty. Her parents had waited three weeks to tell her about her dad's leukemia. They hadn't wanted to ruin her high school graduation, they said. But now whenever she thought back to the four-hour ceremony in the stuffy gymnasium and the string of parties that followed over the next two weeks, she could think only of her parents, quietly suffering, faking smiles and laughter. Three whole weeks she had been kept ignorant.

"It's a risk, I know," Olive said. "Opening yourself up to

rejection. But for Pete's sake, Sherry, don't be selfish. Your son deserves to know."

"Ah, *selfish*. There's that word again." Sherry smirked. "It's been hurled at me many a time, because being a mother and wife is all about *selflessness*, see?" She imitated a perky, syrupy-sweet voice. "Giving up every molecule of your soul. If you want anything for yourself, you're accused of being selfish. Marriage and especially motherhood mean being condemned to play second fiddle your entire life."

"I disagree, but anyway, maybe *selfish* was the wrong word—"

"You disagree on what grounds? Have you ever been married? Have you ever had a child?"

"No, but—" She had witnessed her mom over the years and could testify to the pure love and joy her mom had gained from her role in the family; she always said raising such wonderful children was the accomplishment she was most proud of in her life. Maybe it did take an act of total selflessness to give that kind of love. Wasn't it worth it? But maybe her mom had wanted something more from this life, something separate from them, all her own, but had been too afraid to go after it.

Sherry rose from the table with some difficulty. "Get back to me in about ten years. Then we'll talk about selfishness."

Olive stood, too. "What do you have to gain by keeping this all to yourself? I see it all the time with my patients—having the support of family and friends can make a huge difference. You told me that repeat years are for last chances, Sherry. You think you're just going to get surgery and chemo and everything will be fine? You don't think there's a bigger picture here?"

"I'm tired," Sherry said, her sun hat covering most of her face. "I'd like you to go home now."

"I'm sorry. I'll leave soon, but you know I'm right. You know that you're here this year so you can try to fix things with your son, but you're scared he won't forgive you."

"You don't know anything about my son."

"No, I don't. I don't presume to. I just think—"

"I think you have enough of your own problems to fix this year without nosing into mine." Sherry made her way around the table, opened the glass patio door, and slipped inside. She slid the door back into place with a quiet click.

Stunned, Olive sat alone and waited. She was sorry but not sorry enough to go inside and apologize. She doubted Sherry was torturing herself about dropping the bombshell on her about her mom and Harry. Since January, Sherry had been the one doling out advice. The suggestion to reach out to Heath was really the first time Olive had ventured to speak up. Perhaps she could have said it better, but maybe brusqueness was what it took to get through to Sherry. Nothing else seemed to work.

Sherry didn't come back out. Finally giving up, Olive walked around to the front of the house, returning to manicured lawns, order, and civilization. The sun was hot on her skin, but she knew it would be even hotter in St. Lucia. As she drove back down the bluff, the buoyant feeling she'd experienced on the way there was replaced with heavy reluctance.

Chapter 14

A world of lush green opened up below. Two spectacular mountains rose up out of the green; the helicopter cast a small shadow as they flew over them. Their pilot said something in his melodious accent, but over the roar of the whirling blades, Olive couldn't hear him.

"What did he say?" she asked Phil, who sat on her left, pressed up against the wall of the cabin.

"Pitons," Phil said. "Those mountains are the Pitons."

"Doesn't *pitons* mean 'breasts' in French?" Olive's mom shouted from the other cabin wall. She was a nervous flyer and had had one glass of champagne too many on the plane.

"Yes. I think it's actually a Creole word," Harry said. He was on Olive's other side, and his sweaty knee touching hers was the only thing preventing her from enjoying the helicopter ride. "According to the guidebook, they're called Gros Piton and Petit Piton. You can't tell it from up here, but they're different sizes."

"A pair of lopsided breasts!" Olive's mom exclaimed, and Olive tried not to think about Sherry.

"Why do all mountains remind explorers of breasts?" she asked Phil.

"Perhaps because there's nothing else quite so majestic," he said.

Last year Olive had taken a different flight than her mom and Harry, a later flight. The airport was located in the southern tip of the country, but the resort was located in Castries, a northern city, so she'd taken a shuttle there. Three young couples, all honeymooners, shared the shuttle with her. They'd looked at Olive as though she were an exotic specimen—a single tourist in a lovers' paradise. Solitary, Olive had sat up front next to the driver and closed her eyes every time they motored up a mountain. In St. Lucia, they drove on the left side of the road, and the roads were so narrow and winding that drivers honked perfunctorily to warn other motorists of their presence before plowing ahead. For the whole two-hour drive the newlyweds had snuggled and talked about all the neat wedding gifts they'd just received and the ones they would still need to complete their registries. By the time they had arrived at the resort, Olive's nerves were frayed.

But with Phil by her side, everything seemed better. The bellhop didn't glance at her with pity as he had last time when he left her alone with her luggage in her room. The king-size bed didn't appear to be so ludicrously huge. The pools, hammocks, shuffleboard courts, and lawn chess sets looked more inviting. Some of this, she knew, had to do with the fact that now, as a part of a couple, she belonged here. But there was more to it; it was the way Phil viewed and interacted with the world. He became fast friends with an Australian couple as they waited in line to check in. He made Olive dance with him to the tinny tropical music that emitted from speakers painted to look like rocks along the pathway as they walked to dinner and then wondered aloud if they could make love in a hammock without falling out. His playfulness helped keep her mind off the unpleasant conversation she'd had with Sherry.

The buffet-style restaurant was mostly outdoors, covered only by roof beams painted a cerulean blue with red flowers. Bananas, pineapple, plantain, and a watermelon with a fish carved into its rind were heaped on a central table. The restaurant had a view of the ocean, if the ocean hadn't been too dark to see at that time of night. If everyone at the table stopped talking at the same moment, Olive could hear the ocean rise up onto the beach with a forceful, inhaling rush and then retreat with a soft exhale.

Christopher and Verona, who had taken the late flight this time, arrived as the four of them were just finishing dinner. They both looked a little green around the gills, probably from the shuttle ride, Olive suspected. A pang of guilt shot through her. Her mom invited them to fill up some plates and join their table.

"We're pretty tired, so we're just going to go to bed," Christopher said.

"We want to be fresh for tomorrow," Verona added quickly. "We just wanted to check in and see what's on the agenda."

"Nothing's set in stone," Olive's mom said. "We've been tossing around a lot of ideas. Taking a catamaran to Martinique. Checking out the resort and just relaxing on the beach. Phil found out there's a golf course if anyone wants to golf."

"I'd like to learn to golf," Christopher said, speaking directly to Phil.

"I'd be happy to give you some pointers," Phil said.

"That's a great idea," Harry chimed in. "Why don't the guys play golf, and the ladies can treat themselves to a spa day? I know that's something you wanted to do before the wedding anyway, Kathy. Then we can all meet up for dinner."

Phil looked at Olive questioningly. Her mom scrutinized Christopher with a furrowed brow. The ocean sucked in a deep breath and then spit it back out.

"Sounds good to me," Olive said. On their first day last year—their first day of three excruciating days in limbo before the wedding—they had milled aimlessly around the resort without a plan. They finally settled in at one of the pools. A few hours later, Christopher and Verona had left to play tennis, and then Olive had lingered on awkwardly with her mom and Harry, until she'd come up with an excuse that she needed to get out of the sun and would take a short nap before dinner. Instead, she'd walked to the busiest bar at the resort, where she'd be less conspicuous, and drunk Bahama Mamas.

"It's settled then," Harry said, draping his arm around his fiancée.

However, their plans changed abruptly the next morning when Verona came to breakfast alone.

"Christopher went to breakfast early. He said he really wanted to try some watersports first, and he'd meet up with you guys for golf later." She said this in a voice that let them know she did not condone his behavior. Olive guessed they'd probably had an argument about it.

"We don't have to golf. I'd like to check out what kinds of watersports they have, too," Phil said.

Olive stepped on his sandaled foot under the table. "No. He'll meet up with you later. Go golf. Have fun." She turned to her mom. "Would you mind if I took a rain check on the spa day? You know I'm not that into having my face shellacked with different creams and getting my cuticles pushed back. I think I'd like to join Christopher." She knew she was letting her mom down, but she'd let Christopher down, too. And she needed to fix that first before she could make anything else better.

The Watersports Center stood at the far edge of the resort property. It was a small wooden outbuilding with a blacktopped apron leading down to the sand. The shutters were closed tightly with a sign listing its hours. Presumably it hadn't opened for the day yet. Christopher sat on a large rock facing the ocean.

"It's nothing against Phil," he said when he saw her. "I'd be happy to play golf with Phil. I'm sorry to leave him with Harry, but there's no way I'm spending a whole day with that pompous jerk. It's useless trying to convince me."

"I didn't come here to try to convince you. I came here to rent a kayak."

Almost as if on command, two young men in red polo shirts and swim trunks appeared to unlock the shed. They outfitted Olive and Christopher with puffy red life jackets and signed out to them a yellow two-seater kayak and two double-ended paddles.

"I've never kayaked before," Christopher said as he dragged the kayak to the water's edge.

"Neither have I," she said. "But I've canoed before, and it can't be much different, can it?"

"I've never even canoed. I was planning on renting something more motorized. Like a Jet-Ski."

"You're so lazy. Why don't you sit in the front, then?"

"No. You sit in the front." Christopher stepped into the boat and tried to sit on the back seat. He almost fell out.

"The person in back steers. If you're in the back, we'll go in circles."

They paddled hesitantly along the shoreline, never straying more than ten feet from land, the kayak listing first to the left, then the right, as Christopher got the hang of it. The only sound was the splash of their paddles churning the water. It was ten o'clock, and no one else was on the water. They passed the roped-off swimming area where a few pairs of heads bobbed in the ocean; other people lay like strips of bacon frying on the beach.

"Was Mom upset that we're not joining in the festivities?" he asked at last.

She suddenly realized that he thought she had joined him in his strike today. "What do you think? This is supposed to be a family trip, but instead Mom and Harry are off spending time with our significant others instead of us."

"This isn't a *family* trip. This is Mom getting remarried. I don't get you. You seem so resigned to this."

"Christopher," she started, but then found herself at a loss for words. She'd had a year longer than him to process this. She wanted to tell him it would get easier with time, especially once he saw how happy Harry made their mom. Well, maybe that made it harder at first, but eventually, it became possible to witness her radiance and accept that the cause of it wasn't their dad. She wanted to tell Christopher what Sherry had said about the library reading three years ago and see what he made of it, but she didn't want to add more fuel to his fire of loathing for Harry. She wondered how he'd been able to suppress his anger last year. Had she been so terribly effective at venting it for him?

"I guess I *am* resigned to this. This is Mom's life, not ours," she finally said.

Christopher snorted, but his shoulders relaxed slightly. They passed the resort property line—a pile of rocks and a chain-link fence on shore—and entered the public beach.

"What bugs you the most about Harry?" she asked.

"I could give you a top ten list. Besides him touching Mom all the time? The way he finishes her sentences. Like she's too dumb to complete her own thoughts."

"He does that with everyone, though. Not just Mom."

"Well, then, he thinks he's smarter than all of us."

"That drives me nuts, too. But I've thought about it a lot, and I don't think he does it with malicious intent. I think he does it to show he's really listening to us and that he's in tune with what we're saying. Trying to demonstrate that he understands. It still pisses me off, though."

The shore was forested now, the beach rockier. It looked more like a park in Wisconsin than a beach in St. Lucia. A local family stood on the rocky beach; two naked children splashed each other in the shallow water.

"Let's go out to that island," Christopher said, pointing with his paddle.

"Are you sure? We're already pretty far out." Her biceps burned.

"Is the expert rower scared?" he taunted.

"This isn't Lake Mendota, Christopher; this is the ocean. Right now we're protected by the inlet, so the waves aren't that bad. But once we get out there, it's going to be a lot choppier. And you're going to feel stupid if the resort staff has to send a boat to rescue us."

"I'm up for a good challenge."

She tried to remember that this was Christopher, her twenty-eight-year-old brother, a married man with a mortgage, a gifted journalist, not the stubborn twelve-year-old who'd convinced her it was perfectly safe to ride her bike off the ramp he'd built in the street in front of their house and then broken his own arm demonstrating. She considered bringing this up but then thought better of it. Kayaking out to the island was something Christopher and her dad would have done together before he had gotten sick.

She stared at her brother's back as they paddled to the island. Under his red life vest, he wore a gray T-shirt. A large oval of sweat darkened his collar and upper back. The tendons in his neck bulged from the exertion of paddling, and the skin above his collar looked bright pink.

"Didn't you put any sunscreen on the back of your neck?" she asked him. "You're getting burned."

He stopped rowing and swatted at his neck. "Dammit. Do you have any?"

"Not with me, genius." She rested her paddle across her lap. The current pushed them farther out to sea but away from the island. It felt very symbolic of her year.

"Well, I guess we'd better head back, then," he said.

"That's it? A little sunburn and you're ready to give up?" The waves rocked the kayak.

"You said it was dangerous."

"Yes, but, Christopher—" The island beckoned to her from the horizon. She'd become charmed by the idea of reaching it, and besides, she didn't want to come this far just to turn back around, defeated.

Christopher had always been the changeable, flighty one. He'd given up in fast succession a variety of activities in his childhood—soccer, guitar lessons, sketching, fishing. In college, he'd changed his major five times before settling on computer science. Then after graduating and securing a good position doing tech support for a prominent investing company in Milwaukee, he'd quit his job, moved back to Madison, married Verona, and started submitting articles to online newspapers about same-sex marriage, the Israeli-Palestinian conflict, and violence against women in the Democratic Republic of the Congo.

"It's the principle of the thing," she continued. "We're over three-fourths of the way there. Do you want to give up now?"

"God, Olive. Can't you let a guy save a little face? My arms feel like jelly." He stabbed his paddle back into the water and shoved off, but without Olive paddling behind him, he wasn't making much progress. "That's the problem with you: You're so goddamn stubborn. You don't know when to say when."

"What is that supposed to mean?"

"I don't know. That's what Dad used to say about you. He said I was too fickle and that you didn't know when to say when."

"Dad said that? Give me an example."

"I really don't know what he meant. When to say that you've had enough? When to say you've made a mistake? Can you please help me paddle so we can get this over with?"

"No. I don't want to go to the island anymore."

"Fine. Then let's turn around. Let's just do something so we don't drift out to sea."

Olive dipped her paddle back into the water and, with just a few quick, flat strokes, had the kayak facing the shore. The resort and strip of white sand beach looked very far away, small enough to fit in her hand.

As much as she wanted to write off what Christopher had said as a misinterpretation of what her dad had meant, she couldn't help remembering an instance when he had said something similar to her. Her first year of nursing school she had been so stressed out and unhappy that her dad had suggested it might not be the right career path for her after all.

"If I give up now, just because it's hard, I'll never know if it's right for me," she had said.

"You're exactly right, Olive Oyl," her dad had said. "But if you find out somewhere down the line that it's not what you want, there's no shame in changing your mind. Sometimes I think your brother's flip-flopping made too much of an impression on you. I don't want you to stick with something just to prove you can. I happen to know from experience that it will only make you miserable. Don't be afraid to say, 'You know what? I screwed up. I'm going to try this again.'"

At the time, his speech hadn't made much of an impression on her because she had felt so sure about nursing. She had known all along that it was her calling, so to speak; she had never doubted that. Especially after his battle with leukemia, it had seemed only fitting to devote herself to caring for critically ill patients. But now she realized that it wasn't just careers that he had been talking about; he had been referring to all of life's major decisions.

Was he right? Was she someone who didn't know when to

say when? All of last year's wrong turns and her inability to put on the brakes and turn around seemed to suggest it. Even though she had still loved Phil, she had stumbled blindly ahead without him, because it was far easier than admitting she had made a major mistake and fighting to win him back.

She and Christopher established a rhythm; the kayak slowly but steadily glided back to shore. Overhead the sun beat down on them. Drops of cool water speckled her face and arms with each circuit of the paddle.

A half-formed thought flashed through her mind. Did her dad have something to do with her repeat year? Knowing her flaws, was he somehow watching out for her? Had he given her this second chance as a gift? It was a comforting fancy, one that restored her and gave her a new sense of purpose.

She wiped at her sweaty brow with the back of her arm, and her paddle slid overboard. She started to laugh.

"What is it?" Christopher asked sullenly. When he turned around and saw her paddle, floating already quite some distance from the kayak, he cursed. He tried to turn them around, unsuccessfully, because of his position in the front. Then he tried to paddle in reverse, succeeding only in moving them a few inches back, while the current took the light, buoyant paddle a few feet farther away.

"Give me the paddle," she said.

"No. I don't want you to lose this one, too."

"Oh, for Pete's sake. I didn't lose it on purpose. Well, at least switch places with me so you can turn us around." She stood up. The kayak tilted dramatically to the right.

"No. We'll tip over."

"Fine. I'll go get it." She dove into the water. It felt lovely against her skin after exerting herself in the sun all morning, soothing like bathwater. She swam after the paddle, the life jacket making it hard as it kept tugging her back up to the surface. After an awkward, graceless swim, she managed to wrestle the paddle back to the kayak, where Christopher sat, shaking his head.

"You are a nut," he said.

She felt a sudden rush of tenderness she hadn't felt for him in a long time. He was, after all, a version of herself: a taller, more impulsive, male version with stronger convictions about the world. How could she not empathize with his stonewalling of Harry when she had done the very same thing last year? She understood, better than anyone, that it was a way of championing their father.

"Dad would've loved this," she said. "You know he would've written about this in the Christmas letter."

Christopher shook his head again, but she could tell he was laughing by the way his shoulders were shaking.

"This is what he would've wanted for us," she continued. "For us to have fun. Be happy. All of us—Mom, too."

He grunted noncommittally and extended his arm to help her back into the kayak. It swayed dangerously to the left, but he held it steady long enough for her to climb in. They aimed the kayak toward the now-bustling Watersports Center. A motorboat trailing a water-skier careened across the inlet. Husbands and wives helped each other into life jackets and climbed aboard Jet-Skis and kayaks. A line had formed at the wooden counter.

"I'll put on a happy face for Mom's sake," Christopher said, as he stabbed his paddle into the sand to propel the kayak forward, "but I don't like him."

At this point, she felt that was all they could really ask of him. She herself had done much worse last year. She remembered sitting on the patio of her mom and Harry's honeymoon bungalow, calmly pinning a gardenia in her mom's hair and accusing her of loving Harry more than she'd loved Olive's dad. She remembered standing in the sand beside her mom at the ceremony, refusing to listen to the vows they'd written for each other. Instead she had cast her gaze out to sea, her head throbbing from all the piña coladas she had drunk. Then afterward, she had fallen asleep on a chaise longue on the beach, and Christopher had had to help her back to her room before the tide carried her away.

She wished she could convey these struggles to her brother.

They all reconvened for dinner, this time at the Italian restaurant that required reservations and for men to wear a tie. Harry had lent Phil one of his, a black-and-maroon-striped one that clashed with Phil's cobalt blue shirt. They seemed to be best friends now, rehashing a play-by-play of their game for everyone's benefit. Olive's mom and Verona were more reserved, with the look of women who had just engaged in a serious heart-to-heart. Verona's nails were painted pink, and Olive's mom's face looked taut and shiny. Olive felt excluded. She and Christopher were the only ones sunburned.

After dinner, she and Phil decided to take a walk along the beach to watch the sun set. He wanted to change first, so she said she'd meet him near the pier. The sky was mauve, the color of heart muscle. It was only two days until the wedding now.

She slipped her strappy, high-heeled sandals off and carried them over her shoulder. In all its vastness, the ocean felt like an appropriate metaphor for the cosmos.

"Here I am again," she said. "Do you remember me?" She dug her fingernails into the claylike sand and came up with a fistful of shells, stones, and other muck. She flung it as far as she could into the ocean and heard it plop. "I don't know what your plans are for me, but I sure as hell hope I'm following them."

The ocean rushed up the shore, covering her ankles in muck, returning the tiny shells and stones she had just thrown.

"Ha. That's funny. Very funny. I should've known. Back to square one." She squatted down to wash off her feet and ankles in the shallow water. When she stood up, she could see Phil hurrying toward her.

"Fancy meeting you here," he said.

She took his hand, and they fell into stride together. "You know I appreciate what you did today for Harry, but you don't have to go overboard or anything. We all know that 'Professor Matheson thinks Hoobastank was a city in the Byzantine Empire.' He's a dud! You don't have to pretend to like him so much."

Phil frowned. "I'm not pretending. I *do* like him. He's a really kind, well-meaning guy. I feel like I got to know him a lot better today. I think that if you only gave him the chance, you'd like him, too."

"You're a terrible judge of character. You like everyone." She sat down on a stray chaise longue and stretched out her legs.

"I'm an excellent judge of character. I chose you, didn't I?" He sat at the edge of her chair and began tracing small circles on her bare thigh.

"You chose me? I thought fate brought us together. Fate, some apples, and a defective paper bag."

"Maybe this sounds cliché, but today I could tell that Harry really loves your mom. The way he talks about her and the way every little thing reminds him of her. And he's doing everything he can to get you and Christopher to like him. He asked me all about the ICU, what you do, and if you like it. He really cares, Olive. I think it hurts him that you guys are so indifferent to him."

"Honestly, I don't care." She felt a twinge of meanness and fought to justify it. In her mind's eye, she saw the Richmond library branch and her mom and Harry in the deserted Derleth Reading Room, leaning together much too close across a wooden lectern. "I'm doing all I can right now to support my mom. I don't have the energy to get all buddy-buddy with Harry."

The high tide lapped almost as far as the stone wall, gliding stealthily under the chaise longue. Phil lifted his feet and then moved to another chaise longue and faced her. "You act like those are different things. Supporting your mom and approving of Harry."

"They are to me! I *can't* like Harry. He represents too many bad things to me. He's everything my dad wasn't. Don't you see that I'm doing the best I can?"

"I do. But what you don't see is that Harry's doing the best he can." His tone was resentful.

"Why are you getting so mad at me? You're supposed to be on my side."

"I'm always on your side, Ollie. I guess I just . . . Maybe I'm just jealous. Your real dad was great, and now you have a potential stepdad who's bending over backward to make you happy."

Olive dangled her feet over the edge of her chair. "Well, although Charlie will never win the Father of the Year award, he's trying, too, Phil." She curled her toes into the wet sand.

There was a long silence. The sun had moved behind the island, so they couldn't see it touch the horizon. The clouds left behind were orange and ragged.

Phil straightened up in his chair. "I haven't heard from him since late March. I've tried calling him, and his number is disconnected. I called his sponsor, Maryanne, and she hasn't heard from him in months, either. I even looked up the number for his trucking company, but they said he no longer works there. I think he's fallen off the wagon again."

"Oh Phil, I'm so sorry." She reached out to squeeze his arm, but he had turned away from her, toward the sunset, and she couldn't reach him. "Why didn't you tell me sooner?"

"I don't know. You didn't ask, and—"

"I'm so sorry. I should've."

"That's not what I meant. It just didn't come up in conversation, and I didn't want to make it out to be more important than it really is. He's a drunk and always will be. What more did I expect?"

"Maybe you didn't expect him to change, but you hoped," Olive said.

Phil laughed bitterly. "I'm an idiot for letting him back into my life. What a waste of time."

"No, you're not. You're a good person. A forgiving person."

"A fool."

"He has an illness, Phil."

"I don't want to hear it. I am so sick of all the excuses. It's simple: If I were worth it to him, he'd get his act together. But if I wasn't worth it to him at age eight, I'm certainly not worth it to him now." He closed his eyes and pressed his thumbs into his eyelids.

"Of course you're worth it. The first thing he did when he became sober was contact you. He loves you. He's just a man with a serious addiction."

"That's not love, and I can't put up with it anymore. I'm done with him now." His voice was hard and uncompromising, the way he'd sounded last year when he'd told her goodbye. Olive involuntarily shuddered.

The cloud scraps reflected on the water, resembling large, golden fish.

He was in his own world now, and she wanted him back. "This reminds me of the docks," she said. "How we used to watch the sun set together and you would quiz me on drugs. And almost every time, you would tell me that same story about your childhood. How you thought the sun set only in your backyard."

The best part of the Russells' old farmhouse was the backyard. It faced the west with miles of rolling green fields and red barns and silos as far as the eye could see. The sun would disappear neatly between the cradle of the hills as if it slept there every night. As a little boy, Phil had thought they were the only ones with a view of this spectacle, that the sun set only over their land. When he was six years old, he'd stayed overnight at a friend's house and witnessed the same sun setting as he perched at the top of a jungle gym at the neighborhood playground. He'd been so distressed that he'd fallen off but was too embarrassed to explain the real reason for his fall. He said it was the first revelation that he'd ever had.

"I love that story," Olive said. "I never really knew what you meant by 'revelation,' but I still love it."

Phil clasped his hands over his knees. "Just what every kid learns at some point, I guess. That people and things don't exist just for us. They exist for other people, too. They exist in their own right."

Olive's own similar revelation, she supposed, had come when she realized her parents had names, that their names were not simply Mom and Dad. She had overheard them talking in the kitchen one morning as they made pancakes. "It looks like we're out of syrup, Kathy. I guess I'd better run to the store." "Hang on, Greg! I have some frozen berries and cream we can use instead." It had been like finding out her parents had secret identities.

It was hard not to think about Sherry's claim that motherhood meant giving up your dreams, giving up a secret part of yourself. She tried to imagine this secret part of her mom. A dark corner of her that loved opera and had a passion for trying new foods. A shadowy space devoted to loving Harry. It saddened her to think there was any part of her mom to which she didn't have access.

Back in their room, Olive stepped out of her sundress and untied her bikini top. Phil sat on the bed behind her and rubbed aloe vera onto her shoulders and neck. The aloe vera felt cold against the heat of her sunburn. She felt like she was freezing and burning up at the same time. She collapsed into him, gritting her teeth against his handsome jawbone, digging her fingers into his warm flesh, relishing her physicality and his closeness.

Chapter 15

It was Saturday, June 25, the day of the wedding. The morning unrolled in an identical fashion, as if last year had been merely a dress rehearsal. Olive's mom called at eight forty-five to remind them of the nine o'clock meeting with the resort's wedding consultant, Rowena, to go over the details of the afternoon's ceremony. They met in the lobby, which bustled with arrivals and departures. Luggage was packed and unpacked from white shuttles idling on the cobblestone driveway. Rowena's turquoise blazer was familiar, as well as the room she led them to, with its crystal vase of sweet-smelling plumeria and shelves and shelves of silver-framed brides and grooms hand-in-hand on the beach. Olive felt claustrophobic.

She knew the wedding was central to her year, one of the major sticking points she needed to straighten out, and she'd gotten this far without majorly blowing it; she just needed to hold on a little longer, but she was exhausted and on edge from the previous day's catamaran cruise to Soufrière. Repeat year, okay, but for a really neat trick, how about a pause button? A few days off from Harry, from her whole family. She and Phil could camp out on the beach. She'd let the sun drench her skin, drug her into a stupor, and erase her memory of Sherry's unwelcome gossip. She'd read novels, doze, and move only enough to take sips from a strawberry daiquiri. Rejuvenated, she could endure her mom's wedding to Harry a second time cheerfully and graciously. But alas, there was no pause button, and she was already five minutes late for her appointed time to help her mom get dressed for the ceremony.

Whistling a half-familiar tune, Harry was just leaving the honeymoon bungalow when Olive arrived. He wore a white linen tunic, matching drawstring pants, and leather sandals. Phil was going to keep him company until the wedding. Harry bowed deeply. "My lady's lady-in-waiting."

Olive stared back, unsure how to respond. Was she supposed to curtsy? Call him *my lord*? But he was already ambling down the walk. She slapped her forehead and shook her head, and then hoped her mom hadn't been looking out the window.

She kicked off her sandals and found her mom in the bathroom, wrapped in one of the resort's oversized white terrycloth bathrobes. Her face was pink and blotchy from the shower, her hair tangled in clumps around her face. She looked less like a blushing bride and more like the woman Olive had tried to console in the days following her dad's death.

"Happy wedding day," Olive said and hugged her.

"Thanks. Your dress is just darling. I made the mistake of trying mine on last night, and it's a little tight across my stomach. I wish I'd bought a larger size, or better yet, said no to the dessert table this week."

"You're going to look beautiful." Olive began untangling her mom's wet hair with a wide-toothed comb. "Let me know if I pull too hard."

"You're very gentle." She picked up a jar of face cream and smoothed it under her eyes. "Can you believe I'm nervous? I'm fifty-three years old. God knows what I have to be nervous about."

Had she said this last year? Olive didn't think so. She rubbed some styling product through her mom's hair and wiped her hands on a towel. She tried to remember their exact words, but she could only remember the general impression of an offense-defense match. Olive's mom had raved about the elegant setup on the beach; Olive had asked her how it compared to her first wedding. Her mom's rebuttal had been to ask what Olive would one day like for her own wedding. This had led to a discussion of whether a person had just one perfect soul mate and if marriage was necessary for happiness. And so on until Olive declared that her mom loved Harry more than she had ever loved her dad.

The loud whir of the hair dryer made it unnecessary to speak for the next few minutes. Olive busied her hands spreading out the contents of her mom's makeup bag on the counter and trying to ignore her appraising look in the mirror. The hair dryer clicked off.

"What is all this stuff?" Olive asked. There were tubes, bottles, and plastic squares of creams, glosses, and powders in every color. She held up a vial of bronze-colored liquid. "I don't know if this is for your eyes, your lips, or your skin."

Her mom squinted at it. "I don't know, either. You know I don't wear much makeup. I bought it from one of those department store ladies who gave me a makeover. She said it would all come together quite nicely. Here—this looks like foundation." She handed Olive a triangular bottle.

"And I put this on with what?"

"The lady did it with a sponge. There's a pack of them around here somewhere. Do you think we should call Verona? She always looks so put together."

"No," Olive said quickly. She found the pack of wedge-shaped sponges under a blush compact. "We can figure this out. It's not rocket science."

"Okay, good." Her mom sat down on the toilet lid. "Is Christopher still having a difficult time?"

Olive knelt before her on the robin's-egg blue tile. "I think he's starting to come around. We both love you so much; we just want to see you happy again." She dabbed the foundation on her mom's face with the sponge. "If Harry makes you happy . . ."

"That means a lot to me. He does make me happy." She lifted her chin for Olive, stretching her slender neck, and then grinned at the ceiling. "Who woulda thunk?"

Olive bristled at her mom's use of one of her dad's favorite expressions. She swiped the sponge along her mom's jawline and tried to think of something to say. Something about the drive-in-volcano they'd seen yesterday in Soufrière or a funny memory from her childhood. Something benign and appropriate for the occasion and maybe even sweet. Instead, she found herself saying, "But you must've suspected that when you met him, right?"

Olive's mom accepted the sponge and mirror from her and touched up a few spots around her eyes. "Harry? Well, not at first, no." She turned the hand mirror from side to side, critically studying her reflection.

"How did you meet again?" Olive asked, standing up. She looked away from her mom and pretended to be engrossed in twisting open a makeup brush that fanned out like a palm tree. She held her breath, scared to hear her mom's answer. She didn't know if she was more nervous about her mom lying to her again or telling her the truth.

"Yoga at the Y. In our whole class, Harry was one of only two men." Her mom set the hand mirror facedown on her lap. "What's next? Blush?"

Olive bit her lip. Her hand shook as she twisted the makeup brush again and its bristles disappeared. "That was the first time you met? You didn't meet earlier . . . at the library?" She risked a glance at the mirror and saw her mom staring back at her reflection. Their eyes met, and Olive saw that Sherry hadn't been lying.

"It's not like you think," Olive's mom said softly.

Olive clung to the edge of the bathroom counter. *Why had she pursued this?* Knowing would not make anything better; it would only make things harder. For the first time since the early days of January, she wished she had not been given a repeat year. She wished 2011 were done and over with. Even if she'd been a bitch at the wedding, it still would've been better than hearing this. But a macabre instinct guided her—the same sick curiosity that made her unable to turn her head away when Phil said, “Don’t look,” at cats or dogs dead on the side of the road or particularly gory scenes in movies. She needed to face the worst.

Olive squatted on the floor in front of her mom. “Tell me what to think, then.”

She wouldn’t look at Olive. “Honey, I don’t think this is the time to talk about it. Verona will be here any minute, and the wedding . . .”

“I agree with you. The best time would’ve been a long time ago.” Olive sat back on her heels. Was she doing this for her dad? What else could explain forcing her mom to confess only an hour before the wedding? She knew she was being cruel, but she couldn’t stop.

Her mom gripped the handle of the mirror and turned it over and over in her lap. “Your dad and I had such a beautiful life together. He showed me so much love. I was never wanting for love. Even in the end.”

Olive’s eyes burned as she blinked back tears. She set her trembling lips in a firm line.

“It was wrong, I know. I punished myself for a long time, especially after your dad passed. I told myself it was my fault he hadn’t lived longer; my actions had made him worse. That I deserved the pain and suffering I was going through because I hadn’t appreciated him enough. It was awful. It made getting out of bed even harder. But as guilty as I felt, I still couldn’t make myself regret it.” Her mom carefully laid the hand mirror on the counter.

Her admission was like a hammer to Olive’s memories of her parents’ happy marriage. The hammer swung and struck, and the memories exploded into thousands of sharp crystal shards. Her dad was gone, and now this, too.

"I don't understand," Olive said. "You met at the library three years ago and you've been together since then? After Dad's death, why did you hide it? Why wait so long?" With each question, her tone became more and more accusatory. It was easier to be furious than devastated, or even worse, sympathetic. With her slumped, defeated posture, her mom reminded Olive of herself the night she'd admitted her infidelity to Phil.

"No, no. It wasn't like that." Her mom straightened herself and crossed her ankles. "We met at the library three years ago, that's true. But I told your dad about him that night, about his goofy Middle English accent, and Greg said, 'Gotta love the library dorks. I'm so sorry you have to put up with that.' I didn't think I'd ever see him again. Your dad was very sick then, and taking care of him took up most of my time. Not that I minded, of course. It was a privilege to care for him, when he had given so much of himself to me and our family over the years."

She took a deep breath, as if working up the courage to continue. "A few weeks after the reading, Harry stopped by the library and asked me out for coffee. I told him I couldn't, that I was married, and he acted taken aback. 'Two academics going out for coffee to discuss literature isn't a date,' he insisted."

Olive clenched her teeth at her mom's imitation of Harry. It sounded so like him. So precise. So fussy. How manipulative he'd been. Of all the faults she'd disliked him for, she had never thought he was a scheming sleaze who'd chase a married woman.

"I surprised myself. I went. And it felt so good to be somewhere other than the house or the hospital or the library. I was a woman in a coffee shop with a man who asked her questions she'd never considered before. And he took my answers seriously, like I was an expert. So I went again. And again. We went out for coffee or lunch every week, for about a year. But then your dad's hospice care started, and I broke it off. I couldn't—I just . . ."

"Did you and Dad never have interesting conversations? Did Dad not take you seriously?" Olive pushed.

"No, it's not that. It's hard to explain. Greg's goal in life was to make me laugh, I think. He saw me as this serious creature who always had her head in a book. And though he loved that about me, I don't think he ever understood it."

"So you never—" Olive paused, unsure how to ask her mom such a personal, prying question, but she knew she needed the answer. "You were never intimate?"

Her mom looked up from her lap. Even through her matte cream-colored foundation, her cheeks were flushed and shiny. "It was more of an emotional affair than a physical one. Yet I never told Harry about your dad's cancer. He didn't find out until we started officially dating last year, and he was stunned I hadn't confided in him. But I didn't want sympathy. I just wanted to escape, I guess. To be someone else for a little while."

Sherry's words suddenly echoed in Olive's head. *Being a mother and wife is all about selflessness. Giving up every molecule of your soul.* The thought froze the retort that had been on her lips: *You wanted to escape from us? Why weren't we enough for you?* She tried to take a step back and put into perspective what her mom had just said. In the middle of the bleakest years of her life—her beloved husband of twenty-six years fighting a losing battle with acute myeloid leukemia, her adult children depressed and clingy—her mom had needed to shake free of that life for a little while.

The tiles were slick with sweat under Olive's bare legs. She shifted her position and sat cross-legged, not caring about her exposed underwear or the wrinkles she was probably pressing into the skirt of her dress. "Did you ever tell Dad?"

Her mom shook her head. "I couldn't bring myself to. He was so weak, and I didn't want anything to come between us, especially at the end. I still question that decision. If it was really best for us, or just best for me. But your dad talked about me remarrying a lot. I would get so angry with him. He would say things like, 'When I'm gone, I don't want you pulling off at a rest stop just yet. You've still got a lot of miles in you, Hepburn,' and 'God help the man who falls in love with you. He's never going to be the same again. I know I haven't been since the day I met you.'"

Tears as fat as pearls slid down her mom's face, leaving pale streaks behind. Olive stood and handed her a damp washcloth. Her mom pressed the washcloth to her face. It was so silent in the bathroom that Olive could hear the gravelly sound of wheels on the sidewalk outside. The maid with her cart, probably, arriving to clean the bungalow next door.

Olive's anger and indignation were slowly seeping out of her like air from a leaky beach ball. Her mom, Kathy Watson, née Rogers, soon to be Kathy Matheson, was—surprise!—a fallible human being, just like Olive. Her patience, her generosity, her unconditional love—all of those qualities coexisted with less worthy ones. With secrets. Olive wished she had known this last year when she and Phil had broken up. Maybe it would have lessened her self-loathing.

"I'm sorry, Mom. I'm sorry for making you talk about this on your wedding day."

"It's actually a relief to have finally told someone. It was eating away at me. But I'm sorry if what I did hurt you." Her mom's voice was muffled by the washcloth. She removed it; under the fluorescent lights, her face was a smeared mosaic of pink, white, and beige. "Did I ruin it?"

Olive didn't know if she was referring to their relationship or her makeup. "Let's go out to the patio," she said. "The natural lighting will be better, and we've got only twenty minutes now to get you ready."

Red and purple tropical flowers hung over the edge of the roof and wound their way through the decorative wooden brackets. Olive's mom sat in one of the rattan chairs, and Olive dumped the necessary tubes and bottles on the table. She swiftly reapplied the foundation, covering up the evidence of her mom's tears, and brushed on a rosy, blushing glow, fit for a bride.

"It's so strange, isn't it? You helping me get ready for my wedding. Not the natural order of things."

"Blue, gray, silver, or um, silver-gray?" Olive asked, showing her the squares of eye shadow.

"Silver-gray." She obediently closed her eyes so Olive could dust the eye shadow over their lids. "I'm sorry. I didn't mean to sound like one of those pushy moms who's always nagging her daughter about weddings and grandchildren."

"It's okay," Olive said. "Please don't say anything, but Phil proposed in February."

Her mom opened her eyes and blinked a few times, sparkles of eye shadow raining from her lashes. She seemed to be thinking hard about something, and Olive knew she was probably remembering the engagement announcement dinner in March and how Olive had blown off her concerns about her relationship with Phil then. "You turned him down?" she asked softly, comprehension dawning on her face.

"I wanted to say yes, but I couldn't." Olive passed a tube of pearly pink lipstick to her mom.

She didn't ask why. She held the lipstick distractedly in her fist, like she wasn't sure what to do with it. Then she leaped from her chair and enfolded Olive in the large, white arms of the hotel bathrobe. "Oh, honey."

Olive let herself be enveloped, giving in to her mom's love. Her body relaxed. She pressed her nose against her mom's shoulder, which smelled like bleach and felt scratchy. Barefoot, they were the exact same height.

"We're cut from the same cloth, you and I," her mom murmured into her ear. "Always dwelling on the past. Always second-guessing every single decision." She stroked Olive's hair. "But sometimes you just need to dive headfirst into the water."

But you don't know what I've done, Olive wanted to say. *You don't know how I hurt Phil last year and how he wasn't able to forgive me. And even though I've been given a second chance, my mistake just won't go away, and I can't not tell him like you didn't tell Dad, because it's so important to me that he forgives me this time, that he understands, and that we can live our lives together without secrets. Even if I don't tell him, I'm so scared that I'll screw up again in some way and he'll cast me off. He's been through so much with his dad, and if I let him down, too . . . It's just too much pressure sometimes. And this second chance? Isn't it so that I can fix my impulsive behaviors from last year, the times I "dove in headfirst"? I can't afford to give up my control now.*

Olive pulled away so she could see her mom's face. She was riveted by the beauty and light there; it was like seeing her for the first time. And she realized that even though her mom didn't know about her repeat year or the one-night stand, she understood Olive's fears and worries all the same. Cut from the same cloth, Olive thought. Maybe she was right.

Olive heard hurried footsteps approaching and turned to see Verona clattering up the path in stilettos, three bouquets of flowers in her arms.

"We've got ten minutes to go!" Verona called out to them. "Everyone's there. Even the officiant. You're not dressed?"

"We're a lot further along than we look," Olive replied. She crouched down and retrieved the lipstick, which had rolled under the table. She gave it to her mom. "Put this on in the bathroom. I'll help you with your dress."

Her mom gave her a wide-eyed look and disappeared inside.

"What did you say to her?" Verona asked. "Did she change her mind?"

"No, of course not. The wedding's on. We were just talking and lost track of time."

Verona gave her a disapproving look and set the bouquets on the rattan chair. Olive didn't have time for her disapproval. She rushed into the bungalow, where her mom was just emerging from the bathroom in her dress. The dress was light and gauzy, calf length with a deep V-neck and flowing sleeves like butterfly wings. Her brown hair sailed behind her like its own wedding veil.

"Zip me up?" she asked Olive. "I don't want to be late. I don't want Harry to think I'm standing him up."

She grabbed the beaded handbag on the nightstand and flew to the door.

"Wait," Olive cried. "Your hair. The gardenia." She dug in her own purse for the clear plastic box Rowena had given her this morning; inside was the delicate white flower.

Her mom stood still for her in the doorway. Olive tied her mom's hair back and gently pinned the gardenia's petals in place.

"Beautiful," she said. "You're beautiful."

They were all waiting for them on the beach. Harry in his white linen, Christopher out of place in a dark suit coat and tie, Phil in a green polo shirt that matched the color of the ocean. The officiant stood underneath a bamboo archway draped with organza. It was the same image emblazoned into her memory—except for Phil's added presence—but it looked very different. Olive took her place on the warm sand by her mom's side.

Chapter 16

"A flat-screen TV would look great on that wall," Phil said, spreading his arms out to the size of the imagined TV. He stood in a totally beige living room.

"We don't have a flat-screen TV," Olive said with a laugh. She pulled a pen and notebook from her handbag.

"Not yet. But if the genius of the place requires it . . ." He came up behind her and kissed her neck. She reached around and caught his lips with hers.

"But we haven't decided on this place yet." This was the fourth condo they had looked at today. Olive had to work in an hour, and she was already feeling burned out. "You don't like that there's only a one-car garage, there's not enough cabinet space in the kitchen for my liking, and we both thought the window in the shower was creepy."

"But I like it better than any of the others we saw today. It has more *character*. And it's definitely closer to our price range."

"You just like the gym and tennis courts." She tapped her pen against the chart she'd made in her notebook, outlining the pros and cons of each condo they'd looked at.

"That may have swayed my opinion somewhat."

"Well, we don't have to pick just from the condos we saw today. And we definitely don't have to decide this minute. We have plenty of time." She closed the notebook and returned it to her handbag.

Plenty of time. It was late August, and Olive and Kerrigan's lease on the upper flat of the pink house didn't expire until the end of September, and Phil had his place until mid-October. Not that Kerrigan knew Phil and Olive were looking at condos. Olive had had several opportunities to tell her friend that she and Phil were planning to move in together, but every time the moment presented itself, she got cold feet. The promise she'd made to Kerrigan haunted her. *You don't see me going anywhere, do you? I'm not moving out.*

She rationalized this in many different ways. She wanted to protect Kerrigan from the news until she had some kind of solution for Kerrigan's living situation. She didn't know what this might be. The ideal roommate to take her place? A cute, affordable apartment in the downtown high-rises that Kerrigan had always admired? A condo in the same neighborhood as—or better yet, right next door to—Olive and Phil's?

And when it came right down to it, would Kerrigan really feel betrayed? Moving out was natural, a part of growing up. They were both twenty-five years old, after all, and had lived together for the past seven years. It seemed unlikely that Kerrigan would expect this to go on much longer. Last year Olive had moved out because she needed a change and wanted to be more mature; she could see how Kerrigan would have found this hurtful or insulting. But this year she was moving out because her relationship with Phil was getting more serious. It should be a happy occasion—a celebration of the next step of her life. Surely Kerrigan would understand that and want the best for her friend, especially since Olive wanted the same for her.

Yet even this line of reasoning couldn't dispel Olive's guilt. She kept imagining Kerrigan's misery when she'd found out 2011 held nothing for her to look forward to. Or even worse, when she'd found out that she and Olive had drifted apart as friends last year. But Olive refused to let their friendship dissolve this year. She would make Kerrigan a priority even if they weren't living together. She would prevent the injury she had caused her friend last year.

All of this back and forth wouldn't have been worth it if it weren't for Phil. When Olive had first mentioned the idea, as they lay in his bed and she bemoaned the fact that she still had to drive home and change for work, Phil's eyes had lit up with boyish excitement. And the more they talked about it, the more enthusiastic she became. She envisioned painting the walls together, breakfast in bed, playing with Cashew in their own yard, and best of all, coming home and crawling into bed beside him every morning. It was one step closer to marriage. It was a commitment that wasn't as hard for her conscience to say yes to. And living together would give her more chances to observe Phil, study his mood, and pick the perfect time and way to tell him the whole truth. Or some of the truth, a little at a time, so as not to overwhelm him. She needed him to know and accept her for who she was, flaws and all, before they could progress to the next step in their relationship. The prospect of creating a home together made this task seem less insurmountable somehow.

The real estate agent, evidently hearing a concluding note in Olive's voice, chose that moment to wander back into the living room. "Any other questions I can answer?" she asked. She halfheartedly gave them her card, as if sensing they wouldn't be calling.

Phil dropped Olive off at her apartment so she could change into her scrubs. She walked around to the driver's side to kiss him good-bye. His arm rested outside the window, revealing the golfer's tan lines that were so common for him at this time of the year. His hand was paler than the rest of his arm, as if he were still wearing his golf glove. Suddenly, she felt overwhelmed by how much she cherished each of these little details. His funny tan lines, the dark freckle under his left eye, the Mickey Mouse boxers she knew he was wearing because he was running low on clean clothes and desperately needed to do laundry.

She grabbed his face with both hands, drawing him closer to her, catching him off guard, and kissing him deeply. He responded in kind, nearly pulling her through the car window.

"Wow. What was that for?" he asked breathlessly.

She kissed the back of his hand. "I love you."

"I love you, too," he said, "and I can't wait until we live together."

Kerrigan wasn't home, but Olive felt dishonest as she let herself into their apartment, as if it were a place in which she already didn't belong. She guiltily removed the notebook from her handbag and slid it facedown into one of her desk drawers. She knew this was probably childish and unnecessary, but she didn't want Kerrigan finding out the wrong way and before she was ready.

As she dressed in a pair of pink scrubs and tied her hair up in a high ponytail, she listened to her voice mail messages on speakerphone. The first two were from real estate agents returning her call. The third was from her mom, who sounded distraught. For a split second, Olive wondered if she and Harry had had a fight.

"Olive. How could you not tell me? Sherry Witan and I did lunch today. That poor woman. You know her mother died of ovarian cancer? I just feel so awful. Here I've been enjoying myself these past few months, and she's been suffering all alone. If you'd only told me. Even if she wanted her privacy and wasn't feeling up to visitors, I could've at least been praying for her. Call me back when you get a chance so I can scold you properly. Also we want to invite you and Phil to our Labor Day picnic."

Relief washed over her. It didn't bother her that her mom was annoyed, because she knew that a quick explanation of patient confidentiality would convince her that Olive couldn't have done otherwise. Instead, now that Olive's mom knew about Sherry's breast cancer, her burden was lessened. Her mom would know how to console and encourage Sherry in a way that Olive couldn't. Sherry would listen to her. Olive had tried calling Sherry twice since she'd been back from St. Lucia, and neither time had Sherry called her back. Olive speculated that she was either too sick or still too mad at her to pick up the phone. At least now she could get an update on Sherry's health from her mom.

The ICU was louder than usual when she arrived, but she quickly realized that just one man was making all the ruckus.

A heavyset, dark-haired man in his sixties was arguing with Tina at the nurses' station. He gesticulated wildly, yet Tina, who was only half his size, stood her ground.

"I'm sorry, Mr. Dodge. Visiting hours aren't until eight o'clock. Hospital rules. You can come back and see your brother then."

Mr. Dodge snarled something unintelligible and tried to go around the desk.

"Mr. Dodge! The waiting room is that way! And if you don't listen to me, then I'll have to call security and have you removed."

Hangdog, the large man turned around and retreated to the waiting room, mumbling under his breath the whole way. As he passed Olive, she caught a strong whiff of alcohol.

"Let me guess," she said to Tina. "He's related to one of my patients?" The truth was she remembered Frank Dodge and his ill brother, Ed. They were a pretty memorable pair. Ed had cirrhosis of the liver, and Frank had shown up drunk and insisted that all good old Ed needed to make him feel better was a tumbler or two of Scotch.

Tina nodded. "This always happens. First it looks like it's going to be a slow night—we're under capacity, only eight beds full—and then some basket case comes in to make things complicated." She grinned and handed her two clipboards. "But now he's your problem."

Olive tucked the clipboards under her arm and set off to check on her patients. Sometimes she wished this whole repeat year thing had a fast-forward button. There were moments in her life that just didn't seem worth reliving; there was nothing she needed to change, nothing new to learn, nothing more to gain. She was worn out from her day of condo hunting with Phil and didn't know if she was up to the Dodge brothers tonight.

Ed Dodge had a reddish nose shaped like a summer squash. His hairy arms were speckled with purple, spidery lesions. He was hooked up to everything but the ventilator. She skimmed through his chart before she took his vital signs. He'd gone through a battery of blood tests to measure his clotting factors and liver function markers to see how advanced his cirrhosis was. Fluid had collected in his abdomen, which had led to a pretty serious bacterial infection. There was an important note here. He was allergic to penicillin, and his cirrhosis had made him very sensitive to a lot of other drugs and their side effects.

The drug allergy note tickled something deep and forgotten in her brain. Not something to do with Ed but another patient. She stared at the scrawled word *penicillin* for a long moment. Suddenly, the memory was jarred loose. A patient with a morphine allergy: a young man who'd been in a rollover accident. Not her patient, but Tina's. There had been no note of any drug allergies—no MedicAlert bracelet or pendant, no card in his wallet. But after the morphine had been administered, he had gone into anaphylactic shock. The shot of epinephrine had been too little, too late; he had died only minutes later.

Now here was a chance for Olive to make a difference in this year; she could save the life of someone who had wrongfully died. While she didn't know how critical the young man's injuries had been, she did know he had a one hundred percent better chance of recovering if the lethal morphine was not given to him. She could be responsible for totally changing the outcome of 2011 for someone.

If only she knew when he had been brought in. She remembered only that his death had occurred in the fall, and of course, it happened on a night when both she and Tina were working. That didn't narrow it down much. She would have to be vigilant.

She watched the rise and fall of Ed's massive chest and counted his respirations. Twenty breaths per minute wasn't bad. She jotted the number down and then almost dropped her pen when she saw Alex looking through the window at her.

He leaned against the doorway. "Didn't mean to startle you. I wanted to ask you to tell me when Mr. Dodge wakes up. He needs to meet with a hepatologist to get the evaluation process started for a liver transplant."

"Oh. Of course." She had suspected Ed's liver was totally shot, but no one had told her he was trying to get on the transplant list. It was hard for a person of his age with his habits to get on the national list.

He read her expression. "Yeah, I don't think his chances are good, either. A sixty-eight-year-old chronic alcoholic? They'd be crazy to give him another liver to ruin."

"Actually, I disagree. It's a slippery slope, isn't it? Deciding whose life is more valuable? Whose life is worth saving?" She looked up from her clipboard.

Alex gazed intently at her. "I know what you mean because I once thought that, too. But there's a limited supply of organs, and they have to decide somehow, right? And shouldn't they go to the people who have the best chance of making a full recovery and having long, healthy lives?" He tugged on the ends of his stethoscope, which was draped around his neck. "Let me give you a scenario. A little girl born with biliary atresia or an elderly man who's destroyed his liver from years of drinking?"

She jotted down Ed's oxygen saturation levels and closed his chart. "I took an ethics course, too. I get it. It's just . . . well, alcoholism is a disease, too." She pushed past him lightly to get to her next patient's room.

He followed her. She didn't understand his persistence. Since their chance encounter at Heureux Hasard in April, Olive had doubled, no—tripled her guard. Her behavior toward him was brisk and professional, sometimes bordering on cold and rude, and whenever she found the opportunity, she mentioned her *boyfriend*. She even spoke her mind and disagreed with him more than she had last year, less wowed this time by his white coat and years of medical school.

And still there was something between them. A hidden, illicit past that Olive wanted to repress and Alex seemed to want to uncover. It was like there were magnetic forces at play: Olive repelling, Alex attracting. He mentioned nights he and his friends would be at the little French bar or Concerts on the Square with a picnic blanket and bottles of wine and suggested she drop by. She never did. After some of their overnight shifts, he proposed they go out for coffee and pancakes. She pleaded fatigue. Still he refused to get the picture.

"I didn't mean to offend you," he said.

"You didn't." She stopped just outside her other patient's room.

"Does alcoholism run in your family?" he asked. He was standing close, too close. She could see the day-old stubble, like a smattering of cinnamon and sugar, sprinkled across his face. She could smell his laundry detergent, an almost citrusy scent.

"What? No, but—" She stopped herself and took an awkward step backward.

"I'm sorry. That's a really personal question. I shouldn't have asked. I just thought, judging by your reaction, that someone you love might have a drinking problem. But it's clearly none of my business." He folded his stethoscope in half and slid it into his white coat pocket. "I'm sorry," he repeated. "You can see why I'm not in family practice, though. I could never deal with all the noncompliance issues. People refusing to lose weight, quit smoking, or take care of themselves in general."

Olive understood. But she also understood that knowing what was good for you and following through were two totally different things. She turned around and took a step toward her patient's room, on the threshold now.

"You remember my friend Anoop?" Alex asked, willfully ignoring her efforts to escape. "The internal medicine second-year?"

She grudgingly turned her head toward him. Yes, she did. The kind, thoughtful one. The non-nump.

"Well, he might be dropping out of his residency here for similar reasons. The arguing with the patients, seeing them slowly kill themselves . . . I think he's going to apply for a dermatology residency next year."

"Can you do that?" Olive asked. The whole med school–residency–licensing exams pathway seemed so strict and narrow to her, allowing no divergences or last-minute changes of heart.

"Well, it's not recommended, of course," Alex said. "And he's going to take a lot of flack for it. But this is his life, his career. And if he chose the wrong one, better to suck it up now than live his whole life doing something he hates."

Olive tucked a strand of hair behind her ear and tightened her ponytail holder. "That's very brave of him."

Alex nodded. "You should talk to him about it. I'm having a little cookout at my parents' lake house for Labor Day, and Anoop will definitely be there. You should come."

"Thanks, but I already promised my mom I'd come to her picnic." God bless her mom for giving her a ready alibi.

"Too bad. Well, some other time, then. They live on Nagawicka Lake in Delafield, and they have a pontoon boat and—"

"Watson!" Tina called. "You have a visitor!"

Olive had never been more grateful to hear Tina's bossy voice. She looked from Alex to her patient's room quickly, held up one finger, and then hurried to the nurses' station.

She was surprised to see Phil. She'd been expecting her mom or maybe even Sherry. He looked out of place under the fluorescent lights, like an actor who had wandered onto the wrong set. Phil rarely visited her at work. He didn't like hospitals. He couldn't bear to be around the ICU patients, who to him all seemed to be on their death beds. The proximity of all that pain and illness suffocated him. He didn't understand how she could endure it.

"He brought us burritos," Tina said, holding up a white paper bag. "He even brought me a vegetarian one."

Olive knew Phil had included Tina in his generosity because he wanted to keep her impressed. Tina thought Phil was a phenomenal catch. She always referred to him as a "hunk" or a "hottie." The irony of his ostensibly geeky job teaching high school physics tickled her, and whenever Olive recounted Phil's romantic surprises, Tina would remark, "My ex-husband never did that mushy stuff for me even when we first met, and you guys have been together for ages. He's a keeper, all right."

"Aw, thank you," Olive said and hugged him. He smelled like his usual woodsy soap with a hint of fresh cilantro. "That was very thoughtful." It felt surreal for him to be here; it was like her personal life and work life, two very separate and distinct spheres, were suddenly merging.

"Did I come at a bad time?" Phil asked. He was looking over her shoulder. Olive turned to see Alex walking toward them. Her heart stopped.

"It's never a bad time for burritos," Tina said, unwrapping hers.

"I just need a few minutes to finish up with a patient, and then I'll have more time," Olive said. She left her hand on his arm, worried that if she moved it, he would somehow disappear.

Alex had a large smile on his face as he strode to the nurses' station, and she felt sick to her stomach. She tried to relax, act casual. After all, she and Alex were guilty of nothing. This year. Still, she didn't want Phil anywhere near Alex. She didn't want him to have to unknowingly shake the hand of someone with whom she had betrayed him. She felt like such a hideous person.

"Phil, I don't think you've met Dr. Carpenter. He's one of our new residents this year. Alex, this is my boyfriend, Phil." She was amazed at how calm her voice sounded. The ease with which she deceived them appalled her.

Phil smiled his charming smile and shook Alex's hand. Tina stopped eating and watched with interest. The two men sized each other up but not in an unfriendly way. Alex was slightly taller than Phil, but Phil had a more muscular build.

"It's nice to meet you, Phil," Alex said, and then swiftly turned his attention to Tina. "Did those X-rays come back on Mrs. Litschke yet?"

"Do you think I'm hiding them in my pants?" Tina asked. "You'll be the first to know when they arrive. I promise." She took a large bite of her burrito.

So that was his cover story for coming over here. He was curious about her boyfriend, but he didn't want to seem curious. He glowered at Tina and then avoided looking at Olive and Phil as he self-importantly dashed off.

Phil raised his eyebrow at Olive. She didn't know how to interpret this. Was it in reference to Olive working with a young, handsome doctor who she'd never mentioned? Or in reference to Alex's obvious slight to him? Or maybe he was simply amused by Tina's irreverence?

She tried to smile at him. "I'll be right back," she said. "Wait right here."

The air felt very close and thin. Phil and Alex in the same space together, and Frank Dodge on his way back to the ICU any minute now. She entered the room of her other patient—Irma Vanderburgh, an elderly woman with congestive heart failure—and tried to match her breathing to the slow, steady whooshes of the ventilator. The old woman's powdery, brittle-looking skin and bony forehead reminded her of Betty Gardner. And Betty Gardner reminded her of Alex. And the Family Room.

Olive easily encircled her patient's delicate wrist with her fingers and counted her pulse. Soft like the beating wings of a sparrow. How could she have ever thought moving in with

Phil would make it easier to tell him the truth? It would *never* be easy to tell him. *But was it really necessary?* a small voice asked her. She had set up these rigid rules for herself, but this wasn't a rigid, rule-following universe she was living in now, was it?

"Hang in there, Mrs. Vanderburgh," she murmured as she tucked the blanket around her emaciated form.

Phil was leaning against the counter, paging through a packet when she returned. His white golf shirt nicely contrasted with his lingering tan. *Weren't some things left better unsaid?* she pleaded with her conscience. Weren't little white lies sometimes necessary to make a relationship work? Maybe not white lies exactly, but pale gray lies. Lies of omission when the situation was the furthest thing from black and white.

"What is that?" she asked him, feeling paranoid.

He had a gleam in his eye. His face was so open, so earnest. There were no secrets or doubts there. He completely trusted her. He suspected nothing. This was almost more painful than if he'd narrowed his eyebrows at her and sneered, *Is there something going on between you and that doctor?*

"I found the perfect place for us," he said. "I don't know how we missed it before. Two bedrooms, a full bath and a half bath, a two-car garage, a full-size washer and dryer, a gas fireplace, vaulted ceilings in the living room, tons of closet space, a pool, tennis courts, and a gym, *and* it's in our price range." He handed her the packet. "I printed this from their website."

"What's the catch?" she asked with a smile. She looked down at the paperwork. High Pointe Hills Condominiums. It was where she had lived last year. In their preliminary searching, she had intentionally kept it off their list. How could she possibly start somewhere fresh with Phil in a place like this? In a place where she and Alex had been together? In a place where she'd dallied and messed up her life last year?

"No," she said, shaking her head. "We can't live here."

"Why not? It fills all your requirements. It goes above and beyond your requirements. And if you think it's too much, it's not. Look at the last page. We could make those numbers work with our budget."

Without flipping through it, Olive handed the packet back. "No, it's not that. I've heard really bad things about this place. I knew someone who lived there. She said it was . . . awful."

"Really? What was so bad about it?" Phil was clearly disappointed.

"Oh, lots of things." She struggled to think of her own complaints about the condo, but they were very limited. It had actually been a very nice place to live. "There were all these hidden condo association fees that nobody told her about. And the neighbors were really unfriendly." Phil didn't look persuaded yet, so she continued with something she knew would concern him. "She said after she'd been living there for a while, everything started falling apart. Really shoddy materials and workmanship."

Phil rolled the packet into a tube. "Would you at least check it out with me? Maybe it was just this girl's experience with her unit. It looks really nice to me."

"I think it would be a waste of time, but if you really want to . . ."

His excitement had dissipated. She now understood why

he'd come to visit. To bring her dinner, yes, but also to share his good news and enthusiasm with her. He thought he'd found the ideal condo for them, and she'd just dashed his hopes. She had let him down, but there was no way of remedying this. She couldn't live at High Pointe Hills again.

"Back to the drawing board, then," he said, tightening the tube in his hands.

"I'm sorry, honey."

"It's okay. Well, I should probably get going. I know you're busy. I hadn't planned on sticking around this long."

She wished she could tell him to stay, but she had patients she was neglecting, and his presence in the ICU was really throwing her off.

"Thanks so much for visiting. I'm really looking forward to eating that burrito when I get a free moment."

"You're welcome." He gave her a peck on the cheek. "Have a good night."

"Phil?" she called after him. "We're going to find something soon. Something even better than that place. I promise."

He gave her a halfhearted grin.

Frank Dodge was stumbling through the doors as Phil headed out. Phil stopped in his tracks and turned to watch Frank's weaving progress. Instead of going to the waiting room, it appeared that Frank had decided to spend his time drinking at a bar. His face was red and sweaty, and it looked like he was going to collapse into a heap at any moment.

"I'm back. You can't throw me out now!" he crowed. He leaned across the counter so that his face was only inches from Olive's. The stench of his breath was overpowering. "I'm within my rights. Visiting hours."

"Hey now," Phil said, and strode to the nurses' station. "Why don't you back up a step there, buddy?"

Frank spun crazily to face him. "Don't tell me what to do. I'm within my rights."

"It's okay, Phil. He's harmless. He's here to see a patient," Olive quietly explained.

"I don't like how he's treating you. And it's clear he's drunk. How do you know he's harmless?" Phil put himself between Frank and Olive at her desk.

"Don't you call me a drunk. I have my rights just like anyone," Frank slurred. He raised one of his fists and shook it at Phil.

Phil's eyes widened. He threw up his hands at Olive. "This is harmless? You want me to leave you alone with this man?"

"Phil, you're making things worse. Just go. Nothing's going to happen. But even if anything did happen, I can call security."

"Don't you goddamn call security," Frank said. "I'm within my rights. The gal said to come back at eight o'clock."

"Nobody's calling security, Mr. Dodge," Olive said soothingly. "Do you want to see your brother now? Calm down, and I'll take you to him."

Phil looked betrayed. He scrutinized Frank's every move as if the drunk man might strike Olive at any moment. She knew he wasn't seeing Frank. He was seeing his father.

Olive led Frank around the nurses' station to his brother's room. She looked back and gave Phil a reassuring wave. He crossed his arms.

"Aw, Ed, you look like hell," Frank said when they entered the room. He shuffled to the bedside and then seemed too scared to touch his brother, who was covered from head to toe with wires and tubes. Now that he was finally in the room, he didn't seem to know what to do. He clutched the guardrail of the bed.

"Would you like to sit down, Mr. Dodge?" she asked, and gestured toward a chair next to the bed.

Once he was seated, all the fire died out of him. His imposing body folded inward on itself.

"Do you have any questions about your brother's health?" she asked.

"I know that it's his liver and the drink that done it. Is he going to make it?" he whispered hoarsely, as if he didn't want Ed to hear him.

Olive smoothed Ed's pillow. "He's very sick, Mr. Dodge. The damage to his liver can't be reversed. But if he stops drinking and with the proper medication and an improved diet, it may be controlled for a few more years." She didn't mention the transplant list because she didn't want to raise his hopes for something she was almost certain would not happen.

Frank leaned back in his chair and closed his eyes. Relaxed, his face looked very similar to his brother's. Same summer squash nose, same unruly eyebrows and full lips. She wondered if he was imagining a similar fate for himself.

She stayed longer than she should have, fiddling with Ed's IV. She didn't want to bump into Alex again, and there was something so peaceful about being in a room with two grown men, who were otherwise so boisterous and disruptive, fast asleep like tuckered-out toddlers.

In his sleep, Frank twitched his scruffy head like a dog. Beneath his reddish eyelids, his eyes tracked back and forth rapidly. He moaned something, and his lips opened just enough for Olive to make out the words. "I'm sorry," he moaned. "I can't." And then again and again, slightly more gargled and desperate each time. "I'm sorry I can't I'm sorry I'm sorry I can't I'm sorry I'm sorry I'm sorry I can't I can't."

Olive pressed her palm over her eyes and ducked out of the room.

Phil had left. Had he gone immediately or had he waited to see if Frank would cause any trouble? She walked around the ICU, which was shaped like half of a circle. Tina was pushing meds. Christine was sitting at her computer, monitoring the telemetry on her patients and drinking a cup of coffee. She smiled and said hello to Olive. Kevin was talking to a family with small children in his patient's room. But many of the beds were empty, and while Olive knew this was a good thing, the dark rooms made the ICU feel bereft.

She came back to the point where she had started and sat down at her computer station. Frank was now snoring loudly. From her perch, she could also hear a chorus of steady beeps that filled the ICU. Machines working to regulate hearts and lungs. A constant cacophony reporting back the most secret workings of organs. Normally in such a moment, she felt like the grand conductor of those whirring, clicking, beeping, whooshing machines. Now she felt only Phil's absence. She longed to call him back and have him simply listen to that dissonant orchestra of life. Perhaps then he would understand.

A hand cupped her shoulder, and she nearly leaped from her stool. Alex? Phil? But it was Tina, holding out the white paper bag. "You should eat," she said.

"Thanks." Olive set the bag on the desk but didn't open it.

"So what do you think?"

For a moment, Olive thought Tina was psychic and could read all her innermost thoughts, but then she noticed Tina was gazing into Ed Dodge's room with a tiny smirk. Tina was playing their game.

"Definitely a boxer, when he was in his prime," Olive started, keeping her voice low in case Frank woke up. "They called him The Great Dodger. But he turned to the bottle when his wife left him for his biggest rival." She immediately regretted this last speculation, wondering if it maybe contained a kernel of truth.

"Bah, is that all you've got? I'm pretty sure my lady in bed seven is the second cousin of the Duchess of Kent. You should've seen the sapphire studs she came in with, and when I overheard her daughter talking to Dr. Dominguez, she clearly had a British accent." Tina was obsessed with the royal family and suspected at least a third of her patients of having connections of varying degrees to the throne.

Olive attempted a laugh. "Sounds likely."

Tina turned to leave but stopped abruptly. "Look, Watson, it's none of my business, but—" She put her hands on her hips, her face warring between fierceness and a look of apology. "He's a good guy, Phil. Don't let him get away."

Chapter 17

Olive's African violet looked sickly. It wasn't blooming, and small brown spots flecked the leaves. She wasn't doing a very good job of keeping her promise; she would have to water it first thing when she got to the condo and then find a window with good sun exposure for it. She placed the plant in a shoebox without a lid, carried it out to her SUV, and set it on the passenger seat. She stood there for a moment, hands on hips, wondering what she had done on this day last year.

By October, her life had been on a totally different trajectory. No Phil, no Kerrigan. Even her relationship with her mom had been stretched thin. She had had her job and her condo; it was clear to her now that she hadn't had much more. It made her light-headed to think, *what if?* What if she hadn't been given this chance to repeat the year? What if she'd continued on her set path, isolating herself more and more from the people she loved? Her whole life would have been tragically different.

And although she wasn't diving in headfirst as her mom had recommended, moving in with Phil at least felt like getting her feet wet. She was trying to be brave. She was trying to be happy. But sometimes it was hard to trust her good fortune. She felt like she was on a whirling carnival ride, waiting for the floor to drop out from under her. And for some reason, every step she took forward with Phil seemed to leave Kerrigan a little further behind.

"I don't know if this pizza cutter is yours or mine," Kerrigan said, as Olive reentered the apartment. She was helping Olive pack by sorting through their hodgepodge of kitchen items, which had mingled together over the years. Cardboard boxes and plastic tubs were stacked everywhere; the whole apartment looked like a rummage sale in progress.

"I think it's mine. But you can have it because—" Olive cut herself off. She had been about to say, *Phil already has one*, but something stopped her. "You use it more than me," she concluded.

"Thanks," Kerrigan said, and dropped the pizza cutter into a rectangular container. She rubbed her temples and yawned hugely, looking like a cat revealing the ridged roof of its mouth. "Ugh. I feel like a fire truck ran over my head."

"A fire truck, huh?" Olive had heard Kerrigan stumble in around four this morning and had been surprised when she dragged herself from bed at eleven to offer her assistance. "How long have I been telling you to drink a couple of glasses of water before you go to bed? Alcohol dehydrates you terribly. Hence the hangover."

"And how long have I been telling you that drinking even more at that point makes my stomach feel all sloshy? And there was that one time I wet the bed . . . yuck. It's not worth it." Kerrigan held up another cooking utensil. "I don't even know what this is, so it must be yours."

"It's a lemon zester. I think it came as part of a set. You can put that in the Goodwill pile. I've never used it." Olive sat on one of the bar stools. She peered into a box on the stool next to her. Kerrigan had carefully wrapped all her glasses and plates in paper towels. "Thank you so much for doing this. I was really running out of steam."

"Sure." Kerrigan kept her eyes on the jumble of whisks, spatulas, and wooden spoons in front of her. "I'm thinking of it as a kind of inventory, you know? An opportunity to take stock of everything before I make my next move."

Kerrigan had already donated three boxes of purses, shoes, and University of Wisconsin clothing and paraphernalia to Goodwill, but Olive understood she meant taking stock of more than just handbags and cutlery. "Have you decided what you're going to do yet?" she asked, with what she hoped sounded like an air of nonchalance.

"I've given up trying to find another roommate just for the sake of staying in this place, that's for sure. I mean, look at it!" She gestured to the cheap metal cupboards painted brown to look like wood, the bare bulb with no light fixture covering it, the scratched and peeling pink linoleum. "It's a total shithole. What possessed us to stay here for all these years?"

"We were too lazy to move?" Olive ventured, but she knew the real reason. It wasn't the apartment that mattered. It was the home that she and Kerrigan had made together. "Listen, my offer's still on the table. I'd be happy to contribute to the rent until you can find another place to move. It could take a while in this town."

"Your money's no good here anymore." Kerrigan's tone was playful, but her eyes were bloodshot and solemn. She massaged her forehead vigorously. "What do you think? Hair of the dog that bit me?" She opened the fridge and retrieved a bottle of beer.

"Some orange juice would be better. Maybe you should go back to bed and get some rest if you're not feeling up to this."

"Not feeling up to helping my best friend move?" She took a swig of beer and rifled through a half-filled box. She held up a white coffee mug and turned it around so Olive could read the familiar message in black type. YOU ARE DUMB.

Olive laughed. "Do you remember who originally bought that? Didn't Robin buy it for you as a gag gift for your twenty-first birthday? Or maybe Alistair bought it for me?"

"I don't think it matters now. What matters is who gets to keep it. Who do you think needs it as a reminder more?" Kerrigan's hands fluttered around the mug, displaying it like a game show prize to be won. "Me for making my same old mistakes and never learning? Or you for hiding from every mistake you've made and ever could make?"

Olive leaned forward on her stool, and it gave a disconcerting wobble. It was the one with the loose leg, the one she'd been meaning to report to their landlord but kept forgetting. She stood up. "Kerrigan, I'm sorry. I know I kind of promised you that I wouldn't be moving out anytime soon, and I know it's been a rough couple of weeks for both of us. I'm sorry if you think I'm being hypocritical—"

"Don't bother saying you're sorry unless it's sincere. I'm not in the mood for another lecture disguised as an apology." Kerrigan set the coffee cup down in exchange for her beer.

Olive knew Kerrigan was referring to last weekend, when

Olive had come home from work in the early hours of the morning to find a half-dressed teenage boy smoking in their bathroom. Dark-skinned with black hair and full, perfect eyebrows: Kerrigan's office crush. They had argued about him.

"Six years' age difference is not that big of a deal. You act like he's not legal," Kerrigan had said.

"Nineteen and twenty-five is a world apart. Think of yourself at nineteen. And boys are even less mature!"

"Just say what I know you're thinking. You think I'm loose. You think I'll bring anyone home."

"Of course not! I would never think that about you, and I'm sorry if you think that. I'm not trying to judge. I'm just worried, is all."

"If you're worried about his feelings, don't be. He knows this isn't a relationship."

"And what about your feelings? Do you think this is healthy for you? Where is this coming from, Kerrigan? Is it because I'm moving out?"

Kerrigan had whirled around to face her with the terrible force of a tornado. "Contrary to what you think, Olive, not everything is always about *you*."

"I know that. I just thought that— Never mind. But what if your coworkers find out? What if he spills the beans? You'll get fired."

"Oh, I forgot I was the only one who ever had an affair with a coworker," Kerrigan had taunted, and this had ended their conversation. But Olive hadn't seen the boy at their apartment since.

She walked around the kitchen counter. "I am sincerely sorry that I've hurt you. I guess I earned that mug."

Kerrigan handed it to her. "Don't you forget it. You know,

Olive, I'm not a naïve child who thought we would live together until we were little old ladies wearing dentures and Depends. I knew it was only a matter of time until you and Phil wised up and moved in together. I just thought the circumstances would be a little different when it happened." She let out a world-weary sigh.

"I know. But we'll still be best friends. And it's a brand-new start for both of us."

"Sure it is." Kerrigan looked like she was going to say something more but changed her mind. She turned away and began sorting through the drawer of dish towels.

"I'm going to take another load to the condo. Do you want to come along?" Olive asked.

"No, thanks. I'm kind of on a roll. I think I'll stay here."

Olive's heart sank. In her mind's eye, she saw her friendship with Kerrigan getting packed away and shelved in some dusty corner, as it had last year. Stored like some object she was tired of or a gadget that had no practical purpose, instead of one of the most meaningful relationships in her life. While on the surface Kerrigan was doing all the things a good, supportive friend would, there was a razor-sharp bitterness just below her exterior. *You're hiding from every mistake you've made and ever could make.* Clearly it wasn't just the move that was upsetting her. Her self-destructive behavior and resentment of Olive had started earlier. It had started when Kerrigan found out about her repeat year. In her eyes, it must have seemed as if the universe had cast judgment on them: Olive had been singled out, Kerrigan had not. Olive wished she had never told her the truth.

Despite herself, she enjoyed the drive to the condo. It was a warm day, and she drove with her windows down. Some of the trees had already started changing color: russets and bronze, purples and scarlet. The sunlight and everything it touched had a golden quality. All her worries were carried out the window on a cross breeze. The moment was filled with pure and utter potential.

Brian's red pickup truck was parked in the driveway; the truck bed was empty except for a few ragged blankets. Brian and Jeff had been helping Phil move the heavy furniture all morning: bookcases, dressers, the oak entertainment center. She hurried inside to greet them—the African violet's pot balanced in one hand—and found that the condo was empty. Phil had left a note.

Went to get a game of Ultimate going at the Arb. Be back around 5:00. Love, Phil.

She walked through the house still carrying the African violet. The guys had moved the furniture pieces into their designated rooms and created a mountain of boxes in the otherwise empty dining room. The pile almost reached the dangling gold light fixture. It was too soon to feel like home, but there was something *right* about this place. Olive had felt it the first moment she and Phil crossed the threshold. They belonged here. It was almost as if the condo had been reserved specifically for them, and in a way, it had been. Phil had heard about the place through his principal, whose son and daughter-in-law had lived there and were moving to Boston for a job change. The condo, which wouldn't have lasted long on the market because of its convenient location in a well-to-do neighborhood, had never even been listed.

Her heels clicked on the hardwood floors, and the noise

reverberated off the bare walls. She set the African violet on the kitchen counter next to the sink and then opened the cabinets below. No watering can, of course. And no cups or glasses, either. She settled for turning the faucet on at a slow drip and letting the water trickle into the soil. The room with the best sunlight was the living room, but the windowsills weren't wide enough to hold the pot. She struggled to lift and maneuver one of the end tables to position it under the window. In the direct sunlight, her plant looked even more lackluster.

Her cell phone rang. She clattered through the rooms of the condo, trying to trace the amplified sound of her ring tone and remember where she'd dropped her purse. She found it, just in time, on top of one of the boxes in the dining room.

"Hello?" she answered, catching her breath.

"Hi," her mom said. "How's the move going?"

"Good. Most of the big furniture is in now. We're still packing up some of the minor things at my apartment. Books, knickknacks, kitchen stuff."

"Only you would consider kitchen stuff 'minor.' Well, let me know if you need an extra pair of hands packing or unpacking. I'd be happy to help."

"Thanks. What are you up to today?" Olive leaned against the window and watched a man walk his golden retriever down the street.

"I made banana bread this morning, and I'm taking some over to Sherry Witan's. It's her favorite."

"Sherry? When—right now?" Olive sat down on a tall box marked *DVDS ANIMAL HOUSE THRU GHOSTBUSTERS II*. Phil's collection.

"Yes. Would you like to come along?"

She hesitated. Sherry brought up a whirlwind of emotions: grief and frustration, sorrow and anger. Olive didn't understand how a grown woman could be so petty and immature. She'd walked away from Olive, shut the door on her, never returned her phone calls. All for suggesting she call her son? Olive had wanted to help Sherry through this year, the same way that Sherry had extended an offer of help and guidance. But then she had completely turned her back on Olive.

"Can I?" she asked in a small voice. In spite of all this, she still wanted to see her.

"Are you at the condo? I'll be there in fifteen minutes. Maybe you can give me the grand tour before we go?" She'd seen the condo briefly several weeks ago, when they'd been considering making an offer, but the previous owner's furniture had still been in place then.

Olive's mom arrived shortly, svelte and girlish in her batik-patterned dress. She had brought a loaf of banana bread for Olive and Phil, too. She embraced Olive and then stepped back to inspect the place. "Wow. It's bigger than I remember. Look at the crown molding! Is that a leaf pattern? You don't see that in most houses these days. And the fireplace is simply gorgeous. It really cleaned up well."

Olive grinned. She was especially proud of the cultured stone fireplace. It made her somehow think of both Frank Lloyd Wright and cozy winters in old farmhouses. "Let me show you the kitchen. There's so much cabinet space, we won't know what to do with it all."

Her mom followed closely behind, trailing her fingers over every surface and scrutinizing each room floor to ceiling as if she were touring a cathedral. She had only good things to say about every feature of the house, but her proclaimed favorite aspect of the condo was one Olive had nearly overlooked. The backyard was a hundred square feet of weed-infested grass hemmed in by tall trees. In both Phil and Olive's opinion, it was a less than ideal territory for Cashew, who was staying with Carol until they were officially settled in. There was no fence, and it was too small and close to the woods, where ticks lurked. But in the corner of the yard, nearly hidden by overgrown bushes and shade, was a crumbling stone "sweetheart bench," as Olive's mom called it.

"Oh, your dad would've loved this," she said, sitting down despite its damp, mossy appearance. "Your Grandpa and Grandma Watson had one of these in their garden. It was where we had our first kiss."

"Really?" Olive studied the bench and her mom with renewed interest.

"Yeah. We were seventeen, and what I remember most is all the mosquitoes. We went inside shortly thereafter, and I had bites everywhere. My ankles, the back of my hands, even my forehead. I was so itchy I had to go home."

She'd seen her parents' senior pictures, and she could imagine their seventeen-year-old selves sitting side by side, tentatively reaching out for each other. Her dad with his perpetual doofy grin, skinny and confident as a greyhound. Her mom with soft, soulful eyes—eyes that seemed much too old for her otherwise childlike face—and wavy hair down to her narrow hips. Olive had been raised on their love story and wanted to continue believing in that love story, so she was grateful to her mom for giving her this small gift of their first kiss.

"That sounds magical," Olive said with a laugh.

Her mom peered into the dense grouping of trees. It was a sea of dark green, but mixed in were blazes of red and yellow leaves. "You said there's an entrance to the Arboretum nearby?"

"Yeah. Just a five-minute walk. And it's not too far from both the hospital and the high school."

"That's great." Her mom stood up from the bench and dusted her dress off. "You know I'm a little old-maidish when it comes to my ideas about living together before marriage."

It was her one conservative belief. When Christopher and Verona had moved in together, she'd rattled off unsuccessful cohabitation statistics for weeks, and they'd even been engaged at the time. "They're going to find out each other's annoying habits sooner or later," Olive's dad had joked. "But there's more to it than that," her mom had insisted. "It's about protecting yourself. And making sure you're fully committed to the relationship, not just the fun and convenience."

Now her mom strode to the end of the yard in just seven steps, a few dead leaves crunching under her feet.

"Yes, I do," Olive said. "You made it pretty clear when Christopher and Verona bought their first house before the wedding."

Her mom cupped her hand over her brow and surveyed the roof and chimney. "But I know you're not taking this lightly, and it's the decision you feel comfortable making right now. And if this is the step you need to take to be with Phil, then so be it."

Olive walked toward her and followed her gaze. There were a couple of warped shingles, and one of the chimney's bricks was missing. Little flaws, minor problems, but they were things she hadn't noticed before, and they unnerved her slightly. Why hadn't the inspector noticed them? Why hadn't Phil noticed them?

"How do you know we're not making a mistake?" she asked, sounding more serious than she'd intended. She tried for a more playful note. "Like those couples in the articles you showed Christopher?"

"I don't, honey." She turned to Olive, and her expression was hard to read. Encouraging, yet cautious. "But I feel good when I see the two of you together. And I'm hopeful." She pressed Olive's hand.

Olive squeezed back. Hopeful was nice, but she wanted something more solid to go on. It was addictive, she realized, this foreknowledge and certainty that repeating a year gave her. Knowing what to expect, preparing her reactions, gauging each situation before she entered it. But she was off the map now and no longer knew what awaited her and Phil. How had she lived like this for the first twenty-five years of her life? How did everyone else on the planet live like this on a daily basis? It was distressing, to say the least.

"Well, we shouldn't keep Sherry waiting," her mom said, already at the back door after three paces. "You know she has the patience of a fruit fly. Are you ready to go?"

The inside of Sherry's house reminded Olive strongly of the garden. Teacups, stacks of books, and potted plants covered the end tables, the coffee table, the bookcase, the floor. Olive and her mom perched on the edge of the couch, afraid to disturb any of the precarious stacks. Sherry had greeted them at the door in a black-and-gold kimono-like robe, a black scarf knotted around her head. She looked strangely beautiful, like a forgotten, aging movie star. She hadn't seemed surprised or upset that Olive was with her mom.

"Please let's not talk about my health," Sherry said as she lowered herself into an armchair. "I'm bored to death of cancer. Tell me how married life is treating you."

Olive's mom moved a ruffled pillow to her lap. "Harry's wonderful. He's raking leaves right now. The maple in our backyard always drops its leaves early. We went to the farmers' market this morning and bought some fresh herbs and vegetables. Tonight he's going to make eggplant Parmesan for dinner."

"Ah, newlyweds," Sherry said. She shot Olive a significant look, but what it was supposed to signify, Olive didn't know. She didn't want to know. "I remember when my second husband, Norman, used to read to me in bed. Everything from the *Wall Street Journal* to *Wuthering Heights*. I love being read aloud to."

"Have you read anything good lately?" Olive's mom asked.

Sherry considered the question. She spread out her elbows to rest on the arms of her chair. "Yes, but nothing I would recommend. Have you?"

"Unfortunately, I haven't had much time to read this year. But I am organizing a Virginia Woolf book club at the library if you're interested."

"That sounds lovely," Sherry said and closed her eyes. "'*I can only note that the past is beautiful because one never realizes an emotion at the time. It expands later, and thus we don't have complete emotions about the present, only about the past.*'" When she opened her eyes, she was staring straight at Olive.

"Is that from *Mrs. Dalloway*?" Olive's mom asked.

"No, one of her autobiographical essays, 'A Sketch of the Past.' Do you agree, Olive? Do you ever feel that way?"

Olive sat between them, feeling like a twelve-year-old again. She understood both of them much better than they did each other, and yet, in this living room, surrounded by all these books, she doubted her own insight. She remembered the way the voices of the book club ladies had drifted over her as she'd done her homework in the kitchen. Both her mom and Sherry were watching her.

"Sometimes. But it depends on how you're applying it to your life," she said finally. "Even if we can't fully understand all our emotions and the implications of our actions in the present, we can't keep holding out, expecting to be given another chance to sort it all out. Because by then, it will all be nostalgia. You will be grieving for and missing all the things and people you lost."

"That's a really interesting take on it," Olive's mom said, gripping her crossed legs and rocking forward. "But don't you think Woolf was writing more about the knowledge we gain from having the time to meditate and reflect on our past? As they say, hindsight is twenty-twenty."

"Not always," Sherry muttered, but just loud enough for Olive to hear. She coughed. "Who wants tea?" she asked and tried to lift herself from the armchair. Pain flashed across her face and she fell back into the seat.

"I'll make it," Olive's mom offered. "Stay here and rest." She touched Sherry's shoulder as she left the room.

Sherry steepled her fingers together and gazed intently at Olive. Olive was suddenly reminded of their first moment together in her apartment.

"So you have it all figured out now? One go of it, and everything makes sense?" Sherry's lips were twisted into a sarcastic smile.

"Of course not. I'm still figuring it out," Olive said. She hoped her mom wouldn't take too long with the tea. Something in Sherry's eyes made her uneasy. Something wild and restless.

Sherry arranged her scarf over her shoulder, like a long mane of black hair. "I called Heath. He didn't answer. I left a message, and he hasn't called back. That was over a month ago."

"I'm really sorry, Sherry. Maybe he didn't get the message. Maybe he has a new cell phone. Or maybe he's still thinking about it, and he doesn't know how to react yet."

Sherry dismissed these comments with a wave of her hand. "It's what I deserve, I know. I was never a very good mother to him. I've always been better at being on the receiving end of love than the giving end."

"Do you want me to try to talk to him?" Olive asked, realizing how far-fetched her offer sounded as soon as it escaped her lips. Who was she to Heath? Who was she to Sherry even? "Maybe I can convince him—"

Sherry acted as though she hadn't heard Olive. She turned her head and rested her cheek against the velour fabric of the chair. "I don't know how this is going to work. If this is it—if I'm simply going to die alone at the beginning of next year—or if I'm going to be held by Heath's refusal to forgive me as I held my own mother back." Her pale face in profile looked stricken.

"*Two years* longer I kept her on her deathbed. The first year I wasn't there. I didn't even know she was sick. I was at a women's retreat in Florida. Heath called me and said, 'Nana's gone.' That was all he said. I felt guilty as hell, but I didn't bother begging and pleading for a second chance at things. I knew by then that wasn't how this thing operated. So I was surprised when I woke up in 2005 again.

"It was the first time in my life that I felt like I had a plan. I moved in with my mother. I did the grocery shopping, I gave her her medicine, I washed the drapes and polished the silver. She asked me to take her to Mass, and I did, but I wouldn't come inside and stay for it, and that bothered her. She began preaching on the 'state of my soul' and told me that she couldn't die in peace without knowing that my divorces had been annulled by the church and my son had been baptized. Nothing else I did mattered to her, and I got frustrated. I ran out on her, and she died alone again.

"When I woke up in 2005 *again*, I knew I was being punished. I moved back in with her, and I tried to be the perfect daughter. I went to daily Mass with her. I took communion. I jumped through all the hoops to get my divorces annulled. And all the while, Heath was getting into trouble. He was thirteen then, skipping classes and smoking pot. Norman told me there were days at a time when he didn't know where Heath was.

"But I needed to make amends with my mother first. I stayed with her until the bitter end because I knew I'd caused her so much unnecessary pain. I see her face when I look in the mirror now. And I understand why Heath is staying away." She buried her face in the chair.

Olive leaned toward Sherry. "How do you know that your mother wasn't experiencing the year over again, too? Maybe it was her decision to stay."

"No, she wasn't. Why would anyone want that?" Sherry shrilled, balling her hands into fists.

"Maybe it was more important for her to make things right with you than to relieve her own suffering."

Olive's mom poked her head through the swinging kitchen door. "Tea's almost done," she announced. Her brow furrowed. "Is everything all right in here?"

"Thanks, Kathy," Sherry said. "There are some teacups in the cabinet above the sink."

After a moment, the door swung shut, and there was a long silence. Sherry wrapped the end of the scarf around her hand like a bandage. "I don't know what to do. What should I do?"

Her mom would come back through the door any minute. Olive stretched out her hand to Sherry and squeezed her knee. "Keep fighting. Keep getting your treatments. Keep taking your medications. And call Heath again. Go visit him if he won't answer. Tell him what you just told me. Make him understand how much you love him and how sorry you are."

Olive's mom reentered the living room, carrying a wooden tray with three teacups. She smiled at Olive as she handed her one. "I added milk and honey to yours because I know you don't like tea. Try it; you may like it."

The teacup was made of delicate fine china; a chain of tiny purple flowers encircled its waist.

"Isn't the pattern lovely?" Olive's mom said when she saw Olive admiring it.

"Thank you. This was my mother's wedding china," Sherry said. "All the plates were broken or lost. I have only these few cups left."

"Greg and I didn't get any china for our wedding. We were

too young for that. I think we got mostly Tupperware." Olive's mom laughed.

Olive took a sip of her tea. It did taste better with milk and honey. Less bitter. She studied the spines of the books stacked next to her. *Ultimate Transcendence. The Spiritual Art of Dying. Tibetan Wisdom on Reincarnation. Prepare to Meet Your God.* Her heart ached for Sherry. Atop the pile was an African violet with star-shaped pink flowers.

She turned back to Sherry. "How did you get your African violet to bloom?"

Sherry straightened up in her chair. "African violets are tricky. You have to convince them they're living in Tanzania—the right light, the right water, the right humidity."

"How do you do that?"

"The watering technique is really important," Sherry said. "How do you water your violet?"

"Usually just tap water from a glass. I don't have a watering can."

"You should never water your violet from above. You don't want to get the leaves wet. Never use cold water, either. You need a deep saucer to put under the pot. Fill it with small rocks. Always pour room-temperature water in the saucer, never directly in the pot. Whatever water the violet doesn't drink within an hour, you should dump out of the saucer."

So she had been caring for her African violet all wrong. It hadn't occurred to her to invest more time into researching what she was doing wrong and how she could make it healthier. She had expected it to grow and flourish because she wanted it so badly. But of course that wasn't enough.

Dusk was descending when her mom dropped her off. The

red pickup was gone, and in its place was Phil's tan Mercedes. A few of the lights were on, but Olive couldn't see Phil through any of the windows.

All of her worries, all of her hopes seemed minuscule next to Sherry's. She felt like she had just lost a patient at the hospital. It was hard to pull herself back up, reenter her life, and care about the things she'd been so excited about only hours ago—organizing furniture and choosing paint colors—when Sherry's body was slowly losing a war. Part of her resented Sherry for this. Olive was young, she was in love, she'd been given a second chance. Was it so wrong for her to want to enjoy this?

"Your lives are entwined for a moment," Gloria had told Olive on one of her first days in the ICU. "Your patient depends on you for his or her very life. And you give back the care and respect you would give a family member. Then your patient moves on—either leaving this hospital or leaving this life. The roles you have played in each other's lives are over. And you need to take from the experience what you can and move on, too."

Olive didn't know why she and Sherry had been thrown together. She didn't know if they were the only two people in the Madison area or the only two people in the world reliving this year. Was Olive's mom the connection? Something with Sherry's breast cancer? Was Olive supposed to somehow save her? It seemed impossible: the same Herculean task she had assigned herself when her dad was diagnosed with acute myeloid leukemia. Find a loophole, find a cure. Make a miracle.

Perhaps the link between Olive and Sherry was not predestined but only coincidental. Perhaps they were just two women who had hurt people they loved. Two women who were both in need of redemption.

She walked up the driveway. Phil came into view. He was standing in the living room in a white T-shirt. He bent down, dipping gracefully out of her sight, and reappeared holding a large framed painting. He set it on the fireplace, took a few steps back, and eyed the picture with a thoughtful gaze. God, she loved him. She would do anything to keep him. To hold on to this life they were building together.

Chapter 18

It was November 5. Olive's twenty-sixth birthday again. Outside, the first snow of the season was falling, a mix between sleet and rain. Inside a crush of bodies filled the living room and kitchen. A fire blazed in the fireplace, the Killers blared over the speakers, and there were martinis and cosmopolitans and chocolate fondue. Phil had planned a party for her, inviting all their closest friends. In an echo of a year, he had still managed to surprise her.

Last year she had gone out to lunch with her mom and then worked a twelve-hour shift.

"Gosh, I wish I could find a place like this in Milwaukee," Maggie said, admiring the fireplace. She wrote for the food section of the newspaper there. She and Alistair were Olive's oldest friends.

Olive bit into a chocolate-dipped strawberry. "Yeah, but you know Madison. Places like this are few and far between. We got lucky."

Alistair leaned over the couch and handed her a cosmopolitan. "For the birthday girl." He worked in IT for the university and sent her dirty forwards almost every day.

"Thanks," Olive said. This was her third cosmo, and it was only ten o'clock. She surveyed the living room. It felt surreal to have so many of her friends—some of whom she hadn't seen since 2010—together in one place. It felt a little like the old TV show *This Is Your Life*. There was Claire, Olive's good friend from nursing school. After graduation, she'd moved to Milwaukee to work at Children's Hospital. There was Tina, flirting with one of Phil's best friends, Jeff. There were Robin and Lisa, who'd lived on the same floor as Olive and Kerrigan freshman year and then followed them to the pink house and lived in the lower flat until a few years ago. It was strange that Kerrigan wasn't here yet.

"I'll be right back," Olive said, and hoisted herself from the couch. She found Phil in the kitchen with Brian and his girlfriend, Kristin. Brian was shaking a martini shaker; he worked part time as a bartender.

"Was there not enough vodka in your cosmo?" Brian teased.

"Probably too much," Olive said. "Just the way I like it."

Kristin wrapped her in a sideways hug. "Oh, to be twenty-six again." She had just turned twenty-nine last month.

"I know," Olive agreed. "It's weird." She should be turning twenty-seven. She wondered if her body had stopped aging. If even at a cellular level, she was really only twenty-six. "Phil, you invited Kerrigan, right?"

"Oh crap. It never occurred to me to invite your best friend." Phil slapped his forehead. "Of course, I did. She's not here, yet? Well, you know Kerrigan. She's probably out shopping for the perfect birthday gift at the last minute."

Kristin handed Brian a martini glass, and something sparkly caught Olive's eye. A big fat diamond. An engagement ring.

"Oh my God. Are you guys engaged?"

Was there a split-second hesitation, or did Olive imagine it? Kristin thrust her hand toward Olive, wiggling her fingers so that the diamond refracted the light and glittered. "Yes! Brian proposed last week. He picked the ring out himself. Isn't it beautiful?"

"Gorgeous. Congratulations. I'm so happy for you guys!" She hugged them and then caught Phil's reserved expression over Kristin's shoulder. He looked wary. Of course—he had already known about the engagement and withheld the news from her. "Why didn't you tell me?" she asked him. She tried to keep her tone light and teasing, rather than hurt and angry. He had just thrown her a surprise birthday party, after all.

This time she was sure she wasn't imagining the hesitation or the look that passed between the three of them.

"I'm sorry," he said. "It just happened on Sunday, and I've been so busy planning for this party."

But Brian was his best friend, and Olive suspected Brian had told him about his plan to propose well before the fact. Phil was undoubtedly going to stand up in the wedding, probably even be his best man. How could it simply slip Phil's mind to tell her something of this magnitude? Something that meant so much to him? Although she could hardly compare this to the magnitude of her own secret.

"Men," Kristin said, shaking her head with a smile. "I was

on the phone with my sister thirty seconds after I said yes. Gosh, and there's so much to do because we're planning a Valentine's Day wedding. Four months is a bit ambitious, I know, but our first date was on Valentine's Day, and you would not believe how many wedding reception sites are available in February." Olive could tell she was trying to smooth over the situation.

She suddenly wondered if Brian and Kristin had known about Phil's proposal. Perhaps Phil had told Brian, and Brian had told Kristin, and that was why everything was so awkward now. Because Kristin had said yes, and Olive had not. Olive trained her eyes on Phil. He was pulling out another plate of strawberries and pineapple slices from the fridge. They hadn't talked about the proposal since March, when he'd told her he still had the ring. But now that they'd moved in together, she wondered if he was planning on asking her again. More than anything she wanted to say yes, but the truth had to come first. The truth made the kitchen feel hot and close.

"That sounds so lovely," Olive said. "Sorry, but I've got to make the rounds. Congrats again." She took the fruit plate from Phil to set on the coffee table by the fondue pot.

Kerrigan had just arrived, and she wasn't alone. A tall man with shaggy blond hair and wire-rimmed glasses was helping her out of her coat. He was good-looking in a scholarly, middle-aged way. He was probably somewhere in his late thirties. He didn't look like Kerrigan's type at all, but he seemed somehow familiar to Olive.

When Kerrigan spotted her, she started playing air guitar and singing loudly, "They say it's your birthday. Nur-nur-nur-nur-nur. It's my birthday, too, yeah. Nur-nur-nur-nur-nur."

Next she used her clutch purse as a microphone to serenade Olive with the song that had become their tradition over the years. "Happy birthday, girlfriend!" Kerrigan concluded. She shook snow crystals from her hair as she danced toward Olive. Kerrigan embraced her and whispered in her ear, "I want you to meet Fritz."

"Fritz?"

"Dr. Fritz Morgan. We met at Heureux Hasard. Remember that swanky little bar by the Capitol we went to a few months ago? Where we ran into your coworker Alex? Well, apparently, it's the hangout of a lot of cute doctors."

Olive blanched at the mention of Alex. Fritz stepped forward and shook her hand. He seemed amused by Kerrigan's antics.

"Happy birthday," he said. "It's nice to meet you. I work at Dane County General, too. You're in the ICU, right? I'm in surgery."

Dr. Morgan, the surgeon. She'd seen him in the ICU on a few occasions. He looked different without his white coat and hanging all over her friend.

"Nice to meet you, too," she said. "Thanks for coming. I'll take your coats." She carried their damp coats to the bedroom and tossed them on the heap that had already formed on the bed. She paused for a second, relishing the quiet and solitude of the bedroom. Cashew crept out from under the bed when he realized it was her. She squatted down to scratch his head, and he licked her fingers.

They had purchased a new, more gender-neutral duvet cover for Olive's down comforter. It was a peaceful blue and green that reminded her of Lake Mendota. Matching nightstands flanked the bed. On Phil's were his watch and a neatly folded *Wall Street Journal*. On hers were a paperback novel her mom had recommended and a framed photo of her family in front of the Blue Ridge Mountains, a snapshot from a trip they'd taken in 1998 to watch the monarch butterfly migration.

It thrilled her that this bedroom was theirs. That their clothes were mingled in the closet. That they slept together in this bed every night.

She gave Cashew one last head rub and then returned to the party, where Kerrigan was introducing Fritz to Tina and Jeff. Olive could tell from Tina's body language that she was unimpressed. Doctors were a dime a dozen to her. Jeff and Fritz, however, seemed to have hit upon something in common and were talking animatedly.

Olive set off to talk to Claire, whom she hadn't had much of a chance to talk to tonight, but Kerrigan intercepted her. "I need to talk to you in private." Carrying a nearly empty martini glass, she led Olive down the hallway to the one unfinished room in the condo. Boxes were stacked in one corner of the extra bedroom; in the other stood Phil's Bowflex.

"You couldn't have told me whatever you wanted to tell me in the kitchen or the bedroom?" Olive asked. "This seems kind of antisocial."

Kerrigan ignored her and shut the door behind them. "I have awesome news. Guess what?"

Olive sat on the black leather seat of the Bowflex and swung her legs. "What?"

"I found the perfect solution to my living situation. I'm moving in with Fritz. He has this awesome apartment in one of the high-rises downtown. Ninth floor. He has a view of Lake Monona."

"That sounds great, but isn't this a little fast?"

"We've actually known each other for a couple of months now. I didn't tell you, because—well, I know it's fast, but it's kind of serious." Kerrigan paced across the room. "He's really amazing, Olive. He adores me and he's gentle and sweet and he's great in bed and he loves to travel and I feel like I can tell him anything and he won't judge me or tell me I'm stupid. When I told him that I've been wanting to go back to school to get my MBA, he told me to go for it and not wait another minute. He takes me seriously. He likes me for who I am." She stopped to take a breath. "Aren't you going to say anything?"

Olive looked down at her hands in her lap. "I don't know what to say. I have to gather my thoughts first. You kind of caught me off guard."

"You don't know what to say? How about 'I'm happy for you, Kerrigan'? Is it too much for me to expect you to be happy for me for once?"

"Of course I'm happy for you! I'm glad you met someone. I'm just a little worried. You haven't known each other for very long. What if you move into his place and things don't work out? It could be a big mess."

"You and Phil moved in together. You bought a frickin' condo together. Like that wouldn't be messy if things didn't work out!" Kerrigan crunched the olive from her martini between her teeth.

"Yes, but we've been dating for four years now, Kerrigan! We know each other pretty well."

"You don't know everything about each other. You keep secrets."

"Kerrigan, I—"

"Fritz and I don't keep secrets. We've known each other

for only two months, but we don't lie to each other. We don't pretend we're perfect. For example, I know that Fritz is married, and I'm okay with that."

"Oh, shit. Fritz is married? Nothing good can come of this, Kerrigan."

Kerrigan glowered. "I knew you were going to make a big deal out of this. I just knew it, because that's the kind of person you are. His wife lives in New York. She's finishing up her PhD in biochemistry or something. They've been married four years, and three of the four years, they've lived in different states."

"Does she know?"

"She will soon. Fritz wants a divorce."

"Does he really mean that, or is he just saying it so you'll be with him?"

Kerrigan kicked one of the boxes. "He means it!"

"Don't do that. You might break something."

Kerrigan turned to face her. The flush of exhilaration had drained from her face. Even her provoking demeanor had passed.

"It's my birthday, and you're my best friend. I don't want to argue with you. I just want what's best for you. If you think this is it, then I'll be happy for you." Olive stood up from the Bowflex.

Kerrigan didn't say anything for a long time. "He wasn't wearing his ring when I met him," she said at last. "He says he never wears it because he doesn't want to lose it inside somebody during an operation. That none of the surgeons do. If he had had a ring on . . ."

"I know, Kerrigan. You're not like that." Olive reached out to touch her shoulder.

"I'm not like that? Like *what*, Olive?" She whirled away from her, out of her touch. "A cheap slut? Say what you really mean. God, you're so judgmental. You think you're so much better than me, so much better than everyone, just because you think you've got a free pass with this whole time warp thing. But really you're just hiding from your mistakes, while the rest of us have to deal with the consequences."

"That's not what I think," Olive objected.

"I'm so sick of your holier-than-thou attitude. The week after Phil tried to propose to you, you screwed a doctor in the Family Room of the ICU. Don't you think he would be interested in knowing that?"

"Please, Kerrigan, lower your voice." Her blood pumped through her veins like a speeding train rattling its tracks. "You know it's not that straightforward. That happened the first time I lived through 2011. This time around I didn't do it. I've been—"

"Oh, is that how it works?" Kerrigan widened her eyes. "Right. Cheating in an alternate universe doesn't constitute cheating. Rule Number One in the Olive Watson Handbook to Perfect Fucking Relationships."

Olive tried to keep her voice level because she was afraid if she didn't, a scream might erupt. "I'm going to tell him soon. About everything. But I need to break the news gently. When the time is right."

"It's November, Olive, and time's a-wasting. Ten months have passed, and the time was never right? Will it *ever* be right?"

"I don't know. Probably not. But the purpose of this year is not to make me pay doubly. It's to free me—"

"If you think you're free, you're lying to yourself," Kerrigan snapped. She set her martini glass on a box and fled to the door.

"Kerrigan, please!" Olive hurried to the door to block her exit, but Kerrigan was too quick for her. She shut the door in Olive's face and was already halfway down the hall by the time Olive could open the door and follow her. Olive's heart was trying to jump out of her chest. Where was Phil? Was Kerrigan going to expose her here in front of everyone? At her birthday party? Olive was nearly running to catch up with Kerrigan now. She overtook her just as Kerrigan was reaching a clump of people in the living room—Fritz and Phil were among them.

"Get our coats," Kerrigan hissed to Fritz. "We're leaving."

Phil raised his eyebrows at Olive. She hurried to his side and tugged on his arm, effectively pulling him out of the circle and away from Kerrigan.

"We had a fight," she whispered. "Kerrigan's really angry with me."

"Really? About what?" Phil asked.

"I'll tell you later. Just don't listen to anything she says, okay?"

He looked suspicious, but Robin and Lisa came up then and diverted his attention. "Who made the fondue?" Robin asked. "It's delicious."

While Phil explained to Robin that it was actually just a pre-made mix, Olive positioned herself more and more between Phil and Kerrigan. She eyed the hallway, waiting for Fritz to emerge with the coats. For every minute that passed and he didn't appear, Olive grew more panicked. Kerrigan was going to say something. She could feel Kerrigan's resentment as if it were a hot, itchy blanket she couldn't shake loose.

The room was too loud, too crowded. She couldn't hear what Phil was saying, but his lips were moving. She squeezed his hand, and he looked down at her. He seemed to be asking her a question, but she couldn't make it out. He said something to Robin and Lisa and then wrapped his arm around Olive's shoulders and guided her to the bedroom. They passed Fritz on the way.

Suddenly she could breathe again. Her ears came unplugged. She could hear the tinkling of Cashew's collar as he paced in front of the bed. Phil pushed some of the coats aside so they had room to sit down.

"Are you okay? You looked like you were going to pass out."

"It's just so hot out there. I felt kind of light-headed."

"Are you feeling better now, or do you need to lie down?" He passed his cool hands over her burning cheeks and forehead.

"I'm better now. I just need a moment." She closed her eyes.

"What happened between you and Kerrigan?" He sounded concerned, not accusatory.

She took a couple of slow, deep breaths and opened her eyes. "I really don't want to talk about it right now, but I'll give you the condensed version. That doctor she's dating? Well, he's a married man, but they're moving in together. I told her I didn't think that was the best idea, and she went off on me."

"Wow. Really?" Phil stood up from the bed and walked to his scratched mahogany dresser. It was the only piece of furniture in the room that was his, and it stood out as such. He seemed to be waiting for her to say more, but Olive was resolved to say as little as possible right now, for fear that everything else would come tumbling out. "Do you think this has something to do with us moving in together?" he asked.

That surprised her. Sometimes she forgot how perceptive he was. "I don't know," she said. "Maybe."

He came back to the bed and stood in front of her, cupping his hands loosely behind her neck and pulling her face close. "I'm sorry this had to happen on your birthday, but I'm sure you'll both work it out somehow. You're being a good friend, Olive. The person that Kerrigan can count on to tell her the hard truth when she really doesn't want to hear it." He kissed her nose.

He gave her too much credit, thought too highly of her. Really it was Kerrigan who was trying to make Olive face the hard truth. She was a horrible friend. An even worse girlfriend.

"Phil, I . . ."

He unlocked his hands and let them run down over her hair, smoothing it over her shoulders. "It's okay, Ollie. If you want me to ask everyone to go, I will. Or if you want to stay in here, I can tell everyone you're not feeling well—"

"No, don't do that! I haven't gotten to talk to everyone yet, and so many of them came all the way from Milwaukee. I just need a moment to collect my thoughts, and I'll be okay. Just give me a few minutes, and I'll be right out."

The door clicked softly in place, and Olive fell back on the bed. She was safe for now, but she didn't know for how long. She would have to tell Phil before Kerrigan got to him. The coats next to her smelled musty like damp wool. She rolled onto her side and tried to imagine a scenario where all her words came out right, where Phil understood and instantly forgave her, and their lives continued on almost as though nothing had happened. But what she kept imagining was her life with Phil slipping away.

A cell phone in someone's purse or coat pocket rang and startled Olive from her reverie. She steeled herself to return to the party. Claire was hovering outside the door when she opened it.

"Oh no. Are you leaving already?" Olive asked.

Claire smiled sheepishly. "I'm sorry, Olive. I've still got a long drive ahead of me tonight."

"Oh, of course. I understand. I only wish I'd had more time to talk to you. I promise I'll make a trip to Milwaukee sometime soon so we can catch up. How's Nathan doing?"

Nathan was Claire's husband of two years. Olive had stood up in their wedding.

Claire plucked her coat and purse from the pile. "He's good; thanks for asking." Her cheery tone seemed forced.

"Is everything all right?" Olive walked with Claire down the hallway. They stopped at the entrance to the living room.

"Yeah, everything's fine, it's just hard sometimes." Claire fiddled with the zipper pull of her purse before meeting Olive's eyes. "I'm sure it's the same way for you and Phil sometimes, too. Being with someone who isn't in the medical profession and doesn't quite understand."

Olive nodded. She couldn't see Phil from where they were standing, but she could hear his distinctive voice among the other guests.

"Nathan doesn't understand my crazy hours or why I come home depressed sometimes," Claire continued. "And now he wants to start having kids, and I'm not ready for that professionally or emotionally." She shielded her eyes with her palm. "You know me: I love babies. That's why I chose to work in the neonatal unit. Those babies are so beautiful, but once you start to see everything that can go wrong . . ."

Olive hugged her friend. "I'm sorry, Claire."

"It's fine. We're fine. Please do come visit, though. It would be nice to have another nurse to commiserate with."

It was after midnight, and the other party guests were still going strong. Somebody had replaced the Killers with rap music and moved the coffee table up against the wall to make room for dancing. Alistair and Maggie pulled her into the mix. Brian made her another cosmo. The bass was so loud she could feel it in her spine. She shook out her hair and raised her arms above her head and felt utterly, recklessly, frighteningly out of control.

Chapter 19

Olive spent the next three days planning what to say. In the shower, she crafted soliloquies. When things were slow in the ICU, she drafted notes in her head. *Dear Phil, You are the most important person in the world to me, and I never intended to hurt you.* Or: *I have never regretted a mistake more. You are the only person I want to be with. I hope you can find it in your heart to forgive me.* Stale, tired-out sayings seemed to be the only words left to speak the truth.

She tried composing a letter to him on her laptop but found she couldn't stand being indoors for one minute longer. Full-on winter hadn't even arrived yet, and already she had cabin fever. She zipped herself into her fleece jacket, grabbed her laptop, and headed for the backyard. After tying Cashew out on his rope, she settled herself cross-legged on the sweetheart bench with the laptop balanced on her knees.

Dear Phil, she typed. The cursor waited patiently for her to continue.

As I write this, you're at school. It's 1:23, so let's see, that puts you in seventh period. That's your favorite class, isn't it? The one with some of your golf boys in it? I can't remember what you said you're doing this week, but I bet it's something fun. Well, maybe not "fun" by most people's definition, but I bet you're trying your hardest to make it interesting and engaging for your students.

I know I've told you this before, and you don't believe me, but you would've hated me as a student. Physics was my least favorite class my senior year of high school. I was one of those students about whom you're always saying, "I just don't get how someone so bright can be so uninterested in the way the world works." But I do. Light, color, sound, electricity, the whole shebang. They're beautiful and amazing, but they can also be explained by some mathematical equation and replicated and expected to behave the same way time and time again. I know that's probably what you like about them. When you pass out prisms in your class for lab work, you can count on your students to see ROY G. BIV, in that exact order, right? Not some totally new pattern or color. Class period after class period, year after year. But I guess that's why the way people work has always been more interesting to me. We're not always predictable or explainable. You can put us in the same situation ten times, and we might react differently every time.

I don't know what this repeat year is exactly. If it's the world's way of having a bit of fun with me: "See how predictable and explainable I am now, Olive! Take that!" Or if it's an invisible part of nature that's been going on for as long as evolution and has been affecting many people over the centuries, or if it's some sort of divine intervention intended just for me and a few select others. I don't know what to make of it, and I don't think your laws of physics would help much to explain it, either. But maybe the Mayans were right. Maybe if we started thinking of time as cyclical instead of linear, people and the world would make much more sense.

The laptop fan whirred gently, heating her lap. She tucked her cold fingers underneath it briefly to warm them. Cashew had found a stick twice his length and was gnawing on it contentedly in the middle of the tiny yard.

For the sake of giving my repeat year some context, let's call it an experiment. The first time the experiment was performed, combustion, so to speak, occurred. We fought. I lashed out. You retreated into yourself. I had sex with someone else. Everything turned to ash, and we couldn't get it back to its original form. But we had another opportunity to do the experiment, and we were so much more successful this time. And maybe one time isn't enough to convince you this is the way it's meant to be, because you've got that other time still fresh in your mind, but I can promise you that I could be sent back to live this year a hundred times, and I would always choose you. I would always. Choose. You.

She reread the letter through tear-blurred eyes. It was gibberish, she realized, shrouded in analogy. The only line he would understand would be "I had sex with someone else." She tried to close the letter, but a gray box opened up. *Do you want to save changes to Document1?* it inquired. She clicked no. The box, and the letter behind it, vanished. What good was saving changes to a stupid document? Where was the gray box that allowed her to save the changes in her life to make those permanent?

Back to being between a rock and a hard place: the ultimatum she'd given herself a long time ago, and the ultimatum Kerrigan had recently implied. *It's November, and time's a-wasting . . .*

There had to be some way she could convince Phil first of her repeat year before easing him into other, less pleasant areas of revelation. Sports scores? Spot-on weather forecasts? A prediction of a major national or global event? But she knew that Phil's rational mind would require something truly spectacular—or horrifying—to convince him of the truth. It seemed that people were always willing to believe the worst.

The next day, Olive came home from work early in the morning. Phil's alarm clock was just about to go off, so she slipped carefully into bed, not wanting to rob him of his last minutes of sleep. He lay with his left arm across her side of the bed, as if he had been reaching out for her. She gently moved his arm away and studied his sleeping face. Beneath his closed eyelids, his eyes fluttered back and forth quickly, almost as if he were reading a book. He was having a dream. A tiny furrow of consternation creased the skin between his eyebrows. A bad dream.

She propped herself up on her elbow and stretched her other arm over him to turn off his alarm clock before it could start its obnoxious beeping. She rubbed his back and kissed his lips. "Time to wake up, honey."

He opened his eyes and seemed disoriented for a few seconds. Then he smiled and kissed her back. "Good morning, Ollie." He folded the comforter down. "How was your night?"

"Long." She sighed and curled her body against his. They lay like that for several contented minutes, before Phil glanced at the clock and announced he really needed to get in the shower if he wanted to make it to school on time.

He kissed her forehead and tucked the comforter around her. "Sweet dreams."

It took her a long time to fall asleep. She heard the shower running and then cupboard doors opening and closing and finally the front door as it clicked behind Phil. The silence was oppressive after he left; the truth sat on her chest like a sack of flour. She tried to think of something else. She thought of her recent patient, a thirty-two-year-old woman in a coma after a suicide attempt. She tried to think of nothing, and Kerrigan's angry face rose unbidden in her mind. She imagined Lake Mendota right before sunset, ducks gliding across the glassy surface. Her last thought before she fell asleep was Phil telling her about the moment he knew he wanted to marry her. *You were laughing and trying to toss the bread far to the little ones who couldn't get up close to the pier. You're always looking out for others. Even the timid ducks. You're so loving. So kind.*

She woke up abruptly, heart pounding, not sure why. Everything was quiet. There were no garbage trucks, no children playing in the cul-de-sac. Her T-shirt clung to her sweaty skin. The alarm clock read two fifty-five. She was still tired, so she tried to go back to sleep, but she couldn't. Something felt off.

She hurried to the kitchen to get a pot of coffee brewing.

She would definitely need it today. She froze when she reached the living room. Phil sat at the end of the couch. The TV was off, and he wasn't reading. He was simply staring off into space.

"What are you doing home so early?" she asked. Wright High School let out at two thirty, but Phil was always staying after for golf practice or tournaments, physics tutoring, or meetings. He normally got home around five or five thirty. She wondered if it had been a rough day and he'd needed to get out of there. Or maybe he'd been feeling sick? But he'd seemed fine earlier.

He didn't answer, and he didn't look up, either. Had something happened to one of his students? A car accident, a drug overdose? Something was very wrong. He sat totally still with his hands on the knees of his khaki pants. He raised his eyes to meet hers, and suddenly, she understood that he knew. She didn't know how. She didn't know how much. But he knew.

There was a lag time between her brain's understanding and her body's reaction. She stood before him in her T-shirt and yoga pants, hair askew, eyes still blurry from sleep. She had to repress a mightily inappropriate yawn. She had imagined how this moment would unfold so many times, but now that it was finally here, she could feel nothing but sharp, cold relief. It felt like the morning of a major surgery. After months of dread, after all the sleepless nights, it was finally about to be over soon. She was going under.

"What's wrong?" she asked. The sweaty T-shirt against her stomach felt chilly.

"Judging by the expression on your face, you already know." He rubbed his temples. "You look like a deer in headlights."

"You surprised me. I wasn't expecting you'd be home."

This was the wrong thing to say. He arched his eyebrow. "Were you expecting someone?"

"No. You just usually don't get home until five. Did something happen at school?" She felt odd standing, the coffee table between them, but was too anxious to sit down.

"Yes. Something happened at school. I got an e-mail from Kerrigan."

It shouldn't have surprised her—there was no other explanation, really—but the realization that Kerrigan had betrayed her stung. They had been best friends for more than eight years. What had she done to make Kerrigan want to hurt her so badly? How could she? *How could she?* Playing the part of the good Samaritan, confessing the truth to Phil, a truth he couldn't possibly understand without all the facts, and somehow keeping her head held high the whole time as though she herself weren't sleeping with another woman's husband. And in an e-mail, no less!

She imagined him on his off period, eating a turkey sandwich and checking his e-mail. What had the e-mail said? What had his face looked like when he read Kerrigan's accusations? And then for him to have to keep his cool and teach two more classes before storming home to confront her. *Oh, Phil.* Her heart was breaking for him. If only she weren't the cause of his pain.

"About what?" she managed to choke out.

Phil shook his head. "This is more awful for me than it is for you. Please stop pretending you don't know what's going on here. Tell me the truth: Was Kerrigan lying or are *you* lying?"

She collapsed into one of the papasan chairs near the fireplace. She tried to remember the soliloquies she had rehearsed, the letter she had written. Where were the words she needed to answer him? To make him understand it was all just a mistake, and it was really him that she wanted?

"Answer me, Olive. I can't bear this anymore." His hands were clasped in a pleading gesture, and his eyes were filled with pain. "Are you cheating on me?"

"No," she answered, and wished desperately that this were the whole truth, that there were nothing more she needed to explain. That this were a second chance with no strings attached. She couldn't meet his eyes.

"Last year—in February—we had a fight, and I thought everything was over between us. I was distraught. You're my whole world, Phil, and the thought of losing you was unbearable. I had to work that night, and I lost a patient. I know it doesn't make sense, and I'm not trying to justify my actions, but I felt so low—about our relationship, about my patient—that I sought comfort from one of my coworkers. But it only happened once. And I've regretted it every single day since."

Phil squeezed his eyes shut, as if this information were a harsh, blinding light he could block out. He rubbed his forehead with one hand and clutched his knee with the other.

Olive hugged herself. She felt like she was trapped in last February—the first time she had broken the news to him and he had ended things. His anguished expression was the same, the rigid shoulders, the growing distance in his voice. It didn't matter that she hadn't slept with Alex this year. It didn't matter that she had shunned him and instead devoted all her time and energy to strengthening her relationship with Phil. It was all so *unfair*, yet the word seemed too small and whiny to fully describe the shitstorm of false hopes and battered expectations that were whirling around her now. She could be given an infinity of repeats, and this mistake would still haunt her, would still ruin her happiness.

"What happened last February?" Phil asked suddenly.

She looked up at him, but his eyes were cast away. "What do you mean?"

"What did we fight about?"

She paused, uncertain how to proceed. "Phil, there's something I need to tell you." She moved to the opposite end of the couch from him. He refused to look at her. "I should have told you this in January, but I didn't know how."

"Oh boy. Two big surprises today." His sarcasm was scathing.

"This February you surprised me with the trip to Lake Geneva, and we had a wonderful time. You proposed to me, and I turned you down, not because I don't love you, but because I wasn't ready yet. There were still some things we needed to get sorted out."

"Like you cheating on me."

She tried to ignore him. "Last February, you also surprised me with a trip to Lake Geneva, but things didn't go as well for us." Phil looked like he was going to protest, but she held up her hand and continued. "Your car broke down on the way there—the fuel pump. When we finally got to the cabin, we were cold and tired. I was worried about a patient, so I called in to check on his condition. You got really irritated with me for never being able to detach myself from my work—not even on a romantic weekend. You were so upset with me, that you didn't even propose and we left early."

Phil rolled his eyes. "What is the point of this?"

She inched closer to him on the couch. She wanted so

badly to take his hands in hers. She wanted to pin him down until he believed her. "That I've already lived this year through once. After that weekend the first time, I made a huge mistake. I slept with my coworker, and I totally ruined things for us. But then New Year's happened. I woke up in the same year—2011—and I could see that I'd been given a second chance to make things right between us. So we went on the trip again, and you proposed this time. And I didn't cheat. My coworker has no memory of us being together because to him and almost everyone else that first 2011 doesn't exist. And you and I have been so happy together this year, Phil, building a life together. Haven't we been happy?"

She laid her hand on his knee, and he flinched away.

"Don't you think that one lie was enough?" he asked. "Do you think inventing a whole slew of lies is going to make this better?" He stood up from the couch.

Exasperation seized her. Why did he have to be so damn hard to convince? Why couldn't he just take a leap of faith for once in his entire life and believe in her?

"I'm not lying! Ask me anything. I'll prove it to you. What do you want to know? The weather? We're going to have record-breaking highs in early December. In the fifties."

"Stop. Just stop. This is absurd. I had to find out you're cheating on me from an e-mail your roommate sent, and now you're hiding behind some kind of magical thinking." He grabbed his jacket off the back of a kitchen chair and slipped it on.

Olive stood up, alarmed. She was losing him! "I know it sounds crazy. I didn't believe it at first, either. But if you'd only let me explain—"

"There's only one thing I'm interested in hearing you explain, Olive: *How could you*? If you supposedly love me so much, how could you have cheated on me? How could you do that to me and even entertain my proposal? How could you let us buy a condo together? How could you sit back and let me make such a fool of myself? Do you not have any respect for me?"

She leaned on the couch for support and closed her eyes. "I tried to do things differently. But no matter how hard I try, I can't take it back—"

"I need to get out of here." He pushed past her on his way to the door, as thoughtlessly as if she were a stranger in a crowd he was trying to escape.

"Where are you going?"

"I don't know. Somewhere to think. Somewhere I can be alone." His hand was on the doorknob.

"Please stay," she begged. "I'll give you your space. And then when you're ready, we can finish talking about this."

"I don't think so."

Then he was out the door. She flew to the picture window and watched him walk to his car and then back out of the driveway. Even after he was out of sight, she continued to stare, not really seeing the skeletal limbs of the trees in their neighbors' yards or the overcast sky.

Some time later, she found herself curled up on the couch in the spot Phil had vacated. The clock informed her that it was a little after four. Only eight hours ago her world had been intact. She and Phil had lain in bed together. She had kissed him awake, and then he had tucked her into bed. The morning felt like days ago.

Oh, the irony. The cruel, cruel irony. It didn't count that she was innocent this year; she was damned either way. She had done nothing but love Phil, yet she had still earned his scorn for a mistake she had made in a year that was starting to feel more and more distant and dreamlike to her. She tried to convince herself that this was different from last year's separation. Phil just needed some time to digest the bizarre information. Even though she was the one reliving the year, it had taken her at least a full day and a half of craziness to admit that it was 2011 again. She had convinced Kerrigan, which had been her downfall, of course. Phil would believe, too. And once he did, once he understood the magnitude of this year, and how it meant they were destined to be together, he would forgive her. He had to.

Twilight came and drained all the light from the living room. She didn't get up to turn on the lights or close the blinds. Instead, she sat motionless, letting her eyes grow accustomed to the dark. Every so often, headlights flashed through the windows, temporarily illuminating the room. Her neighbors were coming home from work, preparing dinner, discussing their days. She wrapped a cotton throw around her shoulders and wondered where Phil was. She didn't want to get up, not even to use the bathroom, in case he came back and she missed him. She wanted him to see her sitting here like this, penitent, remorseful, filled with sorrow. A testament to her love and loyalty for him. But he didn't return.

She was slowly coming back to herself. Cashew was curled up against her side. He looked up at her with his dark, liquid eyes, almost as if he understood her grief. Was he trying to console her with his nearness? No, he was probably just anxious for dinner. She flipped on all the lights in the living room at once and snapped the blinds shut. Closed in, she felt less vulnerable. She filled Cashew's dish with kibble and then found some mandarin oranges in the cupboard for herself. She ate them straight from the can with a fork, pacing the condo and admiring the office walls that she and Phil had painted Mint Julep. The wall she had done was easily identifiable by the sloppy brushstrokes. Phil's walls were neat and streak-free.

She left him a voice mail. She wanted to say, *I lost you once already; I've come too far to lose you again. We're meant to be together. I know that now. That's what this year is all about.* But he would be resistant to this since he didn't believe yet, so instead she said, "Phil. You have the right to be angry with me. I understand. But we owe it to each other, to the four years we've been together, to try to talk this out. Please. Just give me a chance to try to explain. I love you. Call me when you're ready."

She sat down on the edge of the unmade bed. She had no intention of sleeping; her head was awhirl with thoughts of Phil and the hurt she had caused him, anger toward Kerrigan, and a numbing fear that it was all over. She'd been provided with a fresh start and she'd blown it. She didn't know which was worse—the prospect of having to relive the year again as Sherry had done or the thought that she *wouldn't* get to live it over again. That this was it: Phil would never forgive her and she'd be condemned to a life without him.

She fell into a fitful sleep where she had dreams of the ICU. One of her patients was Heath. She had never met him before, but she knew it was him. He was seizing violently in a fishbowl room, but the door was jammed, so she couldn't get to him. She ran to get someone to help her open the door, but another patient came in with a bloody head, and then another in the throes of cardiac arrest, and then another and another. She could never get back to help Heath.

She woke up with the sheet twisted around her legs almost as though she'd been trying to run in her sleep. Why Heath? Of all the people she could've dreamed about right now, why him? But dreams didn't always make sense. After her dad had died, she'd had a recurring dream about missing a flight. She turned over; part of her knew that Phil was gone, but the other part denied the reality and still wanted to check. It was nine o'clock in the morning. She wondered where he had slept last night. Before depression slowed her down, she needed to get up and going, get inertia on her side. She couldn't bear another day like yesterday, trapped alone in the house with her wretchedness.

It was becoming more and more apparent that the cosmic forces that had granted her this repeat year were no longer her friends. Phil called when she was in the shower—the first time she'd been away from her phone in twenty hours. She immediately tried to call him back, but he had already turned his phone off. The voice mail he had left was terse. "I'm going to stop by the condo to pick up a few things while you're at work tonight. I'll be staying with a friend for a few days. I'm not ready to talk yet."

She tried to take hope from the fact that he had called, but he was shutting her out the same way he had shut her out last year. She needed to make this right somehow before things continued any further down that path. She needed to talk to someone, and there was really only one person.

Sherry didn't answer her door. Olive alternately rang the doorbell and knocked for about five minutes. Then she walked around the side of the house. It was only thirty-five degrees out, but the sun was shining, so maybe Sherry was outside soaking it up. But the garden was empty, and it looked nothing like Olive had remembered it. Now everything was brown and decaying. The leaves and vines that had given the impression of the backyard being its own island of tranquillity were gone, leaving gaping holes in their place, and now Olive could see the house behind Sherry's, a three-story brick monstrosity with a swimming pool.

Slightly panicked, Olive called her mom at work. "Hi, Mom. Have you talked to Sherry lately? Is she okay?"

"We talked on the phone earlier this week, and she sounded like herself. Why?"

"I'm at her house, and she's not answering her door, and I'm really worried." Olive sat in one of the wicker chairs. The seat was wet with rainwater, and it dampened her pants.

"Well, honey, maybe she went out. Maybe she's at the grocery store or a doctor's appointment." There was a meaningful pause. "Is everything okay? You seem rattled."

Tears rolled down Olive's cheeks, and she brushed at them quickly with the back of her hand. "Everything's fine. I'm just worried about Sherry. I know it's stupid. I should've called her first."

"That's very sweet of you, honey. If there's anything you want to talk about, feel free to come over tonight, okay? Harry and I are making samosas and chicken curry."

"Thanks, but I need to work tonight."

"I'm happy to talk whenever. Just the two of us."

"Thanks, Mom." Olive couldn't imagine telling her mom that Phil had left. To tell her would mean accepting sympathy that she didn't deserve. To tell her would make the situation seem more real. More permanent.

She resolved to wait until Sherry came home. Despite the sunshine, it was still November in Wisconsin, and she hugged her jacket to her chest. A mourning dove cooed plaintively at her from the leafless trees. It turned out she didn't have to wait for more than an hour. The sound of a car coming up the driveway woke her from her frozen stupor. She peered around the side of the house and saw a young woman helping Sherry out of a white car. They both glanced at Olive's parked SUV. The young woman left the car running, so it appeared she was simply dropping Sherry off and not staying. Sherry hobbled like an old woman. The car drove away, and Olive counted to ten. Then she hurried around the side of the house and rang the doorbell.

Sherry opened the door a few inches. She wore a rust-colored terrycloth turban, and there were hollow spaces around her eyes. She looked as cold and detached as she had at the New Year's Day party, sitting alone at the end of the couch, eavesdropping on Olive. "This isn't a good time. I just went through another round of chemo, and I'm sick as a dog." She started to shut the door.

"Sherry, wait! I'm sorry you're not feeling well, but I really need to talk to you."

Sherry peered at her through the crack for a moment and then held it wide open. "I'm warning you—I'm really ill. But I'll try to give you ten minutes without vomiting."

Olive stepped into the house. A wave of humid air met her. "Doesn't your doctor have you on any anti-nausea medications?"

"Yes, but it gives me such terrible headaches that sometimes I don't take it."

"There are a lot of drugs out there. There's got to be one

with milder side effects that will help with the nausea. Do you want me to make you some toast?"

"No food. Just talk." Sherry lay down on the couch and threw her arm over her eyes. She was not the most welcoming conversation partner, but Olive needed her.

She took off her coat and sat in Sherry's usual armchair. "My boyfriend found out."

"About the repeat year?"

"About my cheating on him last year. He doesn't believe in the repeat year. I tried to explain it, but he thinks I'm lying to explain away the cheating."

Sherry's chest rose and fell heavily. She didn't respond for a long time, and Olive wondered if she'd fallen asleep. "How long did it take you to believe?" she finally asked.

"At least a day. And then you came to my apartment—"

"Right. So give him some time. It *is* a time warp we're talking about here. Not the easiest story to swallow." Sherry pulled a purple afghan from the back of the sofa and covered herself, despite the house's balmy temperature.

"But you don't understand. I went through it, so I couldn't deny it. Phil won't even give me the chance to explain, so he'll never believe it. He's distancing himself from me. He left yesterday afternoon and hasn't been back to our condo since. He won't answer my calls. He's purposely coming over tonight to pack a bag while I'm at work so he can avoid me."

"Give him some time," Sherry repeated drowsily.

Her faith in Sherry was obviously misguided. Sherry was too sick; she had too many troubles of her own. She wasn't an oracle; she was a dying, middle-aged woman whose life had taken innumerable wrong turns. Olive stood up. "But I'm afraid if I give him too much time, it will all be over, like last year. And I keep asking myself, did I screw it up beyond repair? Am I going to have to live 2011 over again? Or even worse—was this my one shot and now I'm never going to get Phil back?"

Sherry moved her arm to her stomach and looked up at her. "Someone once told me that I should keep fighting. That I should keep calling my son and that I should visit him if he wouldn't answer. That I should make him understand how sorry I am and how much I love him."

Olive sighed. "But it's not that easy."

"I know."

She sat back down. "Have you heard from Heath?"

"Yes, actually. I got a letter. He said he was on some kind of pilgrimage in Spain this summer. El Camino de Santiago. No cell phone reception. He didn't even bring it."

"And?"

Sherry tried to prop herself up. "He was thinking about me on his pilgrimage. Even before he knew about the cancer. But he still doesn't want to see me. He doesn't think the cancer changes anything. He wrote, 'I don't believe in pity forgiveness. Forgiveness needs to be earned.'"

"I thought forgiveness was something granted, not earned."

"I guess not." Sherry bundled the afghan around her shoulders.

Olive rubbed her fingers against the worn arms of the chair. "I had a dream about Heath this morning."

Sherry cocked her head. "Really? What was it about?"

"I'd rather not say. It was a bad dream, but I'm sure it didn't mean anything. I've never even met him. I don't even know what he looks like. I think I'm just anxious about everything and everyone right now. I feel like I'm falling apart."

"At least not literally." Sherry slowly returned to her supine position.

"You're right. I'm not dying. That's the one thing I have going for me."

Sherry let out a bark of laughter. "That's a damn good thing to have going for you."

Olive resisted at first. She was tired of this contrast, tired of feeling her troubles were insignificant compared to Sherry's. Yes, thankfully, she wasn't at the end of her life. But sometimes she wished she were traveling through this year with the young Sherry who'd had a failing marriage with a lawyer husband. Or the Sherry who'd gone through a second divorce and tried to create a new life for herself in Madison as a single mother. Perhaps Sherry would've empathized with the loss of the love of her life more. Now Sherry was jaded. She didn't believe in happily-ever-afters, so Olive's loss was no surprise to her.

But Sherry's laughter was hysterical and contagious, and soon Olive found herself joining in, simply because Sherry's loud guffaws and teary eyes were so funny. She sat on the floor next to Sherry and laughed until she had a hard time catching her breath. She dried her tears with the purple afghan.

"Stop it, stop it. I'm going to throw up," Sherry warned in between laughs. "Oh, my stomach hurts."

Olive left her with two slices of dry toast and a cup of tea. As she walked to her SUV, she felt better, even though no progress had really been made. But on her drive back to the empty condo, despair twisted its icy fingers into her heart.

Though it would've been the typical time of day for Phil to arrive home from work, the driveway was empty, and all the windows were dark. He wasn't coming home. She knew she needed to be practical, to walk the dog, make a quick dinner and get ready for work, but tonight she didn't feel up to playing the part of solid, dependable Olive. The nurse who never called in sick. The nurse who (almost) never let her personal life interfere with her work. She didn't feel like smiling and speaking in soft tones and dealing with everyone else's shit. For once, she needed to face her own problems first.

Toya didn't seem to believe that she had flu-like symptoms, but she didn't push the issue. When Olive set her phone down, a mixed sensation of escape and surrender filled her. Escape from a night of having to pretend nothing was wrong, and surrender to a night of wallowing with no distractions. If she was being honest with herself, one of her major reasons for calling in sick was the chance that she would see Phil and they would have a nice long talk.

After taking Cashew for a brisk walk around the neighborhood, she set a pot of water to boil for spaghetti, poured a glass of red wine, and clicked on the news. She avoided watching it most days because it gave her such a helpless feeling. If she hadn't been so wrapped up in her own life last year, perhaps she could've remembered the dates and places of some of these tragic events and prevented them. She turned away from the photo of a three-year-old girl who had perished in an apartment fire.

The water was burbling in the kitchen. She hurried to add the noodles and start warming the sauce. When she returned to the living room, wooden spoon in hand, a traffic report was on. Helicopter footage showed an overturned car lying diagonally across two lanes of traffic. "A one-car rollover accident caused traffic delays of up to an hour on the westbound Beltline between Mineral Point and Old Sauk Road late this afternoon. Our sources tell us that only one person was inside the vehicle, a young man. He suffered critical injuries and was airlifted to Dane County General. His status is still listed as critical."

The anchors cut to a new segment, but Olive was blind to it. The image of the flattened car was burned into her corneas. A rollover accident on the Beltline. A male airlifted to the hospital. This was the patient with the morphine allergy, she was sure of it. Had he been transferred from the ER to the ICU already? It was nearly seven o'clock now. The anchor had said "late afternoon." The young man would be in surgery for at least three hours before they had him stabilized. Another five minutes to transfer him to the ICU. At least twenty minutes before they assessed his vitals and started him on a course of morphine for the pain. She dashed to the kitchen to turn off the burners.

Only moments ago she had been feeling powerless to change the outcomes of the events on the news, and now here was one outcome she had had the potential to change, but she had called in sick. There was a year's worth of deeds that she could not accomplish. She could not erase her betrayal of Phil, and she could not make him forgive her. She could not cure Sherry's cancer and reunite her with her son, *but she could save this man's life.* She needed to get there before the fatal drug was administered.

Chapter 20

The drive to the hospital, which took only fifteen minutes, stretched out before her like a five-hour journey. At every red light, she braced herself against the steering wheel and saw the young man's swollen face—his bottom lip the size of a nightcrawler, his thick tongue trying to escape his lips as he struggled to breathe.

She tried to imagine what she would say if—no, there was no *if* about it, she *would* get there in time, she had to—*when* she arrived. What would she say to convince them of his morphine allergy without sounding like a lunatic?

As she ran up the stairs to the second floor—no time to wait for the elevator—she remembered the look of horror on Tina's face when she realized that she had been the one to inject the lethal drug. It didn't matter to her that a doctor had prescribed it, that no known drug allergies had been indicated on her patient's chart—in her mind, she had still been the one responsible for his death. Olive knew she would have felt the same way.

The ICU was in total upheaval when she burst through the doors. No one was manning the nurses' station, so Olive hurried past. The bulk of the chaos was concentrated in one fishbowl room. Alex, Tina, and Kevin were all crowded around the patient's bed.

When Olive saw the young man, she thought she was too late. There was no way someone who looked so bad could still be alive. Both his left arm and leg were immobilized in braces; burgundy abrasions and lacerations mottled his skin. A bloody bandage covered the right side of his head. Tubes and wires coiled out of his body as though he were an insect held in place by a spider's web. But his lips were not swollen nor his face severely flushed; he had not yet gone into anaphylactic shock. There was still time.

Kevin noticed her first. "What are you doing here? I thought you called in sick." His tone was accusatory; it was clear he was the one filling in for her tonight.

Olive drew in a deep breath. Now that she was here, it was hard to keep from simply shouting at them about morphine. But she had to do this in the smartest, most efficient way. It took all her strength to keep her voice calm yet commanding. "Tina, can I please talk to you outside? It's urgent."

Tina's eyes widened. She dropped the man's chest tube, and it swung against the bed rail. "Are my kids okay?"

"Yes, they're fine. It's not about them. Can we please step outside? It will only take a minute."

Olive guided Tina a few paces away from the fishbowl room. She didn't want to be seen or overheard. There were painful crescent moons indented in her palms; she hadn't realized she'd been squeezing her fists. Tina studied her warily. Despite Olive's reassurance, she still didn't seem convinced that her daughter and son were safe and healthy.

"This is about your patient," Olive started.

Tina's shoulders relaxed. She tilted her head toward the room. "Ryan Avery?"

"Ryan Avery." Saying his name made the situation feel even more critical. "It's not in his chart, but he's allergic to morphine."

Tina didn't look as bowled over as Olive had expected her to look; instead she looked skeptical. "Do you know him?"

"It's important that you record that in his chart. Give him anything else for the pain—fentanyl, Toradol—but not morphine."

Tina pursed her lips, the look of an experienced nurse who was not about to be outsmarted. "A true morphine allergy is extremely rare. A lot of people think they're allergic—they have a small reaction, some itchiness—but it's a common side effect. Nothing a little Benadryl can't fix."

"I know it's rare, but Ryan Avery has a *true* morphine allergy. If you give him morphine, he will go into anaphylactic shock and die."

"How do you know that?" Tina's skepticism had been replaced with stunned astonishment.

"There's not enough time to explain. Please just trust me, Tina. His life depends on it."

"But, what if—" Tina wasn't a by-the-book nurse, but she was a good nurse, and Olive could see a flicker of hesitation in her eyes. Writing something unsubstantiated in a patient's chart, administering a different drug than the one the doctor initially prescribed—this was serious stuff.

"Trust me. You won't regret it." She remembered how Tina had gone home early last year and then taken a week off. The young man's death, accidentally on her hands, had really shaken her.

Tina studied her for a long moment and then threw up her hands. "Okay. I don't know why I'm saying this, but okay. I'll get Alex to prescribe something else." She hurried back into the fishbowl room.

Olive crumpled onto a stool at the computer station. She doubled over, touched her forehead to her knees, and took several deep breaths. She had made it in time. She had prevented something terrible, and now Ryan Avery had a chance at recovering from his injuries. She thought of his parents, his siblings and friends, his girlfriend maybe, all the people to whom she had restored him. There would be no funeral, no grieving, no lawsuit against the hospital. Instead there would be long months of rehabilitation and then years returned that had been stolen away. Maybe there would be a wedding. Maybe there would be children who wouldn't have existed if she hadn't gotten here in time today. She saw a whole life spool out before her eyes for the young man she didn't know.

Some time later, everyone but Tina left the room. Ryan's parents had arrived. They were dressed elegantly, as if their plans for tonight had included an opera, not an emergency trip to the hospital. Seeing them dressed like that reminded Olive of the way Ryan's mother had thrown herself weeping over his body, her black evening gown leaving sparkles all over his ruined skin. It was time for Olive to go. She had accomplished what she had come here to do, and she knew what came next would still be hard to witness. Even though he had survived this time, his parents would still be devastated by his condition. She wanted to leave, but something kept her transfixed in her seat. Perhaps she was waiting to see that moment of pure relief when his parents learned that he was still alive.

But it didn't come. Alex led them into the room, and Ryan's mother sobbed and held her son's hand, while his father stared intently at Alex's face, as though by the sheer power of listening he could overcome his son's circumstances. Olive felt like a voyeur, and yet she couldn't turn away. It was like looking through a window into last year. *He's alive,* she wanted to call out to them. But of course, sorrow and pain were all relative, and thankfully, they did not realize how close to losing their son they had been.

She needed to leave now; viewing this was not helping her state of mind, and maybe Phil would still be at the condo if she hurried. But as she stood up from her perch, Alex walked out of the room and laid his hand on her shoulder. A shadow of stubble covered his face, and his white coat was rumpled.

"Can't get enough, huh?"

Olive backed up a step. "Excuse me?"

"Tonight's your night off, right? I've been on for almost twenty-four hours now, and of those twenty-four hours, I've gotten maybe an hour's sleep. I'm so tired that I'm seeing floaters in my peripheral vision, and then all of a sudden, here you appear, like the angel of the ICU, watching over all of us shortsighted mortals. Sorry. It's the sleep deprivation talking."

She pretended not to have heard that last part. "What's his prognosis?"

Alex rubbed his eyes furiously. "Fucked."

Olive gasped. "He's not going to make it?"

"No, I'm sorry, that's not what I meant. He'll live; his life will just never be the same. He suffered a transection of his spinal cord at T10 in the crash. He'll never walk again, have sex again, have control of his bladder or bowels . . ."

She didn't know what to say. Her earlier sense of triumph was eroding. "And you told his parents?"

He scratched at his chin stubble. "Yeah. One of my least favorite conversations. It's right up there with telling someone they have cancer." Despite his sarcastic tone, his eyes were tearing up. He rubbed at them again. "His dad seems to think it would've been better if he had died."

"No, he doesn't mean that," she whispered, but she wasn't entirely sure. "He's just heartbroken for his son right now. All his hopes, his dreams for the future—that will all have to change now. But I know for a fact that losing him would not have been any easier for them. He'll still be the same person inside, the same Ryan that they love. There will just need to be some accommodations. And maybe after some rehabilitation, his prognosis will improve." She squeezed Alex's hand. Even to her own ears, the words sounded hollow.

How could she have been so naïve? She was furious with herself. Only moments earlier, she'd been patting herself on the back and imagining a fairy-tale ending for Ryan Avery. But no one just walked away from a rollover car crash. She'd stopped the morphine, but so what? It hadn't been enough. In this year, nothing she did was ever enough. She would've needed to stop the car, and as Sherry had pointed out to her from the very beginning, they weren't superheroes. When it came right down to it, they didn't have the power to change much of anything. Instead of changing events for the better, Olive just kept fouling things up more and more. And it was one thing to mess up her own life, but to toy with someone else's? Would Ryan Avery have wanted this for his life? She didn't know the guy, and yet she had taken it upon herself to tamper with his fate.

Alex grabbed her hand and held on, stroking her palm with his thumb. "Thanks, Olive. I really needed to hear that right now. You're amazing in that way." He looked down at her through his eyelashes, straight and thick as the bristles of a broom. "Sometimes I feel like there's this connection between us."

She watched those eyelashes as they flicked up and down, and she wondered how he could not recognize the pile of bullshit she had just fed him. And if he did recognize it, why not call her out on it? Why ingratiate himself to her? Why the constant barrage of flattery, especially when her defenses were so weak? His eyelashes were the type that could flirt with you of their own accord, and she hated him for sleeping with her last year and for continuing to unknowingly be an obstacle between her and Phil and for being a symbol of everything that was wrong with her year, standing there telling her that Ryan Avery would be a paraplegic and trying to hold her hand at the same time. Beneath those gorgeous eyelashes, his irises were the same intense blue of Lake Mendota, and it was clear he wanted her, wanted her as if she were a cool drink on a hot day. He wanted her without asking for anything more than her body. No promises. No expectations. Only sweet, superficial intimacy.

She should have pulled her hand away, but it was such an innocent gesture. Consoling a coworker. Grieving for a patient's prognosis. Never mind that the slow circles he was drawing on her palm reminded her of the slow circles he had drawn on other parts of her body once upon a time. Never mind that the Avery family was only a few feet away, weeping over their son's broken body, or the fact that this was the kind of behavior that had gotten her into trouble in the first place. She was so sick of everything: trying, fighting, resisting. What did it ever amount to? It would be so much easier to give in. Her heart was heavy with everything that had happened in the last forty-eight hours, and Alex was willing to help her forget that burden.

"Alex, I—" His fingertips were brushing back and forth across her own. She looked up at his face, which was kind and intelligent. But it wasn't a face she loved. "Alex, I need to go now."

Footsteps were approaching behind them. He released her hand, and she turned guiltily, expecting to see Dr. Su or one of the nurses.

But it was Phil. It took her eyes a few seconds to confirm that this was the real Phil, not some hallucination sprung from her desire to see him or her guilt over this exchange with Alex. Unfortunately, it was the real Phil, made of flesh that was quaking and blood that was boiling with anger. In a blur of action, he raised his fist as though he were going to punch Alex in the face, suddenly dropped both hands to his sides, and then turned and stalked away.

She ran after him. "Phil!" she cried. He was walking so fast that even though she was almost sprinting to keep up, she couldn't catch him. She hardly noticed Kevin or Brenda, the night nurse manager, and their scandalized expressions as they watched them fly by the nurses' station. Phil exited the ICU and rushed past the waiting room, where a handful of family members were watching what sounded like *American Idol.* Olive was at his heels. The elevator wasn't there, so he jerked open the door to the stairwell and disappeared inside.

She yanked the door back open. "Phil! It's not what it looked like. Please stop. We were talking about a patient. He was in a car accident and now he's paralyzed!"

Phil spared her a fleeting glance as he spiraled downward, but he didn't stop. She barreled down the stairs, afraid of losing her footing in her hurry. She was breathing heavily, and her heart seemed to have given up on her. Its pumps were steady and indifferent, unaware of the trauma that had been inflicted.

They reached the ground-floor landing at the same time. Phil seemed to be slowing down. He pushed through the metal door and halfheartedly held it open for her. The lobby was almost empty. A tired-looking woman read a book at the front desk; she didn't look up when they entered. The only sound was the peaceful patter of the water fountain. Olive passed it every day on her way to the ICU, but she had never truly taken the time to see it before. It had two tiers with what looked like a caduceus on top; both the stone of the smaller basins and the water in the pool had a greenish tinge. Spotlights under the water made the droplets spilling over the tiers shimmer. Phil paused in front of the fountain, too.

"Why did you come here?" she asked his back. "Were you ready to talk?" *Were*, not *are*, in case what he had just seen upstairs had changed his mind. Still she was hopeful.

"I went to the condo," he started. "The lights and the TV were still on, there was food on the stove, but nobody was home. I was worried about you." He sat down on the fountain's edge.

She stood before him. "I was watching the news, and I saw this awful rollover accident happen on the Beltline. They said the victim had been brought here, and I thought—I thought

I could somehow help. I had called in sick because—well, you know—and then I felt guilty for not being there when I saw that."

Phil was watching her strangely. She wasn't sure if he believed her. Did he think she had dropped everything and rushed to the hospital to be with Alex? The light from the fountain cast a hazy glow over his handsome features.

"Someone stopped by when I was there," he said. "That friend of your mom's. Sherry Witan."

Olive froze. How had Sherry, in her weakened condition, made it to her condo? And what for? She seated herself a few feet away from Phil. Tiny drops of water pelted the side of her face.

"I told her you weren't there," Phil continued, "but she invited herself in anyway, and she looked so sick, I couldn't turn her away. She told me everything about this year, Olive, everything you've been going through."

Warmth bloomed in the pit of her stomach and spread to her extremities. It was nothing short of a miracle. Sherry—opinionated, jaded, self-absorbed, tough-as-nails Sherry Witan—had performed an act of love for her. An act to save Olive's love. She had forced herself from her home to talk to someone she had never met before, to convince him of the truth in a way that no one else, not even Olive, could have done. Olive dipped her fingers in the fountain and touched the water to her forehead like a benediction. There was hope after all.

She was ready to launch herself at Phil and envelop him in a hug, but his face warned her away. All was not forgiven. There was still a very long conversation ahead of them.

He glowered at his hands in his lap. "I still can't fully wrap my head around it, it's so bizarre, and I felt like I'd wronged you in some way by not listening to you and letting you explain. I felt like I needed to give you that chance, so I came here, and what do I walk in on? You and that bastard holding hands, looking like the coziest couple in the world."

"It wasn't what it looked like. Alex was upset about his patient"—he winced when she said Alex's name—"and I patted his hand. That was all there was to it. We were talking about how his patient's life was going to change now, how his family was going to handle it."

His eyes burned into hers. "Really? That was all there was to it? So you can honestly tell me that if I hadn't walked in when I had, things wouldn't have gone any further? History wouldn't have repeated itself?"

Her cheeks grew warm. A rush of embarrassment tinged with anger coursed through her. She wanted to snap at him, *Maybe if you stopped treating me like a yo-yo, bringing me in close only to fling me away again, I wouldn't be so out-of-my-mind confused*, but she held her tongue. "Of course not. I don't want him. I want you. You're the only man I want to be with. I've never felt otherwise—not even in my one lapse of judgment."

He stood up and loomed over her. "How can I ever trust you again, Olive? Maybe you didn't cheat on me this time, but how do I know you don't want to? How can I know that you're not going to run into his arms every time things get rough between us? Why is it that you never seek comfort from me? Why is it that everybody else—this prick, Kerrigan, even your mom's book club friend—is your best buddy, while you keep me in the dark?"

Because she had wanted to protect him from the truth.

Because she hadn't thought he would believe her. Because she hadn't wanted something like this to happen and ruin her beautiful second chance. "Because I didn't want you to think less of me. And I really didn't want to hurt you."

The front desk lady had looked up from her book and was staring at them. Phil shook his head and walked to the automatic double doors; Olive followed. The fluorescent lights of the drop-off zone overhang buzzed and made everything look lurid and dingy. It was freezing outside. Had she driven here without a jacket? She hadn't noticed the biting cold in her haste.

"Do you think we could go back to the condo and talk about this?" she asked, rubbing her goose bump–covered arms.

"I don't think there's much more to talk about." Phil buried his hands in his jacket pockets. "This isn't how I thought tonight would turn out," he muttered.

"We can change it."

"No, we can't." His tone was resolute. "I'm tired of being made a fool. It's like—it's like with my dad. How many chances can I give you to break my heart? There just comes a point when I need to say no. I love you, but no."

A siren wailed in the distance.

"You should go inside, Olive. You're shivering." He lightly touched her arm and then melted into the jumble of cars in the dark parking lot.

The ambulance would be arriving soon with its red-and-white flashing lights and matter-of-life-and-death commotion. She stepped out from under the concrete overhang. The sky was an electric blue. Clouds dark as soot scudded across, making her feel she was on a world that was spinning much too fast. Her thoughts were moving as quickly as those clouds.

The siren was a constant, high-pitched whine now, probably only blocks away. She crossed back under the overhang and glided through the automatic doors.

Chapter 21

The world continued to turn too quickly, each day chasing the tail of the next. Olive was torn between wishing it would accelerate even more and wanting the hurried days to slow down. She was reminded of the story of Sherry's mother's death. Sherry and her mother had been so close to reconciliation at the end of the year, and then Sherry had run out on her. Another year, another try. Chastened and subdued, Sherry had finally conformed to her mother's expectations so the old woman could die peacefully. So what was the lesson Olive was supposed to be learning here? To always tell the truth? To never *ever* tell the truth? The strength of her conviction—that the universe had rolled back time to reunite two fated lovers—was flagging. She was confused and heartsick.

Phil had moved out and taken Cashew with him. She coped the best way she knew how: She threw herself into her work. She bathed and turned patients, comforted their families, administered medications, ordered chest X-rays and ABGs. She suctioned out air passageways, changed colostomy bags, irrigated wounds, collected sputum and urine. She was her patients' advocate and guardian angel. She was everything they needed her to be and nothing of her own. She stayed late. She took extra shifts. She kept her distance from Alex.

When Thanksgiving approached and Olive remembered it would be a depressing day alone with her mom and Harry like last year (since Verona and Christopher were spending the holiday in California with her family), she eagerly volunteered to cover Jennifer's day shift and then apologized profusely to her mom, saying there was no way to get out of it. But then her mom and Harry showed up in the ICU that day with a plate of turkey, mashed potatoes, and green bean casserole, and a whole pumpkin pie to share with her coworkers, and Olive felt like the most unworthy, selfish daughter on the planet.

Her unworthiness was a recurring theme these days. She had been avoiding Sherry as well; she hadn't even thanked her for the generous act she had performed. She was too ashamed to tell her that even after the perfect setup, she had still managed to wreck things. Even a miracle hadn't been enough. But Sherry didn't call her, either, and Olive started to fret. She ignored her broken heart and her shame and called Sherry, but several days later, Sherry still hadn't gotten back to her. Olive was planning a visit to Sherry's house when she received a call from her mom. They'd found a lump in Sherry's left breast; the cancer had metastasized. The surgery was scheduled for the next day.

Olive sat alone on a love seat in the waiting room of the

surgical ward. Her mom had to work until five o'clock and would join her then. Glittery snowflakes hung from the ceiling tiles by paper clips and string. On the walls, the framed pieces of artwork were wrapped like presents. A fat fleece snowman sat on the counter of the nurses' station and blared "Frosty the Snowman" whenever someone walked past it, which was often. It was hard to get in the Christmas spirit when she felt so numb inside.

The procedure had started at nine o'clock this morning, and it was now almost two, and still Olive hadn't heard a word from the surgeon. It had been a while since she'd been on the waiting-and-praying end of things—not since her dad—and it was all she could do to keep herself from barging into the operating room and demanding an update. She jiggled her crossed legs. She wondered why Sherry's doctor hadn't encouraged a double mastectomy from the start. The pain of going through the operation twice—Olive shuddered. Yet she was encouraged by the fact that Sherry had undergone the surgery at all. That meant she was still fighting.

The small waiting room was crowded and tense. A middle-aged black woman held the hand of her elderly mother in a wheelchair, a teenage couple passed a fussy baby back and forth, a young man with spiky black hair had his nose buried in a thick book. A bearded man talked on a cell phone, saying over and over, "They won't let me see him yet, Aunt Gladys. I don't know if they've fixed his heart. They won't let me see him." A Hispanic woman sitting back-to-back with Olive was praying the rosary, her soft whispers spoken almost directly into Olive's ears. *Santa María, Madre de Dios, ruega por nosotros pecadores, ahora y en la hora de nuestra muerte. Amen.*

She thought of Ryan Avery's mother, who had sat at his

bedside every day of his hospital recovery, mouthing the words to the prayers and rubbing the rosary beads between her fingers until Olive thought the beads would crumble into dust. His dad had stopped coming after those first few days of demanding miracle cures from doctors, and even Ryan's girlfriend—a heavy girl with a Celtic tattoo on her ankle—began to visit less and less frequently. But his mother was there every day. She combed his hair and read aloud to him from *Field & Stream* magazines.

He had been released from the hospital a week ago to adapt to his life as a paraplegic. She hadn't been working then, but Tina had described to her how Ryan had sat tall in his manual wheelchair and rolled it forward himself.

"I still don't know why you did what you did the night he came in," Tina had said to her, holding up her hand as if to stifle any explanation that Olive might try to offer, but Olive remained silent. "I'm willing to explain it away as some kind of intuition, like the moment I had when Conner wanted to ride a pony at the county fair, but I had a really bad feeling—achy like this intense pressure in my gut—and I told him no, and then the next little kid who rode that pony was bucked off. That kid scraped up his hands and knees pretty bad, but Watson, you saved this man's *life* with your intuition. I've been having nightmares about what would've happened if you hadn't stopped me from giving him the morphine. Really bad, wake-up-at-three-o'clock-in-a-cold-sweat nightmares. And every time I wake up like that, I think, *Thank God Watson stopped me.*"

Olive interrupted. "Tina, I really don't think you should give me that much credit."

"You're being too hard on yourself, forgetting one of the

cardinal rules of ICU nursing. You can't expect perfect outcomes for our patients. They come to us very, very sick, and we do our best, but it's not always in our hands. Ryan Avery is alive today because of you. He would thank you if he only knew what you had done for him. Don't pity him because he's in a wheelchair—that's closed-minded. He's coming to terms with it, and I think you should, too."

Olive started to protest again, but then stopped herself. Tina was right: His outcome was not perfect, but what in life, she thought, ever was? There were car crashes and cancer and Alzheimer's and alcoholism. Fathers died too young, and their families just moved on. Lovers were weak and careless with one another's hearts. Living meant playing with fire. It was amazing that anything ever went right at all with all the bad things lurking around every corner.

She closed her eyes and tried to tune out the noise and anxiety that was rolling off the other people in the waiting room in overpowering waves. But with her eyes closed, she remembered the way Phil had held her hand and brought her cold cans of soda from the vending machine while her dad was in the hospital. Maybe perfection didn't exist in the long term. Maybe it existed only in brief slices that happened so quickly you didn't even realize you had been happy until months or even years later. She sighed and opened her eyes. The snowman was singing again. She pressed her fingertips to her temples.

The spiky-haired man leaned across the aisle. "If I have to hear that song one more time, I'm going to throw that thing out the window."

Olive smiled politely. She didn't feel like making small talk with strangers right now. She looked down at the stack of magazines next to her, as if seriously considering which one to read.

"It's sad when all the meaning is stripped from the holidays because everyone is trying to be so PC," he added. "No Christmas trees, no menorahs because we don't want to offend anyone. And this"—he pointed to the singing snowman and the snowflakes on the ceiling—"*this* is what we're left with."

Olive looked up from the magazines. His eyes were a dark, piercing blue. He was younger than she had thought at first. Maybe only twenty or twenty-one. "It is awfully depressing."

He set the heavy book on his lap. "Are you here for a family member?"

"Friend. You?"

"To be perfectly honest, I don't know why I'm here. Because I like to be tortured, I guess." He patted the top of his hair lightly, confirming that each spike was still perfectly gelled in place.

She didn't want to collect another sad story—she had enough of her own—but the expression on his face was so troubled that she couldn't give him the cold shoulder now. Yet she still didn't want to hear his tale of woe. "What are you reading?" she asked instead.

"*The Da Vinci Code.*"

"That doesn't look like *The Da Vinci Code.*"

"No?" He flashed a handsome smile. Olive wondered if he was flirting with her. "Dante's *The Divine Comedy,*" he amended.

"So which circle of hell are we in right now?" she joked, before she could wonder if he would misconstrue this as flirting back.

He laughed. "I'm not sure yet." He tucked the book under his arm and stood up. "I seriously need a cup of coffee. Do you want to join me?"

Olive nodded toward the double doors of the surgical ward. "I'd better stay here. I need to be here for my friend."

"Right. Can I bring you anything?"

There was something oddly familiar about the sly curve of his lips. She studied him for a moment too long. "That's very nice of you to offer, but I'm fine, thanks."

"Be back soon." He turned down the hallway that led to the hospital cafeteria.

Olive endured curious stares from the teenage couple. She crossed her legs at the ankle. An efficient-looking nurse returned to the desk, and she leaped up to talk to her.

"Excuse me. Is there any word on Sherry Witan?"

"Why, yes. I wasn't aware there was any family present." The nurse paged through a pile of forms.

"Not family. A close friend. Is she out of surgery yet?"

"Yes. She did quite well. She's been out of surgery since noon and under observation in the recovery room." The nurse checked her watch. "I'd say we're just about ready to transfer her to her room on the oncology floor."

Olive moved to the waiting room on the oncology floor. The same chintzy snowflakes dangled from the ceiling there as well; a jar of miniature candy canes adorned the counter of the nurses' station. She called her mom to let her know Sherry was safely out of surgery and that she should come directly to oncology on the fourth floor when she arrived. While she was on the phone, a scrawny, bundled body that looked like it had once been Sherry was wheeled on a gurney from the elevator to the patient rooms. It was hard to believe that only months ago she had thought of Sherry as a large woman; she had become so reduced.

It was another half hour before they let Olive back to see her. Sherry's fragile body seemed swallowed up by the large pillows supporting her. There was nothing covering her head, only wisps of fine gray curls dotting her scalp. Her chest looked sunken in. She had only been wearing a prosthetic, Olive realized, and now both her breasts were gone. Despite her wretched condition, Sherry's thin lips actually curved into a smile when Olive entered the room.

"On the home stretch," she murmured hoarsely, and beckoned Olive with her pulse oximeter–clamped finger.

Did she mean that they were nearing the end of their repeat year or that she was nearing the end of her life? Olive pulled a chair to her bedside and wrapped both her hands around Sherry's cool and bony hand. "I'm so glad you made it through," she whispered.

Sherry turned her head. Her brown, all-seeing eyes were still just as sharp. "Me, too. There's not much more they can take from me. I'm practically just a shriveled-up corpse right now." She squeezed Olive's hand, and the sly smile spread across her face again. "If I make it through to January, though, I'm finally going to undergo that reconstruction surgery, and then I'm going to have the perkiest pair of knockers a fifty-eight-year-old woman has ever had. I won't even need to wear a bra, they'll be so perky."

"Well, then." Olive laughed. She released Sherry's thin hand and leaned back in her chair. Something had changed. Sherry seemed almost optimistic now. What had happened? Had her doctor given her a promising prognosis? But she was worried Sherry's buoyant mood had come from her good deed toward Olive and Phil. She didn't want to let on that Sherry's kind overture had not panned out. "Do your doctors think they've removed all the cancer?" she asked.

"Yes, for now. I'll have to go through more chemo, of course, and there's always the chance of the cancer metastasizing to somewhere else, but I have a good feeling about this. I don't think it's going to come back. I think I've suffered enough." Her face was practically beatific.

"That's wonderful. I hope you're right." Despite her numbness, she caught a tiny spark of Sherry's serenity and let it warm her. Sherry was going to make it. She had won her battle at the eleventh hour. The universe had allowed her a second chance at life. At least one of them was making something worthwhile of this year.

"He just needed some more time," Sherry murmured, and her eyelids fluttered drowsily. "More time to work things out."

"Yes," Olive agreed because it seemed like the wrong time to tell her the truth. It seemed egotistical and cruel to break through Sherry's moment of bliss. "I wanted to thank you," she choked out.

Sherry's eyes flickered open again. "No, I want to thank *you*. For telling it like it is. For pushing me to take a risk and reminding me what it means to be a mother. I never would've swallowed my pride and called him without your constant nagging. I couldn't have done it without you, Olive. You're the reason he's back."

It was quickly becoming apparent to Olive that they were not talking about the same *he*. Her thoughts spun in a sloppy, graceless pirouette. "Do you mean . . . ? Are you talking about Heath?"

"Yes." Though her body was blanched and wasted, Sherry beamed like a woman in her prime.

Everything clicked into place. This was the reason for Sherry's beatific smile. Heath had come home. Olive wondered how long he had been in town and what had passed between them. It was unsettling to her that he wasn't here with his mom now. She had so many questions for Sherry, but she didn't want to tire her out after her mastectomy.

"Oh, Sherry. That's terrific." Her face hurt from a combination of smiling so hard and suppressing tears. Overcoming the cancer, reuniting with Heath—it was all too much. The wall between Sherry and the rest of the world had seemed too high, too impenetrable, but here it was, crumbling down, and all these good things were flowing in effortlessly. Sherry had been through so much in her life, and God knew she deserved this. But just behind Olive's happiness for Sherry lurked an envy that she didn't even want to acknowledge because it was so mean and low. *Why Sherry? Why not me? I've been working ten times as hard as she has.* But she ripped the envy away as though it were a spiderweb obscuring her view and told herself to be happy for Sherry.

"He arrived three days ago. He was so mad, I could hardly bear to look at him. He was mad at me for having cancer, can you believe it?" Sherry rasped.

Olive swallowed. Actually, she could. She remembered all the ugly stages of grief she'd been through with her dad.

"I told him, 'Excuse me for inconveniencing you with my life-threatening breast cancer.' We went on like that for a long time, and I thought for sure it was going nowhere and that he would leave any minute, and I'd never see him again. But then he showed me some pages from his journal that he took with him to Spain."

In her eagerness to tell the story, Sherry tried to lean forward, her diminished body pulling against the various tubes and wires, but Olive gently restrained her. Sherry relaxed against the pillows as if that had been her plan all along.

"He had actually made a list of every wrong I'd ever done him! Can you believe it? God, that was hard to look at. But after I read the list to myself, I started to read it aloud to him, item by item, saying, 'Heath, I am sorry for leaving you at Camp Loon Lake even though you wrote me twenty times that summer to come get you. I am sorry for promising to take you and your friends to Six Flags Great America for your eleventh birthday and then blowing it off. I am sorry for never learning that you hate peanut butter. I am sorry for bringing Robert to your cross-country awards banquet even though you asked me not to.' He told me I was being stupid and to stop, but I told him I needed to do it."

Her breathing sounded more like panting now. Olive didn't know if it was from the emotion or the recent surgery, or both. Sherry's heart rate and blood oxygen levels looked normal on the monitor. Olive stroked her forehead. "Take a breath. Easy now. You need to rest, Sherry. Don't strain yourself."

Sherry scowled at her but took a few slow, deep breaths. "I didn't know what to expect when I finished. Neither of us said anything. But then Heath asked me if it was okay if he stayed with me for Christmas, and of course I said it was."

"That's progress," Olive murmured. "Definitely a step in the right direction." She held up the cup of water the nurse had left on Sherry's tray, but Sherry shook her head.

"It was so awful looking at all the mistakes I'd made with him. I've always suspected I was a bad mother, but seeing it all stacked up like that in his neat, angry handwriting . . . it hurt." Sherry curled her fist over her newly missing breast. "It hurt worse than this."

"But you've acknowledged those mistakes now, and it seems like he's willing to give you a second chance." *Unlike Phil.* She swallowed back her own unhappy story, which was aching to trickle from her tongue. Sherry didn't need to hear this from her now.

"To do what? Go to Great America together? I know nothing about being a mother to a college kid."

Olive forced a smile. "Neither do I. Maybe you can talk to my mom. But I think the important thing right now is just to be there for him."

"One go of it, and you have everything figured out," Sherry said. It was the same thing she'd said when Olive and her mom had visited her in October, but this time it wasn't a sarcastic accusation. Instead, Sherry sounded impressed. Maybe even proud of Olive.

Olive's chest tightened. "Not everything."

There was a light tap on the open door. The same young nurse with glasses who had cared for Sherry last time stood in the entryway. Olive feared that she had come to kick her out. "You have another visitor, Ms. Witan. Are you feeling up to it?"

Sherry widened her eyes and managed to look alert. "Yes, of course."

Olive turned her head, anticipating seeing her mom with a cheery smile and a bright bouquet of flowers. Instead, it was the spiky-haired young man from the waiting room. He looked just as surprised to see Olive as she was to see him. His eyes flashed from Olive to Sherry and then back again.

"Heath," Sherry whispered—she was the only one in the room who didn't seem surprised—and he took a tentative step into the hospital room.

Olive pushed back her chair to make room for Heath as she struggled to comprehend how two people who looked nothing alike could be related. Sherry with her fair complexion, red hair, and once-rounded body. How could this dark, lean young man be her son? But then she remembered the strikingly familiar smile on the young man's lips—it was Sherry's smile—and the comment Sherry had made about Heath after her first mastectomy. Handsome like his father, Norman, but stuck with Sherry's temperament. That seemed about right.

"This is Olive Watson, the daughter of a good friend," Sherry explained. "And a good friend in her own right."

Heath studied them skeptically. He still hadn't moved beyond his first step into the room, even though Olive had pulled up a chair for him. "Yes, we've met," he said. "In the waiting room."

"Oh." Now Sherry was surprised. She looked at Olive. "So you already knew that Heath was home for the holidays?"

"We didn't introduce ourselves, and I didn't put two and two together until just now," Olive said. She gestured to the empty chair next to her, and finally Heath took the hint.

"Mom," Heath started, and it shocked Olive to hear him call Sherry that. He sounded so young. "You look like shit." Apparently, tactlessness was a family trait. Heath's eyes drank in everything but his mother's face—the partially open door leading to the bathroom, the blank TV, the call button, the IV bag and stand, the bedside monitor.

"I know. I *feel* like shit." Sherry sounded almost apologetic.

They didn't say anything else. Heath slouched forward with his eyes on the tile floor, gripping *The Divine Comedy*. Sherry stared at his spiky head fervently. It was a far cry from a Hallmark moment, but there was definitely something powerful there. Heath's presence spoke volumes. The broken bones of their severed relationship were slowly starting to knit back together.

"Read to me?" Sherry suddenly asked in a way that would've seemed almost coquettish to Olive, had she not known how nervous and afraid of rejection Sherry really was.

Heath's face reddened, and Olive was worried he would turn her down. But then she realized he was simply embarrassed. "I haven't gotten very far," he admitted, showing his mom the few thin pages his bookmark separated from the rest. "Should I just start at the beginning?"

"Please," Sherry said. "Hearing about a journey through hell and purgatory and on to paradise seems fitting right about now."

Heath cleared his throat and ducked his head low. "This is the Longfellow translation." There was another long pause before he began. " 'Midway upon the journey of our life, I found myself within a forest dark, for the straightforward pathway had been lost.' "

His reading voice was gentle and rich, nothing like the blasé tone he'd taken with his mother earlier. Olive felt like she could close her eyes and stay there all day and all night letting the poetry wash over her and erase everything else.

But she knew this moment belonged to Sherry and Heath, who still had such a long way to go. She had played her part in their reunion, but now it was time for her to leave them.

"I should get going," she said when Heath paused to take a sip of water after completing the first canto. "It was nice meeting you, Heath. I hope you recover quickly, Sherry. Please call me when you're feeling up to it. If there's anything I can do for you . . ."

Sherry attempted to prop herself up against the pillows. Her brown eyes were intense, and Olive thought she could make out Sherry's former fiery self. The Sherry who let her garden grow wild. The Sherry who read Hardy, Chopin, Brontë, and Woolf. The Sherry who conned men out of their money betting on baseball games and claimed she didn't believe in happily-ever-afters. "Thank you, Olive," she said softly.

It was almost five o'clock, and Olive knew her mom would be leaving work and heading to the hospital soon. She called her from the lobby to give her one more update. "I'm just leaving the hospital now, Mom. You might want to stop by a little later tonight."

"Why? Is Sherry okay?"

"She's doing fine. But her son is here right now, so it might be better to visit later."

Olive's mom took a sharp breath. "Heathcliff? Heathcliff is there? How wonderful! I know that will mean a lot to Sherry."

Olive involuntarily lingered at the fountain. "Yeah, it does. I'm sorry I'm not sticking around. I know we planned on doing this together."

"That's all right. I'm just happy Sherry's doing well. And

I'm thrilled that her son showed up. I'm glad he had a change of heart." She paused, and then added softly, "Sometimes it just takes time."

She was insinuating that Phil might eventually forgive her, too, but Olive knew otherwise. "Time and a life-threatening disease," she said sarcastically. "There's nothing like cancer to bring families together. And then rip them apart."

"Well, the cancer may have helped things in a way," her mom admitted. "But I don't think it was so much on Heathcliff's part as Sherry's. It gave her a reason to reach out to him finally and give it her all."

Olive didn't say anything; she was watching the basins overflowing and trickling like tears into the pool below. Her chest felt constricted by sorrow. She wanted to go home to Phil, but he was like a house that had been torn down. His shelter no longer existed for her.

Chapter 22

It was easy to prepare for Christmas when she already knew which gifts to buy. She felt a tinge of guilt recycling the same gift ideas from last year, but honestly, besides herself, who was going to know? She had too much on her mind right now to worry about coming up with the perfect presents. And her family had seemed to enjoy the gifts she'd given them last Christmas, so presumably, they would enjoy opening them up again. She purchased a watercolor kit for her mom, who had recently taken a painting class; a wok for Harry; and a cashmere sweater for Verona, and she made a donation to World Vision's clean water fund for Christopher, who was against the extravagant holiday consumerism.

Her family knew that she and Phil had broken up and were no longer living together. But besides the short Thanksgiving Day encounter with her mom and Harry, Olive hadn't spent any real length of time with her family since the breakup. It wasn't something she was looking forward to.

They had all been distraught, particularly Christopher, last February when she'd broken the news the first time.

She pulled up in front of the gray-and-white Cape Cod at the exact time her mom had specified, but Christopher and Verona's car was already in the driveway. She braced herself for the day ahead. It bothered her that a holiday she had once so looked forward to now filled her with a sense of dread. She knew that would've been different if Phil had been by her side.

She closed her eyes and tried to remember happy Christmas Eves past. When Olive was in seventh grade, her dad had unwittingly started the family tradition of eating anything *other* than a typical Christmas dinner when he forgot to thaw the ten-pound turkey. That year they ordered pizza. In subsequent years, they did tacos, calzones, a fish fry, hamburgers, waffles, fried chicken, and for one particularly memorable Christmas, five kinds of pie. The December her dad passed away, they hadn't celebrated Christmas, and the following year, her mom had reverted back to traditional Christmas dinners so she could invite Laurel and their elderly father, and the house wouldn't feel so lonely. But even then, her mom would throw in an odd side dish, a stack of blueberry pancakes or a tray of chicken nuggets, as a kind of tip of her hat to her late husband. Last year, Harry had presided over the dinner with the standard fare: turkey, chestnut stuffing, mashed potatoes, cranberry sauce, acorn squash, pumpkin pie, and gingerbread cookies.

But when Olive entered the house, the rich smell she'd been expecting—a warm burst of cinnamon, nutmeg, molasses, and turkey roasting in the oven—didn't greet her. She sniffed cautiously as she unwound her scarf and hung up her coat. It was four o'clock—hadn't they started cooking yet? Although there were no food smells, she detected a hint of pine as she made her way to the living room. The tree Harry had picked out was beautifully symmetric and proportional, almost as tall as the living room ceiling. It was covered with Olive and Christopher's childhood ornaments—laminated paper hearts with grade school photos pasted inside, Santas with buttons for eyes and cotton balls for beards, God's eyes, gingerbread stars. In front of the tree, Christopher and Verona sat playing Christmas checkers at the coffee table. Olive's mom relaxed on the couch with a glass of wine, watching their game. Harry stood before the stereo, apparently putting on some music. Nat King Cole's velvety voice crooned from the speakers.

It was too much. It was too perfect, but still somehow all wrong. Just like watching the moment in Sherry's hospital room, observing her own family felt like intruding. She didn't belong here.

Almost as if he'd heard her thoughts, Harry suddenly turned around and spotted her in the doorway. "Olive!" he called. "Merry Christmas!"

Olive forced a smile and reluctantly stepped into the room. "Merry Christmas, guys!" She unloaded her bag of presents under the Christmas tree and sat next to her mom. "Who's winning?" she asked.

"Rona, of course," Christopher said with a frown. "She sits here and calculates the mathematical probability of every single move before she lifts a finger. It sucks."

"I play winner," Harry said.

"Looking forward to it." Verona smirked at her husband, as she jumped another of his checkers and removed it from the board.

"Can I get you anything, Olive?" her mom asked. "Eggnog, wine, soda?"

"Thanks, but I can get it myself," she said, and started to stand up.

"No, no. Let me get it," Harry protested. "What would you like?"

"A soda would be great, thanks. Whatever lemon-lime kind you have." Olive craned her neck to peek into the dining room. The table was naked except for a porcelain angel centerpiece. No plates, no silverware, no linen napkins, no silver gravy boat.

"I'll take an eggnog," Christopher called after him. He dejectedly moved one of his last checkers forward. "Go on. Take it."

"Has he always been such a poor sport?" Verona teased.

"Always," Olive and her mom both agreed.

"Are we done yet?" he complained, rocking back on his heels. "It's clear I don't have a snowball's chance in hell of winning this game."

"Do you surrender?"

"I surrender." He propped both his elbows on the coffee table with a glum expression, as Verona started putting all the pieces back on the board.

"What's going on with dinner?" Olive asked, running her fingers along the braided seam of a paisley pillow.

"Oh," her mom said, as if she were caught off guard by the question. She glanced over at Christopher. "We thought we'd do something different this year and order Chinese. It should be here any minute."

"Harry's not cooking?"

"No. You like Chinese food, right?" Her mom's forehead

scrunched with worry. "Christopher thought spring rolls and kung pao chicken were your favorites, so we made sure to get some of those. Honestly, we got a little of everything off the takeout menu. I don't know how we're going to eat it all."

"No worries," Christopher said, patting his stomach. "I'll handle it."

Olive stared at her brother in his oatmeal-colored cable-knit sweater, which clearly had been purchased by Verona. Could it be that he was actually on board with this Chinese food idea? It was so reminiscent of the dinners with their dad that she couldn't tell if it was a good thing, a kind of tribute to him, or a disrespectful act, a taking over of his unique tradition, like the New Year's Day party. It was also hard to know what to make of this seemingly random departure from last year. What had changed? Whose idea had it been and why?

"It's fine. Chinese sounds fine," Olive said stiffly, and accepted her soda from Harry. She thanked him, took a sip, and set the glass down on a coaster next to the potted poinsettia on the coffee table. The plant's hearty leaves and red silken petals provided a stark contrast to her African violet. She had discovered it lifeless last week—its leaves parched and gray, its shriveled buds lying atop the soil—and she couldn't revive it. She'd failed to keep her promise, and it seemed to her then, as it did now, that she hadn't done one single thing right this year. It was all a waste. A terrible, stupid waste of cosmic magnitude.

Harry and Verona started their game of checkers, and Christopher settled into an armchair across from Olive, drinking his mug of eggnog.

"Hey, Olive, I've been meaning to ask you—" He started, and Verona looked up from the game and shot him a warning look, but he continued anyway. "Are you planning on selling your condo?"

"Christopher!" their mom scolded sharply. She surveyed Olive, as if to measure how much damage had been done.

"What? What's wrong with that?" Christopher asked. "It's a legitimate question. I have a friend who'd be really interested in buying it from you if you are. For good money, too, and this way you wouldn't have to pay an agent commission or go through any of that other rigmarole."

"Don't mind him, Olive," Verona said. "He's actually quite torn up about you and Phil. Being an insensitive ass is just his way of showing it."

"No, I'm not selling it." The decision had been a difficult one. Should she cling to the hope that they would work things out, or should she prepare to start over alone? Selling the condo seemed so final. She worried that if Phil didn't have a home with her to come back to, he wouldn't ever come back to her. But living in the condo without him was torture. Everything reminded her of him—the Mint Julep walls; his forgotten, slowly rotting oranges in the fridge; her Chagall painting that he had hung over the fireplace. There were large, empty spaces like black holes where his belongings had been. The house that had once been bursting with happiness and potential now felt like a mausoleum. She and Phil had conversed brusquely about it over e-mail. He seemed indifferent to the fate of their condo, and since she had put down the majority of the money for the down payment, and they hadn't made many mortgage payments yet, he said he didn't care if she kept the condo and transferred it solely to her name.

"Really?" Christopher looked surprised. "But Phil moved out, right?"

"Yes." She hugged a pillow to her chest. "He managed to get his exact same apartment back. Can you believe it? The place stood open for three months, and no one rented it."

"I can believe it," her brother said. "That place is a dive. Who else would want it?" He gulped his eggnog, which left a wisp of a white mustache.

"How can you drink that stuff?" Olive asked. "You know it's like a million calories and grams of fat."

"Thank you, Nurse Killjoy," Christopher shot back.

"It's only once a year," her mom said. "Let him enjoy it."

"Actually," Harry interjected, "the way I make my eggnog is slightly different from classic recipes, and quite low fat. I use skim milk and mostly egg whites, but to make it thicken, I—"

The doorbell rang, sparing them from further details.

"I'll get it!" Harry jumped up, nearly overturning the checkerboard. Verona, who was on the verge of jumping two of Harry's checkers, Olive could see, blew out a heavy sigh and sat back.

Olive made a motion to move to the dining room table, but no one else did, so she remained seated on the couch, feeling almost like a propped-up doll, a shell of herself. She wished she could exchange glances with Phil and see what he was making of all of this, but of course, he wasn't here, and he never would be again. She closed her eyes momentarily, remembering the reassuring pressure of his hand on her thigh, the way he'd been a cheerful conductor between Harry and Christopher, between all of them, really.

Harry returned with two large paper bags. Her mom slid off the couch and knelt on the floor, moving the checkerboard and poinsettia aside, and then helped Harry unpack the small white cartons and arranged them on the coffee table. *We're eating here?* Olive thought, but Christopher was already opening a pair of chopsticks, and Verona was situating herself cross-legged beside him on the floor. "Ooh, beef and pea pods," Verona said, as she untucked the flaps of the carton closest to her. Olive sat down next to her mom. It was like the nineties again with flimsy paper plates and reindeer napkins and greasy food and companionable silence and stocking feet and inexplicable Christmas cheer. But her dad wasn't here. And Phil wasn't here, either, and Olive wasn't going to let herself be tricked into enjoying herself.

"Is Aunt Laurel coming over tomorrow?" Christopher asked around a mouthful of fried rice.

"No, she's working," their mom said. "We're going to exchange gifts on New Year's Day instead." Olive's heart flipped over at the mention of the New Year. "Harry and I are probably just going to sleep in, make a big brunch, maybe catch a matinee. You're welcome to join us if you'd like."

"Thanks," Verona said. "We wouldn't miss it for the world. We won't be able to stay very long though because my parents are flying in, and we're having a little dinner for them at our place."

"Oh, how nice," Olive's mom said.

Out of the corner of her eye, Olive could see her mom watching her with great tenderness, and then she tucked a strand of Olive's hair behind her ear. She murmured, "I hate to see you so sad, honey."

Harry, with his preternatural hearing, looked up from a losing battle with his chow mein. *He really should be eating it with a fork,* Olive thought. She waited for him to say something cheesy and meaningless. Instead, he stared at her with a sad little smile of understanding.

"Hey, there are only four fortune cookies in here," Verona said, holding up a little plastic bag. "We're short one."

"That's okay. I don't want one," Olive said. She backed up from the table and pulled her knees to her chest.

"No, no. You take it. I don't need one," Harry said. "I'm the luckiest man alive. I have all the good fortune I'll ever need." He patted Olive's mom's shoulder, and she smiled back at him.

Christopher turned to Olive and pretended to stick his finger down his throat.

Olive's mom cracked open her cookie and read aloud, "Those who have love have wealth beyond measure."

"Aw," Verona said.

Christopher rolled his eyes and then pulled the folded slip out of his broken cookie half. "He who laughs at himself never runs out of things to laugh at."

"Ah, that's a good one for you." Verona chuckled, and Olive's mom unsuccessfully tried to hide a smile.

"Ha, ha. Very funny," Christopher said. "What does yours say, Rona?"

Verona held up her tiny white slip of paper and read dramatically, "Get ready! Good fortune awaits you. Lucky numbers: five, seventeen, thirty-three, sixty." She chewed her cookie. "I guess I'd better go buy a lottery ticket. Olive? What does your fortune say?"

The cookie still lay in front of Olive untouched. She didn't want to open it. What good were fate and fortune anyway? If there was some sort of plan she was supposed to follow, it was unreadable to her and impossible to stick to. She was tired of fate, which was probably just a made-up concept invented by humans to feel like something or someone was guiding them anyway. God, spirits, cookies, whatever. She was so sick of buying into the idea that there was actually meaning behind any of this. It was just her, blind and alone, making a mess of her life on her own, thank you very much.

"I don't want it," she said, and hugged her knees tighter.

"Come on. It's supposed to be fun," Christopher said. He snatched her cookie away before she could stop him. His eyes scanned it a couple of times before he read it aloud. "Many a false step is made by standing still."

Was that the best the universe could do? Olive raged silently in her head. It was a slap in the face, really. What a cop-out. What a generic piece of crap. And yet her face was heating up and her eyes were starting to sting.

"I'm sorry. I need a minute," she whispered, and fled to the kitchen.

The kitchen was clean and bare. The only clue that it was Christmas Eve was a tin of cookies on the marble countertop. She leaned her forehead against the fridge door and tried to quell the flood of overwhelming sorrow and helplessness that was threatening to rise up and drown her.

Her eyes flickered downward, and she noticed a photo on the fridge. She plucked it from its magnet to get a closer look. It was Phil and Harry playing golf in St. Lucia. Phil, radiant and athletic, good-naturedly enduring the sweaty arm Harry had slung around his neck.

The kitchen door swung open behind her. She didn't look up from the photo.

"You know I'm not one to meddle," Christopher started,

"or talk about feelings, for that matter. And I don't know why your relationship ended, but it's obvious you're still in love with Phil. And if I knew the guy at all—which I think I did—he's still probably very much in love with you. That kind of love just doesn't go away because of some stupid fight."

"It was more than a fight. I ruined it. He doesn't feel the same way about me anymore." Olive returned the photo to the fridge and turned to face Christopher.

"Now would be a good time," he muttered under his breath.

"A good time for what?" she returned angrily.

"A good time to say *when*, Olive. Dad was right. You don't know when to say when. When to admit you're wrong. When to really lay it all on the line and take a chance."

"You don't know that! You don't know how I've tried!" she cried. "I admitted I was wrong. I apologized. I've tried really hard to make things right."

"Well, you obviously haven't tried hard enough."

She stood there seething in the frustratingly calm, quiet kitchen. Christopher stared her down. They had the same eyes, she knew. The same chocolate brown eyes as their dad, who could laugh with his eyes one minute and shoot daggers out of them the next. She remembered Phil's admission—that he had asked for her dad's blessing before his death. She remembered the crazy thought she had had kayaking—that this whole year was somehow her dad's doing. Maybe it was his way of watching out for her and saving her from herself.

It galled her to admit it, but for once, her brother was right. She *hadn't* tried hard enough; she had let Phil walk away from her twice. She had been too reserved, too passive, believing she deserved whatever punishment was coming to her for a mistake she had made in a parallel year. But she had been punishing herself all along. When would she have fully atoned for her transgressions? When would her conscience be finally clean? She had done the right thing this year, and that meant something. She needed Phil to forgive her. She needed to forgive herself.

She whirled away from Christopher and flung open the kitchen cabinet where her mom always kept a calendar hung. It was the same tropical beaches calendar she had given Olive as a Christmas present last year, but she hardly noticed. Her eyes narrowed in on the last week of December. Seven days. Seven days until the new year. Sweat dribbled down the back of her neck, and her hand trembled as she gripped the corner of the cabinet door.

Phil Russell. She saw his beautiful face; his strong, brown hands; the solid line of his shoulders, almost as if he were standing before her. He was a good, honest man. He saw positive qualities in people that others overlooked. He had helped her through one of the most difficult periods in her life. He had given her the kind of love that made her feel protected and cherished. He made her want to be a better person.

The cabinet door slammed shut, snapping her out of her reverie. Her conviction and clarity of purpose were suddenly, blindingly restored. She loved him, and she was going to do everything she could to get him back. She hadn't come this far just to walk away. He was the love of her life, dammit. The man she wanted to marry. The world had reversed its orbit to bring them back together, for Pete's sake, and she wasn't going down without a fight. Fate could only do so much; the rest was up to her.

Chapter 23

The Russell farmhouse had never looked prettier than it did that Christmas Day. Crisp, virgin snow blanketed the hills, capped the trees, and concealed the discarded car parts and broken flowerpots that normally littered the landscape.

With trepidation, Olive surveyed the scene from her idling SUV. The driveway was lined with minivans and sporty station wagons—the vehicles of Phil's aunts and uncles—but his old Mercedes wasn't among them. Perhaps he was parked around back by the dilapidated barn. Perhaps he wasn't even here.

She turned off the engine and trudged through the snow to the house. Despite the cold, it felt unbearably warm inside her down-filled jacket.

She didn't allow herself to pause before knocking on the side door, which was the entrance everyone except salespeople and Jehovah's Witnesses knew to use. Inside, she could hear loud, happy voices. Minutes seemed to pass, and then abruptly, the door was thrown open by a blond girl in a red dress with a taffeta skirt. She was Phil's seven-year-old cousin, Leah, who was a particular favorite of his.

"Hi!" Leah exclaimed brightly, swishing her skirt from side to side.

"Merry Christmas, Leah!" Olive remembered how Phil had bought sidewalk chalk for Leah two Easters ago and the three of them had knelt on the asphalt driveway drawing rabbits, eggs, and rainbows. *I love you, Olive*, Phil had chalked inside a lopsided pink heart, and Leah had giggled and then pouted until Phil had drawn a heart for her, too.

Olive could hear scrabbling claws trying to find purchase on the linoleum, and suddenly a brown blur skidded across the kitchen to her and jumped at her legs.

"Hi, Cashew," she said, crouching down and letting him lick her cheek. "Good boy, good boy," she murmured. His tiny body was so warm and compact, so energetic, so affectionate. He was a bundle of pure love, gift-wrapped in fur. She wanted to scoop him up and hold him to her chest and never let him go. Leah squatted down, too, and started scratching his back. Cashew flopped to the floor and squirmed from side to side, giving her easier access to his tummy.

"Silly dog," Leah pronounced. She turned and shouted into the kitchen, "Aunt Carol, Phil's girlfriend is here!"

Olive couldn't help feeling a tinge of pleasure at being called that, even though she knew a seven-year-old would not understand the abstract concept of a breakup. She patted Cashew's rump and then leaned through the doorway, hoping to catch a glimpse of Phil, but all she could see was a group of women clustered around the kitchen table.

She hadn't anticipated an audience. As she'd lain awake last night envisioning how their reunion would transpire, she had imagined a string of scenarios—Phil slamming the door in her face, Phil sweeping her into his arms, Phil coldly asking her to leave, Phil bending down on one knee. The closer her brain had fluttered toward sleep, the stranger the scenarios had become. Standing on the frozen surface of the lake, the ice cracking and popping all around her, she had reached out her hand for his and waited to see if he would save her.

Phil's mom broke away from the cluster. She was a petite woman with Phil's thick, brown hair, but streaked with gray. Her apron had a row of poinsettias embroidered across the bosom. The expression she wore was often guarded and unfriendly, the toughened façade of someone whom life hadn't handled with care. At times, Olive could glimpse Carol's stark, unadorned beauty, the stunner she must have been in her twenties. At the present, however, she was studying Olive with the look mothers reserved for people who had hurt their children.

"Oh, Olive," Carol said, and her voice sounded more sad than angry. "I suppose you're looking for Phil."

"Is he here?"

"No, you just missed him. He said he was going for a walk along the lake. He didn't say which lake; he didn't say for how long." There was a silent threat in her brown eyes.

"Thank you," Olive said. There was so much more she wanted to say to her. *You don't know me like you think you do. I love your son just as much as you do, and I only want to make him happy. I'm never going to hurt him again.* But promises like these had been made to Carol before, and she had no reason to trust them now. She wore her apron like a coat of armor. “Have a nice Christmas.”

Olive hurried back to her SUV so quickly that she almost fell in the snow.

He was at Lake Mendota, of course. On the lakeshore path. It was the place he went to clear his head and the site of so many of their happy memories together. Bike rides; long walks; stolen kisses in the woods; talks about their future careers, their parents, the afterlife. After their first serious argument—on a Sunday afternoon in early spring, she remembered, but not what the fight was about—they had angrily parted ways only to find each other an hour later, brooding on the same pier. They had instantly made up.

She was certain he was at the lake now, but it was difficult to rein in her hopes that he was there for *her*: thinking about their relationship, missing her, maybe even wishing she would find him. She tried to remind herself that it had been almost a month and a half since he’d left her alone outside the hospital, and since then, he hadn’t returned any of her calls or tried to see her. But still—still there was this, Phil at the lake on Christmas Day, and she couldn’t drive back into the city fast enough.

She had the radio tuned to the only station that refused to play Christmas carols during the holiday season. For the first part of her drive, the music had fallen on deaf ears, but ironically, as she drove to the University of Wisconsin campus, Cher’s “If I Could Turn Back Time” came on and caught Olive’s attention. *If I could turn back time, if I could find a way, I’d take back those words that hurt you and you’d stay.*

“Oh, Cher, you make it sound so easy,” Olive said aloud. She sang the rest of the lyrics at the top of her lungs.

With the dorms closed for winter break, no one had cleared the snow from the sidewalks or parking lots, but Olive's SUV had no trouble plowing over the foot and a half of untouched snow. She parked in the lot next to the old cream-brick dormitory where she had spent her first year of college; hers was the only vehicle. If he was here . . . she guessed that Phil had parked at the Union instead.

The snow crunched underfoot. She would've found the shushing rhythm of her footfalls peaceful had she not suddenly become so anxious to find Phil and confirm the hunch she was aching to believe. What if they missed each other, somehow circumventing one another like true star-crossed lovers? What if he had already headed back home? What if he had never been here at all? The serendipitous prospect of their meeting each other here seemed tenuous at best.

It was impossible to run in the deep snow, so she half walked, half hurdled over the drifts as fast as she could. The docks were packed away for the winter, and the frozen lake looked oddly forlorn without these branching arms. The wind sent the powdery snow dancing in swirling patterns across the dull gray surface of the lake. Dark circles marred the ice like pockmarks, where ice fishermen had drilled.

Olive tried to imagine how Phil would view this landscape. Would it remind him of another frozen lake and how he had proposed to her beside it? Would he remember how it looked in fairer weather, when they had sat on the docks together and watched the sun set? Or would it appear to him a bleak backdrop with all meaning drained from it? Was he here, then, to grieve? The last thought made her shudder, and she struck it from her mind.

She came to a fork in the path. Should she go left toward

Picnic Point or right toward the Union, where they had fed ducks? She lingered uncertainly at the junction, facing the open expanse of silvery ice and sky, letting the stillness of the landscape seep through her many layers of clothing, into her bones.

A loud crack suddenly exploded in the quiet of the abandoned path. A fallen tree? Breaking ice? It was probably just wishful thinking, but it had sounded almost like a golf club connecting with a ball. She remained stationary, watching her puffs of warm breath evaporate in the frosty air. *Crack!* The earsplitting noise ricocheted off the trees. She strained her ears, trying to determine which direction the sound had come from. It was close by.

She whirled to the left, nearly losing her balance. About forty feet away, a stone bench nestled among the naked trees, and beyond that, a small clearing revealed a view of the lake. As she approached, she caught the dark shape of someone standing there. She held her breath and continued walking, and when Phil's solemn profile came into focus, it no longer seemed necessary to breathe.

He's here, he's here, he's here, she repeated silently to herself in an effort to convince her brain of what her eyes were seeing. She had been right about this much. He stood in his golf stance with his head down. While she watched, he twisted his body gracefully and then struck the ball with vicious force. *Crack!* The little white ball sailed over the lake, skittering onto the hard surface at least two hundred yards away.

Phil had either heard her approach or sensed her presence because he suddenly turned his head. He blinked against the glare of the snow and held up his hand to his forehead like a visor. There was a long pause. "Olive?"

"Phil." She slipped through the trees, feeling unaccountably shy.

Here was the moment she had been waiting for, but it was hard to live up to the fearlessness and passion of her dream self. It was easier to fight everyone else's battles; it was much harder to feel bold in the face of such painful rejection. To act bravely when her own heart was at stake.

"How did you know I was here?" he asked, managing to sound casual, as if they had been separated for mere minutes rather than months.

"Your mom."

"But I didn't tell her I was coming *here*." He leaned on his driver.

"I had a feeling," she said, chasing after the words to describe it. "I was thinking about the fight we had in college, and how we both came to the pier, and I hoped . . ." She drifted off, unsure how to qualify her hopes, which felt too large and weighty for the mere beginning of their conversation to sustain.

He bent to retrieve a golf ball from the worn leather bag splayed open on the stone bench. "Do you remember what that fight was about?"

"No," she said apologetically, and dug her numb fists into her pockets.

"It was about Brian, actually, of all things. Do you remember? He backed out on that spring break trip with me, and I was out five hundred bucks, and I was so furious with him. I didn't want to speak to him ever again, but you tried to get me to see his point of view, and I got mad at you for taking his side. It wasn't really ever our fight to begin with. You were just trying to save me from myself." Dropping the ball in the flattened snow, he hardly waited for it to settle before whacking it nearly to Picnic Point. *Crack.* "It's ridiculous to think about now, but I remember how indignant I felt at the time. But I was clearly in the wrong."

Olive gave him a wary smile. "Clearly." As it was also clear that she was the one in the wrong this time. In a major way.

He plunked another golf ball in the snow. "You want to hit some balls?"

The unexpected turn in the conversation threw her off; she hadn't hit a golf ball since college when he'd taken her to the driving range. She took another step into the clearing. "Sure."

He handed her the driver. Was this some kind of test?

She accepted the club, the leather grip still warm from his hands. She imitated Phil, positioning her feet shoulder width apart and leaning slightly forward. She raised the golf club over her shoulder, vaguely remembering something Phil had taught her about an L shape, and then took a hack at the ball in front of her. It popped off the hill and then dribbled across the ice about twenty feet.

"That was abysmal," Phil said, but he looked amused. "You look like you're playing baseball. I'm surprised you even hit the ball."

"Is this how you coach your boys?" she asked, arching an eyebrow.

"Most of my boys start off with a little more skill. And besides, didn't I teach you all this once before?"

Her heart gave an encouraged thump. "It was a long time ago."

He sighed and passed her another ball. "You don't remember, huh? Your swing should be like a wheel—not quite vertical, not quite horizontal. Angled. And make sure you follow through all the way. You stopped almost right after you hit the ball, and that's not going to give it much distance."

She lined up her shot and tried to follow his directions, swinging the club in a self-consciously angled wheel—up, down, and over. This time she missed the ball completely and sliced the snow instead.

Phil reached for the club. If this was a test, she had failed it.

He strode over to where she was standing and motioned for her to back up. It took her a moment to realize he hadn't given up on her; he was just demonstrating his stance and swing. "See how I'm pivoting my body? It's not just my arms—the real power comes from the rest of my body turning into my swing. Come here and try this."

She stepped closer to him, and he didn't back away. Instead, he stood close behind her, his chest nearly brushing her back, his arms draped loosely over her arms, swinging the golf club back and forth in a slow, exaggerated curve. Her breath caught in her throat as he gripped her hips, pushing them gently toward the lake. Even through her thick winter coat, his touch felt electric.

"Let's try it together," he said. "Okay? Swing on three. One. Two. Three."

Olive gave herself over to him, letting her arms move with his arms and her torso turn with his torso. The club connected with the ball. The ball flew at least fifty yards in the air this time, rolling neatly into a large, grayish divot in the ice. A frozen-over ice fishing hole.

"A hole in one!" Phil laughed, not letting her go.

She stood very, very still, hoping he hadn't realized he was still holding her. Or that he had realized it and wanted to. His body felt warm and substantial against hers. She closed her eyes.

"Why are you here?" he whispered into her hair.

She shivered. "I wanted to ask you the same thing."

He paused, his arms still around her, but his grip loosened ever so slightly. "I guess I came here to escape for a little while. From my family and their chaos. From all the holiday cheer and goodwill to mankind. From you."

"From me?" she asked, startled.

He grinned sheepishly. "It didn't work, though."

She stepped out of his grasp, and his arms fell away easily, like he wasn't trying to hold on to her at all. She felt exposed. "Do you want me to go?" she asked more coldly than she'd intended.

"No, no. That's not what I meant. You were here even before you got here." He gestured to the lake and the snow-buried path behind them. "You're in every single one of my memories of this place. In the trees, in the sky, in the contours of the lake. There's no escaping you, Olive."

Hopefulness swelled inside her chest, but a flicker of anger tempered it. *Then why must you try?* she wanted to ask. *Then why don't you give in and come back to me?* Because he hadn't last month, and he hadn't last year, and even now she was the one who had come to him. If he loved her enough to see her in the "contours of the lake," why didn't he love her enough to give her a call and make her heart stop aching so badly?

"On my end, it feels like you've made a pretty clean break," she said, looking down at the ground beneath her, where her boots and Phil's had stamped diamonds and spades into the snow.

"There's no such thing as a clean break." He laced his fingers behind his neck, elbows pointed out like wings, as if surrendering. "There's just hurt and regret. Second-guessing and trying to figure out how such a right thing could go so wrong."

They stood facing the lake without speaking, together yet also apart. Time felt as thick and impermeable as ice, and Olive wondered if the world had finally slowed. She sought the language that would express how sorry she was and how fervent her wish for their reconciliation, but all she could think of were the three little words that would be inadequate. *I love you, but no*, he had said.

Phil punctured the silence. "This whole time, I've been trying to solve our relationship like it's some equation that I couldn't get to balance. I couldn't figure out if your not-cheating the second time canceled out your cheating the first time, and then if lying to me all year somehow multiplied the whole mess." He released his interlocked fingers, letting his arms swing at his sides. "And then I realized that I hadn't even factored in my side of the equation. I know I can be rigid in my thinking sometimes, and I must have made it really hard for you to want to talk to me about all of this. And I know I shut you out and walked away from an otherwise really good thing because that's what I tend to do. But then I didn't know which of these was worse, which way the equation tipped."

She craned her neck to look up at him, her thoughts

fluttering around like moths trapped in a jar. Phil's eyes flashed at her, green as ivy in the wintry light. She stared back, hoping he could read everything she was thinking and feeling in the depths of her eyes. He scrutinized each of her features, as if he'd forgotten her face, as if he'd like to kiss her.

"Laying eyes on you, Olive, makes all of those imaginary calculations fly out the window. I see you, and I suddenly forget why I was keeping score. That's why I stayed away, I guess. It was a last-ditch effort to protect myself. Because you totally, utterly undo me."

Her heart was straining to lift right out of her body like a helium-filled balloon. "I'm going to try to never hurt you again. You don't need to protect yourself from me."

"You're probably right," he said, "but it's a hard habit for me to break. Ever since I was a kid, I've been trying to protect myself. It's like I'm trying to keep the bad away with one hand while holding on to the good with the other, and it just doesn't work. It's stupid. I need both hands. So I guess I just have to spread out my arms and accept the bad with the good."

She reached for his hand, bridging the distance between them. "I hope there's more good than bad."

"You never answered my question," he said softly. "Why are you here?"

"I'm here," she started, praying for the right words to come to her, "because I couldn't bear to let another day pass without you knowing how sorry I am for hurting you. I'm here because our relationship is such an important event in my life that the *universe* propelled me backward in time to restore our love. I'm here because it only took a few days of being with you again, loving you, and having you love me back so completely, for me to remember how happy I could be." Teardrops streamed down her face, and she distractedly wiped them away with her free hand.

"I'm here because I could never want to be with anyone but you. I'm here because I could never find someone as compassionate and honest and fun as you, someone who sees so much beauty and good in the world and in me. I'm here because as clichéd as it sounds, I know you're my soul mate. I'm here because I love you, Phil, and living without you is unbearable. And I really believe we're both here, drawn to this spot, because we're meant to be together."

He squeezed her hand. "I thought you didn't believe in fate."

"I still don't," she said. "At least not Fate with a capital *F*." How could she possibly believe in the Fate of the Greek tragedies, just one path, just one destiny for the hero when there were multiple fates, numerous possibilities, infinite outcomes, so many different routes? Wasn't her repeat year really just a vehicle for her to see that? To see all the different choices she could make before realizing that Phil had been the best choice for her all along?

"But I believe in us," she said.

He pulled her into his arms and crushed her to his chest. She could feel his rib cage and beneath it, the steady thump of his heart. The bitter wind whistled around them, but immersed in Phil's embrace, she felt only protected and warm. Something was loosening inside her body. The burden she'd been carrying for almost two years was dissolving now. Absolution entered her pores, filled her bloodstream, and circulated to every cell in her body. Her happiness and relief were so intense that she felt weak.

Phil bent his head downward to kiss her, still cradling her.

Carefully backing toward the stone bench, he pulled her onto his lap. She leaned against him, letting him support her. They clung to each other and kissed desperately as if he were going off to fight a war. Even in the oppressive cold, she could smell traces of the soap on his skin, fresh as evergreen trees and cut grass. She folded back the collar of his jacket and pressed her lips against the bare hollow of his throat. He moaned and smoothed his hands down over her hair. It felt so good, she had to stifle a sob.

"God, I've missed you," she whispered into his neck.

"I've missed you, too, Ollie." He raised her face and stroked her cheek. His fingers sent tiny tingles across her skin. "Your face is really cold."

"But my lips are warm," she murmured.

He tightened his grip on her, hugging her closer. "We probably shouldn't stay here. I don't want you to freeze. Where are you parked?"

"In the dorm lot," she said.

"I'm over by the crew house. Let's head to my car since it's closer."

At that moment, she didn't care if they walked all the way home as long as they were together. They set off through the shin-deep snow, Phil with one arm around her waist, the other carrying his golf bag and club. The snowdrifts seemed like half the obstacles they'd proved earlier, and the blocky crew house was just up ahead.

"So tell me about this alternate reality," Phil said, lifting her over a particularly deep snowdrift. "Gosh, if you'd told me sooner, can you imagine all the space-time tests we could've done?"

She laughed and then started to chronicle the differences

between her mom's two weddings: her opposition the first time and Christopher's opposition the second, how Phil's presence had made the events go more smoothly. She told him about Sherry's battle with breast cancer and her reunion with Heath. She explained why she hadn't wanted to live at High Pointe Hills, even venturing to mention that she and Alex had dated briefly and unsuccessfully. She divulged the real story behind her rupture with Kerrigan. She told him of all the trials she'd experienced and lessons she'd learned from repeat patients—Sarah Hutchinson, Betty Gardner, the Dodge brothers, Ryan Avery. They sat talking and then kissing in his Mercedes with the heater blowing full blast until the sky turned lavender. She felt empty yet full, spent yet bursting with energy, drowsy yet wide awake. She felt love.

Chapter 24

The new year was only an hour away. Olive and Phil stood in Kristin and Brian's crowded living room. The TV was on; New Yorkers were already celebrating the arrival of the new year in Times Square. Kristin passed out glasses of champagne while big band music filled the room. A silver-lettered banner expressed the deepest desire of Olive's heart—*Welcome, 2012!* Phil must have caught her anxious look because he squeezed her hand. "It's going to be okay," he reassured her.

They had enjoyed days of bliss before the cruel possibility had dawned on her. What if—like Sherry in 2005—she was forced to relive the year yet again? She had struggled to evaluate the year's failures and successes, but for some events it was difficult to decide under which column they should go. Had she been good enough to her mom, Harry, and her brother? Though she had won Phil back, she had caused him and herself an unnecessary amount of pain and sorrow by lying for so long. Also, by saving Ryan Avery's life, she had subjected him to a life of paralysis. And what of her ruined friendship with Kerrigan? Did her successes outweigh her failures, and who was the judge of all this? She hoped whoever it was, he or she was much wiser than her.

If she *was* sent back . . . she didn't think she could bear to wake up in 2011 again, in bed beside an unknowing Phil. It would be an innocent Phil who loved her, but not one who had forgiven her and grown with her. The insights she had gained this year were hard-won, and to do it all over again . . . The thought was suffocating, but not as suffocating as the fear that this year was all an elaborate prank of the cosmos—a cruel "this is how your life could have been" gag, before shepherding her back to 2012. The 2012 she had already started constructing for herself—one living all alone at High Pointe Hills, dedicating her every waking moment to her job. Sherry had never suggested the possibility of this to her, but Olive suspected she didn't know all the rules of time travel. Perhaps the only pitfall of happiness is the fear that it will vanish. Every time she closed her eyes, she imagined everything she had worked so hard to gain being swept away in the blink of an eye.

"Champagne?" Kristin offered with a shrewd smile. She and Brian were ecstatic that Olive and Phil were back together. Because they had kept so much to themselves during their breakup, very few of their other friends even knew that they had been separated for the majority of November and December. But Phil had stayed with Brian and Kristin and then his mom for a couple of weeks before he'd managed to move back into his old apartment.

"Thank you," Phil said, accepting two flutes. "It's funny to think that the next time we'll be toasting will be at your wedding. I guess I should get started on my speech, huh?"

Olive sipped her champagne, enjoying the fizzy bubbles on her tongue. She was trying to live in the moment and ignore the reality of tomorrow, but it was a ridiculous notion. She envied the other carefree party guests moving around them. Phil had persuaded her to come in the hopes of preventing her from watching the clock all night. After listening to her description of both years, he had such renewed faith in her goodness that he couldn't imagine she would be condemned to repeat again. All the same, she couldn't help noticing that he seemed particularly affectionate tonight—holding her hand, putting his arm around her shoulders, lovingly tucking strands of hair behind her ear. It was almost as if he were afraid she would be whisked away suddenly, too.

She caught a glimpse of herself in the large gilded mirror hanging across the room. Pretty in her midnight blue cocktail dress, but with the somber face of someone attending a funeral. Standing next to her, looking stylish in his suit coat and dark blue jeans, was the object of her affection. She turned away from the mirror reflection to face the real man. If these were the last few hours she had to spend with the Phil of the present, she was going to savor every second.

A new peppy song was playing. "Do you want to dance?" she asked.

He raised his eyebrows in surprise. They had taken a ballroom dancing class together their last semester of college and been notorious as some of the worst dancers in the class. The concluding unit had been swing dance, and in their final exam, during one of their jumps, Olive had lost her shoe, hitting another dancer in the head with it.

"Sure." He grinned and held out his hand.

No one else was dancing, but a large enough space was open in front of the sliding glass doors leading out to the balcony. He spun her out onto the empty floor and then guided her into an underarm turn. They rock-stepped and sidestepped, snapped their fingers, and did the occasional spin. Olive smiled to catch Phil mumbling the steps aloud. A short while later, Alistair and Maggie, who proved to be much better dancers, joined them. Maggie rolled across Alistair's back; he leapfrogged over her body and then pulled her through his legs. Somehow they managed to make these maneuvers look effortless and graceful.

"Do you think we should warn them of the possibility of flying shoes?" Phil teased.

"I think they'll be safe as long as we don't try to keep up with them."

Kristin and Brian joined them next, and then another couple Olive didn't know. By the time the next song started, almost everyone in the apartment was swing dancing or attempting to swing dance. Olive was having so much fun that she had glanced at her watch only once (it was eleven twenty). Benny Goodman's "Sing Sing Sing" trumpeted from the speakers. Then suddenly, as Phil pulled her into a tuck turn, she caught a glimpse of a familiar blond head twirling past them. Kerrigan. They hadn't seen each other or spoken since Olive's birthday party. Kerrigan had never returned any of her calls. Olive completed her turn and their eyes met in an obstinate stare.

Her feelings about Kerrigan had fluctuated since she and Phil had gotten back together. Her anger had lessened in a way that wouldn't have been possible if her relationship had been permanently over, but she was still disturbed by Kerrigan's conduct. She didn't understand how Kerrigan could've been so malicious and spiteful. What other possible motive for telling Phil could she have had?

"Let's take a break," she suggested to Phil, and they left the bustling dance floor.

He snagged a spot for them on the recently vacated couch. The couch and armchairs had been pushed together in a corner to make room for the dancing. The jumbled-up furniture felt surprisingly intimate.

"Don't look now," he said, "but Kerrigan's over there with her doctor friend." He had told Olive about Kerrigan's e-mail in more detail. And while he faulted Kerrigan for misleading him into thinking that Olive was having an affair, he still felt gratitude for her attempt at honesty and believed her intentions had been honorable.

Olive casually scanned the dance floor for a glimpse of Dr. Morgan. She wouldn't have recognized Kerrigan's date if Phil hadn't identified him first. He wore a faded black T-shirt, and his wire-rimmed glasses were conspicuously absent. Kerrigan had his wrist in a tight grip as she wiggled her hips and tugged him from side to side.

"Remind me again what Kerrigan said in the e-mail," she said.

Phil sighed. "I don't remember her exact words, but she wrote that she didn't think it was fair for me to be in the dark anymore, that I needed to know the truth, just as much as you needed me to know the truth."

"What was that last part? You didn't say that last time."

"Olive, I just told you I can't remember her exact words."

"Do you still have the e-mail?"

"It wasn't exactly something I wanted to keep for posterity."

She chewed on her thumbnail and fidgeted with her watch. It was eleven thirty-five. There were twenty-five minutes of 2011 left, and while the thought of missing out on precious minutes spent with Phil dismayed her, there was someone else she loved almost as much as Phil and had known even longer with whom she needed to reconcile. Ending the year estranged from her best friend felt all wrong.

"I need to talk to Kerrigan."

It wasn't difficult to persuade Kerrigan and Fritz to quit the dance floor; Fritz didn't even seem to know the dance steps well enough to count them under his breath. Relieved, he joined Phil on the couch, and Kerrigan, with an impassive face, followed Olive to the tiny kitchen. It was the type of kitchen where the fridge door and a cabinet couldn't be opened at the same time. Kerrigan leaned against the counter with her arms crossed; Olive stood in front of the refrigerator. They were only a few feet away from each other. Olive didn't know what to say; this was as far as she had planned.

"So you and Dr. Morgan are still dating," she said.

"We are," Kerrigan said defiantly, and uncrossed her arms. "And I see you and Phil are back together."

Olive gritted her teeth. So she had known that they had broken up. Of course, it wasn't too surprising an outcome after what Kerrigan had told Phil. Her hands trembled as all her pent-up anger struggled to be released. She longed to shake Kerrigan by the shoulders and shout at her, *How can you just stand there like that? You do realize that Phil and I spent two months apart? That we almost didn't get back to-*

gether? You're my best friend. How could you betray me like that? Instead, she bit her lip and tried to believe in Phil's conviction that Kerrigan had had a noble motive. She tried to remember all the good times she and Kerrigan had had together.

"You didn't return my calls," she said.

Kerrigan shrugged. "Sorry. I figured you were calling to yell at me."

Olive had to admit to herself that this wasn't too far from the truth, but Kerrigan's flippancy and lack of remorse still stung. She was starting to regret this conversation; it seemed nothing productive could come of it. "Why would you think I'd want to yell at you?"

"Because you blame me for your breakup."

This was also partially true. Though she knew it was her own lies and infidelity that had caused the cracks in the foundation of their relationship, it seemed that Kerrigan had been the dynamite that blew the whole thing wide open. She couldn't help thinking that if Kerrigan hadn't broken the news to Phil first, she would've somehow found a gentler way to tell him everything, and he would've understood, and weeks of hardship and agony could've been prevented. But if Kerrigan hadn't told him, would Olive have ever really done it?

"Why did you tell him?" Olive asked. She tried to sound merely curious, but she knew her question was infused with vehemence.

Kerrigan exhaled heavily. "There are a lot of reasons, actually. Some of them I'm not proud of. At first, I was just really hurt and mad. Hurt that you were moving out on me after you said you wouldn't. Mad that you had the nerve to be so judgmental about my relationship with Fritz. And maybe I was also a tiny bit jealous."

"Jealous? Of what? My repeat year?"

"Yes, but also your relationship with Phil. I've been looking for something like that for almost four years now." She absentmindedly twisted a clump of her hair. "But I was *never* vengeful, I promise you that."

"What do you mean? That you didn't want to hurt me?"

Kerrigan seemed to ignore the question. "At the party, I was pissed off at you, so I threatened to tell Phil. But I actually had no intention of telling him—not at first; I just wanted to scare you. And boy, were you scared. White as a ghost and shaking like a leaf. The more I thought about your reaction, the more I realized how destructive keeping that secret from Phil was. It was killing you. There you were, at a surprise party thrown by your adoring boyfriend in your beautiful new home together, and you couldn't enjoy it one bit. And then I remembered when you first told me about Alex, how you looked at me with these scared eyes, like I was going to condemn you, but you know that's not my style. You confided in me, Olive, because you didn't know what else to do. I realized you could never be truly happy with Phil if you had this lie on your shoulders, but I also knew you were too chicken to ever tell him. So I had to be the friend you needed and do it for you."

Olive was incredibly touched by her friend's speech, but there were still some things that didn't add up. "But why did you tell him the way you did? Sending him an e-mail proclaiming that I was cheating on him?"

"That wasn't how I wanted to do it," Kerrigan said. "But I

couldn't think of a better way. And I wanted to tell him about the repeat year, but I didn't know how, and I didn't want him to think I was a nut job. But it sounds like he really latched onto the whole affair thing."

"Well, how did you expect him to react?" Olive snapped.

Kerrigan's eyes widened. "I knew he would be upset. But I also knew that if you guys were strong enough as a couple, like I thought you were, that you would get back together and would be the better for it." She paused for a beat. "And I was right. But I'm sorry I caused so much collateral damage in the process."

Olive felt a little unsteady on her feet. She leaned against the cool door of the fridge. Kerrigan's explanation had comforted her, but it had also illuminated her own weakness and indecision this year. Kerrigan had known her better than she had known herself. She had been stronger and more principled than Olive. Oddly enough, without Kerrigan's interference—and Sherry's and Christopher's—Olive didn't think she and Phil could've pulled off a happy ending this year.

"I guess I should thank you," she said, embarrassed by the warm rivulets running down her face. She wiped them away quickly with the back of her hand.

"Aw, shucks. No thanks needed." A lopsided grin spread across Kerrigan's face. "Just a big fat 'I was wrong, and you were right, Kerrigan,' would suffice. For someone who can see the future, you sure are fallible."

"Tell me about it," Olive muttered.

"Okay, I will. You were wrong about Fritz."

"That was meant to be rhetorical, you know." Olive toyed with a fancy corkscrew lying open on the counter.

"I know, but I'm intentionally ignoring that. Or trying to, if you'd stop interrupting. Fritz and his wife filed for an uncontested divorce at the beginning of the month, and it'll become official in March. So she's staying in New York doing her own thing, and he's staying in Madison doing his own thing, and they're both much happier people for it. We're moving in together next week."

"Next week? You mean you're not already living together?" She suddenly lost interest in the corkscrew.

"No. I've been staying with Ciara. I told Fritz I wouldn't be his mistress. That I deserved better." Kerrigan's eyes were shining. "You're not always *totally* off base."

"That's wonderful news!" Olive exclaimed.

"What? That Fritz is a free man or that you're not always off base?"

"Both, I guess."

She burst out laughing, and Kerrigan joined her. A long, awkward pause followed in which Kerrigan fussed with her hair and Olive studied the labels of the empty bottles lined up on the counter. Abruptly, at the same time, they both spread their arms for a hug.

"I'm so glad you're not mad at me anymore," Kerrigan said into Olive's shoulder. "You have no idea how much Christmas shopping sucks without you. You know how helpless I am in malls! And my sister's hair isn't long enough to braid, and she's an even bigger neat freak than you. This past month I've been so happy with Fritz, but it didn't feel like real happiness, because I couldn't share it with my best friend."

"But now you can," Olive said, squeezing her arm. "I know the feeling. I finally made it through this year relatively in one piece. I have Phil back, and we're stronger than ever. But I didn't have you, and it's taken me way too long to realize that *that* was one of my biggest mistakes last year—letting us drift apart."

"Oh, Olive Elizabeth, you're going to make me cry." Kerrigan blew a lock of hair out of her eyes and then smiled mischievously. "It seemed rude to mention it earlier, but—oh, never mind."

"No, what is it?" Olive leaned forward, concerned.

"You're wearing my dress."

"Really? I could've sworn this was mine." Olive smoothed the intricate pleats and folds of her satiny skirt. "But didn't I wear it to Claire and Nathan's rehearsal dinner?"

"You did. It was still mine then. You can keep it, though. It looks way better on you with your coloring. It would also make me feel a lot better about keeping your red halter dress." She stuck out her tongue, and Olive laughed.

"Five minutes to midnight," Brian announced as he poked his head into the kitchen, which was much too small for three people all at once. Olive squashed herself up against one of the cupboards so he could open the fridge. He pulled out three bottles of champagne and tucked them under his arms. "There are going to be some lonely guys out there if you ladies don't come out."

Five minutes! Olive checked her watch to confirm that he was right. The night had flown by. Suddenly, in retrospect, it seemed like the entire year had flown by. She wished she had just one more day, one more hour even, to make sure that everything was in order. Perhaps she should've visited Sherry today.

"Looking forward to the new year?" Kerrigan asked with a wink as they rejoined the party.

"Desperately."

She found Phil next to the balcony, looking as apprehensive as she felt. He was holding both their jackets. "Did everything go okay?" he asked.

"Yes. She actually explained a lot. I'll tell you more later."

"Good. Look, I've got the perfect spot staked out. We have the whole balcony to ourselves. No one else wants to go out here because it's so cold and they want to watch the TV countdown." He helped her into her jacket before opening the sliding door.

They stepped outside. Kristin and Brian lived on the top floor of a seven-story apartment building on North Hamilton. While they didn't have a view of the lake, they had a pretty awesome view of downtown, and if Olive craned her neck to the right, she could see part of the Capitol dome. The night was clear and brisk and full of stars.

"This is perfect," she said. "I can't think of a better end to the year."

"I think you mean a better start to the year."

They stood at the railing, looking out over the city. The row of decrepit two-story houses across the street looked festive with their lit windows and gaudy Christmas lights. Snow clung to the slanted rooftops in thin patches. Looking down the street, they could see the blocky outlines of banks, restaurants, and bookstores. The moon looked like a slice of honeydew melon.

"How will we know when it's midnight?" she asked.

"Oh, we'll know." He wrapped his arm around her waist.

A short while later, the countdown started inside. Their friends chanted in unison. Olive could make out Kerrigan's boisterous voice among the others. *Ten, nine, eight.*

She squeezed her eyes shut and gripped Phil's arm as if it were a life preserver. *Seven, six, five.* She held her breath and hoped for the best. *Four, three, two, one. Happy New Year!*

Phil's warm lips met hers, gently opening her mouth. He tasted sweet like champagne and felt solid against her. She never wanted their kiss to end. She never wanted to let him go.

At last, they opened their eyes at the same time and grinned at each other. "You're still here," he said.

"I know!" she said with a laugh. "But remember I said it might not happen at midnight? It might happen in a less dramatic way, like while we sleep."

"Then we won't sleep."

A purple firecracker exploded in the sky. From where they stood, they could see only the top half of it. The smoke tendrils lingered in the black sky. A few more fireworks were shot off, and suddenly the balcony was where everybody wanted to be. Olive and Phil made their way back inside. After a couple more hours of talking and dancing, they said their good-byes to everyone and headed home to the condo.

Olive turned on the lights in every room. Phil made a pot of coffee. It was like the early days of their relationship when they had pulled all-nighters to cram for final exams.

"I know something that will help us stay awake," he said, tracing the lines of her bra through her cocktail dress. "Let's go to the bedroom."

"You know you'll fall asleep afterward."

"No, I won't. I'll stay awake."

But he did fall asleep after they made love, and Olive could do nothing but stand sentinel over an epoch of her life that she was deathly afraid would disappear. She lay watching Phil's sleeping face, until he turned away from her, and then she hugged his body to hers. *Please don't make me go back,* she prayed to she didn't know who—God, the universe, her dad, and any other tricksters conspiring in her fate. *I've learned my lesson and I'm finally happy. Please don't take it all away.*

The sheet stuck to her feverish skin. She pulled it away and exposed her body to the air for a while, but then she was freezing. She consulted the clock on her nightstand. Four o'clock. Four ten. Four twelve. Four twenty-one. Four thirty-six. Her eyelids felt itchy and grainy. She knew she would fall asleep soon. She shook Phil's shoulder.

"Wake up, Phil. I need you. I'm going to fall asleep."

Disoriented and only half awake, he rolled over to face her. "It's okay. It'll all be okay," he whispered as though he were a father reassuring a child who had just woken up from a bad dream. He wrapped both his arms around her and held her close. She felt enveloped by him. "I won't let them take you away."

When she woke up, she was still in his arms. She glanced around the room wildly to determine where they were. The condo or Phil's old apartment? She struggled to sit up, but he was holding her too tightly. She strained her eyes to look for the white vertical blinds. No vertical blinds; instead there were curtains. She threw one arm out to feel around on the nightstand for her watch and the earrings she'd taken off the night before. She knocked something onto the floor that clattered. The watch, maybe.

"Phil, Phil. Wake up."

He moaned something unintelligible but loosened his grip on her, so she was able to pry herself loose and sit up. They were most definitely in the bedroom of the condo. Even in the dark, she could make out the blue-green pattern of the down comforter, the hulking pair of mismatched dressers, her full-length standing mirror, Phil's gym bag on the floor by the closet. The time was eight o'clock.

"Phil." She rolled him over so he was lying on his back and climbed on top of him. "Phil. Please open your eyes. Look at me." She needed him to confirm what she was too afraid to believe in.

He opened his eyes. "You're still here, Ollie," he said with a yawn. "I knew you would be."

"What year is it?" she demanded.

"Two thousand twelve," he said. "Happy New Year."

"Thank you, God." Her eyes watered, and she snuggled against his chest to dry her tears. Everything that she'd been too scared to count on—the bright lights of her future—hit her with the blinding force of a thousand headlights. All the battles that she had fought and won last year would not have to be fought again.

She knew exactly how she wanted to spend the first day of her brand-new year—with the people she loved at her mom's New Year's Day party. She wanted to see her mom, Christopher, Verona, even Harry. She hoped Sherry would be there. She was worried that Sherry hadn't graduated into 2012, or perhaps even worse, that she had, but that her health was now fading fast.

Her mom and Harry were surprised when Olive and Phil were the first ones to show up on the dot at noon, bearing a tray of vegetables and dip they had picked up at the grocery store on the way. "Well, isn't this a nice surprise," they chimed as Olive and Phil stepped into the house.

The Pintos from next door and Christopher and Verona

were quick to arrive next, and the party was in full swing by the time Olive's aunt Laurel showed up and cornered her in the kitchen to congratulate her on getting back together with Phil. "I always knew you two were perfect for each other," Laurel said and squeezed Olive in a bear hug. "Do I hear wedding bells?"

Olive spied Phil through the doorway in a conversation with her brother. He was laughing.

"I don't know," she said honestly. "But I really hope so."

She excused herself and gravitated toward the picture wall, which had been the cause of so much revelation one year ago today. Here was the photo she had been looking for, but with a slight, yet significant, change. Six people barefoot on the beach this time. She looked up to see her mom watching her with a broad smile.

The house was not timeless, as she had once thought. The paisley print couch still hunkered in the living room, somewhere under the dining room table was a crayon scribble of a dog that Olive had drawn when she was six, the deck her father had built continued to hug the side of the house—even the New Year's Day party tradition had been revived—but the house was not the same. Many of the same people were here today, celebrating all the possibilities and the potential for change that the new year offered, and while it could've been almost any year—1982, 1997, 2005, even 2011—Olive appreciated the importance and magnitude of 2012 like no one else in the house. She didn't know what this year had in store for her, but instead of feeling scared and directionless, she felt refreshed and exhilarated because she knew Phil and her friends and family would be by her side.

The noise of the party surged around her like a symphony.

Her mom's laugh, Harry revealing the secret ingredient in the salsa, Phil and Christopher talking about dogs. Amidst this babble, she thought she caught the tones of a proud, familiar voice. She whirled around, and sure enough, Sherry Witan was standing in the foyer.

Sherry wore a vibrant, bright orange wig, cut into a chic bob with bangs. Her face was pale and drawn, but she looked more animated than Olive had ever seen her before. Sherry must have felt Olive's eyes on her, because she suddenly turned toward her and held out her arm in a sweeping gesture as if she were the hostess, welcoming Olive to the party.